The Disappeared

Ali Harper writes feminist crime fiction. *The Disappeared* is her first novel. An option for TV and film rights has also just been signed with Yorkshire-based Duck Soup Films. Ali lives in Leeds, where she teaches creative writing, has just completed a PhD, and plays netball badly.

🐦 @AliHarperWrites

aliharperwrites.wordpress.com

The Disappeared

ALI HARPER

KillerReads
an imprint of HarperCollins*Publishers* Ltd
1 London Bridge Street
London SE1 9GF

www.harpercollins.co.uk

This paperback edition 2018

First published in Great Britain in ebook format by HarperCollins*Publishers* 2018

Copyright © Ali Harper 2018

Ali Harper asserts the moral right to
be identified as the author of this work

A catalogue record for this book
is available from the British Library

ISBN: 978-0-00-829266-9

This novel is entirely a work of fiction.
The names, characters and incidents portrayed in it are
the work of the author's imagination. Any resemblance to
actual persons, living or dead, events or localities is
entirely coincidental.

Set in Minion by
Palimpsest Book Production Limited, Falkirk, Stirlingshire

Printed and bound by CPI Group (UK) Ltd, Croydon, CR0 4YY

MIX
Paper from
responsible sources
FSC FSC® C007454

This book is produced from independently certified FSC™ paper
to ensure responsible forest management.

For more information visit: www.harpercollins.co.uk/green

For Harvey and Maggie

Chapter One

Had I known our first client would be dead less than twenty-six hours after signing the contract, I might not have been so thrilled when she pushed open our office door.

I once read that hindsight is always twenty-twenty, but I disagree. Hindsight distorts the picture, makes us believe we could have done something different, something better. Hindsight opens the door to 'if only' and the 'if only' is what kills you.

It had been five weeks, four days and six hours since we'd opened for business and in all that time no one had so much as glanced through the window. Despite adverts in every local listings magazine, the only phone calls we'd fielded were cold ones – did we want double-glazing, roof repairs, a conservatory? Jo had been getting increasingly aggressive with each caller. The strain was getting to both of us.

I was alone in the office that Friday afternoon. Jo had nipped out in the company's battered Vauxhall Combo, ostensibly to buy printer ink – but really, I knew she'd be checking out the latest surveillance equipment at The Spy Shop, down on Kirkstall Road. Jo's my best mate, business partner, and a gadget freak: not always in that order.

I'd been at my desk when I'd noticed the woman pacing the

pavement opposite. I'd watched her through the gaps in our vertical strip blinds. She'd smoked two cigarettes, crushing out the stubs with the heel of her boot. Truth is, I'd been willing her to cross the street and come on in.

So when she did step through the door, my pulse quickened and my mouth went dry. I slid my packet of Golden Virginia into the top drawer.

She was nervous, obviously so. She had blonde hair, cut kind of choppy round her face and she kept touching it, scratching at the back of her neck.

'Hi,' I said. I almost fell over the desk in order to shake her hand. She allowed our palms to touch for less than a second, but long enough for me to register the coolness of her skin. 'Welcome to No Stone Unturned.'

She glanced around. Our office used to be a corner shop, situated at the end of a red-brick terrace, so it has windows on two sides. The rent is cheap, and the interior walls are panelled in a wooden laminate that wobbles whenever we shut a door or slam a drawer too hard.

I watched her drink in the details – the cheap brown carpet tiles, the battered filing cabinet we'd bought from Royal Park Furniture Store – purveyor of cheap crap to low-class landlords. I noticed the pot plant Jo had supplied was looking thirsty.

'Are you missing someone?' I asked.

'Sorry.' Her voice was soft, well-spoken – the kind of voice that could have worked for The Samaritans.

'That's OK,' I said. 'It must be diff—'

'Could I speak to an investigator?'

I straightened my spine, remembered to ground myself through the soles of my feet. 'You are. I'm the …' I wanted to say proprietor but settled for 'lead investigator.' Jo would have punched me.

2

'Oh.' A crease appeared on the woman's forehead. I cursed the fact we'd given up wearing suits on day four.

'I'm Lee,' I said, 'Lee Winters.' It still felt like a lie on my lips, even though three months before I'd made it official. I wasn't born Lee Winters. The Buddhists believe you shed your skin every seven years, and changing my name was my way of forcing the process. I pointed at the two armchairs and coffee table in the corner of the room. 'Take a seat.'

She didn't move. I positioned myself between her and the exit and gestured at the seats again.

'I shouldn't have come,' she said.

'Give it a chance. Why don't you tell me what the problem is, and we'll see if we can help?'

'I didn't know where else to turn.' Her right hand twisted the gold band on her wedding finger. She turned it round and round, over and over. The ring seemed loose, a little too big on her slender fingers. I examined my own bitten fingernails, the silver rings I wear like knuckledusters. As she opened her mouth to speak, I heard a noise behind me. I turned to see Jo pushing through the door, a box of paper in her arms and a Spy Shop carrier bag dangling from her wrist.

'Hi, Jo.' I raised my eyebrows and nodded, trying to telepathically answer her unspoken questions.

Jo dropped the reams of paper on the edge of my desk and beamed at the woman. 'You've come to the right place,' she said.

Jo sounded so certain I felt my shoulders relax. The woman stared at Jo. Most people do. Jo inherited her Afro-Caribbean curls from her Jamaican grandfather on her mother's side. Her startling blue eyes came from her Liverpudlian dad. They make a stunning combination. It must have been windy out – her hair was wild even by Jo's standards. The woman turned to me.

'Is there somewhere private we can talk?' she said, pushing up the sleeve of her dark jacket.

'Go through to the back room,' said Jo, putting a casual arm

3

across the woman's lower back and propelling her forward. 'I'll make you a nice, strong cup of tea. Looks like you could use one.'

We've got three rooms out back. I use the word 'room' in its broadest sense – you have to step outside the kitchenette in order to open the fridge, and how anyone could ever use the gas cooker is a mystery. There's a toilet next door, but when you sit on it, your knees graze the door. The windowless back room contains a punchbag, as well as a small wooden table covered with decaying green felt, and three chairs. The bag came from the boxing gym round the corner and dangles from the ceiling. I'd spent much of the previous six weeks in there, punching till my arms ached and beads of sweat flew, trying to fight the worry that I'd blown my inheritance on a business that wasn't ever going to see a client.

The back room also has a broom cupboard – now converted to Jo's spy equipment store – which has a safe cemented into the brick wall at the back of it. That small metal box had sealed the deal when we'd been looking for premises. We figured the previous tenants must have been dope dealers.

I cleared a space on the table by stashing the playing cards to one side and setting the ashtray on the floor.

'You smoke in here?' She didn't miss much, I thought.

'No. Well, only in emergencies. I mean, sometimes clients—'

'Would you mind if I smoked?' she asked.

'Oh. No, not at all. I'll open the kitchen window.'

When I got back, she'd lit a long, dark brown cigarette, and I noticed the tremor in her hands. Jo popped her head round the door and handed me a new client file.

'Right, yes,' I said. 'Thank you.'

I heard the click of the kettle from the kitchenette. I opened the file, spread it on the table in front of me and cleared my throat. 'So, how can we help you?'

'I don't think you can.' She blew a cloud of smoke into the air. 'I was stupid to come.'

I bristled at that. It's personal – the business; my chance to

4

put right what I've done wrong. OK, this woman was our first potential proper client, but it wasn't like we didn't have previous experience. Besides trying to track down my own dysfunctional family, last year Jo and I travelled to the other side of the world to find a missing person – Bert's wife. Bert lived next door to my mum, took care of her in what turned out to be her last years. Me and Jo managed to track down his missing mail-order bride, in Thailand, despite not knowing the language. We have a natural flair for finding people.

'You had your reasons,' I said.

'I saw your ad. About reuniting families.'

I extracted Jo's Initial Enquiry Form and read the tag line out loud. 'Are you missing someone?'

'Yes.'

I waited a moment, but she didn't expand. I coughed again and wished I had a glass of water. 'Who? Who are you missing?'

'My son.'

Another silence. 'What's his name?'

'I don't know what to do.'

I tried to sound like a well-seasoned investigator, battle weary. 'Start with his name.'

'Jack.'

I made a note on the form as she exhaled. Instinct told me to stick to simple questions. 'Age?'

'He's 22.' She stubbed out the first cigarette, which was only a third of the way smoked, and lit another straightaway. 'I was very young,' she said, in answer to a question I hadn't asked. But it did make me think. I stared at her, but she held her cigarette to her lips almost permanently, so that her hand obscured the bottom half of her face. It was hard to put an age to her. Older than me, but I'd be surprised if she'd hit forty. 'He's had problems.'

'Problems?'

'He's driven us to our wits' end. We've given him everything. Cash. Car. You name it.'

'And now he's missing?'

'Not a word in three months.'

I wrote that down. 'Tell me about the last time you saw him.'

'Christmas. He came round for dinner, borrowed twenty pounds.'

'This was to your house?'

'Yes.'

'In Leeds?'

'Manchester. But he came back to Leeds. He's a student here. Or he was.'

'Where does he live?'

She sat a little straighter in the chair and leaned in. 'That's why I chose you. You being so close, I mean. The last address I had for him was a squat on Burchett Grove. It's not very far from here.'

I got a shot in my veins; the feeling's hard to describe, like I'm kind of coming alive. A trail, a scent of someone. I knew Burchett Grove. Locals called it Bird Shit Grove. It was ten minutes away, in Woodhouse, an area of Leeds favoured by the politically earnest. This was my neck of the woods.

'Which one?'

She put her hand in her jacket pocket and took out a piece of paper, ripped from the pages of a spiral bound notebook. She handed it to me. 'I hate going round there.' Her whole body juddered as if to prove her point. 'The last time I went, they said he'd moved. I don't know if they were telling the truth.'

I probably grinned, reading the address. There are two squats on Burchett Grove, and I've known people living at both of them over the years. If he was there we could have the case cracked in minutes. I might even know the guy. 'You got a photo?'

She picked her handbag up from the floor and flicked the clasp. After some rummaging she pulled out a photograph of a lanky teenager in school uniform.

I frowned at her. 'A recent one?'

She closed her eyes for a moment. 'He hates having his photo

6

taken. That's the sixth form. He dropped out a few months after that.'

'When did he move to Leeds?'

She scratched at the back of her neck again. 'Five years ago. Hired a van, insisted on doing it all on his own.'

'What will you do if we find him and he doesn't want to see you?' This was a standard question we'd agreed to ask everyone. We weren't naive. Families often split for good reasons.

She squared back her shoulders. 'I can live with that,' she said. I caught a glimpse of an inner steeliness and I believed her. 'I just need to know where he is, that he's OK.'

I told her what we charged, and she nodded. Jo had included a blank contract in the file. I passed it to her and read upside down as she printed her name. Mrs Susan Wilkins. As she filled in her address details, she glanced up at me.

'There's another thing. You have to promise you won't contact my husband.'

She stared at me with piercing blue eyes. I shrugged. No skin off my nose. 'You're the boss,' I said.

'He's washed his hands of Jack. He'll go berserk if he knows what I'm doing.' She pushed the contract back to me, the still-damp ink glistening in the fluorescent overheads.

'You haven't put your mobile.'

'I dropped it,' she said. She raised her eyebrows at me. 'Silly of me. They're replacing the screen. I'm staying at the Queens. Could we perhaps agree a time each day where I call you and you give me a progress report?'

'OK.' I handed her a business card with my mobile number, and she tucked it into her jacket pocket. I cleared my throat. 'So, there's just the matter of the fees.'

'Yes.' She opened her bag again and paid the deposit – two hundred pounds – in cash, counting out ten-pound notes from a brown envelope. No Stone Unturned, Leeds's brand new missing persons' bureau, had its first client.

And it promised to be a straightforward case – middle-class kid, starts college, smokes dope, forgets to ring his mother. We'd have this in the bag by the weekend, I remember thinking. I had no sense of what was in store for us. Now, as I sit here, trying to write this report and pick through the pieces of the last few days, it's easy to see that the signs were all there, I just didn't read them. We fit the pictures to the story we want to hear. And what I wanted to see was a middle-aged, middle-class woman, desperately seeking her son.

Chapter Two

Mrs Wilkins didn't stay for the cup of tea that Jo had made. She had to get going, she said. I fed Jo the details while our client nipped to the toilet and then we escorted her out of the offices and back onto the street, doling out promises like those lanky kids in town hand out club fliers.

'This'll be a piece of cake,' I remember saying.

'You'll know as soon as we do.'

That last one from Jo as we made our way to the back street where we keep the van parked.

I turned to Mrs Wilkins. 'Do you need a lift somewhere?'

'I'm parked down there.' She gestured towards the Royal Park pub, and I wondered what kind of car she drove. I hoped it hadn't been nicked in the time she'd been in our office. She didn't appear worried, but then she didn't know these streets like I did. Royal Park is an area of Leeds that's an uneasy mix of local scallies and the poorer students. It encourages a healthy, non-materialistic outlook among its residents. As Proudhon said, property is theft. Round here, anything worth nicking is nicked.

Mrs Wilkins's parting comment was that she'd ring us first thing the next day. Saturday, 9 a.m., she said. The clock ticked, and my pulse raced alongside it. I couldn't wait to crack our first case, Jo was desperate for a smoke, and Mrs Wilkins had less than twenty-five hours to live.

We jumped into the van. True, we could have walked. Burchett Grove is less than half a mile away; but getting Jo to do any kind of exercise is harder than getting a decent pint in the Hyde Park.

Burchett Grove sits at the top of a triangle of narrow streets that form Woodhouse – a mix of students and locals – mainly long-haired, cloth-capped hippies accompanied by dogs on pieces of string. There's also the local pub, The Chemic, and, best of all, Nazams – the best curry house in Leeds.

We pulled up at the far end of the street, just before the scruffy rows of brick-built terraces meet The Ridge. The Ridge always scares the hell out of me – a long strip of woodland and ankle-deep mud that separates Woodhouse from Meanwood. Woodhouse is students and hippies, Meanwood is Leeds born and bred. The Ridge feels lawless, a no man's land, a sea of used condoms, empty cans of Special Brew, and spent syringes – the Russian roulette of country walks. Most women I know have got at least one tale of being followed by some random pervert down there. I avoid it whenever I can, preferring to do four times the distance but stick to the roads and the streetlights.

The curtains weren't drawn at number 16 but the house was in darkness. The last time I'd been here we'd smoked so much I'd got tunnel vision and had had to walk all the way home with one eye closed.

We marched up the small path, and Jo pounded on the door. A minute later a head appeared at one of the upper windows. I saw a flash of black hair.

'What the fuck do you want?' a voice called out.

We both stepped backwards. 'Just calling,' said Jo, her leather jacket and Afro more effective than a warrant. I held up a hand. It was obvious we belonged.

He opened the door a moment later. I had the idea we'd woken him up but I'm not sure why, because he was dressed, although his feet were bare, his toenails clean and square. I vaguely recognized him from around.

'Jesus,' he said, 'thought you were the cops or something. What you hammering on the door like that for?'

'Looking for Jack,' I said. I tried to keep my tone steady. 'Jack Wilkins.'

He shook his head. 'Wrong house. Never heard of him.' He moved to close the door, but Jo put the palm of her hand against it.

'Don't make this hard,' she said, in a voice I didn't recognize. 'It really doesn't need to be.'

'Is he in?' I asked.

The guy rested his arm on the doorframe, so that his T-shirt rose up and I caught a glimpse of black hair just beneath his belly button.

'He doesn't live here anymore.'

'When did he leave?'

'What's it to you?'

I hesitated, uncertain whether answering his question would breach client confidentiality, but before I'd decided one way or the other, he sighed heavily and held the door open wider.

'I get it.'

Got what? It struck me as an odd choice of sentence, but before I had chance to ask what he meant, Jo had stepped on to the doorstep.

'We need to speak to him,' she said. 'Urgently.'

'The gear,' he said. He took a step backwards. 'Wait there.' He turned and walked towards the rear of the house.

'Play nice.' I rested my hand on Jo's arm. 'We want him on our side.'

'What gear?' she said, as she shrugged my hand off and trailed after him inside the house.

I waited on the doorstep for a minute or so, unsure what to

do. A group of students were making their way up the hill. I felt weird just standing there, so I followed Jo, pausing in the hallway to close the front door. By the time I caught up, the two of them were in the kitchen, glaring at each other, Jo with her hands on her hips. I caught the end of her sentence.

'A few details.'

There was a table in the middle of the room and washing-up stacked to the left of the sink. The room smelled of fresh paint and bleach. The guy said nothing.

'Nice place,' I said. 'You lived here long?'

'Could murder a brew,' Jo said. 'Stick the kettle on.'

'Murder.' He nodded his head. His dark fringe got in his eyes and he kept pushing it away with his hands. 'Nice.'

'It's a figure of speech,' I said. I had the feeling I wasn't keeping up with the conversation.

''Course it is.' He turned to fill the kettle with water. 'A brew.'

There was something in his tone that made me doubt his hospitality, but Jo didn't seem to notice. 'Ace,' she said, pulling out her tobacco pouch. 'Mind if I smoke?'

'Knock yourself out,' he said, retrieving three mugs from the draining rack. He wiped each one thoroughly with a clean white tea towel.

'You said you've got his stuff?' I said. 'Could we take a look?'

'You used to be in Socialist Students, didn't you?' he said to Jo.

I flinched inwardly. Jo hates being reminded of that time, especially since she'd been asked to stand down as branch secretary when they'd found out she was seeing a copper. Of course, Jo hadn't exactly been thrilled about what Andy did for a living – but you can't choose who you fall in love with. Anyway, since that time she's been more of your freelance revolutionary.

'Saw you at the Corbyn rally,' he continued. 'Pants.'

I wasn't sure whether he was saying the rally wasn't good, or

Pants was his name. Jo didn't seem bothered either way, shrugging his comments off, like she was engrossed in rolling her cigarette. Her tongue stuck out between her plump pink lips.

'Class War,' he said.

Still no comment from Jo.

'So, Jack,' I said, feeling a change of subject was called for. 'When did he leave?'

He ran a hand through his floppy dark hair. 'I have no idea where he is.'

'But he lives here?'

'Used to. He skipped. A week or so back.'

'Oh.' My thoughts of a quick and easy solution to our first case sloped off into the middle distance. 'Know where he went?'

He shook his head. 'I have no idea, I swear. Did a runner, proper moonlight flit. Took Brownie's PS4 with him.'

I took a seat next to Jo as the kettle boiled. 'Any clue where he might have gone?'

'Uh uh.'

'Did he leave a forwarding address?' I knew as the words came out of my mouth that they were overly naive.

'Ever heard of someone doing a moonlight flit and leaving a forwarding address?'

'Pants, what's your problem?' said Jo, folding her arms across her chest and leaning back in the chair. 'It's not like we're not asking nicely.'

Pants stared at her, like he wanted to say something, but he checked himself.

'You said you had his stuff,' I said. 'Does that not mean he's coming back?'

'No idea. He didn't tell me his plans.'

'Can we see it? His stuff?'

'You mean the stuff from his room?'

'Yeah, I guess.' I still had the feeling we were speaking in riddles.

Pants thought about this for a moment, then he shrugged.

'What do I care?' He moved across to a door in the corner of the room and flicked back the bolt. 'It's in the cellar.'

I glanced at Jo. Was it wise to follow a man we'd only just met into a cellar? Possibly not, but six weeks of punching a leather bag had made my biceps swell and there's a confidence that comes with that. Besides there were two of us, and he was barefoot.

'After you,' Jo said to him.

Pants went first, I followed, and Jo brought up the rear as we made our way down the narrow stone steps. When Pants got to the bottom he flicked a light switch. He nodded towards half a dozen bin liners in the corner of a small room that might have been where they once delivered coal. My first reaction was to grin.

'That's everything.' Pants said. 'I mean, apart—'

'Can we look?' asked Jo, already inspecting the bags.

Pants looked at me like he was daring me to say something. I shrugged as he squared back his shoulders. OK, we hadn't got Jack, but we'd got his stuff: surely the next best thing. There had to be something in there that would tell us where he'd gone, who he was with. An old phone would be great. And we had something we could tell his mother. I practised the words in my head. *Yes, that's right, Mrs Wilkins, we've a few leads we're working on.*

'Can we?' I asked.

'Bring them up. It's freezing down here.'

I hadn't noticed the temperature, but Pants's bare toes were crunched up against the cold concrete.

Jo and I grabbed the necks of the nearest bin liners.

'Pen's supposed to be taking them to the charity shop.'

'What's in them?' asked Jo, as we followed him back up the stairs, lugging the bags behind us.

'Crap,' said Pants. He returned to the kettle, poured the just boiled water into the mugs, while Jo and I went back for the last bags.

When we'd brought them back upstairs, Jo said: 'They're not very heavy.'

'Clothes mainly.'

That wiped the grin from my face. I frowned, trying to make sense of what we knew. 'He took Brownie's PlayStation but left his own clothes?' I tried to undo the knot at the top of the first bin liner, but it was tight.

'Don't open them in here,' Pants said to me. 'I've just hoovered.'

'Has he got any mates?' Jo asked. 'Anyone who'll know where he went?'

'Only Brownie, and he doesn't know.'

'Where is Brownie?'

'Out.'

'Out where?' said Jo, in a voice that said she was trying to be patient.

'He's gone to try The Warehouse again.'

We waited for him to expand.

'Jack works there. Or he used to. Brownie's gone down, looking for him.' He opened the fridge and took out a carton of rice milk. 'You're not the only ones, you know. He owes his share of the gas bill.'

That surprised me. People living in squats pay gas bills? Struck me as a bit pedestrian. 'Not the only ones what?'

'How do you know he left?' asked Jo, sitting back down at the table and returning to her roll-up.

'What?'

She lit the end, her eyes screwed up against the smoke. 'How do you know he's not dead?'

Sometimes I hate Jo. She has this way of putting into words the things that lurk in the corner of your mind, the things you don't want to think about. She just puts it right out there, like there's nothing to be scared of. Pants kicked the fridge door shut with his foot.

'He's not dead.'

'How do you know?' Jo stared at Pants without blinking.

Pants didn't say anything.

'He might have fallen in the canal,' Jo said.

'What you trying to say?'

Wasn't it obvious enough? I flinched as Jo continued to bat around the possibilities.

'Been mugged, got run over?'

Jo listed the various tragedies as I tried not to think how plausible each of them sounded. More plausible than someone doing a runner in the buff with his housemate's PlayStation.

'Did you try the hospitals?'

Pants raised his eyebrows.

'How do you know it was him that took the PS4?' Jo paused and tapped the end of her cigarette into the ashtray on the table.

'It's obvious.' He put two mugs on the table in front of us with a bit too much force, so that a splash of hot liquid leaped over the rim. 'Who else? There was no break-in.'

I thought I saw him frown, his features darkened for an instant.

Jo didn't let up with the questions. 'Have you rung his family?'

He mopped at the spilt tea on the table with a dishcloth and then rinsed it in the sink. 'He didn't—'

'Sounds like you didn't give him much of a chance,' said Jo.

I took my first sip of scalding tea. I love it so hot it burns the skin off the roof of your mouth. 'She's right,' I said, after I'd thought about it for a moment. 'If my flatmate went missing—'

Jo didn't let me finish either. 'Ever heard of the benefit of the doubt?' she asked.

Pants folded his arms across his chest. The beginnings of a tattoo poked out under his T-shirt sleeve. 'You didn't live with him.'

'He could be dead in a gutter for all you know,' said Jo.

I got a sudden flash of my Aunt Edie, although she'd have said 'dead in a ditch'. Guilt clawed my stomach lining. She's my only living relative, and I hadn't rung her in weeks.

16

'Don't you take the moral high ground with me,' he said, his voice lower, quieter. He turned away.

I didn't understand the sneer in his voice. My gaze followed his. I could see the tops of the trees on The Ridge through the kitchen window, still bare from winter and fading against the darkening sky.

'His family's not heard from him for three months,' I said. 'You can understand why they're worried.'

He reached for a packet of Silk Cut that was on the high up mantelpiece above a gas fire. He lit one, inhaled in a way that made me think my initial hunch was right – he'd only just got up. As he exhaled he turned back to face us.

'Oh, we heard from him.'

My patience snapped. 'He's rung?'

His gaze flicked to me like he'd forgotten I was in the room. 'Would have been nice,' he said. 'But no.'

'Then?'

'Wait on,' he said, disappearing through the kitchen door towards the hall.

Jo pulled a face, like she didn't know what he was on about either.

He returned a moment later carrying a brown envelope. He held it upside down over the table and an Old Holborn tin fell out – the old-fashioned kind, orange and black with a row of what looked like Georgian houses on the lid. It clattered onto the table. Jo and I glanced at each other, a weird feeling blooming in my chest.

'Go ahead,' he said. 'Open it.'

17

Chapter Three

A feeling of dread crept over me. Don't ask me why. I'm starting to believe in sixth senses and I'm learning to trust my gut. It's taken years, but, after what happened, well, let's just say I learned the hard way. I knew whatever it was in that tin it wasn't good. It had its own aura, a bad vibe, or some kind of shit.

Jo picked up the tin. It didn't rattle, and I knew by the way she held it in her hand it had weight to it. She glanced up at Pants, then me, and she prised off the lid. I held my breath.

Inside was a small plastic bag plump with brown powder. I kind of hoped it was demerara sugar but a voice inside me said I was clutching at straws.

'Smack,' said Jo, her voice rising like she was asking a question, but one to which she already knew the answer.

'Really,' said Pants, the sarcasm hard to miss.

'So …' My brain tried to make sense of the messages my eyes were feeding it. 'What? He posted you heroin? In lieu of the bills?'

'Read the note.' He tugged it out of the brown envelope, a piece of scruffy A4 paper, folded into quarters, and handed it to me. He dropped the envelope on the table. Jo held the bag, still

18

inside the tin, to her nose. Then she gave it to me, and I did the same, like we were seasoned sniffer dogs. Pants went to stand back by the sink.

I unfolded the note and read it out loud.

"'Soz, guys. Leeds does my head in. When they come looking for me, give them this and tell them I'll sort the rest when I can. Sorry bout …'" There was a word crossed out and I couldn't make out what it said. Instead he'd continued, "'everything, but the less you know the better. Keep the faith. J.'"

'Did you know he was into smack?' asked Jo.

Pants looked uncomfortable. 'Dunno. I don't want to know.'

'Who's "they"?' I asked, as I read the note again.

'Funny.' He glared at me. 'Just take it and don't come back.'

'What?'

'I'm serious.'

'No,' I said, as the realization of what he was thinking crept over me.

'This isn't how it was supposed to be,' he said. 'Not when we set it up. I don't want to get involved.'

'No,' I said again. I've been accused of a few things in my time, but heroin dealer was a new low. 'We're private investigators, working for his family.'

'Yeah, right.' From his tone it was clear he didn't believe me. 'His family.'

'Did you call the police?' Jo asked as she replaced the lid on the tin.

'What, to come to our squat to talk about the heroin one of our housemates just sent us?' Pants stood with his arms folded across his chest. 'Take it and go.'

'Can we take his stuff too?' asked Jo. She stuffed the tin into her jacket pocket. I frowned at her. She took a slurp of tea as she got to her feet.

'I guess. We're not planning a car boot.'

My cheeks felt warm. I hate misunderstandings. But in my

experience, these things are hard to unravel. The more you pull, the more you tangle. Still, I gave it a limp shot.

'We're not drug dealers, you know.'

He didn't show any sign that he'd heard me. Instead he continued to speak to Jo. 'I just want it out of here. We're on dodgy enough ground as it is.'

Jo had already stubbed out her cigarette, readying herself for the task of moving the bin liners. I folded the note, picked up the envelope and shoved both in my pocket. Pants helped us lift the bags out to the pavement in silence.

There were seven bin liners in all, added to the Old Holborn tin full of smack, and we had quite a haul. We crammed the sacks into the back of the van.

'If anything happens, will you let us know?' I handed him a business card.

He frowned, like he'd seen everything now. Smack dealers with business cards. I couldn't think what to say. The more I protested the lamer it sounded. I stuffed the last bin liner into the van, and when I turned round Pants was already back in the house. The front door banged closed.

'Don't think he likes us,' I said to Jo. She was crouched in the road by the driver's door.

'Whatevs,' she said.

'He thinks we're dealers.'

'Who cares what he thinks? He's a bloke.'

Jo's never been what you'd call a man's woman and you can't really blame her. When she was twelve, her dad ran off with her Girl Guide leader. He's just had twins with his latest girlfriend, Stacey, who's only three years older than Jo. Jo says he's trying to be the Paul Weller of gastroenterology.

But lately she's got worse. Five months ago, she caught her last boyfriend – Andy, the copper – in bed with the station typist, and since then she's declared herself a political lesbian. Whether a political lesbian is the same as an actual lesbian, I've yet to discover, but Jo ranks men only a point or two higher than amoeba on the evolutionary scale.

I watched her trying to prise open the plastic cover on the inside of the driver's door with a screwdriver. 'What you doing?'

'Trying to find somewhere to stash this. Case we get pulled.'

My discomfort grew. I wasn't in a hurry to have anyone else suspect us of drug dealing, and particularly not the police. We drove back to the office in silence, the sky turning a dusky pink.

The offices felt safe, familiar. As soon as we'd carried all the bags inside, I locked the door and flicked the lights on. I made us a cup of tea while Jo quickly devised an inventory form on our second-hand PC. We sat in the front office, and Jo printed off a copy as I opened the first bin liner. Pants, or someone from the squat, had tied big knots in the top of each one, and it took me a few moments to prise it undone, the black plastic straining against my stubby fingernails.

'Right, one thing at a time,' said Jo. 'Remember, this could be evidence.'

I paused. 'Should we wear gloves?'

'Shit, yes,' said Jo, and I could tell she was pissed off she hadn't thought of it. 'I'll run to Bobats.'

Bobats is the local hardware store. It's open more or less twenty-four hours a day, and it sells everything from firelighters to lock cutters. I wasn't sure it would sell gloves though; but sure enough less than five minutes later Jo was back with a box of disposable ones. We grinned at each other as we both pulled on a pair.

'Remind you of anything?'

I shook thoughts of plastic speculums and wooden spatulas from my mind. 'Probably should have thought before we handled a tin of heroin,' I said.

21

Jo held the tip of her pen against the paper she'd attached to a plastic clipboard. 'OK, what've we got?'

'First up. A black jumper. Men's.' I looked at the label. 'Marks & Spencer. Anarchy in the UK.' I grinned. Jo didn't respond. 'Size: Large.'

Jo scribbled down the information.

'Yeuch.' I pulled out a pair of blue-grey underpants, glad of my latex. 'Undies.'

That was all the first bag contained – clothes, and not all of them washed. The second one was a bit more interesting – a handful of textbooks, a biography of Bowie. A couple of ring-binder files with notes and hand-outs from the university sports psychology department and what looked like an advert dated May 2013 cut from the pages of the *Manchester Evening News*. '"Three Unforgettable Years. You will always be in my heart. *Ciao*. Roberto Mancini."' I turned it over. It had traces of Blu-Tack in the four corners. 'Who's he?'

'Philistine,' said Jo. 'Manager at Man City, till he got sacked. Used to play for Italy.'

I put the advert to one side and carried on searching. At the bottom of the second bag I found a wallet containing an array of plastic cards – one for the National Union of Students complete with his photograph. I put that up on the desk as the photo was newer than the one we had. Also in the wallet were a couple of credit cards, past their expiry dates, and one that confirmed him as an organ donor. I tried not to see that as a sign. There were a couple of cardboard cards tucked in a pocket behind the leather – a library card and an out-of-date membership card for Alderley Edge Cricket Club. I guessed the wallet hadn't been used for years. There was no money.

Jo continued checking the pockets in the heap of clothing in front of us. I'm not known for my colourful wardrobe, but it seemed Jack didn't wear anything but black. She held up another pair of trousers, and a pair of underpants fell out of the leg. I shuddered. They say clothes maketh the man. If that's the case, the man we were dealing with was shapeless, full of holes and had a bit of an issue with personal hygiene.

It wasn't until the third bag that we discovered there was a whole lot more to Jack Wilkins.

Chapter Four

Jo had taken off her gloves and given up writing everything down. Mainly, I think, because she couldn't keep coming up with alternative ways to write, 'shapeless black jumper' or, 'pair of black canvas trousers with ripped hole in the knee'. As I watched the mountain of jumble grow higher, I did wonder what Jack was doing for clothes. It was March, but still bitterly cold – hardly time to be dispensing with jumpers. Had he decided on a whole new wardrobe direction or had he gone somewhere that clothes didn't matter?

Which, of course, begged the question, where don't clothes matter? I sparked up a fag and mulled it over. Two answers came to mind: a nudist beach in the South of France and the bottom of a lake. For some reason I couldn't get the second one out of my head. I glanced at the clock. Four hours we'd been on the case, and I'd been quietly confident we'd have something for Mrs Wilkins by now. If not her son himself, at least news of his current address. Instead, all I could tell her was that he was mixed up in the supply of Class As and was probably naked.

Jo stood and crossed the room to retrieve the third bin liner. She left behind her a space on the floor, the brown carpet tiles resembling an island in a sea of black clothing. I watched her wrestle the knot for a few seconds, before giving up and ripping a hole in the side of the bag. A volcano of balled-up pairs of socks erupted. Jo frowned.

'How many?'

The contrast of the neatly paired socks, different colours – blue, grey, tan – next to the heap of the rest of Jack's clothes struck me. 'They're all brand new,' I said, picking up the pair that had rolled closest to me. They had that unwrinkled freshness of having never been worn or washed. 'Why would you have a million pairs of brand new socks?'

Jo freed two socks from their conjoined ball. She held them up, like Christmas stockings, then cocked her head to one side, her eyebrows knotting. I thought I heard something, a scrunching sound. Jo let one sock drop to the floor, and I watched her wrinkle up the other, like she was about to put it on. She turned it inside out, and as she did a wad of tightly folded paper popped out. Jo's blue eyes shone. She's got the most amazing eyes has Jo and the make-up she wears accentuates them, so that sometimes I catch people transfixed as they're talking to her. She grinned at me as she smoothed out the bundle, and I realized what it was we were looking at.

'Wowzer.'

I did the same to the pair I was holding. An identical wad of cash fell out. I picked it up and smoothed out the clutch of twenty-pound notes. I counted them out, as Jo snapped on another pair of gloves. When I'd finished I stared at her.

'Ten. Ten twenty-pound notes. Ten times twenty? That's two hundred quid.'

Jo nodded, indicating she had what I had. We both checked our second socks. Same result.

Jo grabbed a third pair. I didn't, I was too busy trying to do the maths. I assessed the piles of socks. At least fifty pairs. Two hundred quid in each sock, two socks in each pair. That's like what? My brain refused to do the sums, so I reached for my phone off the edge of the desk, as Jo popped out another wedge of cash.

'Twenty grand.' I sat back on the floor, propped up against the wall. 'Give or take ...'

Neither of us spoke for a moment. I felt a shiver, like someone had breathed down the back of my neck. I ran to the window and tugged the string that pulled the vertical blinds closed, making sure every centimetre of the dark glass was covered.

'Get me some envelopes,' said Jo. 'We need to get this straight.'

Jo un-balled sock after sock and counted out piles of cash, every so often stopping to tuck a wedge of notes into a brown envelope and write something on the front.

I sat back and tried to work out what was going on in Jack's life. If he owed his dealers, why didn't he just hand over the cash? Why leave it at his house, wrapped in pairs of black, brown and blue socks? Why leave his clothes behind? Had he been planning on coming back?

'Sixty,' said Jo, when she'd sealed the last pile of cash into an envelope.

'Sixty grand?' I felt light-headed.

'Sixty pairs of socks. Twenty-four grand.'

I crossed my legs and reminded myself to breathe from my belly and let the weight sink into the floor through my sitting bones.

'Well. Our first case has been good for business, even if we haven't solved anything,' said Jo.

'We can't keep it.'

'You think we should give it to his mum?' From the tone of her voice, I gathered Jo didn't think much to this idea.

'I'm thinking his dealers are bound to come looking for it sooner or later. His note.' I pulled it from my pocket. 'It says, "when they come looking for me". They must know where he lives.'

Jo reached up to help herself to a handful of rubber bands from the desk tidy and bundled the envelopes together.

'Why would he post smack but not mention the cash?' I asked out loud. Another thought hit me. We'd just removed heroin with a street value of God knows what and twenty-four grand in cash. 'Shit. They're going to go to his house and—'

'We left them our business card,' Jo finished the sentence for me. She straightened up from her position and stretched out her back. 'Might not be a bad thing. They can come round here; we can give them the money; they tell us where Jack is. Everyone's a winner.'

'Mmm.' I wasn't convinced. 'If it's that easy, why didn't Jack give them the money?'

'He got greedy?'

'If he got greedy, why'd he leave it behind?'

'Maybe he got scared.'

'If he got scared, why'd he run without his clothes?'

'I dunno.' Jo was obviously bored playing twenty questions, which was a shame because I had a whole stack more. She got onto her knees, used the desk to pull herself to standing. 'I'll lock this in the safe for now.'

She went through to the back room with twenty-four neatly labelled envelopes, a thousand pounds in each.

'Don't forget this.' I lobbed the tin of heroin at her, and she caught it one-handed. While she was gone, I stuffed Jack's clothes back into what was left of the bin bags. There were two more bags still to open.

'The safe's full,' said Jo, coming back into the room. 'Find anything else?'

'More clothes. Some copies of the *Socialist Worker*, an old bus pass. Not much to show for a life, is it?'

'He's not doing bad. Twenty-four grand in savings.'

'Hardly think they're savings.'

'But still—'

'What's not here?' I asked. 'If these are all his worldly goods?'

'No computer, no iPad, no phone,' said Jo, sitting on the edge of the desk.

'Good point. Pants said he'd nicked Brownie's PlayStation. So he's taken electrical goods.'

'To sell.'

'Doesn't make sense. Why nick a PlayStation and leave behind twenty-four grand?'

'No toothbrush. No toiletries.'

'We should ask Pants about that. Maybe they're in the bathroom. It would be useful to know if he took his toothbrush.' I scrawled a note on the pad on the desk.

Jo yawned. 'What now?'

It wasn't like we had much to go on. 'Let's try The Warehouse. They might know something there. And we might bump into Brownie.'

It struck me that I should have taken a notebook to the squat. My memory's not great at the best of times. I felt like a schoolgirl with an appointment to see the headmaster. How was I going to explain this to Mrs Wilkins?

When I first had the idea for this business, I'd had visions of the kind of experiences Davina McCall and Nicky Campbell preside over on *Long Lost Family* – the ecstasy on people's faces as I reunited them with lost loves. Not that I'm in it for the gratitude, but I want to make a difference. I know what it's like to live with the ghosts of the disappeared.

But I had this quiet but persistent voice inside me, saying that that kind of arm flinging, oh-my-god-I-can't-believe-it's-you, tears, laughter, hugging experience wasn't going to be happening. In fact, the monologue inside my head continued, I should keep my nose out. Dealers, large sums of money, smack. It was obvious nothing good was going to come of this.

But it's like I've got this kind of death wish when it comes to family. I'm driven by something I can't explain, something about

28

belonging and the self-awareness, the understanding that comes with it. I need it to work out.

I need to find the family that works. Because Christ knows, mine didn't.

Chapter Five

We took the bus into town. Perhaps not the obvious mode of transport for professional investigators, but it's a habit that's hard to break. Besides, the number 93 rattles down Woodhouse Lane at a rate of about one every minute, ferrying students into town and college. And there's never anywhere to park in Leeds.

It was early enough that The Warehouse hadn't opened for the night. The big black doors were closed and there wasn't a doorbell, so we hung around outside till we saw a young blonde woman turn the corner and push through the side door. We jogged to catch up with her before the door banged shut. Jo asked her if we could speak to the manager, and she said to come in.

Once inside, she told us to wait by the main door. No one goes to The Warehouse for the décor, but even so I was taken aback at the state of it, empty of its clientele and with the lights on. Bare, damp walls, the floor littered with cigarette burns, the seating areas stained and ripped.

I watched the woman who'd let us in cross to the bar and speak to a bloke with a straggly beard. She returned and told us Bill wasn't in yet, but wouldn't be long. She invited us to wait, asked if we wanted a beer. Jo nodded at the same moment I held up a hand to say no. I sighed, but on the inside.

At first, me giving up drinking had been a bit of an issue to our friendship, but Jo's adapted now. We'd both known if something didn't give, well, if something didn't give, something would have given. Probably me. That didn't mean it didn't hurt watching Jo swig from a bottle of Tiger beer that had beads of condensation on the glass.

Jo sat while I opted to stand, rehearsing my lines for Jack's mother: *It's not gone quite as well as we hoped, Mrs Wilkins, but ...*

A tall, gangly man made his way across the dance floor towards us. He must have been six foot seven, a long, lean streak of piss. 'You're looking for me,' he said, and it didn't sound like a question.

'You the boss?' asked Jo.

'Bill,' he said. I held out my hand but he either didn't see or he ignored it.

'Nothing going at the moment, but if you come back next week, I might have something.'

'Sorry?'

Jo stood up. She has this trick of making herself look taller than she actually is, but they still looked like a comedy duo as they faced each other. She wasn't much above his waist.

'We're not looking for a job.' She made the word 'job' sound like something you might scrape off the sole of your boots.

We followed him as he made his way towards the bar. He turned his head and spoke to us as he walked. 'What then?'

The dance floor stuck to my boots as we crossed the room. The seating areas looked manky under the harsh lights, and the heat of the bulbs was making me sweat. God knows what the temperature would get like when the place filled.

Bill ducked beneath the bar and lifted a crate of beers onto the black melamine. He pulled half a dozen bottles out by their necks and stacked them on the shelves behind him.

'We're looking for Jack,' I said. 'Jack Wilkins.'

He froze for a brief second, so brief I wondered whether I'd imagined it and then resumed his shelf-stacking. 'Why?'

'He's a friend. We're worried about him.'

'You and the rest of the world.'

'Pardon?'

'No idea.'

'What?' Jo was on tiptoe at the bar, straining to hear him.

He turned round, wiped his hands down his trousers. 'He was on the rota, last week, three shifts. Didn't turn up for any of them.'

'Has he rung in sick?' I asked.

'Still don't see why this is your business.'

Jo leaned over the bar, and I saw Bill's eyes drop to her cleavage. When he got back to her face, he flinched as Jo glowered at him.

'We're looking for a friend who appears to have disappeared. No need to be defensive.'

Bill's gaze flicked to the outskirts of the room, and I knew he was looking for the door staff. No sign of them, which was fortunate, as Jo'd had an altercation with one, heavily tattooed, the last time we were here. The list of places we haven't been escorted out of is getting shorter; although since I stopped drinking I've adopted the role of minder. As soon as Jo shows signs of wear and tear I steer us back up the hill. It's not that she goes out looking for trouble, but she can't keep her mouth shut when she's had a few – insists on intervening in any situation, particularly if there's a political or feminist perspective that needs raising. She's obliged to rescue women from unwanted male attention, or to point out issues of gender inequality that may have been overlooked by pissed-up blokes who are out hunting, looking to get their rocks off.

Bill turned his attention back to Jo. 'Don't come in here—'

'We're private investigators,' I said. 'We've been hired by his family. No one's seen him or heard from him and they're worried. About to call the police.' I shrugged my shoulders in what I hoped was a disarming manner. 'We're trying to find him before that happens.'

He scooped his hair back and tied it with a piece of elastic he had plucked from his wrist. 'Still don't know where he is.'

'When did you last see him?' I asked.

'He came to collect his wages.'

'When?'

'Pay day's Friday.'

'So you saw him last week?'

'Week before.' He dumped another crate of beer bottles on the counter and unpacked it, turning his back to us in order to stack the shelves. We waited a few moments before he glanced over his shoulder at us and said: 'In fact, when you do find him, you can tell him from me, he's sacked.'

'Are you worried for his well-being?' asked Jo. 'Have you alerted the relevant bodies?'

'Come again?'

'An employee doesn't turn up for work, doesn't ring. Don't you have some kind of duty of care? To make sure he's OK?'

Bill pulled himself up to standing and turned to face Jo. 'Who do you suggest I ring?'

'The guy's disappeared and no one gives a fuck,' said Jo. 'Who said society is dead?'

I moved to stand on the left-hand side of Jo so that I was between the two of them. I tried to ease her down the bar, away from Bill, using slight pressure from my right hip. Jo stood firm.

'Do you know anyone who might know where he is?' I asked.

Bill continued to stare at Jo. 'You want me to ring his mother every time he don't turn up for work?'

I felt genuinely sorry for Bill. He'd ended up on the wrong side of Jo, and when that happens you've got no chance.

'Did you ring him even?'

'Dint need to. His housemate came here. Said he'd done a runner and took his Xbox.'

33

'Pants or Brownie?' I asked.

'Come again?'

'The housemate?'

'The guy with the piercings. Dint catch a name. Carly'll know.'

'Who's Carly?' I asked, but Bill clearly considered the conversation over.

He lifted up the part of the bar that snapped to the wall, allowing him an exit route, and picked up the two empty crates. He strode off back across the dance floor without saying goodbye.

I put my hand on Jo's arm. 'Steady tiger,' I said. 'Doesn't help to get people's backs up.'

'It was a PlayStation last time we got told that story.' She turned round and leaned against the bar.

The blonde girl returned, the one who'd let us in originally, and took over the space behind the bar that Bill had left. Jo persuaded her to sell two bottles of Tiger beer and asked her to point Carly out to us. She glanced around the cavernous space then gestured towards a young woman coming out of the women's toilets. She carried industrial-sized toilet rolls, wearing them like bracelets. I led the way across to her, Jo still swigging her ice-cold beer. Leastways, I assumed it was ice-cold. Ice-cold and smooth as honey.

'Hi,' I said to Carly.

She frowned, an I-don't-think-I-know-you kind of a frown. She had green eyes, and freckles splattered across the top of her nose like paint drops.

'Bill says you might be able to help us?' I waved in the direction of the bar even though Bill was long gone. 'We're looking for Jack.'

A burst of noise splintered through the sound system, bringing the place to life. Sound echoed off the walls as the lights dimmed. The DJ had obviously arrived.

'What you want?' Carly shouted to be heard.

Jo raised her voice to compete with the music. 'We're looking for someone and Bill says—'

'You found him?' Even in the dim light I could see her face grow pink.

Jo was still shouting out the remainder of her sentence: 'know where his mate is?'

'You know Brownie?' I asked, my throat feeling the strain. Was the music always this loud in clubs? I haven't been in one since I gave up the booze. I've somehow always managed to persuade Jo to get out of town before last orders. I realized as we stood there that I'd never come clubbing again because nightclubs are not intended for sober people. Being out of it is part of the deal.

'How?' Carly shouted.

'What?' yelled Jo.

We all frowned at our separate conversations. My eardrums pounded. Carly beckoned us into the toilets she'd just stepped out of. A hundred memories assaulted me. I always end up in the toilets, no matter what club I go to. In fact, most of my happiest memories of nightclubs are in the toilets. There's something safe about the confined, women-only space. The volume decreased by a decibel or three as the door closed behind us.

'You know Jack?' I asked.

At the same time as she said: 'Who are you?'

'We're looking for him. Know where he is?' said Jo, offering her one of the bottles of beer she'd just bought.

'Oh.' Carly's face fell. 'No. Wish I did.' She stacked the toilet rolls on top of the counter next to the sink, and I caught sight of the watch on her wrist. Almost nine.

'When did you last see him?'

'What's it to you?' she said, taking the bottle of beer Jo held out and putting it down on the side, next to the sinks. 'I'll get sacked.'

'We need to find him.'

'Why? Who are you?'

35

'Do you know where he is?'

'No.'

I didn't trust her. There was something about the way she refused to make eye contact.

'We need to find him,' said Jo. 'We believe his life is in danger.'

Carly turned away from us and sank her face into her hands. Silence. I watched her run her fingers over her skin like she was washing her face. Finally, she peeled her fingers from her eyes and said: 'He's disappeared off the face of the earth.'

I stared at her. She reminded me of someone, but I couldn't think who. She looked like she might cry as she picked the beer back up. 'I shouldn't really.'

'Do you good. You're upset. Not heard from him then?' said Jo.

'No, not a word,' she said. 'Who are you?'

'Friend of a friend,' said Jo, as I wondered where she was going with this.

'What friend?'

'One of his mates. From college. She's worried about him. What about you?'

'I work with him, is all,' she said. '"Friend of a friend"? Who?'

'She doesn't want people to know,' I said.

Carly turned to stare at me. 'I don't believe you.'

'You don't have to believe us,' said Jo.

'Is it Liz?'

I glanced at Jo and we made a face at each other, like maybe we were nervous that Carly was on the right track.

'You can tell her to get lost. He's not interested.'

'Because he's interested in you?' Jo asked, her voice sceptical.

A silence followed; well, as silent as you can be when there's drum and bass throbbing in the background. Don't be afraid of the silences, someone once told me, they tell you more than the bits in between. Sure enough, she cracked.

'We've been seeing each other, a bit. On and off. You know.'

'Fuck, yes,' said Jo, with heartfelt meaning. She checked her lipstick in the mirror. I love that Jo wears make-up. I've never got further than black eyeliner, which I can't live without. But beyond that, I've never understood how women know what goes where. Jo's an expert. Watching Jo get ready for a night out is to watch an artist at work. She can paint herself into a whole different person. 'When was it last on?' she asked Carly.

Carly took a mouthful of beer then turned to the mirror so that she was side by side with Jo. I stood back, observing their mirror reflections from a distance. Carly tugged at her curls, like she was trying to get them to stay in one place. They disobeyed her immediately, springing back into their own chaotic arrangement. She sighed and gave up. Carly looked about nineteen, cute in an Annie kind of way. If I had to guess, I'd say she was one of those students who probably came from some poxy little village in Cumbria or Northumberland and was thrilled to be living it up in the city. She pulled a stick of mascara out of the back pocket of her jeans.

'That's the weird thing, you know?'

I felt like a voyeur – didn't know what to do with my hands, so I turned and studied the signs on the condom dispenser.

'We've been, like, seeing each other nearly four months. Always more off than on. His choice.' She stuck out her tongue at her own reflection. 'He's got … issues. Wouldn't walk down the street with me when we first got together.'

'Been there,' said Jo.

I tried not to let anything show on my face, but inside I marvelled at what women put up with. Carly went out with someone who didn't want to be seen in public with her? And Jo had too? What the fuck?

'But then, lately,' Carly continued, 'we've been more on than off. I thought we'd turned a corner. Even talked about going travelling together. Said he wanted to get his head sorted.'

'Heard that too,' said Jo, cynic to the core. 'They never mean it.'

I abandoned the condom dispenser and watched for Carly's reaction. Her eyes grew brighter in the mirror.

'Two weeks ago, he said he loved me. First time ever.'

'You believed him?'

'Yes.'

'Then what happened?' asked Jo, puckering up her lips like she might just kiss her own reflection.

'He disappears.'

'Typical,' said Jo, and I braced myself for a diatribe.

I watched their reflections, half-fascinated, half-repulsed. So intimate and intense, the kind of scrutiny I could never face. Jo took a deep breath, applied a deep red smudge of colour to her lower lip.

Carly wiped a finger under the eyelashes of her right eye, creating a soft black line that made her eyes appear bigger. 'He was supposed to meet me at the Hyde Park cinema, week last Sunday. Never showed.'

'Did he ring?'

'No.'

'Has he disappeared before?' I asked.

'Not for this long.' Carly's voice wobbled again. 'It's been nearly a week.'

'Tell me about the last time you saw him,' said Jo.

I watched her hesitate. 'It might help us find him,' I said, trying to draw the words out of her.

Water drizzled from the tap at the far sink. I tried to turn it off, but it wouldn't budge. Carly shrugged at her reflection.

'Just over a week ago, last Thursday. We both worked here. Thursday. Normal night. Afterwards he came back to mine. We hung out, watched a film. Then, you know.' She paused, and I envied her the memory as a small smile flickered across her face. 'That's when he told me he loved me.'

The sadness returned, and she drank more beer. 'He got up the next morning, we got breakfast at Chichini's. Said he had to go see someone but asked if I wanted to go to the pictures on Sunday. Said to meet him outside at eight. That's it.'

'Did he seem worried about anything?'

'You know what he's like. Always worried about something, but he never lets on. He can't sit still, always has to be doing something.'

'What does Brownie think?' asked Jo.

At the mention of Brownie's name, a wall sprang up. Carly's tone, her whole demeanour changed. She straightened up. 'I don't give a fuck what Brownie thinks.'

'Bill says he might be in later,' I said.

'He's always in later.'

'He might know where Jack is.'

She shook her head so that her curls bobbed. 'He's looking for him. That's why he comes here every night. He's following me, thinks I'll lead him to Jack.' She wiped at her eyes in the mirror. 'He's bad news.'

'Bad news how?'

She tucked the mascara brush back into its bottle and turned to stare at Jo. 'Come on, *friend of a friend*? Balls.'

Jo glanced at me, and I nodded.

'We're private detectives,' Jo said, handing over another of our cards. She hitched herself up onto the worktop next to the sink, next to the toilet rolls, sitting with her legs swinging as she lit a fag. 'We've been employed by his mum. She hasn't seen—'

'Jack's mum?' The disbelief in Carly's voice was about the same I'd expect if Jo'd said we'd been hired by the Tooth Fairy.

'Yeah,' said Jo, exhaling smoke into the small room. 'She's not heard from—'

'Jack hasn't got a mum.'

That stopped us. The music continued to bounce off the walls and the tap at the far sink continued to drizzle, but I had the feeling everything else stood still.

'Everyone's got a mum,' said Jo eventually.

'Yeah. And Jack's died when he was 5.'

40

Chapter Six

The three of us stood there in the women's toilets, staring at each other as we let Carly's statement sink in. This time it was me that cracked.

'She can't have.'

Carly turned to face me, so I could see the back of her head in the mirror. She folded her arms across her chest. 'She did.'

'Jack's mum *died*?' I repeated. I saw Mrs Wilkins in our offices, twisting the wedding ring on her finger.

'He could be telling you a sob story,' said Jo. 'Blokes'll tell you anything if they think they're in with a mercy shag.'

Carly shook her head in a way that didn't brook any argument. 'She was killed in a car crash. He was in the car. He survived. She died. He's never got over it.'

No one spoke.

Jo frowned at me. I felt panic stir in my belly.

'You need to be careful,' said Carly. 'This woman could be anyone. What did she look like?'

'What about his dad?' Jo asked.

'Never talks about him. Never talks about his past. All I know about his dad is that he's a workaholic. They have no relationship. Jack never goes home.'

'Where is home?'

'He doesn't have one. He was sent to boarding school when he was like 7.'

'His dad must live somewhere.'

'Some posh village outside of Manchester but, I'm telling you, Jack has nothing to do with him. He sells cars,' she said, like this was the worst thing a man could do. 'He's only into making money. Jack hates him. Wherever Jack is, it's definitely not with his dad.'

She seemed certain on that fact, so I didn't press it.

'What were you going to see?' I asked.

'What?'

'At the Hyde?' The Hyde Park Picture House is a small, independent cinema nestled among the red-brick terraces. It shows arty films, often subtitled – the kind of film I can never understand.

Carly stared at me without recognition.

'On the Sunday, when Jack didn't show?'

'Oh, right. The Ken Russell one – what's it called it – Daniel something.'

'I, Daniel Blake,' said Jo. 'Awesome.'

It was difficult to think of anything else to ask, so we left Carly in the toilets. She wrote her number down on the back of one of our business cards, and I promised her we'd be in touch if we heard anything.

'The custard thickens,' said Jo as we hit the pavement and the chill evening air.

'Do you believe her? About his mum being dead?'

'Dunno.' Jo shrugged her shoulders – like the fact our client may have told us a pack of complete lies was a mere blip in an otherwise ordinary day.

I pictured Mrs Wilkins in our offices. Remembered the shake in her hands as she crushed out a cigarette. 'She's got to be his

42

mother,' I said as we headed through town, no real idea what we were going to do next. I felt the need to burn off some energy, see if I could outrun the smell of beer that was clinging to my clothes. My throat ached. 'If she's not his mother, why would she want us to find him?'

'He'll have been spinning Carly a sob story. You know what blokes are like. Lying, cheating—'

'You reckon?' I clutched at the paper-thin straw Jo offered.

'We need to talk to Brownie.'

'She could be his stepmother. Maybe his dad remarried.'

'Maybe,' said Jo, but her voice lacked the conviction I was looking for. 'When you next speaking to her?'

'She's ringing at nine tomorrow.'

'So, ask her then.'

'We can't wait till tomorrow. We need to know who she is.' The words fell out of me, without me really knowing what was coming next. 'She's our client, the whole fucking point of why we're here. She said she was his mother. Why lie? Maybe that's a thing – we need to get ID from people.'

'Ring her then,' said Jo. 'That's why I bought you a phone.'

'She didn't give me her number.' I tried not to notice Jo's raised eyebrow. 'She's staying at the Queens.' I grasped her arm. 'She said not to ring her husband. Said he'd go apeshit if he knew what she was doing.'

'Might be true,' she said.

'Or she might not be Jack's mother; in which case, 'course she doesn't want us ringing his dad.'

Jo put a calming hand on my arm. I shrugged it off. 'Why don't we drop by?' she said. 'It's not that far.'

The Queens Hotel underlines Queens Square – the first thing you see when you come to Leeds by train. Even in the dark it stands out – a huge silver-white building that looks up at the whole city, while its doormen in funny suits look down on the mere mortals milling around its streets. Mind you, at that time

43

of night – half past nine on a Friday – I could understand their disdain. On the walk down, I hadn't seen a single person who wasn't rat-arsed.

One of the doormen gave us a questioning stare as we climbed the front steps, but he let us in all the same, once Jo announced we were meeting someone.

Jo marched up to reception. She's never fazed. 'We're supposed to be meeting one of your guests,' she said to the male receptionist. 'Could you let her know we're here?'

The receptionist looked cynical. 'You have a room number?'

Jo glanced at me. I shook my head. 'It's Mrs Wilkins,' she said. 'Mrs Susan Wilkins.'

He hesitated but turned to the screen in front of him. He typed in a few letters, then turned back to Jo and smiled without warmth. 'I'm afraid we don't have anyone of that name staying at the hotel. Was there any—?'

'You're sure?' I asked. 'Late thirties or something, blonde.'

'We have over two hundred guests—'

'From Manchester? Staying the whole weekend.' I leaned across the desk. He tilted the screen away from me. 'Wears big, kind of round, earrings. Like pearls.' I made weird hand signals in order to help him imagine what a woman wearing earrings might look like.

'I'm afraid I can't help you.' He turned to indicate our opportunity to waste his time was now over. The telephone rang, and his hand shot out to pick up the receiver. 'The Queens. How may I help?'

Jo grabbed my arm and moved me away from the desk.

'Maybe she used a false name,' I said. 'She doesn't want her husband to know what she's up to.'

'Maybe,' said Jo. I had the sense she was humouring me. She led us through the foyer and back out the front doors.

'She's got to be his stepmother. Who else would be looking for him?'

44

Jo pulled a face at me while I realized that was possibly a silly question.

'She wasn't a drug dealer,' I said. A middle-aged couple on their way out for the night frowned at me as they passed us on the steps. I lowered my voice. 'She didn't even smoke fags properly.'

Jo shrugged, grabbing my arm to pull me across the road, ducking between the cars.

'Drug dealers aren't going to hire private investigators.'

'They might,' said Jo.

'If she is his stepmother, and she's disappeared, she could be in trouble. Maybe the dealers have found her. Maybe they're trying to get her to pay up to cover her son's debts. She did say they'd helped Jack out financially in the past. She could be in trouble.'

We crossed the square. 'There's nothing we can do,' Jo said. 'We haven't got a phone number.'

I bristled at that, couldn't help feeling that Jo was blaming me for not correctly completing the form.

'We have to hope she rings tomorrow like she said she would.'

'I did ask,' I said. 'She said it was better if she rang us. Maybe she knows about the drugs. Maybe he's been in this kind of trouble before.'

Jo shrugged, and we walked up through the city in silence, both lost in our own thoughts. It wasn't until we reached the Town Hall, right in the centre of town, I realized I had no idea where we were headed.

'Where we going?' I asked Jo.

'Brownie,' she said, rolling a fag as she walked.

'How do we find him?'

'It's quarter past ten, Friday night, he's an anarcho-hippy, lives in Woodhouse. Where do you think?'

When you put it like that, it was obvious. 'The Chemic,' I said.

Chapter Seven

The Chemic is the local pub in Woodhouse, with a taproom full of anarchists and hippies. The lounge is a bit more upmarket, but not much. Everyone in the pub, including the bar staff, either is or was a student, once upon a time.

It was heaving, as always on a Friday night. I waited in the corridor outside the toilets until Jo came back from the bar with two pints of lager.

'Soz,' she said, when she saw the look on my face. 'Force of habit. What do you want?'

'Nothing. Actually, a bag of peanuts,' I said, just because I wanted to have something to do with my hands.

She thrust the two pints into my hand and disappeared back into the lounge. I felt the coldness of the glass through my fingertips. My taste buds moistened, and I tried to swallow. Of course it's tempting, but not really, not when you know where it ends.

I decided to go through to the taproom, see if I could find a spare five inches of space before someone knocked the drinks from my hands. I'd already had a guy with a rat's-tail spill the best part of his pint of Landlord down my back.

Jo came back the second time. 'Brownie is the guy in the black eyeliner.' She shrugged a shoulder in the direction of the far corner. 'According to the woman at the bar.'

I turned to observe a group of blokes, all in their twenties, sat round a table. I hazarded a guess that they'd graduated five or so years ago, were probably signing on while trying to avoid the onset of real life, life outside of The Chemic.

We squashed into a corner near the dartboard and waited. I tried not to stare at the guy with the eyeliner, but his collection of facial piercings didn't help. He had spikes coming out of his top lip that made him look like a porcupine.

'Wouldn't want to get too close,' I said. 'How does he kiss?'

'Careful,' said Jo. 'You're in danger of sounding like Aunt Edie.'

Jo had drunk both pints by the time Brownie finally got up and made his way across the room towards the toilets. I elbowed her in the ribs, and she downed the last dregs as I followed him out of the taproom towards the gents.

'Brownie?'

He turned and struggled to focus on me, wondering who I was, how I knew his name. Up close I counted four spikes through the skin under his nose, each one nestled in a bed of stubble that would classify as a moustache if he didn't shave soon.

'Yeah?'

'Hi,' I said. I smiled with the confidence that comes of being the only sober person within a hundred-yard radius. 'I want to talk to you.'

'I need a piss. Can you wait a sec?'

Jo bustled into the corridor behind me. 'Just a few questions,' she said. 'About Jack.'

'Jack? What about him?'

'We're private investigators,' Jo said.

His expression changed. He glanced up and down the short corridor, like he was looking for the camera, or the police, or something. 'Private investigators? Fuck off.'

'Honest, we are.' I nodded, still feeling a sense of pride and disbelief at the idea. 'We just have a few questions. Only take a minute.'

'Looking for Jack?'

'That's right. People are worried about him.'

'Hang on a sec. I'm desperate. I'll be right back.'

He pushed through the door of the gents.

I turned to Jo. 'Did you see that look on his face?' I asked.

I noticed Jo's eyes weren't focusing and realized she was hardly going to provide any kind of insights at this stage in the evening.

'He looked scared,' I said.

'Scared?' said Jo. 'What, of us?'

'Go outside and keep an eye out.'

'For what?'

'Case he does a runner.'

Jo sloped off through the back door. I paced the small corridor for a few seconds. Another bloke lurched past us, wearing a purple tie-dye T-shirt. He pushed open the door into the toilets and went in. I caught a whiff of men's urinal before the door closed in my face.

How long did it take for a man to take a piss? Not long in my limited experience. I counted to ten, a feeling welling inside me, a kind of certainty.

I cursed my own naivety as I pushed open the gents' door. The guy with the purple T-shirt stood swaying at one of the stalls, his back to me. Otherwise the room was empty. Fuck. I must have sworn out loud, because the guy turned, frowned and ended up pissing over the floor, his pee splashing my Docs. I clocked the open window and swore again.

'Did you get him?' I yelled to Jo through the open space but there was no reply. I sprinted back through the corridor and out into the car park. Fifty metres ahead of me, his head ducked into the wind, Brownie was sprinting at full throttle. Jo stood in the smoky back porch. 'That's him,' I shouted. 'He's done one.'

48

'Shit,' said Jo. 'Where's he off to?'

There was only one way to find out.

I filled my lungs with oxygen and took off after him.

The Chemic stands at the bottom of the hill on which the red-brick terraces of Woodhouse are built. There must have been a quarry somewhere close because the streets all have names like Back Quarry Mount Terrace and Cross Quarry Street. Brownie had taken off up the hill, away from the main road. That direction would take him through a dense warren of back-to-backs to his house on Burchett Grove.

Before I gave up drinking, I wouldn't have run for a bus. But these last few months, I've had to do something with the time I used to spend getting wasted. That's a lot of time to fill, I've discovered, and as I took off after him I realized that I'm actually quite fit. I've always been skinny, some would say malnourished, but lately I've added stamina to my frame.

I heard Jo running behind me, but I knew I was leaving her behind. That was another thing in my favour. Brownie and Jo both had alcohol in their systems, disrupting coordination and slowing their pace. I caught up to Brownie in next to no time, three streets past The Chemic, up a flight of stairs that led between the houses. The question mushrooming in my mind, as I grew nearer and nearer, was what I was going to do when I caught him.

'Wait,' I shouted after him. 'Only want to talk to you.'

He didn't reply, instead found an extra burst of energy and zoomed forward. I glanced behind and saw Jo appear round the corner of the street I'd just run up. Even from this distance I could see her breath like clouds of smoke around her. I hesitated a second or two, but then something pulled me forward, a natural desire for answers. Why had he legged it like that? He couldn't be scared of two women. I increased my pace, noticing he'd crossed the street ahead, veering to the left. He wasn't going home. I knew in the pit of my stomach where he was headed.

'The Ridge,' I shouted behind me, no idea whether Jo could hear me. 'He's running for The Ridge.'

Sure enough, he took the small side street that led nowhere. I heard the click of the gate that opened onto the scrub waste ground. Great. Did I mention I hate The Ridge?

Adrenaline pumped into my veins, endorphins kicked in – a heady combination. Like the acid freaks, who believe they can fly. I only wanted to ask him a couple of questions, for fuck's sake. I pushed through the gate and followed into no man's land.

It was pitch-black, obviously. It was past last orders and there are no streetlights on The Ridge. As soon as I'd taken five, six steps inside I knew it was a stupid thing to do. But then, I reminded myself, the same had to be true for Brownie. He had to be somewhere close, hiding out. He couldn't keep running: too many tree roots, too many obstacles. And he'd make too much noise.

Instinct made me crouch, squatting on my haunches, allowing the air to go still so I could listen. Sure enough, as the silence settled around me, I heard a low panting to my right. It sounded like a dog, biding its time.

I stayed down, figured no one would be looking for me at ground level. My eyes grew a little more used to the dark, silvery light from the moon occasionally appearing between the clouds. I didn't move until I spotted him, a dark shadow, huddled against a clump of bushes. I calmed my heart rate by breathing deep and waited for my moment.

When the moon ducked behind a cloud, I launched myself. I hit him at waist height, fastening both of my arms around his torso and using the whole of my body weight to knock him off his feet. We slid down the slope together, him desperately trying to stay upright, me pushing for horizontal momentum.

I won.

We crashed through bushes, through small clear patches of mud and grass. Halfway down his legs finally gave up the fight and we rolled the last half together, getting bashed by rocks, discarded glass bottles and broken branches. We didn't stop until we reached the path at the bottom, the one next to the stream. The gravel hurt my knees as I threw myself on top of him, eager to maintain my advantage.

'What the fuck did you run for?' I shouted. Pissed off, because I'd caught my cheek against something on the way down and it hurt like hell.

I could barely make him out. All I knew was I was sitting on his belly and his legs were behind me.

'Bitch.' He didn't shout, just said the word, like it was a quiet statement of fact. His tone made me madder, and I punched him right in the chest, dead centre, just below the solar plexus – took the wind right out of him.

He tried to throw me off, and I had to ride him like a bucking bronco. I had his arms pinned and his coordination sucked. He was fatter than he'd looked running up hill.

'Don't talk to me like that,' I said, when he'd got his breath back. 'I wasn't rude to you.'

'Jesus, lady. What's your problem?'

I don't know whether the moon came out at that moment, or my eyes had become still more accustomed to the dark, or whether I had a moment of psychic illumination, but I realized something. The guy I was sat on didn't have porcupine-pierced lips. This guy was old and smelled of piss and Special Brew. This wasn't the guy I'd chased through the streets of Woodhouse.

This guy wasn't Brownie.

Chapter Eight

I scrambled to my feet, brushed down my trousers like I could rub off the smell, the dirt, the bits of leaves and God knows what I had stuck to me.

'What you doing hiding out in the bushes, you freaking weirdo?'

'Can't a man take a leak without ...' He tried to sit up, but he lacked the coordination skills required for the task.

Please let his trousers be up, I thought, praying now for the moon to duck back behind its cloud. Pitch-black was preferable to the reality I was facing. But the moon resolutely ignored my pleas. Instead it seemed to brighten, illuminating the man on the ground in front of me.

He was dressed against the cold, some awful stinking anorak tied round his middle with what looked like a piece of rope. He had a woollen hat on his head. His breathing was shallow and fast, and an awful thought struck me. What if I'd caused him to have a heart attack? He didn't look in the best of health. Guilt flooded my system. I held out my hand and tried to pull him to his feet.

'Sorry. I thought you were someone else.'

He got as far as his knees and put a hand on the ground to

steady himself. He bent over, almost doubled up and I braced myself for his collapse. I'd be charged with murder. I deserved nothing less.

'Don't suppose you've got a cigarette?' he wheezed.

''Course.' I dug out my packet of Golden Virginia. 'Help yourself. Here, let me make one for you.'

As he pushed himself upright, I tried to roll him a fag. My hands shook, and my mouth was so dry I could hardly summon up the spit to seal the paper, but I managed to produce a fat one. He took a seat on a fallen tree trunk and reached for the cigarette.

'Light?'

'Yeah, sure.' I handed him my lighter and watched him attempt to spark it into action three or four times. When the burst of flame finally came it illuminated his face for a brief second, so that I could see the ruddiness of his skin and the weather-beaten lines that zig-zagged across his forehead. I said nothing as he slipped my lighter into his pocket.

'Could have killed me,' he said.

I didn't tell him the thought had already occurred to me. I didn't say it because I knew there was still time.

'Minding me own business, nice and quiet like.'

'I am so sorry.'

'Crashing through the bushes …'

'Do you think you should go to hospital?' I didn't like the way he was breathing. His chest rattled like someone shaking a tube of Smarties. It didn't help when he inhaled a long, deep lungful of smoke.

'A wild animal.' He coughed and spat onto the ground.

'I've got a phone.' I patted my pockets. What had I done with my phone?

'Nearly finished me off.'

'I could ring an ambulance.' Please don't make me ring the police, I found myself thinking, and cursed my own selfishness. I couldn't leave him here.

'Me leg might be broken.'

'Lee?' Jo's voice floated down across the valley, filling me with relief. She'd know what to do. 'Lee?'

'Jo.' I cupped my hands around my mouth to make my voice carry. I tried to think what directions I could give. 'Down. Down here.'

The man stood up. 'Who's that?'

He looked terrified. The sounds of Jo crashing through the undergrowth didn't help. I could hear her swearing as she stumbled down the hill.

'Got the price of a cup of tea?' he asked. 'Something for the shock.'

''Course.' I rooted around in my jeans pockets, emptying all the cash I had. I handed him a fistful of loose change and a couple of scrunched-up notes as Jo appeared, a small twig caught in her bleached blonde fringe.

'What happened?' asked Jo, panting like a steam train. She frowned at the old fella. 'Where's Brownie?'

'I've just attacked this poor man.' They say confession is good for the soul. For me, it just meant another flood of curdled guilt. 'Thought he was Brownie.'

'Could have killed me,' the man said, for the second time. 'My time of life.'

'Well, she didn't,' said Jo. 'So perhaps you'd better be on your way.'

'Dodgy ticker.' He banged his chest. 'Doctor says it's bad for me to get stressed.'

'But you're all right now,' said Jo.

'We don't know that for certain,' he said. He brushed the dirt off his coat. 'Could have internal bleeding.'

'Serves you right,' said Jo.

'Jo!'

'Go find someone else to wave your willy at,' said Jo, ignoring me. 'Else I'll call the cops.'

Just as I was about to take issue with her lack of care for the elderly and the infirm and the disadvantaged, just as I was about to argue about stereotypes and jumping to conclusions and judging a book by its cover, the man leaped to his feet, turned his back to us and sprinted off in the direction of the beck.

'How did you know?' I asked, as we watched him go.

'Obvious, innit?' said Jo. 'Come on, let's get the fuck out of here. This place gives me the creeps.'

Chapter Nine

We climbed back up the embankment hand in hand, taking it in turns to pull each other up through the undergrowth until we found the top path, which leads to the gate. 'Why didn't you answer your phone?' said Jo. 'I've been ringing you for the last ten minutes. I didn't know where you were.'

'I think I left it at the office.'

'Useful.'

The sarcasm wasn't hard to miss. Jo knows I hate mobiles. I hate the idea of being permanently available, that anyone can just crash into your world, without warning. My hatred isn't my fault, it's genetic. According to Aunt Edie, my grandmother would never have a landline in the house because she thought the whole concept was plain rude. And we never had one at home because there was no one my mum wanted to speak to.

I tried to deflect the conversation onto another path. 'How come you missed him climbing out of the window?'

Jo didn't reply so I linked arms with her and we headed back towards Woodhouse. As we got to within a hundred yards of the gate I heard it click. A moment later an Asian guy in a dark jacket entered the woods. I felt Jo tense beside me, but we carried on walking, although our pace slowed. He hadn't seen us, and we had the advantage, because he was nearer the gate and hence nearer the streetlights of Hartley Avenue. I don't know what it was, but there was something about the way he was looking around that made me wary. Like he was checking out whether he could be seen by anyone in any of the houses that back onto The Ridge.

Then he saw us. I felt Jo straighten her posture, and I did the same, remembering to stare him straight in the eyes. He turned from my gaze, said nothing as we passed. I told myself I was paranoid, that I was seeing danger in everyone and everything.

My heart rate didn't return to normal until we got back onto the pavements and the streetlights burned out their reassuring orange glow. We saw students threading their way through the streets on their way home from The Chemic and life felt safe and normal again.

'Something's not right,' I said. 'Why did Brownie take off like that?'

'Guilty conscience?'

'Why?'

'Involved in the dealing?'

It wasn't outside the bounds of possibility, but I couldn't shake the feeling that he'd been frightened when I'd told him who I was. Not just frightened, terrified. In fear of his life terrified.

'What now?'

It had to be getting on for midnight, and after my sprint and subsequent excitement in the bushes I was exhausted. And sober.

'Nothing we can do,' said Jo. She stooped to retie the laces in her Docs and brush off some of The Ridge which had stuck to her clothing. 'Let's go home. Sleep on it.'

We linked arms again and the warmth of her body next to mine felt comforting, but I knew I wouldn't be able to sleep until I'd made some sense of the last few hours.

'You can, if you want. I'm going to the office,' I said. 'I want to write everything up. We're missing something. Something obvious.'

I knew as soon as we turned into the street. For starters, we hadn't left any lights on, and yet pools of light fell onto the pavement outside the office windows, no sign of our discreet vertical blinds. We both started jogging, slowly at first, turning into a sprint the closer we got. By the time we were a couple of hundred feet away I could see that the door had been kicked in, boot marks still present on the wood. My heart pounded in my chest.

I've never had anything before, nothing that I've owned. I'd never bought a stick of furniture in my life before we started the business. To see it all trashed broke my heart. By the time Jo followed me into the main office, I'd realized everything we had had been destroyed. The computer lay on the top of a heap of broken furniture, its screen smashed, wires trailing. The hard drive was missing. All Jo's neat files had been ripped up, jumped on and added to the pile of debris in the centre of the room. The coffee table, Jo's pot plant, everything we had, destroyed.

The blinds lay on the floor, next to the slashed cushions with their foam insides spilling out. I picked up a pair of Jack's trousers, and the pieces of cloth fell from my hands. They'd been shredded.

'The safe,' said Jo, sprinting through to the back room. I followed her but didn't get far. As she ran out, a figure ran in, cannoning into us both, knocking Jo to the floor and pushing me into the wall. I banged the back of my head, and by the time I'd got my balance, the person was out the door.

'You OK?'

'Twat,' said Jo, getting to her feet.

I turned and followed. By the time I got outside, the figure was halfway down the street, dark trousers, trainers. He ducked his head as he passed under a streetlight, but I caught a glimpse. Enough to see he was a white lad in a hooded top. He turned

58

and lobbed something at me, but it missed, and I continued the chase. I was faster than him, even if this was my second track event of the evening. I caught up as he tried to dodge round the corner of Royal Park Road. I threw myself at his legs, grabbed him around his knees. He stumbled but I didn't bring him down. He kicked out and caught me in the chest, which made me lose my grip. I scrambled back to my feet and rounded the corner, just in time to see him throw himself into the open rear door of a car parked at the kerbside. The car must have had its engine running, because it took off, tyres screeching to get traction with the road before he'd closed the door. I stopped running, knowing I had no chance. I'm shit at cars, no idea of make or model. All I saw was that it was dark coloured. Kind of square-looking.

Two chases and nothing to show for either of them. I kicked the wall and collapsed to the ground in pain. Thought I'd broken my toes. I sat on the pavement for a moment, trying to catch my breath, my lungs cracking with the sudden influx of cold night air. When the throbbing in my foot subsided, I stood up and retraced my steps, stopping to pick up the item he'd thrown at me. A tin of black spray paint.

Jo was waiting for me on the doorstep of the office. 'Complete and utter twat.'

She led me into the back room. The table and chairs had been smashed against the wall, you could see the indentation of chair legs in the laminate. The padlock remained on the door to the broom cupboard, but a great big hole had been smashed through the bottom panel. Jo's equipment store had been plundered, most of the contents smashed on the floor. 'Didn't get the safe though,' Jo said. She'd already unlocked the padlock and she threw back the door. The poster was still on the wall, and the safe behind undiscovered. I felt a rush of pride in that little metal box. Something had survived.

'What's the landlord going to say?' said Jo as we stepped back into the main office and stared at the spray painting on the wall.

'"Be scarred"?'

'Think it means "scared",' said Jo.

They could fuck off. I wasn't going to be scared. Or scarred. Not of sneaky cowards like this. Anyone can break in when there's no one home.

'Well,' said Jo. 'We've obviously rattled someone's cage.' She said this like it might be a good thing.

'Come on,' I said, the pain in my toes helping to focus my thoughts. 'See if the kettle still works. I'll make a start. Better add burglar alarm to the list.'

We had an office toolkit, basic, but we'd bought a hammer and nails to hang pictures, and a screwdriver to put up a set of flat-pack furniture. I found the hammer by the back door and with a bit of effort I managed to get one of the desks back into a vaguely usable condition, although I had to prop it up with the remains of the coffee table. The other desk was a write-off. Luckily, we hadn't splashed out on anything state of the art.

Jo came back into the main room to report that the tea bags had been nicked, which added insult to injury. She turned her attention to bagging up Jack's clothes. The furniture that was beyond repair, the green felt table from the back room and the office chairs, I smashed up into smaller pieces before collecting up the sticks of wood and building a small bonfire in the backyard. I swore as I worked that whoever had done this wasn't going to get away with it.

The upstairs tenants returned from a night's clubbing not long after two. They were wasted, but that made them so sympathetic I nearly cried. They kept hugging us, pupils wide as jammy dodgers, and one of them went up to their flat and returned with tea bags, milk and two new mugs. I swept the remains of our old crockery into the bin.

We all knew what it was like to be burgled, living in Leeds 6: LS6. No one even mentioned calling the police. We hadn't got round to sorting out insurance, so there seemed little point in trying to get a crime reference number.

'We should ring a locksmith,' I said. 'Oh, shit. They've nicked my phone.'

'Lee.' Jo put her hands on her hips.

'It's not my fault,' I said. 'I'm the victim of a crime.'

'It's twenty quid a month we pay for that phone. For the next two years.'

'Lend me yours.'

'No.'

'Fine, I'll use the landline.'

Jo held up the broken body of the telephone.

I was saved by one of the ravers. 'Don't worry. I've got an old one my mam gave me,' he said, and he scampered off, this time coming back with a white plastic phone with a built-in answer-machine.

'Thanks,' I said, fighting back the tears again. Any act of kindness was bringing me to my knees. I tried to get a grip by calling an emergency locksmith. He promised to be there within the hour.

After a while the upstairs lot left, promising to help us redecorate in the morning. I knew they'd be lucky to have come back to earth by then, but I said thanks anyway. They trotted off back to their upstairs flat, not seeming unduly concerned. Burglaries happen all the time in LS6.

But I knew better. This wasn't a burglary. This was a warning.

Chapter Ten

We got the office as straight as we could and then went home. I didn't sleep at all and by the time I heard Jo's alarm clock go off on Saturday morning, I'd made a full set of notes, including a timeline that started with Jack's Christmas visit to his parents, and ended with our burglary.

'He must have started seeing Carly just before he stopped contacting his parents. And that's another thing that doesn't add up.'

'Morning,' said Jo, coming into the front room in her Snoopy pyjamas.

'Mrs Wilkins said she hadn't heard from him for three months, but he only disappeared a week ago.'

'Tea?'

'Why didn't he contact his mother in all that time before?'

Jo yawned and stretched her arms. 'We're sticking with the theory she is his mother?'

'Stepmother. If his real mum died when he was 5, it stands to reason his dad's going to remarry. No man's going to stay on his own all that time, not with a young kid to look after.'

Jo moved her head from side to side like she was trying to find the balance on a set of scales. 'OK.'

'So why didn't he contact them in all that time?'

''Cause he had a new girlfriend? Too busy shagging to ring?'

'I hate that word.' I pulled on my Docs and tied the laces. 'A new girlfriend doesn't explain three months of not ringing. I'm thinking his drug-taking's getting out of control.'

'Did you get any sleep?' asked Jo.

I knew there was a piece of the jigsaw we were missing. I couldn't get the thought to properly form in my head. I had a list of questions – like why had Jack told Carly he loved her the night before he disappeared? Why had he left the cash behind? And why had he posted the smack to the squat and not the dealers it belonged to? If he owed them cash, why hadn't he just paid them out of the money he'd left behind? And why hadn't he taken his clothes? Or got in touch with Carly?

Next to each question I'd written as many possible answers as I could think of. They ranged from 'because he didn't know' to 'because he's dead'. The money was the most puzzling thing of all, and I couldn't help thinking that if I could find the answer to that, I'd be a whole heap closer to discovering what had happened. The only thing that made any sense was that either Jack had been taken away, against his will, or he didn't know the cash was there. Perhaps the dealers had kidnapped him. But then who would pay up?

Jack's letter, plus the fact that there hadn't been a ransom demand, at least not one we knew about, suggested he hadn't been kidnapped, so I was working on the second theory. Jack didn't know the money was there. Which, of course, begged the questions: who would hide twenty-four grand in someone else's socks? And why? One thing was certain, Brownie knew something.

'Hello?' said Jo. 'Tea?'

We needed to go back to the beginning, and to me the beginning spells the nuclear. We'd met Jack's mother, or at least someone who claimed to be his mother. Stood to reason we now needed to meet his dad. See what light he could shed. Was Jack's mother dead? Was Mrs Wilkins really a stepmother? And if she was, what kind of stepmother? The kind her stepson confided in? I hoped so, for his sake. Because I know better than anyone, if you've lost your mother, and your dad's an arse, you need someone on your side.

Mrs Wilkins said Jack's dad had washed his hands of his son. I already knew what I thought of Mr Wilkins. 'We're going to speak to his dad,' I said to Jo.

'Thought you promised we wouldn't?'

'That was when Mrs Wilkins promised me she was his mother. And that she was staying at the Queens.'

'Fair enough.' I noticed Jo's pyjama buttons were done up wrong. 'How?'

'She wrote down the address on the client contact form.'

'Like that's going to be right. Face it, Lee. Everything she's told us has been a lie.'

'I'll google him.'

'What? Mr Wilkins, Manchester?'

I pushed her in the direction of the door. 'Get dressed. We need to get to the offices. She's supposed to ring at nine. If she can't get through on my mobile, she'll ring the landline.'

Jo disappeared into the hall and came back a few moments later with a wooden rounders bat that she kept in the understairs cupboard. Not that she'd ever play rounders, but she'd read somewhere that if you beat up a burglar with something that you could reasonably be expected to have in the house, you wouldn't get arrested. Fortunately, we'd never been called upon to test this theory. She swung it lightly, like she was warming up. 'What about the dickheads that broke in last night?'

'We'll deal with them later.'

The offices were depressing but I didn't intend to hang around too long. It was almost nine by the time I got there. Jo detoured via Bobats to buy padlocks and more bin liners. I didn't want to miss Mrs Wilkins's call. I was fairly certain Mrs Wilkins would ring; she'd been desperate the day before. That kind of desperation doesn't go away.

Sure enough, at three minutes past nine, the phone the upstairs neighbours had given us trilled. I grabbed the receiver, but Jo got to the hands-free button before me.

'Hello?'

'Hi. It's Susan. Susan Wilkins.'

I exhaled.

'What news?' she said. 'Did you get into the squat?'

'Where are you?'

'My hotel.'

'How is it at the Queens?' asked Jo. 'I hear the breakfasts are pretty good.'

'Never mind that,' said Mrs Wilkins. 'How are you getting on?'

'We've run into a couple of problems,' Jo said, and I hated her for being so blunt, for not shying away from the truth.

'Nothing serious,' I lied, as I took a seat on the broken coffee table that was propping up the desk. 'But there's a few questions we need to ask.'

'The main one being—'

I cut Jo off with one of my hard stares. I don't do them much, so when I do, Jo takes notice. I felt the skin on the back of my neck prickle.

'What's happened?'

I guessed what she was thinking. It's obvious, if you've ever lost someone. You think the worst. You think about dead bodies, and possible suicides, cold canals, horrific car smashes. You think about the pictures you thought you'd never have to imagine, the headlines that used to read like fiction, things that would never happen to you. I wanted to reassure her, but I wasn't sure I had the words.

'You see, the thing is, Mrs Wilkins, we spoke to his girlfriend and she says—'

'Carly?'

'You know her?'

'No. Not really.'

'You know her name,' I said.

'He mentioned her, the last time I saw him.'

'At Christmas,' Jo said, her voice rising like she was checking a fact.

'I wasn't sure whether it would develop into anything serious. I assumed they'd split up. Does she know where he is?'

'No. She hasn't seen him. He was supposed to meet her, and he didn't show up.'

'Meet her where?'

Jo opened her mouth to answer, but I didn't give her chance. Something about the whole situation was giving me the heebie-jeebies. 'We can't give out that kind of information. Not at this stage in the investigation. We're eliminating people from our enquiries.'

She paused, and I heard her light a cigarette. 'What did they say at the squat?'

'Same. He disappeared last Friday – no one's seen him since. Well, no one we've spoken to.'

'He was good friends with someone in the squat. Brownie, I think he said. Have you spoken to him?'

I didn't like the way she seemed to know more than she'd let on the day before – *yesterday* she knew nothing, now it was like she was directing us around our own investigation. I decided to grasp the nettle. 'I'm afraid we're going to have to ask you a couple more questions.'

'Like?'

I inhaled. There was no polite way to put this. 'His girlfriend, Carly, is under the impression that Jack's mother, well, that Jack's mother passed over.' I know, don't ask me why – I've never said 'passed over' in my whole life before. 'When he was 5.'

Mrs Wilkins muttered something that sounded to my ears like: 'Never talks about it.'

'What?'

'Nothing. Just, obviously they're very close.'

'So,' I said, when it became obvious she wasn't going to volunteer any information. 'Do you know why she might have said that?'

'I do.'

Another silence that seemed to stretch into the distance. 'Why did you tell us that you're—'

'Jack's stepmother. I married his father after his mother died.' She cleared her throat. 'He was heartbroken. Still is. It's taken years for him to come to terms with it. She was an amazing woman.'

'Must be hard. To match up to a dead, amazing woman,' said Jo, pulling a face at me as she spoke into the phone.

'I don't look at it like that,' came back Mrs Wilkin's voice. 'I feel grateful to her.' Jo stuck two fingers down her throat and pretended to vomit. I don't know whether Mrs Wilkins had an inkling of what was going on in our offices, but her next sentence seemed pointed and directed at Jo. 'Women shouldn't be in competition with each other. If more women—'

'Why didn't you tell us?' interrupted Jo.

'Didn't seem relevant,' she said, and I heard her light another cigarette. 'To all intents and purposes, I am Jack's mother. He's a lost soul, was a lost soul, when I met him. Haunted, really.'

'You got any other children?'

'Am I under investigation in my own investigation?'

There was ice in her voice and an awkward pause as Jo and I glanced at each other.

I flinched first. 'It's just the more background we have, the better and the quicker we'll find him. Has Jack got any siblings?'

'Have you managed to find out anything? Besides he's got a girlfriend?'

Jo and I had rehearsed this on our way down to the office that morning. How much to tell.

67

'He's moved out of the squat,' I said. 'And he didn't leave a forwarding address.'

'And he hasn't been into work to collect his wages,' Jo added. 'No one's seen him for a week.'

'We were wondering whether we should go to the police,' I said.

'I hire a team of private investigators and your first idea is to go to the police?'

I screwed up my courage. 'We're worried something may have happened to him. Something, you know, something bad.' I prayed Jo wouldn't revisit the list of possible catastrophes.

'No.' Mrs Wilkins's voice was firm down the phone. 'No, I'd know if something, something like that had happened to him. I don't want the police involved, not until I know what this is about.'

I glanced at Jo. Neither of us had been particularly keen on the police idea. We'd always seen them as the enemy, the hard black line on demonstrations, the invisible tail on stoned car journeys, the possible tap on the line as we ordered our recreational drugs. And, of course, after what happened with Andy. Well, let's just say it's hard to contemplate the idea of voluntarily involving them in our lives.

'Did his flatmates say anything about where he might be?'

'Not really.' We'd decided not to mention the letter. Or the drugs. 'He did a moonlight flit.'

'What about Brownie then? Have you spoken to him?'

'We've still more interviews to do,' said Jo.

'What's the plan?'

Interesting question, and at that point I couldn't put into words the sense of unease that was hanging around my shoulders like a cloak. I knew she wouldn't be that chuffed if we told her our next move was to track down her husband. I knew she had a very clear idea as to how we should run the investigation and poking around, testing the edges of her story, wasn't it.

'We need a phone number,' I said. 'We need to be able to contact you. We're out and about for the rest of the day.'

'Where?'

'Following up some enquiries on the girlfriend,' I said.

'What enquiries?'

That was as far as I'd got. 'She's from Huddersfield,' I improvised. 'Her parents might be hiding Jack.'

'I want an address,' Mrs Wilkins barked down the phone. A pause. Her tone softened. 'I'm sorry. It's a difficult time.'

I could feel the tension emanating from her down the telephone line. I raised my eyebrows at Jo. 'We'll get back to you as soon as we have something concrete. But we need a number.'

'What happened to your offices?'

'Ah.' I fingered the telephone wire. 'You've been?'

'The front door is boarded up.'

'We're having some work done.'

'You've been burgled. Who by?'

'Kids. It's a crime-ridden area. It's nothing—'

'What did they take?'

'Nothing. There's nothing to take. We have a security system. Nothing of any value is left in the office.'

'The place looked trashed.'

'Just kids—'

'This isn't happening fast enough,' she said.

'Give us a chance.' I know I sounded petulant. 'We only started yesterday. We're making progress,' I said as I crossed my fingers behind my back. 'These things don't solve themselves overnight.'

'I can't stay here,' she said.

'Where's here?' I asked at the same time as Jo said: 'We went down to the Queens.'

A barely perceptible pause. 'I had to move,' she said. 'I think ...' her voice trailed off and for a moment I suspected that she was holding her hand over the receiver and talking to someone else. When she returned to the phone call, she spoke slower. 'I think someone's following me. I'm frightened Jack's involved in something, something bad.'

'Who would—?'

'I'll give you a number. Got a pen?'

Jo pulled one out of the front pocket of her dungarees, and I took down the number that Mrs Wilkins repeated twice.

'Ring me on that, two o'clock. I've got to go.'

The dial tone sounded before I had chance to say goodbye.

'Did you buy that?' I asked Jo.

'What, that about her being his adopted mother?'

'Step,' I said. These distinctions have always mattered to me.

'She sounded worried,' said Jo. 'Why'd you tell her Carly's parents might be hiding Jack?'

'She sounded stressed,' I said, refusing to recognize Jo's look of bewilderment. I glanced at the biro marks on my left forearm. 'Why would anyone be following her?'

'You made it sound like we'd produce her son in time for lunch.'

'I had to tell her something.'

'We've got more chance of finding Madeleine McCann.'

'You don't know that. His dad might know something.'

I wasn't convinced. All we were beginning to discover was how little we actually knew.

The next thing was to see if I could get the number for Mr Wilkins. I knew this was going to get us into deep trouble with our own client, but I needed some facts confirmed.

'Where's the form?'

The filing system, such as we'd had, had been three lever arch files that stood on top of the cupboard that housed the electricity metre. All those files had been torn apart and discarded in the middle of the room and then I'd bagged their ripped contents into bin liners as part of the tidy up process the night before. 'Bollocks.'

I prised open the knot of one of the bin bags, the one that

crunched, and sifted through the papers in there, but I couldn't find the form.

'It's not here.' I upended the only other bin liners that contained paper. The rest were full of the remains of Jack's stuff.

Jo came over to help me search and we went wordlessly through the papers, now strewn all over the floor, one more time. And guess what? It wasn't there. There wasn't a single piece of it in evidence.

'That's weird. They wouldn't take the form, would they?'

'They might. Whoever burgled the office is looking for Jack. Maybe they're on their way round to his dad's house too.'

'Give me your phone.'

Jo passed it across, and I googled 'Wilkins + Manchester': 800,000 results. The first twenty or so pages were about Ray Wilkins, a defender for Manchester United. Apparently.

'This is hopeless. We'll have to go there.'

'Where?' said Jo.

'Manchester.'

'Why Manchester?'

'Mrs Wilkins said she was from Manchester.'

'Only we can't believe a fucking word she tells us,' said Jo.

'Didn't Carly say he was a car salesman?' I added 'cars' to the search bar, which narrowed the results to a mere 65,000.

I stared at what remained of Jack's possessions, scattered on the floor. 'The thing from Mancini – he's a Man City fan.'

'There's people living in Japan that support Man City.'

'You're forgetting our clue.' I pounced on the wallet.

Jo stared at me. 'We have a clue?'

I opened it up and rang a finger through the various pockets. Nothing there. I rummaged through the papers on the floor. 'Jesus, that's gone as well.'

Jo's forehead scrunched. 'His blood donor card?'

'The membership card – remember? Here it is!' I pounced on the small rectangular piece of cardboard among the debris. 'Alderley Edge Cricket Club. Junior member.'

71

'Junior member?'

'It's expired. But that's where he's from. Bet you.'

'Alderley Edge? Was that where Beckham lived?'

'Google it,' I said, chucking her phone back at her.

Jo tapped the screen. '"Alderley Edge",' she read. '"A village and civil parish in Cheshire – fourteen miles south of Manchester".'

'Carly said a village.' We were on the right track, I could feel it.

Jo frowned. 'So we're going to drive around Alderley Edge looking for Jack's dad?'

'He's got a car dealership. He wants people to find him.'

'You don't know his business is in Alderley Edge.'

'Any better ideas?'

Jo pulled a face. 'We should tidy this lot away again.'

'Let's just get there.'

'Wild fecking goose chase.'

'Worth a shot,' I said.

While Jo scooped the crap back into the bin liners, I paced the office, stopping only to scribble a few more questions on my notepad. Even if we didn't find Jack's dad, I wanted to see a bit of where Jack was from, get some of the background – and not just through the eyes of his stepmother. What does a stepmother know? Even assuming Susan Wilkins was who she said she was.

One fact remained. Jack had done a runner and I suppose the thought was in my mind that he might have gone home. We reach for the past in times of trouble, it's instinctive. The same way I still think about my mother anytime there's a success or a failure. No matter she's been dead four years. No matter that even when she was alive, she'd be too wrapped up in her own misery to take any notice of me, or my life. It's in all our bones. We want someone to share the highs and lows with.

We were on the road less than twenty minutes later. Jo stashed the rounders bat on the back seat and then climbed behind the steering wheel. I can drive, but I'm not a natural. I'm more your wing pilot – roll cigarettes, read maps, watch out for signs, that kind of thing.

The clock on the dashboard said twenty to eleven as we arrived in Alderley Edge. It was the first day of the year that felt like it had any warmth to it, and I felt like I was coming out of hibernation – like I was waking up. It was obvious, we needed to come to the beginning to work out what had happened at the end.

Chapter Eleven

Alderley Edge is posh. Wide verges, houses set acres apart from each other. Doesn't fool me though. Life is never like the chocolate box, no matter how much cash you have.

'So,' said Jo, as we drove past the village green for the second time. 'What's the plan?'

'The newsagents.'

The man behind the counter couldn't have been more snooty if he tried. He took one look at me and wouldn't give an inch, no matter how much I tried to persuade him I was a professional. It struck me again that we needed proper ID. A business card wasn't enough. I gave up and went back to the car.

'Not keen to lend a hand?' said Jo.

'We'll have to go door to door,' I said. 'A place this small, someone's got to know.'

It was almost eleven o'clock and it appeared most residents of Alderley Edge did stuff on Saturday mornings. There was no answer at the first four houses we tried. A lanky streak of a teenager answered the fifth door we knocked on, but didn't seem to know his own name, let alone anything about Jack Wilkins.

We marched up and down the drives of the next dozen or so

houses, encountering hostility at every turn. One woman shooed us off the drive with a broom. The only person who was anything approaching polite was a harassed-looking young woman who I guessed was the nanny. She invited us in for a cup of tea, which I took as a sign she was desperate for adult company. I didn't blame her – I could hear the wail of at least two children in the background.

'This could take all day,' said Jo, as we trudged back down a rhododendron-lined drive towards the village centre.

When a man who must have been 90 opened the next door we knocked at, I was all for packing up and going home. He was wearing a brown dressing gown that looked like it was made out of felt, rope like icing piped round the edges.

'We're looking for Mr Wilkins?' said Jo. 'We believe you might know him?'

'You'll have to speak up,' he said.

'Mr Wilkins,' I said, raising my voice. 'Owns a car dealership somewhere around here.'

'Or Manchester way,' Jo muttered under her breath.

'What about him?'

'You know him?'

'I know everyone.'

My heart lifted, and I couldn't resist turning to Jo and smiling.

'Pardon?' said the old man.

I faced him. 'Do you know where his business is?'

'What business?'

'Mr Wilkins's,' I added, my throat feeling the strain.

'You'd better come in. Don't want everyone staring.'

We followed him in to the strangest house I'd ever been in to. On the one hand, it was probably the wealthiest house I'd ever been inside, but it was also the dirtiest. And believe me, I've been in dirty houses. Antique furniture sagged under the weight of piles of books, papers, dust, tins of opened cat food, the tin lids still attached but peeled open. Ashtrays, empty bottles of whisky, wine. Bowls that may have once upon a time contained fruit now contained light bulbs, rotten vegetables, cans of WD40.

'Sit yourselves down. Don't get many visitors these days.'

He lifted a fat ginger cat from one of the kitchen chairs and dropped it to the floor. It hissed at me, before finding itself a corner on a pile of newspapers.

'So what do you girls want? Tea, wine, whisky?'

'Tea, for me,' I said. I glanced at the washing-up next to the sink. 'I'll make it.' It would save me the problem of deciding where to sit seeing as how Jo had grabbed the chair the cat had vacated.

The sink was one of those white pottery ones that are square and fashionable now, but this one was probably from the first time around. I tried to organize some kind of system, stacking as much as I could on the worktop. I eventually found the plughole, scooping out the heap of rotting tea bags that had congealed there. The dark gloopy liquid drained out, and I had an empty bowl. I even found a plug.

'So, Mr Wilkins. Do you know him?' asked Jo.

'Lived here fifty-seven years. Know everyone.'

'Know his son, Jack?'

'Who?'

Jo repeated the question louder as the old fella lit a Dunstan. Jo took the one he offered to her.

'Terrible business,' he said before coughing.

'What was?'

'Pardon?'

'What was a terrible business?'

'They moved here '94. Day after Blair got elected.' The old man shook his head, like it was more than the neighbourhood that was going to the dogs.

'Blair was elected in '97,' said Jo.

'Leader of the Labour Party, not the Government, sweet cheeks. Dawning of a new era. New money, you know. You can always tell by the plants.'

76

'The plants?'

'Got no idea, these young ones.'

I glanced out of the kitchen window. The back garden was like a field – at the far end were so many trees it looked like a wood and made it impossible to see where the garden actually ended.

'You seen Jack lately?' asked Jo, her tone nice and conversational.

'Who?'

'Jack Wilkins. The son.'

'Don't get out much these days. Too much to do in here.' He waved an arm around as if he was showing us a load of unfinished projects. He poured himself a slug of whisky into a glass, three-fingers deep. For a moment I envied him. The guy was rich and old. What did he have left to fear? Might as well get pissed from the moment he woke up till the moment he collapsed.

'What about Mr Wilkins?' said Jo.

'Nick Nickerless, I call him. Ladies' man.' He drank from his glass without flinching. 'Women love him. God alone knows why.'

For a moment I thought he was going to cry, but instead, he fell backwards into the only comfy-looking chair in the room. Another cat squawked and made a beeline for the door. 'Young whippersnapper. I've told him a thing a two, in my time. You mark my words.'

Jo pulled a face at me, and I had to agree. Trying to make any sense of what he was saying was giving me a headache.

'Should never have put a woman in charge. I said it right from the start. Knew there'd be trouble. Bite like a black widow.'

'Who?'

'Thatcher. She was responsible for New Labour.'

'Well, you know. Equal opportunities and all that,' said Jo. 'Men screwed it up for years, might as well let a woman have a turn.'

He looked at Jo like he was seeing her for the first time. I could see his watery blue eyes fighting to focus. 'What do you want with Wilkins, anyhow?'

'We want to buy a car.'

'Pull the other one. It's got bells on.' His eyes glinted as he turned and reached for a brass bell that I hadn't noticed in the pile of crap on the sideboard behind him. He rang it, and it hurt my ears.

'We're trying to find his son,' I shouted, in a bid to make the ringing stop.

He returned the bell to the sideboard. 'Friends of his, are you?'

'Yes, sort of. Do you know where we can find Nick? Mr Wilkins?'

'He'll be where he always is.'

'Where's that?'

'Never stops. Bump into him in the De Trafford and he'll try and sell you one.'

'Where does he work?'

'The car place. You passed it on the way in.'

I shook my head.

'Sells those massive ranger things that every sod round here aspires to drive. Take the main road into Manchester, it's on the left-hand side, just after the crossroads with the church. Can't miss it. Probably got a card somewhere.'

He pulled himself up from his armchair and began rummaging through a charity shop's worth of clothing and bric-a-brac. He wrestled open drawer after drawer in the wooden dresser, then the sideboard, before turning his attention to another cupboard that was built into the corner of the room. I noticed odd socks, old curtains, and perhaps something that had once been a ladies' evening dress, dark blue and sequinned, but eventually he came up with an envelope full of business cards. He emptied them out on the table and after a couple of moments shouted, 'got the bugger,' and held aloft a small card. 'Bought the Rover from him. 1999.'

I snatched the card from his hand and almost laughed aloud when I read the header:

Wheels Motor Sales Ltd Big cars for big people.
Proprietor, Nick Wilkins

'Never throw anything, drove Piers potty, but I told him, you never know. You never bloody know.'

I grinned at Jo and passed her the card. She flicked a finger against it. 'Think he'll be there? On a Saturday?'

'Saturday, Sunday, Christmas Day. Always there,' said the old man. 'Has to be, doesn't he?'

'"Has to be"?'

'Devil makes work for idle hands.' He coughed again and had to sit back down. A black cat came to sit on the arm of his chair, headbutting him like it was trying to remind him to take his pills or something.

'You married?' I asked.

'Confirmed bachelor, m'dear.' The old man reached across for the whisky bottle and poured himself another measure.

'Steady on,' I said. 'Have you had breakfast?'

He glared at me, dipped a finger in his whisky and held it out for the cat to lick.

'What about Mrs Wilkins?' asked Jo. 'Does she work there too? What does everyone say about her?'

'Enough.' He pushed the cat from the arm of the chair. 'You want more, you come back another day. My time of life, got to be careful.'

'We only have a couple more questions,' I said. 'Why don't I make you a piece of toast or something?'

'Out,' he said, clambering to his feet. He swung his arms at me, ushering me in the direction of the door we'd come in through. 'Out, out, right now.'

He shooed us as far as the entrance hall. He pulled his dressing gown cord tighter around his waist. 'And listen to me, Missy. If I wanted Meals on Wheels, I'd sodding well ring them. Go on, off.'

'I'm sorry, I didn't mean—'

Jo linked arms with me. 'All right, granddad, keep your hair on. We're going.'

'Spend a term at university, think you can solve the problems of the world. I fought wars for girls like you. Wars.' He made the last word last about five syllables.

The door slammed behind us as we stumbled back onto the drive.

Chapter Twelve

Wheels Motor Sales Ltd was on the outskirts of the town, on the road into Manchester, not the road we'd used to drive into Alderley Edge. On the forecourt stood about twenty-five plush cars, everything from your little sporty two-seaters to those ridiculous semi-land rovers that are the size of tanks – driven by people who wish they were part of the landed gentry. Each one gleamed in the watery sunlight.

'How we going to handle this?' I asked Jo.

A young man strode across the forecourt towards us, a smile plastered across his face. 'Ladies,' he exclaimed, as Jo popped open the door.

I winced and pretended to look for something in the passenger well.

'Cut the crap,' said Jo, climbing out of the van. 'You don't need to sell me anything. I'm here to buy a satnav. How much and how quick?'

I watched through the windscreen. The smile slipped, wobbled but then reappeared. 'A woman who knows her own mind.' He pointed both index fingers at Jo like she was the prize in a coconut shy.

Jo was already halfway across the forecourt. I clambered out of the van.

'Is Mr Wilkins in?'

'I'm the chief sales negotiator.'

'Congratulations. I want to speak to Mr Wilkins.'

He frowned, revealing well-worn grooves in his forehead. 'Are you an acquaintance?'

'No, just like to put a face to the business. Know who I'm buying from.' I tried to sound convincing.

'Ah, well he only deals with car sales. I'm all you need for GPS, satellite navigation, and in-car entertainment systems.'

'Good,' I said, squaring my shoulders and lengthening my spine. 'Tell him I'm in the market for a car, something like,' – I cast my eyes around the lot and picked out a sporty little number – 'something like that baby over there. Tell him I want to take it for a test drive, then you can go and fix my friend up with an in-car satnav entertainment system.'

He might have doubted me, but I pulled my gold-plated American Express from my back pocket. Normally, I'm embarrassed by my trust fund status but, at times, it has its compensations.

'Righto!' He practically skipped across to the office, a campness to his step I hadn't noticed before. He was back two minutes later. 'He'll be with you in a mo. I'll go and take care of your friend.'

He crossed the forecourt to the door that Jo had slipped through.

Less than a minute later an older man appeared on the forecourt. He had a small beer belly that nestled over the top of his smart suit trousers, but other than that he looked fit. Tall, silver-haired, would have been handsome in his younger days, that much was obvious. He stalked across the parking lot like a man used to getting attention. His smile slipped a little as he took a look at me.

'Don't judge a book by its cover,' I said. 'Just think of me as your average, spoilt, badly-behaved trust-fund kid.'

That cheered him up. 'You're looking to buy?'

'Good to go.'

'What d'you have in mind?'

No contest. I turned to the banana-yellow sporty number on the far left of the forecourt. If I was going to go for it, I might as well go for it in style. 'How about that?'

He followed my gaze. 'The Mazda?' He nodded. 'The kid's got taste.'

Five minutes later I was behind the wheel. I didn't like to tell him I'd only learned to drive a few months before, and I'd been taught by Jo, who's got more speeding fines than Usain Bolt. The soundtrack to Jo's driving is a cacophony of blaring horns, interspersed with shouts of things like 'stupid bitch' from men leaning out of car windows.

'Wow.' He grabbed the window frame. 'Easy on the clutch.'

We lurched off the forecourt.

'Four-cylinder engine, fuel injected; 115 BHP.'

I had no idea what he was talking about, but I could feel the power of the engine throbbing through the ball of my foot. This was the closest I'd been to taking drugs in ages. He pressed a button on the dashboard and the roof ground back, exposing a bright blue sky. He must have sensed my enthusiasm because he laughed, and his pointed canines reminded me of a wolf.

'So, where's the trust fund from, kid?'

'My granddad.' The worst thing about this conversation was it wasn't far from the truth. I inherited over a £100,000 from my mother's father, a man who died before I had the chance to meet him. Him and my mum were what you'd call estranged, which is why he cut her from the will and put all his money in trust for me, for the day I turned 21. Of course, my mother had never thought to mention it; so, when she died, it came as a shock. A shock that's taken me the last three years to get over. At least now I understand her bitterness. She never had anything, my mum.

I learned early to lie on the floor behind the sofa when the rent officer called.

'What did he do?'

'What?'

'Your grandfather. What did he do?'

That floored me a little. I knew nothing about him. 'He was a solicitor.' Not altogether a lie. The man who'd told me about my grandfather's trust fund was a solicitor. 'He disowned my mother. She was dead by the time I got the cash.'

'What did she do?'

'Eh?' I lost concentration as a lorry swerved round the corner in front of me. I hit the brakes and heard the screech of rubber against tarmac. My heart banged against my chest as I tightened my grip on the wheel and eased off on the accelerator.

Nick Wilkins didn't appear to have noticed. 'To get disowned?'

'Oh. She … she married the wrong man.'

He threw back his head and laughed, and I felt affronted that he took my family dysfunctionality so lightly.

'What's so funny?'

'No such thing as the right man. Haven't you worked that out? How old are you?'

'I'm 24.' I shot him a glance. 'Are you telling me I should give up on Prince Charming?'

'The wrong man – that your dad?'

'Kind of.'

'"Kind of"?'

'They split up.' I didn't see the roundabout until we were already halfway around it, but it didn't seem to matter. A millimetre's worth of pressure on the accelerator and we were out of trouble. 'I never met him.'

'Take the B road, takes you out of town. Give you a chance to let it have its head.' He paused. 'Sorry. About—'

'Can't miss what you never had.' I kept my eyes on the road. A couple of miles in this and already I felt like a better driver.

We drove in silence for a while until I took a bend too fast, and his left hand clutched the elbow rest on the door panel. That's when I noticed the gold band of his wedding ring. 'Your wife think the same?'

'What?'

'No such thing as the right man?'

'She doesn't think anything.'

The landscape changed as we zoomed out of town, the buildings thinned then dwindled to nothing. The road broadened, lost its pavement. I loved the feeling of the wind rushing against my scalp. I couldn't help myself. I let out this kind of animal sound, somewhere between a cheer and a yell.

He slapped a palm against his thigh. 'First time?'

'Only ever driven a Mini before. And the van.'

He laughed again. 'You don't know what you've been missing.'

I nearly missed the bend in the road. 'Do you think I'm too young?' I asked, easing the pressure on the gas.

'Too young?'

'I could go crazy in this baby.'

'You'd soon learn.'

'Would you let your kid drive this?'

'Character building. Imagine how your mates are gonna look at you.'

I tried to imagine the hippies in LS6 being the least bit impressed as I spun around the streets in a banana-yellow tin can. Then I thought about the scallies. If it lasted more than thirty-five seconds outside my house, I'd eat shit.

'What's up?'

'I'm worried it might get nicked.'

'Anti-theft device, great alarm system.'

I didn't point out that LS6 was alive to the sound of ringing alarms – no one ever batted an eyelid. 'Do you have kids?'

'Last time I looked.'

'Bit cryptic.'

'A son. 'Bout your age.'

'Does he drive a car like this?'

'Prefers to pretend he hasn't got two pennies to rub together. Calls it making his own way.'

'What do you call it?'

'Pig-bloody-mindedness. Can't tell him anything. Just like his mother.'

'I hope you're more charming to her face.'

'She's dead.'

'Oh. Oh, sorry.' I hit a bump in the road and bit my lip.

'Happened a long time ago. I'm over it.' He lit a small cigar. 'I'm over women.'

A Vauxhall momentarily blocked my way, but the other side of the road was clear and straight, so I sailed straight past it, and in seconds it became a grey blue blur in the rear-view mirror. 'They all say that.'

'All sweetness and bloody light, until someone crosses you.'

'Can't all be perfect.'

'Gold diggers.'

I raised my eyebrows. Good job Jo wasn't here. 'You're sounding bitter now.'

'The price of experience. Women see a man like myself, self-made, drives a great car, and you see the pound signs light up in their eyes. You talk to them and they don't reply cos they're too busy trying to work out your net worth. Better than a Savile Row tailor. They can judge the size of a man's wallet from ten paces.'

'You can't be that over them.' I nodded my head towards his wedding ring. 'You remarried.'

He held up his hand in front of his own face. 'Wear this to put them off.' He rested his arm out the side of the window, making aeroplane shapes with his hand. 'If there's one thing life's taught me it's don't make the same mistake twice.'

I turned in my seat to face him. 'You didn't remarry?'

'No.'

'Not even once?'

'What?' A frown darkened his features. In slow motion I saw his lips struggle to form the right words. 'Watch—'

I yanked my attention back to the road but saw only a low-slung stone wall and green fields. What the fuck happened to the road? I braked as hard as I could, smashing my foot against the pedal. The car lurched sideways, the back wheels spinning round, so that they overtook the bonnet. I didn't notice the ditch until the bonnet dropped out of sight. Mr Wilkins's hands jerked forward, as he steeled himself against the dashboard.

'Jesus Ch—'

The car stopped. It had to. To continue any further on its trajectory would have meant going underground. I turned in my seat. The back tyres were three feet off the ground, still spinning.

'Shit.' I closed my eyes. Opened them again. The picture was still the same. 'What about your son?'

'What about my car?' He leaped out of the passenger door and examined the front end.

I stood up in my seat so I was looking over the windscreen. 'Didn't he need a stepmother?'

'Jesus. I think you might have got away with that.' He ran a hand along the bonnet. 'Bloody miracle.'

'You couldn't bring him up on your own.'

He stopped rubbing the car and looked up at me, his dark eyebrows almost meeting in the middle of his forehead. 'How the hell are we going to get it out of here?'

He had a point. The car was at an angle of forty-five degrees, its nose stuck in the ditch.

'Can you lift the front?'

I restarted the engine, which had cut out on impact. Luckily the car was small.

'I'm not bleeding Superman.'

'What about if I get out?'

'Kill the engine. We need something under the front wheels.'

I looked up and down the horizon but saw nothing that sprang to mind.

'Get some stones from the wall,' he said, pointing at the dry-stone wall a few hundred yards away. 'The flattest ones you can find.'

I limped my way across through the tall grasses. I'd hurt my knee, I realized. By good fortune whoever had built the wall had saved the flattest ones for making crenulations on the top. I carried four back, one at a time. On my final journey, Mr Wilkins was lying across the rear of the car, using his weight to force the rear of the car down. His hands just gripped the steering wheel.

'We're going to need a heavy one to jam the accelerator pedal,' he shouted.

I dropped my fourth stone, ignored my grazed fingers and made my way back over the grass.

'And another for the clutch,' he yelled.

It crossed my mind to yell back that he could fetch his own bloody rocks, but I figured I was riding my luck already.

When I got back he'd managed to get the flatter rocks under the front wheels. 'We're both going to have to press on the back. Make sure you get your feet out of the way though.'

I sat on the boot and clung to the edge of the back seat. I felt the rear of the car sink down a fraction. He placed one of my squarer rocks on the floor of the car so that it was pressing down the clutch pedal. Then he got the last rock and dropped it onto the front seat. He turned the key in the ignition and jumped onto the boot, next to me.

'Hold on to your hat.'

He leaned right over to the front, and I saw his shirt rise and a flash of muscle on his back as he stretched across to put the car into reverse gear. He was head down in the driving seat, the rest of his body draped over the rear of the car. There were no back seats.

He dropped the rock onto the accelerator pedal and whipped away the one on the clutch. The car lurched backwards.

I gripped tighter and thought back to our initial client assessment form. The only solid thing, the only fact we knew in this case, slipped between my fingers like sand through an egg timer.

Susan Wilkins wasn't Jack's mother. Or his stepmother. Susan Wilkins wasn't even Susan Wilkins, that much was obvious. Which left me with a couple of questions. Like who was she, and why had she paid us to find Jack?

Chapter Thirteen

I pulled the car onto the forecourt, relief flooding me as I clocked Jo, sat on the bonnet of our van, her face tilted towards the sun. She opened her eyes as I pulled up alongside her and beckoned me over.

'Look at this beauty,' she shouted across.

My legs felt weak as I hauled myself out of the car. I noticed a clump of turf clinging to the bumper. I scraped it off and kicked it under the bonnet. 'Do you know anyone called Susan?' I asked Mr Wilkins through the open roof.

He climbed out of the car. 'You're lucky I'm not going to have to put a claim in on this,' he said as he stroked down the paintwork, looking for dents. 'I can probably get that out with T-Cut. You're lucky the ground was soft.'

'Susan Wilkins?'

He straightened up. 'Never heard of her. Who is she?'

I pulled a face at Jo before turning back to Mr Wilkins. 'She claims she's your wife. Jack's stepmother.'

A dark shadow crossed his face, and his eyebrows knotted. 'Jack? What do you know about Jack?'

The vestiges of attractiveness vanished. His eyes hardened, made him look mean. I felt nervous, glad that I'd waited until we were back in a public place before I'd let him know I wasn't a regular punter.

Jo must have picked up on the atmosphere too, because out of the corner of my eye I saw her throw a cardboard box back into the van and slip behind the wheel.

'I don't know Jack,' I said to Mr Wilkins. The Mazda lay between us, for which I was grateful. Having his gaze on me was frightening enough. 'I just met someone who told me she was his stepmother, that's all.'

'You're going to have to tell me a bit more than that,' he said taking a step towards the front of the vehicle. I instinctively took a step towards the rear. Behind me I heard the van's engine growl into life.

'I don't know anymore,' I said, which wasn't that far from the truth.

'Who is she, this woman?'

'Beats me.'

'Why would someone tell you they're Jack's stepmother?'

'Don't know.'

'Why are you here?'

'I'm trying to find Jack.'

'Why?'

'I'm …' The words failed me. For the first time since we'd opened the business, I didn't want to admit to being a private investigator. 'I'm his girlfriend.'

'You just said you didn't know Jack.'

We paced round the car, for every step I took away from him, he took one closer. 'Do you know where he is?'

He increased his stride. 'You don't lie to me, you …'

I didn't hear the rest of his sentence, his words drowned out by the sound of Jo reversing the van at high speed towards me. The passenger door hung open. As she got within a couple of feet of me, I threw myself headlong into it, hitting my forehead on the handbrake. The gears scrunched, and we lurched forward.

'Quick,' I yelled, trying to haul myself into an upright position.

'Making friends and influencing people again?' asked Jo.

I yanked the passenger door shut as Jo raced out of the forecourt and onto the main road. I turned in my seat, saw Mr Wilkins clambering into the yellow Mazda. 'Shit, he's coming after us.'

'Best buckle up,' said Jo. She never hangs around in situations like those. A duck to water, loves the thrill of the chase. She hung a hard right at the first road we came to. I smelled tyre rubber as we screeched across the junction. I thanked God it was Saturday and there were enough cars on the road to make it feel like we weren't alone.

'What's his problem?' Jo muttered as she jumped a set of red traffic lights and ducked the first left.

'Didn't like my driving.'

'No one likes your driving.'

'He's never heard of Susan Wilkins. And he's never remarried.'

'Can't say that surprises me.'

'Stepmother, my arse,' I said. 'Why hire someone and tell them a bunch of complete lies?'

A road sign loomed ahead of us. I scrunched my eyes to make out the words. 'Manchester,' I said. 'Take the right.'

Horns blared as Jo pulled across a lane of traffic. I turned in my seat. The Mazda was three cars behind us, heading in the same direction. I pulled the road atlas from the glovebox and opened it up on my knee.

'Use the satnav,' said Jo.

'We haven't got time.' I'm not as big a fan of modern technology as Jo is. I like the weight of a road map, the solidity of it.

'What's he going to do?' asked Jo. 'He can hardly bump us off the road.'

'We don't want him to know where we live,' I said. 'We've got to lose him.'

'How much petrol did the Mazda have in the tank?' asked Jo.

I shrugged my shoulders. Like I'd notice that kind of detail when I'm behind the wheel of a sports coupe.

'Cos we've not got much,' said Jo.

'Moss Side,' I said, staring at the map.

'What?'

'He's not going to want to take a car like that into Moss Side.'

Jo slapped the steering wheel. 'Fucking ace. We can go to Tan's.'

Tan is Jo's mate from back home, in Merseyside. Tan went to Manchester Metropolitan University, and has a flat in Hulme, on the outskirts of Moss Side. I turned and saw the biggest grin break out on Jo's face. 'Call her.'

'What's the number?'

She threw me her phone, and I scrolled through her contacts and rang Tan. I looked in the wing mirror, the Mazda now only one car behind us. As the road bent to the left, I could see Wilkins hunched up over the steering wheel, his frame far too big for the little sports car. I turned and flicked him the V sign.

Tan was always going to be in at this time on a Saturday morning, but it was obvious I'd woken her up. I had to repeat my name, then describe who I was, even though I'd met her about half a dozen times, usually at Vanilla, the lesbian mecca of the north, where she's one of the resident DJs.

'A guy's chasing you?'

'Yeah. Long story.'

'Where?'

'On the A34, coming into Manchester.' The scenery around me was changing. The houses got thinner, closer together. A sign to Rushholme, and the curry mile. The road bent to the left and, as we rounded the curve, the atlas slid off my lap and onto the floor by my feet.

I heard Tan shout through her small flat. 'Jo and Lee have got a guy chasing them.'

I couldn't make out the muffled response because Jo was bitching about me not using the satnav.

'Car,' I heard Tan shout. Another shout out in the background. 'What's he driving?' she said to me.

93

I glanced in the wing mirror again. 'A bright yellow, two-seater sports car. A Mazda.'

'Dickhead. Why's he chasing you?'

'Don't know. But I don't think he likes us.'

'Dan's getting his pants on. Get to Moss Side. He'll be there.'

'Thanks, Tan.'

I hung up the call and handed the phone back to Jo, feeling like I was part of a clan, a family. 'Dan'll meet us there,' I said.

'Great.' Jo fiddled with the satnav that was stuck to the windscreen and fired up the screen. 'I asked the guy,' she said. 'It's so simple even you could use it.'

I punched her arm and pushed a few buttons on the monitor thing. A message appeared on the screen:

Enter destination.

Jo changed lanes, which made typing 'Moss Side' difficult. It took me three attempts, but I finally got there. I hit the enter key and a map appeared on the screen. Traffic was building, most people probably making their way into Manchester for a day's shopping. Jo weaved between the lanes of traffic, managing to put a few more cars between us and the Mazda.

I noticed Wilkins indicate left. I turned to kneel on my seat and leaned out of the window. 'He's going,' I said, catching a glimpse of yellow sports car on the exit road. 'Why's he going?'

Jo checked the driving mirror. 'Maybe he realizes he can't do anything to us in this kind of traffic.'

A disembodied voice told us we were on the fastest route and would arrive at our destination in a few short minutes. A feeling of anti-climax hit my stomach. 'Dan's going to think we were making it up. Should I ring them back?'

'Wait a minute,' said Jo. 'He might have guessed where we're going and know a short cut.'

We drove in silence for a few minutes. I lit a fag and put my legs up on the dashboard. I kept my eyes focused on the wing mirror, waiting to see if Wilkins reappeared. As we weaved in and out of the lanes of traffic, something caught my eye.

'*In one thousand feet take the left turn on the—*'

'There's someone else following us,' I said.

'What?'

Jo studied the rear-view mirror. 'Which?'

'The dark blue one.'

'The Volvo? You sure?'

'Switches lanes every time you do.'

'Let's see.' Jo stamped her foot down on the accelerator, and the van lurched forward. She waited till the last possible moment then swerved left without indicating. She took the next left, then first right, taking us down the back street of a red-brick terrace. The satnav lady urged us to make a U turn. I kept my gaze on the wing mirror, saw the blue Volvo nudge round the corner, as Jo hung another right, then a left, back onto the main road. The satnav lady went mental. A few seconds later the Volvo reappeared.

'Think it's a mate of his?'

I wrenched the satnav off the windscreen and muted it before the woman started screaming. The screen kept rescaling as we careered round corners. In-car GPS and satellite navigations systems weren't yet cutting the mustard. I chucked it onto the floor and retrieved my trusted road atlas. I don't know why they say women can't read maps. It's one of my top three skills, along with building spliffs and lighting fires. The secret to life, I've discovered, is learning to play to your strengths.

'Whereabouts in Moss Side, d'you reckon?'

'Just get us there. Dan'll find us.'

'OK.' I knelt on my seat, trying to catch a road name. A quick glance behind showed the Volvo still on our tail. 'Second left. Not this one.'

Jo left it as late as she could. Driving fast, then hitting the brakes and hanging a left, no indication or anything. I kept my eye on the wing mirror. The Volvo made the same manoeuvre. We left the three-lane A34 and hung a left onto a much smaller road, past a park. Semi-detached houses. The adrenaline in my gut was pumping all around my body now and my mind cleared. There are no worries, no gnawing anxieties when you're travelling at sixty down a residential road with a guy on your tail. Moments like these, life is simple, clear-cut.

'We need to burn time,' I said, trying to work out how many minutes it would take Dan to throw on some clothes and get into a car. 'Take this next right.'

The roads were getting smaller, tight terraces, the number of trees and bushes thinning to nothing. The streets felt meaner, harder. I was back where I grew up. Frightening to some, reassuring to me. Familiar. No front gardens, red-brick houses straight onto the street. Identical except for the odd random paint scheme.

'Where now?'

'Keep going round. Next right.' I scanned the map. As long as I didn't take us down a dead end, we'd be OK. I wondered who was driving the Volvo and what they were planning. I opened my window and half-turned in my seat. There were no cars between us now, and whoever it was, they were getting closer. The sun was in front of me, making it difficult to see.

'Right again,' I shouted to Jo, my words getting whipped by the wind. As she flung us round the corner I saw what I hadn't realized I was seeing.

'Shit the fucking bed,' I yelled, pulling my head back inside the van. I turned to Jo. 'He's got a gun.'

'Fuck off,' said Jo. She turned left, even though I hadn't told her to. I fell against the van door.

'He has.' I concentrated my gaze on the wing mirror. 'He's holding it out of the window. Why's he got a gun?'

Jo floored the van. It made a horrible sound like it was trying too hard, metal on metal. She flung us round another corner,

96

and I wished I was wearing my seatbelt. I couldn't stay upright let alone focus on the map.

'I don't know where we are.'

'Shit creek,' said Jo. 'I've got to lose him.'

I threw the map on the back seat and concentrated on looking out of the window. The reassuring-ness of everything being the same was now outweighed by no distinguishing marks to give us a sense of where we'd been, where we were headed.

'Just so long as we don't hit a dead end,' Jo muttered.

'He's never going to fire at us. Not in broad daylight,' I tried to reassure Jo, whose knuckles were bloodless on the steering wheel. She'd hitched herself up in the seat, her nose practically touching the windscreen.

I turned and watched as an arm appeared out of the driver's window again.

'Duck,' I yelled.

A car window smashed, but not ours. A window in a car parked at the side of the road.

'You fucker!' I yelled.

'Shit,' said Jo.

I faced front. 'What?'

A car headed down the street towards us, but the parked cars on either side of the road meant there wasn't enough room to pass.

'He has to pull in,' said Jo. She pressed the accelerator harder, to show whoever was driving the car in front that she had no intention of stopping. It steamrollered towards us, heading for a full-on collision, giving no sign that it was going to back down either. At the last minute it ducked into a space on the side of the road and we fled past, the Volvo inches behind us.

'Left.'

Jo swerved.

'Left again.'

'What the fuck?'

A red car was parked perpendicular across the road. Filling the street. There was no way past. No time to stop.

'Brace yourself,' Jo screamed.

At the moment of impact, I screwed up my eyes, waited for the pain, the smash, hurt.

Nothing.

I opened my eyes. We were heading down the road – no sign of the red car. I glanced at Jo.

'Open your eyes!' I screamed, grabbing the steering wheel.

I turned in my seat. The red car was behind us, in the same position, un-smashed. Like we'd just teleported straight through it. A man crouched behind it, holding a baseball bat.

'Dan,' we both said together, as two more cars headed down the street towards us. They both passed us and pulled up behind the red car. I watched the Volvo stop on the other side of the roadblock. Suddenly the streets seemed busy. Another two blokes were jogging down the road, scarves round the lower half of their faces. No jackets despite the cold.

Jo pulled into the kerb and threw herself into the back of the van. A group of lads approached the Volvo, but we couldn't see the driver.

'We need to tell them he's got a gun.'

I opened the passenger door and steeled myself for the sound of gunfire.

'Keep down,' said Jo.

Glass smashed. I stared at Jo. 'What if he shoots them?'

'He's not going to start a war in Moss Side,' said Jo. I prayed she was right as I climbed out of the van, ducked low and headed towards Dan.

She was. I hadn't even got to the red car when I heard a squeal of car tyres and saw the Volvo reversing back the way it had come, its windscreen smashed.

I ran towards it, wanted to catch a glimpse of the driver, to see who it was, but it was going so fast, even in reverse, that I didn't stand a chance. A tall figure, dressed in black jeans and an oversized black hoodie jogged towards me. I kept my eyes on the Volvo, watched it screech around a corner, then come out, forward this time and speed off in the other direction. The next thing I knew Dan had put his arm around me.

'All right?'

'Did you see him? The driver?'

'White guy. Ugly. He won't be back.'

I let Dan steer me back to the van. Jo had opened the back doors and was climbing out, Dr Martens first. Dan grinned.

'Morning.'

'Wow,' shouted Jo. She punched him in the ribs. 'Awesome.'

They hugged, a proper bear hug and I knew Jo was more shaken than she was letting on. My own knees were finding it hard to stay locked.

'You always know how to start a party. Thought you said it was a yellow Mazda.'

'It was when we set off,' I said, unease settling around me.

Chapter Fourteen

Jo drove us back to Leeds at eighty-five miles an hour. The van makes so much noise at that speed we couldn't hear the other speak, and the engine got so hot I had to take my jacket off. As we hit the inner ring road, and our speed fell off to a quieter forty-five, I put my feet up on the dashboard. I'd had time to think a few things over.

'Jack disappeared without taking the money, which means he didn't know it was there. If you're going to take off, you'd take the cash.'

'Come in useful for things like aeroplane tickets,' agreed Jo. 'Who the fuck was the guy with the gun?'

'So, assuming he hasn't been kidnapped or killed, someone else put the money in his socks. Agreed?'

'Agreed.' Jo exhaled a cloud of smoke. 'Who the fuck is Susan Wilkins?'

'And the socks were new. So, someone put the money in the socks and put the socks in Jack's room.'

'We know less than we did yesterday.'

'We need to go back to Pants. Find out who had access to Jack's sock drawer.' I already had a list of potentials in my head – Pants, Carly and Brownie for starters. But as Pants had handed

Jack's stuff over to us, it was unlikely he knew what was inside, and I couldn't see Carly being involved either. She was too green. And if Brownie knew the money was there, surely he'd help himself to enough to cover the PlayStation. And for a man with that much fear in his eyes, I'd expect him to help himself to a whole lot more.

No, there was another force at work here. It was time to find out who and why.

Pants didn't look any more pleased to see us the second time around. And this time there was no doubt we'd woken him up, even though it was almost two o'clock in the afternoon. He used his left arm to open the door. He had to. His right arm was in a cast.

'Jesus,' said Jo. 'What happened to you?'

'Get lost.'

I winced at the black eye he sported. It made my own eyes water.

'No need to be rude,' said Jo.

He tried to close the door but Jo's faster than that. She pushed her way through the doorframe.

'I don't want to get involved,' said Pants.

'You are involved,' I said, turning round, glancing up and down the street. It looked like a normal Saturday afternoon in Woodhouse. Music drifted from a bedroom window further up the street. Nothing out of place. I turned back to Pants. 'Brownie?'

'Don't be stupid.'

'Well, what then? Come on, you might as well tell us. Our offices got turned over last night.'

He stuck his head out the door and did his own survey of the street.

'We've got to find Jack,' I said. 'He's in trouble.'

Pants took a step back and we entered the hallway. He shut the front door behind us but didn't ask us any further into the house. 'Two guys. Showed up yesterday, about an hour after you, asking whether Jack had left something for them.'

'And?'

'They asked for his stuff. I said I didn't have it.'

'You gave them our card,' I said, matter-of-fact. I didn't blame him.

'Didn't have much choice.' He held up his broken arm.

'You could have warned us,' said Jo.

'I spent most of the night in A&E. Six hours to get an X-ray.' Pants moved backwards and took a seat on the bottom step of the hall staircase. 'Came to tell you – on my way home. The door was boarded up.' He took a breath. 'I owe you an apology.'

'Yes,' said Jo.

'You should have said,' said Pants, his dark fringe flopped over his black eye. 'I thought you were Jack's dealers.'

'I did try.' I'm not that familiar with the moral high ground, so when I find myself on it, it's easy to get carried away. I tried to put my own stuff to one side, to focus on the case. 'You owe Jack the benefit of the doubt too.'

He sighed but I knew it was a sigh of defeat. I leaned against the hall wall. 'Who had access to Jack's room, apart from Jack?'

'No one. He kept it locked.'

'He must have had mates round. His girlfriend?'

'Yeah. And we'd go in there a bit, me, Brownie and Pen, but only when he was there.'

'Who's Pen?'

'She lives here. Been here ages.'

'Has anyone tried to get into his room, since he left I mean?'

'No. Although …'

'What?'

'Well, when he left, he left his door unlocked. I know, cos after his letter came, I went in his room. Then, couple of nights ago – Wednesday, no Thursday, Ian, a mate of Pen's, needed some-where to crash. So we told him he could have Jack's room.'

102

'But?'

'But the door was locked. We had to force it to get in.'

'So you think he'd been back and locked his room?'

'Maybe. But then why post us a letter if he's still in Leeds?'

'But who else would have a key?' Jo asked.

'And he didn't take his stuff?' Now I was really confused.

'Well, his stuff wasn't there. When the note came, I cleared his room out.' Pants tilted his chin. 'It was a right state.'

'You didn't think he'd ever come back?'

Pants shrugged. 'I was pissed off. His note said they'd come looking for him – I thought it'd be better if it looked like he'd packed up and done one. His stuff was all down in the cellar.'

My pulse rate accelerated. It wasn't Jack that came back. Jack didn't know about the money. Whoever did know about the money, whoever put the money in Jack's drawers, came back. My veins buzzed.

'Can we see the room?'

'There's nothing in it.'

'Still like to see it.'

'I guess,' he said, pulling himself up on the bannisters. 'You're lucky you caught me. Pen's had a fit – gone back to her folks.' He led us up the stairs to the first-floor bedroom at the front of the house, still mumbling as we went. 'No one wants to stay here now.'

We arrived at a bedroom door on the first floor. It had a Yale lock fitted to the door – the kind of lock you'd expect on a front door. I pushed the door open with my foot. The metal clasp that housed the lock on the other side of the doorframe was gone. I glanced at Pants. 'You kicked it in?'

'Ian needed to crash.' He looked sheepish. 'We were a bit pissed.'

I stepped inside the room. There was a mattress on the floor in the corner, with a duvet on top and a sink in the corner of the room. The furniture was cheap and mismatched – a chest of wooden drawers and an empty bookcase, with a pinboard above it. Other than that, the walls were bare.

'So, who would have a key to this room?'

'Jack.'

'His girlfriend?'

'Maybe.' He sounded doubtful.

'Anyone else?'

'He wasn't that social a guy.'

'If someone came in and locked the door, they must have had a key.'

'Not necessarily. They could have just let the clasp down,' said Jo as she fiddled with the lock. 'It's a Yale.'

I tried a different tack. 'Where's Brownie?'

Pants slumped against the wall, like standing was a strain. 'He's not answering his phone. We were supposed to be doing Morrisons this morning.'

'How long has Jack been using?' I asked.

Pants exhaled. 'I was in Peru last summer. Things haven't been right since I came back. Things that didn't add up.'

'Did you talk to him about it?'

'No. I wasn't sure. Not until the break-in.'

'"Break-in"?'

'Last month. We got back from The Brudenell and someone had smashed the kitchen window and spray-painted, "Pay Up" on the kitchen wall.'

'You might have mentioned that earlier,' Jo said.

Pants turned and limped back down the stairs. I took one last look at Jack's room and then followed him.

'Tell us about it. It's important.'

'It was three, maybe four, weeks ago. A load of us came back after the gig – Brownie, Jack, Pen, and Martha. Someone had taken a baseball bat to the back door.'

'Who's Martha?'

'Brownie's latest.' He led us into the kitchen.

'And a person in her own right,' said Jo. Pants frowned.

'Is Brownie doing smack as well?' I asked.

104

Pants didn't look at me. Instead he picked up the cardboard box that was on the kitchen table and put it on top of an identical box that was on the floor. I noticed the new lock on the back door. 'Jack and Brownie are inseparable. Jack does what Brownie tells him to. Or at least he used to.'

'"Used to"?'

Pants crouched down to the cupboard under the sink. He pulled out a roll of bin liners and a mop bucket. 'Jack's got his stuff, you know? Issues. Who hasn't? But, lately, he seemed to be getting his shit together.'

'He met Carly.'

Pants looked up. 'You know about Carly?'

'We are private investigators,' I said.

Pants closed the cupboard door and stood up again. 'She's good for him.'

'What does Brownie think?' asked Jo.

Pants shrugged. 'Brownie does what Brownie always does when he doesn't want to deal with something. Ignores it. Pretends it's not happening.'

'If they're inseparable, and both into drugs, then along comes a girl, Jack starts cleaning up his act … Stands to reason Brownie might be feeling a bit left out.'

'Jack keeps Carly out of it. Doesn't want her getting messed up in it all, I guess. Wish he'd done the same for us.'

'What's Brownie's girlfriend like?' I asked.

'Who? Martha?'

'What's with the eyebrows?' asked Jo.

'Don't think *girlfriend*'s the right word.'

'What is?' asked Jo.

'They're on and off. More off than on.'

'Where does she live?'

'No idea.'

'Think Brownie might be with her?'

He wrinkled his nose as he put the mop bucket in the sink

and turned on the hot tap. 'Brownie's more your love 'em and leave 'em kind of guy. 'Course, she'll have been in Jack's room quite a bit.'

'Come again?' said Jo.

I knew what Jo was thinking. We've both hung out with anarchists long enough to know they're forever jumping in and out of bed with each other. I'm not judging, just saying.

Pants let the water run for a few moments before he switched off the tap and lifted the bucket out. 'Jack's room used to be Brownie's room. They swapped.'

'They swapped bedrooms?'

'Yeah.'

Jo and I glanced at each other. The significance didn't escape either of us. 'Why?'

Pants turned back to face into the room, a puzzled look on his face. 'Students next door. One of 'em moved his girlfriend in. The sound of them banging away all night kept Jack awake. He couldn't hack it. So, Brownie offered to swap.'

I could hardly bear to look at Pants. His swollen eye made mine sting. I focused on his chest instead. 'When?'

'I dunno. Don't keep a calendar of what goes on around here. Last few weeks have been mental.'

'Recently?'

'Yeah, last couple of weeks.'

'What's this Martha look like?'

'Spiky hair. She's older, thirty maybe. Skinny, bit moody.'

'What's she do?'

'Student, I think. Post-grad.'

'Anything else you can tell us about her?'

'She wears a ring.' He touched his right nostril to demonstrate where she wore it. 'Small, silver.'

Pants asked if we'd given the two guys the tin of Old Holborn containing the smack. I said we hadn't been there to hand it over. 'They'll be back,' he said. 'Be careful.'

106

'Have you told the police?'

'No.' He shook his head. 'I'm off to London. I'm done with Leeds.'

We left Pants packing up what was left of the squat. I'm not sure what I think about anarchy. It sounds fairly cool, but perhaps we all need the structures to live by. I once spent a long weekend in an attic with an anarchist called Martin. He had the tautest belly and pierced, dark brown nipples. Christ, he was good in bed, but the stink of his tiny kitchenette pervaded the whole flat and eventually it got too much, and I had to leave. I'm not exactly a cleanliness freak but there are limits.

Chichini's on Hyde Park corner is perfect for a late breakfast. Jo drove us there, and we both ordered a full English and I wrote notes while we waited for it to arrive. I knew things were starting to add up. I just didn't know what kind of sum they were making.

'Perhaps we ought to go to the police,' I said to Jo.

'No way.'

'Because?'

'Because they're the pigs.' Jo paused as I pulled a face at her. 'It's the principle.'

I didn't ask where her principles were when she was seeing Andy. I may take risks but I'm not stupid. 'OK, comrade.' I raised a clenched fist. 'But it's pretty obvious the bad guys are going to be back for the tin.'

Jo interlaced her fingers and stretched her knuckles till they cracked. 'And the cash.'

I shook my head. 'They don't know about the cash. I don't think anyone knows about the cash.'

'Someone does,' said Jo. 'The person who put it there.'

We were interrupted by the arrival of breakfast. My stomach growled at the smell of it. I couldn't remember when I'd last eaten and I was starving. I picked up the ketchup. 'Who's going to hide twenty-four grand in your sock drawer, without telling you?'

'Your fairy godmother.'

I let my mind wander. 'Your pimp.'

Jo forked an entire sausage, spearing it like a fish. She bit off the end, chewed and swallowed before speaking. 'A very satisfied client.'

'Someone who loves you a lot.'

'Think we should visit Carly again?'

'Maybe.' I shook my head, trying to get my thoughts to settle. 'They swapped rooms. Maybe whoever put the cash in there thought it was Brownie's room. And Pants said Brownie had been trying to ditch his woman, what was she called?' I checked my notes. 'Martha. Maybe she's trying to buy him back?'

'At twenty-four grand for a man?'

'Depends what kind of man.'

'Ain't no man alive worth that kind of cash,' Jo said.

We ate in silence until our plates were clean. I sat back and undid the button on my jeans. Jo flicked a baked bean off the table. It sailed through the air landing a good couple of feet away. 'Still don't see why someone would stash all that cash and not tell anyone?'

'True.' I took a slurp of the orange tea Chichini's is famous for. A thought had occurred to me over my breakfast and the more it played in my mind, the more sense it made. 'Maybe they did. Only, they didn't tell Jack, they told Brownie.'

Jo considered this for a moment. 'Brownie thinks Jack's run off with the money and goes mental.'

'Accuses Jack of running off with his PlayStation or Xbox or whatever – that's just a cover – what he's after is the cash.'

Jo wiped her fingers on a napkin and reached for the tobacco tin. 'We're back to the beginning. We need to find Brownie.'

'And Martha.' I underlined the two names in my notebook.

I glanced at the clock above the counter. Almost four o'clock. Jo must have caught my thought.

'We're late for our phone call with Mrs Whatever-the-fuck-her-name-is-Wilkins.'

The streets outside were filling up as students made their way to the Hyde Park pub – Saturday night drinking started early round here.

I didn't want to speak to Mrs Wilkins on the phone. I wanted to meet her, eyeball to eyeball. 'How do we find her?'

'Tell her we've found Jack.,' said Jo, handing me her mobile. 'She'll come.'

I pulled the piece of paper I'd scribbled her number on from my pocket. She answered before I'd even heard the phone ring.

'You're late.'

'Sue me,' I said.

'You've got news?'

'We need to meet.'

'You found him?' Was it hope in her voice, or desperation?

'Yes. Yes, we found him. The Parkinson Steps. Thirty minutes. Make sure you're alone.'

Chapter Fifteen

I wouldn't have recognized Mrs Wilkins if we'd fallen over her, which was a bit odd given as how we'd arranged to meet her. And she was in the right place and bang on time. The Parkinson Steps lead up to the front of the Parkinson Building, which marks the beginning of the university campus. Jo and I had been standing inside one of the cheap sandwich cafés across the road, watching and waiting for her to show up. We'd seen no one suspicious. Just the usual bunch of students traipsing in and out – the Parkinson Building is home to the university library.

Thirty minutes came and went. There was a lot of activity, even though it was Saturday, because everyone arranges to meet at the Parkinson Steps – part of our reason for choosing it. Students come out of the library for their fag breaks, or to grab a sandwich. The steps face south, towards to the city centre, so if there's any sun, you're always sitting in it. I'd clocked a student, dressed in blue jeans, trainers and wearing a university scarf but I'd not paid her much attention. Only complete geeks wear university scarves. And, although it was obvious she was waiting for someone without wanting to look like she was waiting for someone, she looked nothing like Susan Wilkins.

But as time slipped past and Mrs Wilkins didn't show, I

returned to study the student. I noticed she kept going inside and coming out again. She had short dark hair, clipped back off her face, and her jeans were tight, clinging to her skinny frame. She looked fit, like she exercised, because the bulge of her calf muscles was noticeable, even from our location on the opposite side of the road.

Having made two Cokes last the best part of an hour, Jo and I left the café and crossed the road. It was only as we climbed the stairs and I caught the look on the geeky girl's face that I realized. I started, opened my mouth to say something, to alert Jo, but Mrs Wilkins shook her head, as if to warn me to keep quiet. I felt Jo grab my arm, and I knew she'd made the connection too. We both stood there, gawping, while our client turned and slipped inside the doors. I glanced at Jo and she pulled a face at me before we followed into the foyer of the Parkinson Building.

'You're late,' was the first thing she said.

'You're a different person,' I said.

I don't like change. I hate it when people I know get haircuts. I like certainty. Maybe it's something to do with having a mother who rarely dressed. Predictability is what I know.

Of course, I've had to learn to be more flexible, mostly because Jo likes to experiment. One day she'll bleach her hair, the next she'll get cornrows. She's dyed her hair every colour from blue to pink, sometimes both at the same time.

I'm a creature of habit and visits to hairdressers weren't high on my mother's list of priorities. I've got the lowest maintenance hairstyle possible. Long, dark hair, tied back in a ponytail. No fringe. Washed once a week. Usually Sundays.

But while I remain constant, I've tried to get used to the fact that women change. Might surprise you. Might suddenly show up in a red jacket when they've always worn black. Susan Wilkins made my jaw drop. Her hair was dark and glossy, and you'd never have known the wig was a wig. In fact, I wondered, which was the wig – this or the blonde do, the one she'd had when I first met her?

'We didn't recognize you,' I said, somewhat needlessly. It struck me as we stared like unblinking goldfish that when you looked up close you could tell her skin was a bit older than that of your average student. But, as a mature, late-twenties, biology or earth science graduate, I totally believed in her.

'Let's go to the refec,' she said, leading the way to the left. 'It's busy in there.'

'How old are you?' I blurted.

She didn't answer. We followed her through the vast hall, and as I caught sight of her bum in her tight blue jeans I cursed my own stupidity. I was supposed to be a private detective for crying out loud. Susan Wilkins clearly wasn't old enough to be the mother of a 22-year-old. I'd seen what I wanted to see.

The refectory was in the Student Union building – two minutes across campus. It was half-full, even though it was Saturday. It was getting close to finals time of year. I'd overheard the word 'dissertation' three times by the time we'd bought coffees. Mrs Wilkins led the way to the tables at the far side, furthest away from the doors we'd just come through.

I always feel like a fraud when I'm in the university – 'the' pronounced to rhyme with bee. I studied at the one down the road, Leeds Beckett, which has always lived in the shadow of the University of Leeds – both literally and figuratively. Posh and Becks is how everyone refers to them.

We sat at a table that was littered with empty cans of Coke and Red Bull and the plastic wrap of a sandwich. Jo tidied the rubbish while I faced our client.

'Tell me,' she said. 'Where is he?'

'What's with the hair?' I said.

'I know. I—'

'How old are you?' I asked again.

'I wasn't completely honest—'

'I'm struggling to think of one thing you've said to us which wasn't a total lie.'

'Keep your voice down,' she said, emptying two packets of sugar into her coffee and stirring it with a wooden stick. Goosebumps ran up and down the length of my forearms. Wet wood sets my teeth on edge.

'I want to know how old you are.'

Jo slipped into the seat next to Mrs Susan Wilkins, effectively barring her escape.

'She's thirty-five,' said Jo.

'I'm thirty-three,' Mrs Wilkins fired back. She took a breath and steadied herself. 'All this is putting years on me. Where's Jack?'

'You need to pay us,' said Jo. 'Before we tell you the news.'

'Why the disguise?' I asked, dropping my voice to a whisper.

She glanced around her to assess whether the tables nearest to us were within hearing distance. She obviously decided they weren't because she returned to stirring her coffee. 'I'm being followed,' she said. 'It's freaking me out.'

'You think it's to do with Jack?'

'Did you find Brownie?'

'Money first,' said Jo.

'I paid you a deposit, yesterday.'

'We've done twelve hours, weekend rate,' said Jo, as she pulled a figure out of thin air and gave it to Mrs Wilkins. 'And you've lied to us. You're lucky we're not charging you danger money.'

Our client didn't show a single emotion as she pulled a wad of notes out of her jeans pocket, peeled off a few and handed them to Jo. She hesitated, then added another couple to the pile. 'I know you've been working hard,' she said. 'And I'm sorry about your offices.'

Jo nodded and tucked the money into her denim jacket pocket. In truth, money was the least of our problems, but even so, excitement made my stomach fizz. We were being paid for doing what I love. In that moment I didn't really care who she was, or that she'd told us a whole bunch of lies. She was still our client.

'So,' Jo broke the moment. 'We've found out quite a lot.'

'Really?'

'Yes.' Jo glanced at me. 'Where to start?'

Something inside me just told me to go for it. The whole situation we found ourselves in was caused by people not being straight with each other. Time to lead by example, cards on the table. I took a mouthful of tea and swallowed. 'We've found out you aren't Jack's mother, step or otherwise.'

She didn't stop stirring her coffee, round and round and round.

'We found out Jack hasn't been home for Christmas for years,' I continued. 'Him and his dad haven't seen each other in a long time.'

Mrs Wilkins let go of the wooden stick, and I grabbed my moment. I snatched it from her coffee and added it to the pile of rubbish Jo had moved to the table next to us. When I turned back, Mrs Wilkins had dropped her head into her hands. She had a bunch of silver rings on her fingers, the kind you'd find in hippy shops. No sign of a wedding band.

'Not married anymore?' I asked.

She looked up. 'You didn't talk to his dad, did you?'

'Another thing we've found out is that you're not the only one looking for Jack,' said Jo. 'There are, shall we say, retail suppliers,' – Jo made inverted commas with her fingers – 'searching for him too.'

'Probably something to do with the fact that Jack owes them a lot of money,' I added, compelled to give her something she didn't know. She had paid us, after all. A thought struck me. 'And while we're on the subject, if you're not his mother, where are you getting all this cash from? To pay us?'

'Why don't we start again,' said Jo, smiling like she was a bank teller getting someone to open an account. She took out the notebook and turned to a clean page. 'Let's start with the easy ones. Who are you? I mean, really.'

Mrs Wilkins ran a hand through her fringe and tucked it behind her ear. There was something about the gesture that made me think this hairstyle was the real one, that she was used to having hair get in her eyes. 'I'm sorry. I should have been upfront, right from the start. I didn't want to get you into trouble.'

'We find honesty is the best policy,' said Jo. 'In our line of work it really helps.'

'I thought the less you knew, the easier it would be.'

'Name,' said Jo. 'Tell us your name. If you say Susan, or Wilkins, we're out of here.'

'I didn't want to get you involved in this drug dealing issue.'

'So, you know Jack's a heroin addict?' I asked.

She hesitated. 'I suspected. I wasn't certain.'

'We know he's not your son.'

'He's a friend. A friend of a friend.'

'So, who's the friend?' asked Jo.

Mrs Wilkins blinked. I cut to the chase. 'Are you dealing?'

She nursed her mug of coffee in both hands. 'It's all going pear-shaped. I'm trying to help.'

I leaned across the table towards her. I didn't intend to appear threatening, but the suspense was too much for me. I wanted to shake the words out of her. 'We can't work for you if you don't tell us who you are.'

'I'm a wreck,' she said, and from my close-up viewpoint I couldn't help but agree. Her eyes were bloodshot, had dark circles beneath them. She looked knackered. 'Can't eat, can't sleep. I'm terrified.'

'Who's following you?'

'I've never done anything like this before.' Her eyes glistened. 'I've never felt like this before. Don't know what to do with myself.'

Women. I'd heard these words before and I know what they mean, even though I've never experienced it first-hand. Lust, yeah, but not the love stuff. Thank God. As I stared at her, something happened and inspiration hit me full on, right smack between the eyes.

'Brownie,' I said.

'Yes,' she said, in a voice so quiet it was difficult to hear.

I leaned in closer, so that I could feel the heat of her breath when she exhaled. It wasn't until I saw it, that I knew what I was looking for – the small hole in the right-hand side of her nostril, the hole that would normally house a small silver ring.

'Hello, Martha,' I said.

Tears brimmed in her blue eyes. Jo pulled a pack of tissues from her bag, took one out and handed it to her. 'We've all been there,' she said.

'Start from the beginning,' I said.

Women in love are the same the world over. All they want to do is talk. Having never been in love, I don't know what that feels like – but from the outside it looks like a disease.

The tears cascaded down her hollow cheeks. Her words came out in half-formed sentences, random blurts. 'Met him last summer. Didn't mean it to happen. Not like this. Not my type.' She grabbed breaths like she might be drowning. 'Last thing I wanted.' She grabbed Jo's arm. 'You have to believe that.'

'Always happens when you're not looking for it,' said Jo.

I sat back in my chair and listened to Jo soothing Martha, saying all the right things in all the right places. It struck me then that Jo was back, really back, and for a moment my eyes stung. For a long time after she'd caught Andy with his other woman, she'd been like a zombie – like the light inside her had gone out.

I focused on the stripes on Martha's shirt. They were red or purple, or perhaps red and purple. The lines blurred before my vision.

'Where'd you meet?' I heard Jo ask.

'The Chemic,' said Martha. 'He bought me a drink. We got talking. I knew, straightaway. Have you ever had that? Just. Boom. Told myself I could handle it. We could be mates, hang out. We went out a couple of times. Then he turned up at mine. And that was it.'

116

'Wow,' said Jo.

Martha blew her nose. 'Everyone thinks he's bad news, but he's not, he's just got this exterior, once you get past that he's so gentle, so scared. If you knew what he's been through …'

'Sounds amazing,' said Jo. 'Almost too good to be true.'

Martha pulled a face at her. 'I used to be as cynical as you. I'm not stupid. I've been around.'

'So where is he?'

'He has trust issues.'

'They've all got trust issues,' said Jo. 'That's because they're untrustworthy.'

Martha continued like she hadn't even registered Jo had spoken. 'Specially round women. His mum did her best, but he's damaged.'

'And you think you can fix him?'

'I love him.'

'Sweet Jesus,' Jo muttered.

'You know he's a heroin addict?' I asked.

She looked at me, long and hard. I returned her gaze. 'That's not his fault,' she said after a long time.

I pulled a face. I didn't see how anyone could take heroin without it being their fault. There's always the first time, the time when you could say no. That's the thing about junkies. In my experience they're the ones who think they're a bit better than everyone else, a bit cleverer. Heroin is addictive, but not to them.

'What, he was held down and forced to inhale?'

Anger flashed across her face, turning her blue eyes a shade of purple. 'Ever been in care?'

I shook my head. Didn't say that when I was nine I rang social services and begged them to take me away. They came round once, but decided my mum needed me to remind her to take her pills.

I forced myself to concentrate on what Martha was saying.

'Brownie grew up in and out of care homes. Here, Halifax,

Scarborough. He's been in them all. His mum would get sectioned, he'd get taken into local authority care. One time, he told me, his mum stripped him naked then set the house on fire. He was 5, 6 years old. It's one of his earliest memories. I mean what chance?'

'Doesn't explain the smack,' I said. I know I sounded judgemental. But we all have stuff to bear, our crosses. Not everyone turns to Class As.

'The staff in the care home used to give the kids heroin to smoke, to keep them quiet, manageable. So they could abuse them.'

'No way,' said Jo. But I knew from her tone she didn't have any trouble believing what she was hearing. 'Jesus.'

'I checked it out. Spoke to a drug and alcohol counselling agency in the area. There's more than one allegation although no action's ever been taken. Apparently, they told the kids it was a joint, but it was heroin, not pot.'

'I don't believe it,' I said, which was the wrong thing to say, because the worst thing was I did.

'It'll all come out one day. What chance did those kids have? They were addicts before they had a chance to be people.'

'He should report them,' I said.

Jo turned to me. 'That's making it his responsibility.'

'He can't let himself feel,' said Martha. She was speaking directly to Jo. 'But watch him on a hunt, fighting to save a fox, and you see how much love he's capable of. The kind of guy he is.'

'He loves you?' asked Jo.

'When he gives you attention, when you're under his spell, it's the best feeling in the world.' Her eyes widened, like she was pleading with us to understand. I wish I did. Or maybe I'm glad I don't.

'So where is he?' asked Jo.

She wiped under her eyes with the back of her index finger. 'He's off on one. He thinks he can't trust me. Thinks I'm out to get him, but I swear I'm not. I'm trying to help.'

'How? How are you paying us? Where's the money coming from?' I asked again.

'Everyone's on his back.' She glanced around. 'You know they're in debt, Brownie and Jack, and the people they owe aren't what you'd call patient.'

'Why tell us you were Jack's mother?'

'I didn't want Brownie to think I was going behind his back. I thought if you talked to him, and told him I'd hired you, he'd freak out.'

Martha leaned across the table to me. 'Jack's dropped his best mate in the shit and taken off. Not surprising Brownie doesn't know who he can trust.'

'So, you're not looking for Jack, you're looking for Brownie? Really you wanted us to find Brownie?'

'How does finding Jack help you find Brownie?' Jo asked.

I thought I knew the answer, but I waited for her to explain it to us all the same.

She paused for a moment and then said: 'I think Jack's got the money.'

'To pay off the dealers?'

She nodded and drained her coffee.

'How much are we talking?'

'A lot.'

'About fifty quid? A hundred?' asked Jo.

'Thousands,' said Martha.

'*Thousands.*' I repeated. I leaned back in my chair and laced my fingers behind my head. 'So, problem's over. Jack can pay off the debt, Brownie's off the hook.' I tried to keep my voice casual. 'Where did Jack get that much money from?'

'No idea. The point is Jack's got the money, but he's disappeared. Instead of paying them off, he's taken off.' She took a sip of her coffee.

'You think he's decided to start a new life somewhere else?' asked Jo. 'With twenty-four grand he could—'

Her head whipped round. 'How do you know that?' she asked.

'Pants told us,' I said, before Jo could say anything else. 'The dealers told him, at the same time as they broke his arm.' I tried to slow down my words. 'He said they owe twenty-four thousand—'

'They broke his arm?'

'Last night,' said Jo. 'He's seriously scared. Leaving Leeds.'

'Where did you get the photo of Jack?' I asked. 'If you're not his mother?'

'They've definitely not been paid?' Martha spoke directly to Jo.

I didn't point out that it was highly unlikely that drug dealers would be going round Leeds breaking people's arms if they'd been paid. She was a woman clutching at straws and she knew it. Jo shook her head.

'They're going to kill Brownie,' she said, her voice breaking. 'Where is he?'

'I don't know. He disappeared last week – for a whole week. I was going out of my mind. Then, suddenly, he turns up and—'

'Did he say where he'd been?'

'To see a friend in Newcastle. I tried to talk to him, but he's totally paranoid. I don't know where he's sleeping, what he's doing, whether he's safe.'

It occurred to me as I sat there watching her that she was the addict. Her hands shook, her fingernails were bitten, she had black bags under her eyes and her hair needed a wash. Another junkie needing a fix.

'How do you know Jack's got the money?' I said. 'Maybe he's done a runner because he hasn't got the money and he's as scared as Brownie. Or maybe they've done a runner together. Maybe Brownie knows where Jack is. You said he disappeared for a week, maybe he went to wherever Jack is now.'

'No.' She shook her head. 'He doesn't know. He came round on Wednesday, he's desperate to find Jack. They're so close. Brownie's lost without him.'

'How do you know Jack's got the cash?'

She glanced to her left. 'He's got the money.'

'How do you know?'

She hesitated. 'I went to see him. When Brownie disappeared. He told me he'd got the money and he was going to sort it all out.'

Jo raised her eyebrows at me. Another lie. Jack couldn't have told her he had the money because Jack didn't know he had the money. Jack didn't have the cash. We had the cash. Should we tell Martha? Jo and I stared at each other, mulling over the same question, silently discussing it as Martha continued talking. She glanced around the refectory again.

'I think they're following me. They're hoping I'll lead them to Brownie.'

I sat watching her chewing her fingernails. She was never still, always twitching, her eyes darting around the room. Every time anyone walked into the refectory, she knew about it. We fell silent, each with our own thoughts. It was our moment to tell her that the cash was at our office, that we could stop what was happening, pay off the bad guys, make the world better for Brownie, and perhaps for Martha too. That was our moment and we didn't take it. I shook my head at Jo, a barely noticeable shake. I still don't fully understand why, but a voice inside me, clear as anything, warned me not to trust her.

'What do you know about the dealers?' Jo asked. 'The ones Brownie and Jack owe?'

'I can't get involved,' said Martha.

'A name, anything that might help us?'

Martha hesitated for the briefest second. 'I think I dropped Brownie at their house once. He didn't say that's what he was doing, because he knows I wouldn't have taken him. He told me he was visiting a mate.'

'But?'

'I saw him later that same evening. I knew he'd scored.'

'And where was it, this place?'

Jo asked the question. I didn't want to know. The less knowledge, the smaller the dilemma. If we knew where these dealers lived, we'd have responsibilities – twenty-four thousand of them. I remember frowning across the table at Jo, willing her to shut up. She never takes any notice, so I don't know why I thought she would this time. Martha lowered her voice and gave us an address.

'Perhaps we should pay them a call,' said Jo, raising one eyebrow to me rather than Mrs Wilkins. Martha, I reminded myself.

'What do you do, Martha?' I asked.

'Would you?' Our unreliable client ignored my question and leaned across the table so that her nose was almost touching Jo's. 'If they know Jack's got the money, they might leave Brownie alone.'

'We'd need an advance,' said Jo. 'This is where danger money kicks in.'

'Absolutely,' said Martha, digging into her jeans pocket.

She wrote the address on a piece of paper she ripped out of her notebook and then we left the refectory. We went downstairs – Jo needed the toilet and Martha came with us, talking about her dream of moving out of Leeds, with Brownie, of making a fresh start. I went to get a packet of fags from the Union shop and, when I came out, Martha was standing by the lockers putting something in her bag. I crossed over and Jo came back from the bogs. We said goodbye, and Jo gave her a hug and I noticed Martha briefly close her eyes.

'Don't ring me tonight. I'm out,' she said. 'Got to meet someone.' She forced a smile at us both. 'I'll ring you first thing.'

And that was the last time I saw her alive. The next time we met, her eyes would be fixed, unstaring, her skin translucent. I know hindsight colours the glass, but I remember watching her climb the stairs and having this feeling that she was a lost cause. She loved someone who didn't love her back. Jesus, I grew up on that feeling.

That's the only comfort I can get from this. That maybe, wherever she is now, it's better than where she was then.

Chapter Sixteen

We watched her disappear up the stairs, out of the bowels of the University Union. When I replay those last few minutes there's one thing that sticks in my mind. It's like she knew what was coming, knew she'd already lost.

Once she'd gone we headed out of the Union building and back across campus towards the exit.

'So, Mrs Wilkins is actually a mature student called Martha.' I tried the new information on like a new jacket, trying to see if it fit.

'Who knows?' said Jo.

'If she's a student, where's she getting the cash to pay us?'

'She's Walter bleeding Mitty, that's who she is. Can't trust a word she says.'

I checked the time on the Parkinson Clock. 'It makes sense,' I said, although I admit I was pulling at the material, shaping it to my way of thinking. 'She's in love, wants to help her boyfriend. She thinks his best mate has done a runner with the money he owes. She can't tell us that, so she pretends to be Jack's mum, so we'll help her find him. Might have done the same in her situation.'

Jo wasn't as willing to stretch the seams as I was. 'Something doesn't add up.'

'She didn't have much choice,' I continued, not wanting to hear Jo. 'If she had said she was looking for him because he'd stolen money belonging to drug dealers, no reputable firm would have got involved.'

Were we a reputable firm? If she'd told us the truth would we have got involved? Probably, but she wouldn't have known that.

We turned down Woodhouse Lane and headed towards the labyrinth of streets behind the banks, where the van was parked.

'You said Jack didn't know about the money,' Jo said, 'How does she know Jack has the money if he doesn't know he has the money?'

A double-decker trundled past us, too close to the kerb. Jo grabbed my arm, and at that moment, the truth hit us both, like a bucket of cold water, right in the face.

We stopped dead in the street, Jo still clutching my arm. We both spoke at the same time. 'She put it there.'

We stared at each other as we tried to make sense of the revelation.

'Where would she get that much money from?' I said. 'She's a student.'

'She's not a fucking student.'

'But she wouldn't give it to Jack, she'd give it to …' I tailed off. Christ, it was obvious when you thought about it. 'Shit, she did give it to Brownie. She didn't know they'd swapped rooms.' We stood stock still on the pavement as a group of students weaved past us.

'No wonder she wants us to find Jack. He's disappeared with her cash.'

'Where did she go?' I stared down Woodhouse Lane, the main road that runs from the university, past Leeds Beckett and into town. Follow it the other way and it leads to Headingley and Hyde Park. It's safe to say that there's always least a couple of dozen students walking this road, even on a Saturday. I scanned the groups, looking for the scarf. 'Wait here,' I said to Jo.

I turned and sprinted up the road towards Hyde Park. I got as far as the traffic lights at the junction with Clarendon Road, a three- or four-minute run. But there was no sign of her. Martha had dissolved, like a ghost, into the environment, the perfect place to disappear. Hyde Park lay in front of me, Woodhouse down to the right, and the university campus to the left. Students everywhere you looked. With no clue as to which way she'd set off I didn't stand a chance. I gave up, paused a moment to catch my breath and jogged back down to where I'd left Jo.

'Disappeared,' I said.

'You know what?' said Jo. 'I'm sick of this.'

For a moment I thought she meant the business and my stomach lurched.

'We're being taken for a right pair of patsies,' Jo continued. 'I don't trust a single fucking word that anyone's told us.'

'I know.' I had my hands on my knees still trying to catch a breath.

'We're running around after everyone, when really we've got what they want.'

'What?'

'It's like men. You don't chase after them, you let them come to you.'

'Run that by me again.' I was still having difficulty catching my breath, let alone trying to work out what Jo was saying.

'Flies round a honeypot. I vote we tell them we've got the cash.'

'Tell who?'

'Everyone. Jack, Brownie, Martha.' Jo stood up, and we continued on towards where we'd parked the van as I thought about what Jo had just said.

'We've got to find them first,' I said. 'We don't know where any of them are. Even Pants will have gone by now.'

'We've got an address for the dealers. We could start there.'

'We can't give the cash to them. Not until we know for definite whose it is.'

126

'I didn't say give it to them. I said tell them we've got it. There's a difference.'

I thought Jo was splitting hairs. 'But—'

'We go round, tell them we know where the cash is, but we want Jack in exchange. '

'What if they don't know where Jack is?'

'That's their problem. We can tell them we want Brownie too. Give them twenty-four hours to find them both. Or we'll give the cash to the police.'

'"Give the cash to the police"?'

'*Say* we'll give the cash to the police. Not really.'

'They broke Pants's arm. They might kill us.'

Jo thought about this as she rummaged in her pockets for the van keys. 'They want the cash.'

'What about the guy with the gun?'

But Jo wasn't listening. She was off on one. Again. 'We go round. Say we've got a message for them. We set up a meeting for tomorrow. Somewhere where we're in control. Then we sit back and watch them scramble. I bet you they all come out of the woodwork.'

It was ten past six on Saturday evening. A full twenty-four hours since we'd taken the case and I felt like we'd found out a lot, and yet nothing, all at the same time. Jo's idea continued to play in my mind. I grabbed the van keys from her hand.

'What time does The Spy Shop close?'

'Half five. Why?'

'Damn. We need equipment.'

'I can ring Buzz.'

'"Buzz"?'

'He'll open up for us.'

I frowned at Jo. 'He'll open the shop specially?'

She shrugged. 'He lives in the flat above. It's not like he's got anything else to do.'

'You have his phone number?' I couldn't stop the smile that was creeping across my face.

Jo punched me on my upper arm. Hard. 'He gave me his card. Big freaking deal.'

We'd gone to The Spy Shop when we first had the idea for the business. A small shop, sandwiched between kebab houses and Indian takeaways, it sells a wide range of professional surveillance and counter-surveillance solutions designed for any situation, according to the website. In reality it's for suspicious lovers and unscrupulous entrepreneurs wanting to keep an eye on their rivals. Basically, it's geek heaven. You want a gadget, The Spy Shop is your first port of call.

Buzz was standing in the doorway when we arrived, his hands stuffed into the front pockets of his skin-tight black trousers. He wore black-framed glasses and black and white basketball trainers. I swear his ears pricked up when he saw Jo marching towards him.

'Hey,' he said.

'Hey,' said Jo.

We stood there for a moment. Buzz's attention seemingly transfixed by a piece of chewing gum splattered on the flags of the entrance to the shop.

'Thanks for opening up,' I said. 'We really appreciate it.'

He moved to one side to let us enter. 'Check out the intel?'

'Which?'

'The 6950?'

'Not had time,' Jo said as she marched past him.

'Man,' he said to me as Jo disappeared into the store. 'They run at four gigahertz. These bad boys'll make time.'

I had no idea what he was talking about. I smiled in what I hoped was a friendly way and followed after Jo. Buzz closed the door behind us, locked it and then put himself behind the glass counter.

'We need a bit of kit,' said Jo, once she'd had a brief glance at the shelves. 'We've got a situation.'

'Sick,' said Buzz. 'Let me have it.'

They had a conversation that might as well have been in Japanese from all I understood. No mistaking the body language though. Any fool could have understood that.

When we'd got what we wanted, Buzz rang it up through the till and packed our new purchases into a carrier bag, taking his time over each one. Jo handed over some of the cash Martha had given us.

'So, like, if you did ever want to find out more about the intel, we could—'

'I'm busy for the rest of the year,' said Jo.

I winced, and Buzz's cheeks coloured.

Jo removed the bag from Buzz's grasp and headed for the door.

'I'm sorry,' I said to Buzz, once she was out of earshot. 'She's …'

I scrabbled around in my mind for the right word.

'Awesome,' said Buzz.

'That was a bit harsh,' I said as I caught up with Jo on the pavement outside. I stuffed the receipt Buzz had given me back into my wallet.

'What?'

'Poor lad. He's completely smitten.' I knew I was pushing it.

Jo punched my right shoulder. 'Political lesbianism. It's the only ethical solution.'

'Well, I don't know how you're going to break that to poor old Buzz.'

She punched me again, her carrier bag hitting me square on my right kneecap. 'You can't win the war when you're sucking the enemy's—'

'OK, OK! Thanks.' I held up a hand as I limped along behind her. 'I get the picture.'

When you're really tired it's hard to have confidence in your decisions and I knew my mood wasn't great, but when we got back to the offices it plummeted. We had to squeeze our way in through the boarded-up front door, opening the two temporary padlocks the locksmith had fitted. The writing was still on the wall and the furniture in pieces.

Jo propped the rounders bat against the doorframe leading to the back. We stared at each other, neither of us wanting to stay in the mess. I made a note to pop to Bobats and buy some paint. Couldn't keep reading 'Be Scarred'.

'So, what's the plan?' asked Jo.

'Gipton,' I said.

Gipton. East Leeds. Not much of a tourist spot. Fact is I'd only ever been there once, a really bad drug deal that still brings me out in hives thinking about it. One of my low points, when I wasn't taking drugs for fun but because I couldn't handle the moments they left my bloodstream. The car I was in got done over in the two minutes I was inside the house, and the drugs I scored were cut with Vim.

I wasn't that keen on returning but, on the other hand, I was pissed off. I'd had so many dreams when we'd first rented this place. We'd painted the walls, bought the desks, got the phone lines installed. I'd worked my arse off and for what?

Last night, whoever trashed our office had had the advantage. Anyone can break in when there's no one home.

Jo was right. We were being played and I'd had enough of reacting. It was time to create. We needed to claim the advantage. We needed to surprise.

Chapter Seventeen

We packed the van for a stake-out and made our way across the city. It was half past nine, which, we'd figured, was the best time to pay dealers a visit. Late enough to be dark, early enough to get sorted before heading out on a Saturday night adventure. In other words, prime scoring time.

We drove out to the east, through the city centre, and into the suburbs. Leeds is funny like that. You can drive half a mile and go from leafy community to inner-city nightmare. The tree-lined avenues of suburban Roundhay next to red-brick, ethnic Harehills, with its pound shops and neon-lit takeaways. There's Chapel Allerton, a kind of middle-class, post-grad village a few hundred yards from Chapeltown, where, decades ago, the Yorkshire Ripper stalked his prey.

It was time to stand up, assert ourselves. If we were going to run for cover at the first sign of any trouble, we were never going to make it in the business we'd set up. We'd argued about who was going in – I wanted to, but Jo had said: 'Nah, you can't. You don't have the cleavage for this gig.'

Much as I hated the fact, she was right. I'd insisted on having a go, but after much gaffer tape it had proved considerably easier to hide a recording device between Jo's boobs. Stuck to my chest, the small mic stuck out like a coat hook. What can you do? I gave up wishing for curves a long time ago.

So, Jo was going in and I was there as backup. First sign of trouble and I'd be outside with the engine running. I'd stashed the rounders bat in the passenger footwell. The advantage is all about surprise.

We parked three streets away. Jo stashed her mobile in the glovebox. 'Look after it,' she said, as she stalked off into the darkness. I pulled a face she couldn't see and crawled into the back of the van. I turned on the surveillance equipment and heard Jo's voice crackle through the airwaves.

'Nearly there,' she said. 'Wish me luck.'

I could hear the thump of her heart beating, and then, moments later, a knock on the door. Typical Jo, always manages to make a door knock sound like a drugs raid. It took less than thirty seconds for someone to answer it. I heard Jo, her Scouse accent unmistakable, say: 'Hi.'

Then I heard what I thought was a male voice, low and gravelly. 'Yeah?'

'Message for you,' Jo said.

'From who?' the same voice asked. I marvelled at the technology – even at my safe distance you could hear the suspicion in his tone.

'They didn't give a name,' said Jo, as her heart beat faster down the wire. 'It's about the dosh Brownie owes?' The inflection rose at the end of the sentence, so it sounded like she was asking a question, like she wasn't quite sure of her facts.

'Brownie?'

'Brownie from Burchett Grove, that's what they said.'

I heard a bang that could have been the sound of a door flung open or slammed closed. I thought I heard the same male voice say something, which might have been, 'Come in', but equally could have been, 'Do one'. Then I heard a load of static, followed by a crackle so piercing it forced me to pluck the headphones away from my eardrums. When I returned them, I heard nothing.

I turned the receiver off and on again.

Still nothing.

It was like it wasn't even trying. A dead, blank sound. I cursed Buzz. He'd told us this baby was infallible. The silence through the headphones hurt; my own blood pumped against my eardrums.

I waited a few minutes. Wouldn't do to blow our cover over a technical hitch. I counted the seconds off. Jo only had a few lines to deliver. We had the money. We wanted Brownie and Jack. We'd meet them in Millennium Square at two o'clock tomorrow. All she had to do was give them her mobile number and get out. Great plan. Only I couldn't hear a sodding word.

I waited, counting the seconds off in my mind, maybe three minutes in all, until I couldn't stand it any longer. I tugged Bobats box of latex gloves from under the front seat and pushed a pair into the back pocket of my jeans. What else would come in handy? I grabbed the torch and jumped out the back of the van, locked the doors and jogged down the three streets to the address we'd been given, counting the numbers down. The house Jo had gone to was in darkness. Total blackout. I carried on past without breaking pace. Perhaps I'd get more from the back. I looped round the block, glad I'd worn a hat. There was no one else around, and I knew I was chancing it. No woman in her right mind wandered these streets alone at night.

I found the narrow, unlit back alleyway and ticked the houses off, sensing that the occupants of none of them would be on my side. Communities like this stuck together. No one would help a stranger, especially not one they'd found ducking through the undergrowth outside their back doors.

I found the rear of the house. Again, no light in any of the windows. I paused for a moment, hunched low, and thought what to do. No choice. I slipped through the back gate. Even in

133

the half dark I could see the paint peeling from the window frames. I pulled out my torch, kept the beam low and looked around. A handkerchief-sized back lawn, with grass that was almost waist high, empty carrier bags and crisp packets littered around. It was obvious no one made use of the broom that lay across the back path.

I switched the torch off, shoved it back down my waistband and made my way down the path. As I got closer I noticed the back door had deep grooves scratched into the bottom half. Lots of them. If there's one thing I hate, it's dogs.

But I needed to find Jo. I swallowed my fear and crept up to the ground-floor window. The curtains were closed, no light peering through the gaps. There was a wheelie bin to the right of the back door, rubbish overflowing. I flipped the lid closed as best I could and climbed on top of it. It wasn't the most stable of platforms, but it got me high enough to haul myself up the drainpipe. My heart pounded at the increased activity as well as the threat. I knew if I got caught here there'd be no chance of talking my way out of it. The kitchen window jutted out about six inches from the house and I pulled myself up on top of it. From there I could see into the bottom inch of the first-floor window. Pitch-black.

The first-floor window was divided into two panes, and the right hand one had a smaller window within it, at the top. The smaller window was open a crack – one of those that opens horizontally and is small enough to push a child through.

One of the few positives to my ironing board physique is I'm not much bigger than a child. Longer, sure, but not much wider. I tip the scales at eight stone on a good day, seven and a half when I haven't been taking care of myself. I heaved myself up, managed to get my fingers under the open frame and yank it upwards. Then I slipped through the gap like an eel, closed my eyes and hoped for the best.

Crawling through an open window is easy, it's the dismount

that's difficult. There's no quiet way to do it, especially when you don't know what's on the other side. I wasn't sure whether I'd be landing on a bed, a bookcase or a bathtub. This time, though, someone was on my side and I dropped headfirst onto a mattress on the floor.

I lay there for a moment, steady, listening. You've got to get used to what the normal noises are before you can get any sense of whether they've changed – whether anyone has noticed your arrival. Thudding footsteps on the stairs, for example, could be a washing machine. There weren't either in this case. Just quiet. Dead quiet.

I crouched onto all fours, letting the house settle around me. I like the dark. Was never scared of it as a kid. Basically, so long as I'm awake my troubles are small. Reality always feels safer than my nightmares.

I gave it a minute, maybe a minute and a half. And then I worried. I'd never been in a house with Jo for more than a minute and a half without hearing her dulcet Liverpudlian tones, unless she was comatose. I'd have bet money that Jo wasn't in this house. Or, if she was, she'd been muted somehow.

I pulled at the curtain to see if I could let in some moonlight. As I tugged at it the whole thing fell down in my hands, and I realized it wasn't a curtain but a blanket that had been tucked up over the curtain rail rather than hung. As it dropped to the mattress I was standing on, the room lightened so I could make out that it was small, obviously someone's bedroom, although not a well-loved one, and there was a door that was open a fraction.

I crept across to the doorway, pushed against it and peered out. I couldn't see a thing. Dare I risk the torch? I didn't really have a choice. I tugged it out and flicked it on, directing the beam at the floor. A small landing, three doors off it in total, including the one I'd just stepped out of. None of the doors were locked, all the rooms were empty.

135

I crept down the stairs, feeling the prickle of fear run down the back of my neck. I was unarmed. I mean not even a nail file to my name. That made me think and, halfway down, I paused and tiptoed back up. The bathroom. Had to be something there I could use. Just to make me feel a bit safer.

I fumbled around the edge of the bath and found a mouldy wet cloth and an empty bottle that could maybe once have contained shampoo. There were the cardboard tubes of a few spent bog rolls scattered around. Next to the bath was a built-in cupboard. I pulled it open and swung the torch beam inside. Its walls were lined with silver foil. I felt around the bottom of the cupboard and found a jug, a packet of fertilizer and a small pair of nail scissors. I tucked the scissors up my sleeve, switched off the torch and made my way back to the staircase.

Walking into blackness is a strange feeling. No idea what's coming next, your body's poised for anything and your mind starts playing tricks. Like being on the ghost train – your imagination is far worse than anything a fairground can throw at you. The next to bottom stair creaked, and I heard a sound that made me feel sick. A sound that told me I wasn't alone.

It was the low growl of a dog, coming from the front room.

Chapter Eighteen

Growing up, the only people I knew who had pets were the batty old grannies whose houses smelled of cat piss or budgie droppings, or the puffed-up lads with their pit bull terriers. Let's just say I'm not what you would call an animal person. Dogs are the worst because they're unpredictable.

But I do know that dogs have got small heads and hence small brains, so I had to think of how I could use my larger, human one to score the advantage. I heard the growl again, low and insistent. I reached the bottom step. In the gloom of the hallway I could make out two doors, the nearest one obviously contained the dog, I could hear it sniffing along the bottom edge of the door. Where did the other door lead? Probably to a kitchen. Were the kitchen and the nearest room, the room with the dog, linked to each other? The million-dollar question.

I crossed the hallway to the front door. If anyone else was in the house, they'd be alerted by the growling, so the least I could do was pretend I'd just stepped in from outside. I could play dumb – have you seen my mate, she said she was coming here, blah blah. I tried the handle, but the front door was locked, which added weight to my growing belief that I was alone. Alone, apart from Growler.

I felt around the doorframe for a key, and found one, balanced on the top left-hand side. I slid it down, slipped it into the keyhole and felt relief flood my body as the key turned and unlocked the door.

I could have left the house at that point. The growl had developed to a bark and, believe me, the idea was tempting. I opened the door to see the small front garden and the path to the gate. I could be out of here in less than ten seconds. But freedom wasn't an option. Not for me, right at that moment. I had to get the dog out of the front room. I had to find Jo.

I know dogs can smell fear, and I was excreting buckets of the stuff through every pore in my body. What I really needed was a kamikaze cat to stroll past. I think I actually stuck my head out into the garden looking for one, like I might be able to persuade it to commit suicide in order to save my sorry ass.

I knew I had to out-think the dog. Mind over teeth. I needed it out of the house. I needed to get it to chase me into the garden and then I had to run back in and close the door, so I could search the rest of the house. Simple. Just how?

It made sense for me to be in the garden to start with, but then how to open the living room door? I remembered the broom I'd seen in the back and scurried round to get it. As I passed the front room window, the dog went wild, hurling itself at the glass, its claws clattering and scraping. It was black, the size of a small bear.

I came back with the broom and stood on the front step. I held the front door handle in my left hand, the pole in my right and used it to lever down the door handle on the inner door, the door that contained the dog. It took me a few seconds to get the right angle, my legs shaking, the dog going mental, but I managed to prise the door handle downwards, so that the door popped open, unleashing the dog like a cannonball. It went straight for me. I managed to hit it on its head with the broom – hard enough to get its attention. It grabbed for the stick and we played this

138

kind of tug-of-war game, its white fangs gleaming as I manoeuvred it out of the house and into the front garden. I swung it around 180 degrees, so I was between it and the house and I inched backwards, still pushing and pulling the dog with the wooden pole. Once I'd got on the step, I dropped my end of the broom, jumped inside and slammed the front door shut. Our roles reversed. The dog on the outside, me trapped in the house. There was quiet for about three seconds, while the dog came to terms with its new reality. Once the penny dropped, the barking started. I nearly laughed. I had no idea how I'd ever get out, but that wasn't the here and the now. That was the future. I'd deal with that when I got there.

Jo wasn't in the room that the dog had vacated. No one was. I took a chance and switched on the light. I jumped as the dog hurled itself against the front windows then took a breath to calm myself. I pulled a face at it – some guard dog – having to sit outside while a girl ransacked his house.

The front room contained a massive TV, with surround sound speakers, and various black boxes joined together with miles of cables and headphones. There were two black, fake leather settees and a packing crate that had been turned on its side and was doubling up as a coffee table, with an overflowing ashtray. A filthy duvet lay in the far corner – presumably Growler's grotto.

'Jo?' I shouted, desperate now and not caring who heard me. No answer.

I left the room and opened the other door off the hallway. Certain there was no one home, I switched on the light. A small kitchen, grotty, a set of scales on the worktops, and not the kind you use to weigh flour. Empty dog bowl on the floor. I shouted again. 'Jo.'

The house remained quiet. I stood in the kitchen with no idea what to do next. Fear threatened to overwhelm me. What had they done to Jo? If they'd hurt her, if they'd so much as touched her, I'd spend the rest of my life making them suffer. I opened a kitchen drawer and took out a knife. I don't know what I was thinking at that moment.

I stood in the kitchen with the knife in my hand, and I heard a noise. A thumping kind of sound. I paused, held my breath. The dog had gone quiet. I strained to listen but there was nothing. I stepped towards the hallway, and the noise returned. I couldn't work out where it was coming from. I kept hold of the knife as I checked round the house, turning on every single light, scared of the bogeyman.

'Hello?'

I went back downstairs. The noise was loudest in the kitchen. I moved to the far end of the room and noticed a small passage out to the back door. And off the passageway was a small room, I mean tiny – probably meant for a washing machine, although there wasn't one. I stepped into it and only then noticed that there was another door leading off the small space. I stood outside the door.

'Jo?'

More thumping, some of which was the pounding of my heart against my ribcage. I tried the handle with my left hand.

The handle moved but the door didn't. Which was odd, because there wasn't any sign of a lock on the outside of the door. The thumping grew more insistent. The possibilities ran through my mind. Another dog? But then why wasn't it barking? Were non-barking dogs a thing? Jo? Gagged? I barged the door with my shoulder. Pain shot through me. The door didn't give a fraction of a centimetre. I went back into the kitchen and returned the knife to the drawer. I needed a sledgehammer. I threw open cupboards and found nothing useful until my eyes hit on a tin of dog food and, all of a sudden, I had a plan.

I opened the tin with a can opener I fished out of the sink. I scraped the contents into the dog bowl on the floor and made my way through to the front door. I opened it and called for the dog, my voice breaking. 'Here, Growler, here, puppy.'

Nothing, no sound of pattering feet. I tried a bit louder. Still nothing. Maybe it had run off. I put the bowl down on the ground, just to the left-hand side of the front door, and crept round to the back of the house. The kitchen window was on the left side of the back door – now the lights were on it was easy to make out. On the right-hand side of the back door was a small window, just above my head height, frosted glass, the room behind it in darkness. I jumped up and knocked on the glass. Another sound, muffled.

I retrieved the wheelie bin, dragged it across so that it was under the small window and climbed up. I knocked on the glass again. The thumping replied. Mad dog with no vocal chords or Jo? Only one way to find out. I jumped down, scoured the garden until I found a loose brick in the back wall. I inched it out, only half a brick but good enough. I took off my jacket, wrapped it around my right fist and made my way back to the wheelie bin. I heard a sound that turned my walk to a run.

Growler.

I vaulted on to the dustbin. The dog crashed round the side of the house, licking its chops, having obviously already feasted on the dog food. It didn't appear appeased. But it made my next step easier. I raised the brick. Shouted, 'duck.' Smashed the brick against the window with all my force. The glass shattered. The dog went quiet. For about three seconds. Then it leaped at the bin, nipped my left ankle. I held my arms out in front of my head. Dived through the broken pane.

I crashed into the dark void, glass splintering around me. Landed on something hard. I ended up at a forty-five-degree angle to the ground. My hands touched the floor, my feet caught by something on the windowsill. Whatever I landed on was alive. It squirmed underneath me.

I managed to manoeuvre myself in the tiny cramped space, enough to reach up the wall and flick on the light. The tiny space immediately illuminated to reveal a toilet the size of a broom cupboard. The person I'd hit was face down on the floor. The first thing I noticed was the person was naked.

The second thing I noticed – it wasn't Jo.

Chapter Nineteen

I pushed up with my hands and managed to get to my feet, shaking the broken shards of glass from my jacket, still wrapped around my wrist. The person under me tried to climb to his, but he was hindered by the fact that his feet were bound together with masking tape. As were his hands. There was also a piece over his mouth. He wasn't completely naked, I noticed as I helped manoeuvre him backwards so that he could sit on the lowered toilet seat. Whoever had done this to him, they'd allowed him the dignity of retaining his underpants. Small mercies.

I put my left hand to the corner of his mouth and ripped off the masking tape, figuring short sharp shock was the way to go. He yelped in pain, as the spikes in his upper lip pulled free from the tape.

'We meet again,' I said.

His voice was croaky. 'Did you have to rip it so hard?'

'How long've you been here?'

'What day is it?'

'Saturday,' I said. I frowned at him. He couldn't have been there that long – it was less than twenty-four hours since I'd chased him from The Chemic and onto The Ridge. I unwound my jacket from my right arm and shrugged back into it. Not easy in the confined space.

Brownie licked his lower lip. 'Shit.'

'Did you hear my mate, Jo? She was in the house just now?'

He blinked again, and I knew he wasn't going to be able to provide me with any answers. He wasn't in the right frame of mind for one thing, but also what was he going to have heard sitting out here, locked in the toilet? Jo couldn't have been in the house more than five minutes.

'Where are your clothes?' I heard the dog barking outside the bathroom window and prayed it didn't try to come in. The walls were already closing in. There wasn't room for anything else. 'We need to get out of here.'

The toilet door had a big metal bolt on it that was pulled across the frame. 'How come the door's locked?'

'They locked it.'

'Eh? How did they get out?'

'Same way you got in.'

'They put you in here, locked the door and then climbed out the window?' I tried to peel the masking tape off his hands, but it was stuck so fast I couldn't. The ends of his fingers were blue. I remembered the nail scissors, fished them out of my sleeve and cut the tape free.

He didn't say thank you. 'Where's my kegs?'

'I'm not your mother,' I said. 'Where did you leave them?'

'Funny.' He rubbed his wrists. 'You're the bird from The Chemic.'

'I prefer Lee.'

'What you doing here?'

'I'm a private investigator.'

'Yeah and I'm David Bowie.' The guy was sat on the toilet, in his underpants, with his feet still bound.

I bent down to cut the tape from his ankles. 'Loved you in *Labyrinth*.'

144

'This is all your fault.'

'Mine?' I stopped and stood up. 'I just rescued you. Thank you wouldn't go amiss. Why's it my fault?'

'You chased me, right into them.'

'I didn't.'

'Yes, you did.'

I remembered the good-looking Asian man we'd seen at the entrance to The Ridge the previous night and it fell into place. 'I didn't know he was after you.'

'Wanker.'

'How much do you owe?'

He managed to rip the rest of the masking tape from his ankles without my help. He stood up and the airspace condensed. He squinted at me. 'How do I know you're not working for them?'

I felt his breath on my face. Claustrophobia swept through me. I hate small spaces. Even more when I have to share them. I turned and tugged back the bolt on the door. 'Let's get out of here,' I said, 'before they come back.'

'I can't go out like this.'

'Fine,' I said. 'Stay here.'

'You can't leave me here.' He sat back down on the toilet with such force I assumed his legs had given way. Out in the garden the dog barked again.

'I have to find Jo.'

'Jo?'

'My mate. She came here. Wired.'

He shook out his legs. 'Know how she feels.' He sank his head in his hands.

'No. I mean … doesn't matter. She's disappeared. We've got to get out of here.' I stepped out of the closet and into the kitchen. I listened. No changes in the atmosphere, nothing to suggest anyone had entered the house. I turned to check that Brownie followed me. He held onto the doorframe, white skin pale in the

145

light, two red-brown nipples nestling in a dark patch of chest hair, unsteady on his feet. 'Come on.'

He grabbed for my arm, then settled for resting his hand on my shoulder and we set off.

'How long?' I asked, as we made our way back through the kitchen and out of the house.

'How long what?'

'Since your last fix?'

He stalled. 'What you on about?'

'We might need to run.'

'Shit,' he said, as he caught my thought. 'The dog.'

I opened the front door, looked left and right. No sign. But I wasn't fooled. I knew the thing well enough by now. It didn't give up, wouldn't have taken its chance of freedom and done one. In its small mind it belonged to the house. Sure enough, we had only made it three or four steps out the front door before I heard its stupid low-down growl again. I grabbed Brownie's wrist.

'Run. Fast. Now.'

To give him his due, he didn't need telling twice. He managed to match me pace-wise till we got to the end of the path. I vaulted the gate. I landed two footed flat to the floor on the other side, knees bent to lessen the impact. I managed to get out of the way before Brownie threw himself head first over the side. The dog was at his ankles and, of course, Brownie didn't have the luxury of trousers. I heard him scream and turned and grabbed his torso with both hands, dragged him over the wooden gate. The gush of blood on his left ankle glistened in the glow of the streetlight.

I yanked Brownie away from the gate and down the street towards where I'd left the van. The dog barked but didn't follow us. I tried to think of how I could explain why I was accompanying a near naked man out of a probably known dealers' house, just in case anyone asked.

But really, I was concentrating on that in order to keep my mind occupied. Because Brownie's state of undress was the least of my problems. What I really didn't want to think about was what the fuck had they done to Jo?

I bundled Brownie into the back of the van and took off my jacket. I handed it to him and climbed in, pulling the doors shut behind me. I crawled to the front. The clock on the dashboard said it was almost quarter to ten. Forty minutes since I'd last heard Jo's voice.

'What do you want?' asked Brownie as he zipped up my jacket. It was miles too small for him, made him look like a refugee.

I handed him my tobacco pouch and positioned myself between Brownie and the back doors. I sat on the floor and switched on the camping lamp we've got hanging from the ceiling. It cast little more than a glow.

'I want to know where my best mate is.'

'What was she doing in there?'

My heart hammered my chest, still beating at sprinting pace. I exhaled. 'Trying to find Jack.'

'Jack? What do you know about Jack?'

'I told you. I'm a private investigator.'

'Bollocks.'

'I was hired to find Jack.'

'Hired by who?' He crouched on his haunches, his hands shaking so much he couldn't keep the tobacco in the Rizla paper. I watched him drop a second pinch then took the whole works off him, started rolling.

'His mother.'

'His mother's dead.'

'His stepmother.'

'Doesn't have a stepmother.'

Seemed like everyone knew this except us. 'Martha hired us.' I handed him a rolled fag and lit it for him.

He took an inhale of smoke that was so deep I expected to see it coming out of his toes. 'My Martha?'

'Is she?'

147

'Eh?'

'I thought you two—'

'Why would Martha hire you to look for Jack?'

'She's trying to help you.'

'Bollocks.'

'That's not kind. She's doing everything she can to save your sorry ass.'

He flopped down onto the cushions we'd put in the back. 'Don't trust her.'

'No?' Junkies trust no one, I knew this. 'Weird. Who do you trust?'

'No one knows where Jack is. That's the point,' said Brownie. He spoke like I was an imbecile.

'Martha thinks he's got the money that will get that lot off your back.'

'She's nuts. Where's Jack going to get £20K?'

I wasn't in the mood to answer questions. 'Right, listen, you moron. My best mate is missing and it's all your fault.'

'Mine?'

I needed to focus. 'Do they have a car?'

'Who?'

'The guys back there, dipstick.'

'He brought me here in an Escort.'

'Colour?'

'Dunno. It was dark. Red, I think.'

'Who are *they*? How many? I want to know everything about them.'

'Duck and Bernie. What's to say? Bernie's fat; Duck thinks he's Zayn fucking Malik.'

'Who?'

'Never mind. They're both wankers.'

I shook my head to try and clear some space. 'Tell me about you and Martha. From the beginning.'

'Nothing to tell.'

148

'Listen, you want a ride home you'd better start being useful. Else I'll leave you out there in your under-crackers for the dog.'

'I'm over her.'

I made out I was about to open the door.

He held up a hand. His fingernails were dirty, bitten to the bone. 'OK. OK. What do you want to know?'

'Everything.'

'She turned up a few months back – just moved to Leeds, needed some smokes. Can't remember who introduced her.' He shrugged. 'I helped her out a couple of times.'

'That's not how she tells it.'

'She's all right. Anyway, one thing leads to another, I end up at her place a couple of nights. That's it.' His voice tailed off and he took another drag on his roll-up.

'I need more than that.'

'She's ... different.'

'Different how?'

'Established.'

'What does that mean?'

'Not many people can cook, not vegan. She's ... I don't know ... She's got a good set up – curries, a mean spinach dahl.'

'I get it. She loves you and you're using her for nutrition.'

'She's got a knife sharpener. Like, attached to the wall.' He glanced up at me, made eye contact for the first time. 'She don't love me.'

'Says she does.'

He stared at me for a moment before returning his gaze to the floor of the van. 'Whatever.' He wiped his nose on the back of my jacket, and I made a mental note to wash it before I wore it again.

'She's worried about you.'

He tucked his legs up so that they were under his chin and folded his arms around them. 'Never lasts. A rush of blood and then I'm waking up thinking how the fuck do I get out of this ...'

'Charming.'

'Can't trust 'em, bottom line. Praying bleeding mantis, that's all I'm saying.'

'Let's get back to the story,' I said, climbing over him into the front seat. I couldn't sit doing nothing, and it sounded like this story was going to take a long time to tell. I'd already wasted ten minutes. 'You start seeing Martha. What's Jack think about this?'

'He don't talk a lot, don't Jack. He's a man of action not words.'

'"A man of action"?' I turned the key in the ignition. 'He's a smack addict.'

Quiet from the back.

I turned in my seat to face him. 'You'd better get in the front. I'm going to drive around. See if we can spot them.'

He clambered over and joined me, his long milky legs practically glowing in the moonlight. The bruises looked worse illuminated by streetlights. He winced as he fastened his seatbelt.

'If I'm going to get you out of this, you are going to have to tell me everything,' I said. 'How did you get into smack in the first place?'

He shrugged. 'Long story.'

'I think there's still some tea in there.' I nodded at the Thermos on the dashboard.

He looked like he might cry. He reached for the flask and poured himself a cup. I waited till he'd put the flask on the floor and had the cup in both hands before I pulled away from the kerb.

'You never think you're going to get addicted,' he said in a quiet voice, once he'd drained the tea. 'You've kind of worked out that they'd all lied to you – the "just say no" lot. We got into the party scene – bit of MDMA, loads of speed, acid. Me and Jack were at some squat, the first time, after a party. Someone said it was good for the come down. And it was, for ages.'

I figured a gentle cruise around was better than just sitting there listening. Some of this story I already knew. Some of it was a bit too close to the bone.

'Then, one day you realize, you can't get through a day without it.'

I hit one of those mini-roundabouts before I'd noticed it was there, but we were OK. The roads were quiet. We had a while before pub kick-out time.

'It's OK,' Brownie continued, 'if you don't have to. It's when the money runs out.'

A man with a small but well-muscled dog on a lead crossed the road in front of me. I slowed to avoid hitting him. 'What money?'

'We were tooting more than we were selling.'

'You were dealing smack?'

'No,' he said, affronted. 'Dope. A few pills. But the holidays are bad – students piss off home for the summer, sales are down.'

I had my eyes on every passing car, looking for a red Escort.

'We were in it together, least I thought we were.' Brownie stared out of the passenger window and, for a minute or two, I let him go silent, as we cruised the streets. I knew there was a piece of the jigsaw missing. A thought, half-formed, lurked at the back of my mind, but I couldn't quite grasp it.

'Then Jack meets Carly?' I prompted Brownie.

'Yeah. He gets this job, down at The Warehouse. Part-time, not exactly coining it, but it's something. Bernie's getting a bit unfriendly about what we owe. That's where Jack meets Carly.' He says her name in a funny voice. Like he's imitating a Barbie doll.

'You don't like her?'

'Psychology student,' he said, like that was all I needed to know. 'Regular Little Miss Fix It.'

'So,' I said, anxious to move the story on. 'They break into your house, spray-paint the walls, everything kicks off.'

'How do you know about that?'

'Martha told us,' I lied. Pants had suffered enough.

'See. Not to be trusted.'

151

'Carry on.'

'It's a right mess – we'd all been down to a gig at The Brudenell – can't remember who was playing now. Martha was there, comes back to the house. Truth is, by this time I'm trying to get rid, but she's harder to shake than crabs.'

'Nice.'

'Jack's there too. All bleeding hell breaks loose. Ends up in a fight.'

'Between?'

'Me and Jack mainly. Jack's pissed off cos he gave me his wages and I'd not got round to paying Bernie. So I think, fuck it.'

'And?'

'I left. Went to Martha's.'

'And?'

'And nothing. We had a toot.'

'Martha smoked smack?'

He tried to pour himself another cup of tea, but the flask must have been empty. He dropped it onto the floor and slouched in his seat. 'You should see the way she looks at me. Man, I've told her I'm not relationship material.'

'No shit.'

'She nods like she agrees with every word, but you know she's not hearing you. Women, freaking mental. Wanting to drag things out in the open, put the pieces back together. They don't realize some things are just broken.'

I pulled a face at him. 'Nightmare.'

'That night, we get back, and she's wanting to know all about the money I owe. I think, fuck it, I've been trying to get rid, might as well let her know what's going on – tell her I smoke brown – should make her run. 'Course, she doesn't.'

'You're right. Women are mental.'

'I tell her I can't trust her. It's like she wants to prove a point. She's asking for it.'

'Asking for a heroin habit?'

'But it's …' He faded out on the memory.

'It's what?'

'It's kinda, it's nice.'

'Yeah, you get your girlfriend into smack. Beautiful.'

Brownie didn't respond. We drove in silence, him staring out of the passenger window like there was something more interesting than dark dampness out there. His voice was quieter the next time he spoke. 'I try and see Jack the next day, but he's fuming with me. I've done everything for that guy. I'm like his big fucking brother. Swapped rooms with him last week because the sound of someone getting laid every night does his head in. You've got to ask yourself, what's that about?'

I kind of know what that's about, but I didn't say anything.

'So I do one, I think fuck it, I'll go and stay with Zig for a few days. Get a bit of space, clear my head, know what I mean? I'm not going to tell anyone where I'm going, cos they can all fuck off.'

I nodded.

'So I go to Newcastle. We get a bit wasted. I get back, all fucking hell has broken loose. Jack's disappeared. That pisses me off, cos he's supposed to be giving me his wages. I go down to The Warehouse, Carly's on one. I tell her I need to find him as much as she does.'

'You told them he'd nicked your PlayStation.'

'Yeah, that wiped the smug smile off her face.'

We hit the mini-roundabout at forty again. I'd get the hang of it next time, I swore to myself.

'Pants is going mad. I figure I'll not stay where I'm not wanted, so I go and see Martha, tell her I'm leaving. Figure it's the kindest thing to do.'

'And?'

'She loses it. I mean, seriously. Loses. It.'

'So, everyone's out to get you?'

'Right.'

153

'Brownie.' I hit the steering wheel. 'Drugs mess with your head – that's why everyone says they're not good for you. Jack's your best mate. Martha loves you.'

'She's setting me up.'

'Junkie talk.'

'She's not what you think she is.'

'Did she tell you Jack had got the money together?'

He frowned at me. 'She came out with all kinds of crap. Where's Jack going to get twenty-four grand from? She's setting me up. I'm telling you.'

'Why? Why would Martha set you up?'

'Dunno.'

I switched on the radio. I knew there was no point arguing. House music crackled through the speakers.

Brownie wouldn't leave it alone though. After a minute or two he hit the off switch. 'It's all lies. She's put twenty-four grand in my sock drawer? Bullshit. Must think I'm a right fucking—'

'Hang on a minute.' I swerved into the left, mounted the kerb and killed the engine.

'Don't even have drawers in my room,' Brownie continued.

I turned and faced Brownie. 'She said she put twenty-four grand in your sock drawer? She actually said that?'

He didn't answer. He'd a whole story in his head and he wanted to tell it. 'I start following her. See what she's up to, where she goes. I crash at mates' houses. Sleep in the daytime cos I figure if they come looking for me, they'll come at night. Not going to let them catch me sleeping.'

I couldn't keep up. If Martha put the money there, where did she get it from? But Brownie wasn't giving me time to think.

'I'm watching her,' he said. 'And what does she do?'

Fucking student, my arse, is what I think.

Brownie paused, and I realized he was waiting for me to answer. 'What?'

'That first night?' he prompted.

154

I shrugged my shoulders and started the engine, pulled back onto the road. Jo was right. We couldn't believe a single word our client told us. 'I have no idea.'

He tapped it out on the dashboard. One word at a time. 'She breaks into the squat.'

I was driving so slowly I'd almost ground to a halt. A horn behind me made me step on the accelerator. 'What?'

'Serious. And not like a novice. She breaks in like a complete fucking pro: 4 a.m. Dressed in black, the entire kit. Crowbar, the works. She's out again in minutes, not carrying anything. So why's she doing that then? Eh? Who breaks into a house and comes out carrying nothing?'

In that moment I believed him, believed his story. I had this flash of a picture of Martha dressed head to foot in black, stealthy as a cat. 'Who?' I asked, my voice quiet.

'A copper,' he said, like he's cleverer than Einstein. 'She's a fucking copper.'

Chapter Twenty

I drove in silence for five minutes, running over the information I'd just heard, comparing it to what I had stored in my head. Brownie smoked silently next to me.

Eventually the mist cleared. 'A copper? Piss off.'

'Don't believe me.'

'Why would a copper be after Jack?' As soon as I asked the question I realized I could think of a few reasons, many of them locked up in the safe back at our office. I changed tack. 'Why would a copper come to us for help?'

'Because she's desperate.'

'Thanks.'

'Jack always said she was bad news. Me, I keep by brain down here.' He patted at his crotch area as I kept my eyes on the road. 'And he's right. It's like she's been beamed down from planet Mars. One day no one's ever heard of her, next day everywhere we go she's there.'

'The Chemic?'

'Yeah. She made a beeline for me. I should have known she was after something.'

'A copper wouldn't take heroin.'

'Double bluff.'

156

'Big risk.'

I noticed a red Escort on the other side of the road, driving towards us. As it passed I tried to peer in through the windscreen, but the glare of the headlights made it impossible. Luckily, I now knew the area pretty well. I hung left, did a 360 round the mini-roundabout ahead then headed on after it. I found it again in less than a minute, accelerated hard and overtook it. Driving parallel on the wrong side of the road, I peered past Brownie. An alarmed-looking older man stared back at me. In his fifties, looked like a builder. I took the next right and slowed the pace.

'Roll me a fag, would you?'

Brownie did his best. Passed me something as fat as a Tampax.

'Why hasn't she arrested you then? If she's a copper.'

'Dunno. Keep asking myself that.'

'It's not like she hasn't got enough evidence.'

'Maybe she's after Bernie and Duck.'

'She hasn't arrested them, either,' I pointed out.

'Maybe she doesn't know where they live.'

'It was her that gave us the address.' I shook my head, trying to shake up my thoughts, see which one settled. I went with my gut. 'She totally loves you.'

'That's what got me suspicious.'

'Save the violins.'

'No one loves me.'

'Rubbish. Women love a fuck-up. Florence Nightingale complex.'

We passed the mini-roundabout again and this time I nailed it. But I knew I was wasting my time. I wasn't going to bump into a red Escort carrying Jo. I took three deep breaths, allowed the exhale to last as long as I could hold it, to run to the end of each breath. The thought that had been waiting at the edge of my consciousness crystallized. As soon as it hit, it was so blindingly obvious it made my head hurt. I pulled into the kerb and turned to face Brownie.

'We were set up.'

Brownie scratched his forearms.

'The whole thing was a fucking set up.' I hit the steering wheel with the palm of my hand. 'Someone tipped them off.'

A car honked at me as it passed, presumably indicating its disapproval of my choice of parking spaces. I flicked it the finger.

'Can you give us a lift to me mate's house?' Brownie asked.

Anger boiled inside me. I allowed it to swell. Knowledge is power. A phone rang, and I nearly jumped out of my skin.

'That you?' I said to Brownie. Stupid question. The man was in his underpants. I remembered Jo's mobile in the glovebox and reached across to retrieve it. The screen glowed.

Unknown number.

I swiped to accept the call. 'Yes?'

'We got your mate.'

The fingers on my right hand tightened against the steering wheel. 'And?'

'You want to see her alive again, do exactly what we say.'

'Go on.'

'We want the money and the tin. The tin that Jack sent.' Like there could be any confusion.

I focused my gaze on the rear-view mirror. I watched a pair of headlights get closer then pass me by. 'What do I get?'

'Your mate.'

'What about Jack?'

'We ain't got Jack.'

'I want to speak to Jo.'

'Get the cash, and the tin. We'll ring you in an hour. You can talk to her then.'

'What cash?'

'Brownie knows. You found him?'

'I haven't got the cash.'

'Better find it. You've got sixty minutes and you've just wasted one.'

The phone went dead.

'What did he say?' asked Brownie.

'He wants twenty-four grand and then he'll give Jo back.'

'Jesus.' Brownie slumped in his seat, his chin almost level with the dashboard. 'Nightmare.'

'How did you get through twenty-four grand's worth of smack?'

He didn't answer, and I set off again, my mind racing. What was I going to do? I didn't like reacting to situations as they presented themselves to me. I needed a more proactive approach. Just had to think of one.

'We need to get off the streets,' I said to Brownie. 'Where can we go?'

'The squat?'

'Too obvious.'

'I've got a couple of mates.'

The idea of going to see any of Brownie's mates didn't appeal. It was just past ten o'clock on a Saturday night, the chances of anyone I knew being in were small. The offices were the first place they'd expect us to go, especially now it appeared Jo had told them we had the money. 'We need to go somewhere they don't know.'

'Martha's?'

'She said she was going out tonight.'

'I've got a key.'

I glanced across at him. 'You're in your underpants. You don't have anything.'

He grinned and for the first time I noticed the gap between his front teeth. It was kind of endearing.

'I stashed it.'

'What?'

'Saw him coming. So, I stashed my stuff. The key's in my wallet.'

'Where's Martha live?'

'Burley.'

'Where did you stash your wallet?'

'The Ridge,' said Brownie.

Guilt stabbed me again as I thought back to the night before, remembered seeing Duck slip through the gate, his shoulders hunched. Something had nudged me at the time, a feeling that something wasn't quite right, but I'd been keen to get back to the streetlights and I'd let it slide.

Martha's place. I thought it over in my mind. Either I was right, and she did love Brownie, in which case she'd be delighted to see him again, even, or perhaps especially, if he was only wearing his under-crackers. Or Brownie was right, and she was a policewoman. In which case, she could take over and arrest some people. Including the ones who had snatched Jo.

And, my mind ticked on, if she was the one who had grassed us up to the dealers she would have to take responsibility for what had happened to Jo. I couldn't think of a single reason why she would have, couldn't see what she would have had to gain. But there was one question that she hadn't answered last time we saw her that I needed to ask her again. One question that lent credibility to Brownie's story about the break-in. If she was Brownie's girlfriend, how come she had a photo of Jack in his school uniform? One thing I knew for certain: driving round the streets of Gipton was getting us nowhere. It had been almost an hour and a half since I'd seen Jo and I didn't want to think what was happening to her. I kept trying not to notice the bruises on Brownie's arms and legs. If there was anything like that on Jo, I swore to God I'd kill them.

So, for want of a better idea, I took the next left turn and headed back towards Woodhouse, up to The Ridge. I pulled up outside the last row of terraced houses just before the gate. Brownie didn't move. I turned the engine off, rolled another cigarette and handed it over.

'Well?'

'I can't go back in there.' His hands shook so much he could barely take the roll-up from my fingers.

'I'll come with you.'

'I've not got shoes. It's full of dog shit. And broken glass.'

I sighed. 'Where exactly?'

'Just past the gate, there's a wall on the left. You'll pass a bin, a metal bin, and about three or four strides past it, there's a brick missing, in the wall, at the bottom. There's a rock on the floor, just in front. My stuff's in there. My wallet. Just bring it to me.'

I popped the van door and got out.

'Don't open it,' he called out.

I slammed the door and paused on the pavement for a moment. I could see the tops of the trees looming above the last row of houses but, I realized, I didn't fear it as much this time. Things had happened since last night. Dirty pervy tramps seemed like Toytown in comparison.

I didn't hold out much hope as I made my way to the spot that Brownie had described. Brownie wasn't in a fit state to be relied upon for anything. But I found the bin, saw the rock and when I felt inside the gap in the wall my fingers brushed against a leather wallet, exactly where he said. His wallet and a small bunch of keys.

I don't want to be one of those people who doesn't believe the best of people. I'd rather trust and have things blow up in my face every now and again than live my life in a state of distrust. But I couldn't help myself. I knew that if I was going to get us both out of this alive I had to be tough. People were out there, yanking my chain. I know what it's like to be like Brownie, to live a life with dependency, with need. You never let yourself run out. Because running out isn't an option.

So, standing with my back to the wall, I flicked open the wallet, and rifled through the contents. It had less than a couple of quid in it, which only increased my suspicion. A junkie isn't worried about losing his wallet, a junkie's worried about losing his stash. And sure enough, there, tucked in the corner, was a small paper wrap. I tugged it out and held it in my hand. Drugs are a ticket to another world, a pass out from real life. I knew if Brownie got hold of it, he'd be lost to me and I needed him. I needed someone with me, and while he wasn't there yet, maybe he'd come around.

I knew it was mean, but there was another thought in my mind. Men do it to dogs. Keep them hungry and they work harder. If Brownie needed a score, maybe he'd be more use coming up with ideas as to where the dealers might be. I opened up the piece of paper, unfolding the creases and let the contents fall to the ground. I scraped the powder into the mud with my foot and put the loose change in my back pocket. On the way back to the van, I threw the empty wallet into the bushes.

'Someone's had your wallet,' I said, before I'd even climbed into the van. 'But the good news—'

'You're shitting me.'

'But the good news is I've got your keys.'

I held them up and gave him the biggest grin I could, hoping that I could somehow convince him that the keys were more of a find than a wrap of brown. 'So, what's the address?' I asked, turning the key in the ignition.

He slammed his way out of the van, seemingly no longer worried about his bare feet. I watched him charge through the gate and wondered whether I should follow him. But it was freezing out there and I knew he wouldn't get far. He stalked back less than a minute later.

'Fuckers. They'll nick anything round here. Total fucking scumbags.'

To give him his due he didn't take long to come around, but I knew what he was thinking. Not difficult. Junkies only think about one thing. Where's the next place, that's what he was thinking.

'The address?' I said again.

'Burley. Cardigan Road. The flats at the bottom.'

Had I known what was in store for us at the flats on Cardigan Road, I would have turned the van around and headed straight for the nearest police station, I swear. But at the time, all I could think was that Martha had got us into this mess, and so she was the one that had to get us out. Every time I thought of Jo, my palms got sticky and my chest felt tight. I fastened my seatbelt and prepared for a showdown.

Chapter Twenty-One

I never wanted to believe in sixth senses. I spend most of my life trying to hang on to the rational. What do I know? What can I prove? But once you've noticed something, you can't pretend it's not there. As soon as I turned into the small car park outside the flats at the bottom of Cardigan Road, I knew. I had a bad feeling. Something wasn't right. Which was weird, because I hadn't ever been there before. But something struck me like it was out of place.

Brownie hopped out the van. Whether it was the thought of seeing Martha again, or whether he had an idea that there might be drugs in the flat, he appeared anxious to get inside. I followed behind. Uneasy.

She lived on the third floor, he said. They were small, the flats. Not the high-rise kind of the city centre. There were three or four separate buildings, clustered together around the car park. Low-build, two flats per floor. I followed Brownie up the staircase, struggling to keep pace. He was fit, especially for someone who spent most of his time getting wasted.

It was dark now, like, proper dark, but there was a light switch to press on each floor, which then illuminated the next staircase. My stomach churned, and at that point I put it down to fear.

164

Would Bernie and Duck think of coming here? As far as I knew they didn't know Martha, but then Martha had given me their address. Did that mean they knew hers?

The third floor was the top floor, and there was only one flat door at the top of the staircase. Brownie let himself in with the key without knocking, which I thought a bit presumptuous, but I didn't say anything, thinking I'd feel safer once we were inside. I couldn't escape the feeling I'd had since we arrived, that someone was out there, watching us, and it made me anxious. We both fell over the threshold and into the flat, and I closed the front door behind us, sensing immediately that no one was home. The hall light was on, but there was something about the atmosphere that said empty.

Brownie made straight for the room at the end of the small corridor in front of us. I followed him into a square and sparsely furnished box-like front room. Brownie attacked the set of shelves in the corner, opening up pots, looking behind the row of books. He didn't find what he was looking for because he crossed to the window, opened it and leaned outside.

'What you doing?'

'Nowt.' He pulled himself through the opening, until all I could see was his arse hanging out.

I left him to it – we were on the third floor – he wasn't going anywhere – and glanced into the kitchenette, saw the knife sharpener fixed to the wall. A few empty wine bottles next to the bin, three burned-out tea lights and a couple of side plates stacked by the sink.

Back in the front room, Brownie closed the window. I noticed a half glass of red wine on the coffee table and an ashtray empty of butts, but full of ash. I remember a shiver ran down my back, like someone had stepped on my grave. I sloped back down the hallway and opened the nearest door. Another box-sized room, a double bed taking up most of the floor space. I flicked on the light switch, half expecting to see a figure under the sheets.

Nothing. The bed was made. A chair in the corner of the room with a pair of jeans folded on it, trainers on the floor, a purple-and-red striped shirt hanging over the back. The shirt she'd been wearing that afternoon. I skirted the bed to the bedside table and opened the drawer. Inside was a Patricia Cornwell novel, and when I flicked the pages a photo of Brownie and Martha fell out. I picked it up and looked at the pair of them, arms around each other, Martha grinning, Brownie with a small smile playing around his lips. He wasn't a bad-looking bloke with his clothes on.

I replaced the photo between the pages of the book and put the book back in the drawer. I turned to leave and trod on a set of keys that were sticking out from under the bed. I crouched to see if there was anything else under there but nothing, not even fluff. I picked up the keys and examined them. Three on a single ring. One just like the one I'd given to Brownie to let us in here, the second a car key and a third, a smaller one. I slipped them into my pocket and hesitated. The curtains were drawn, and the room was warm. Too warm, I realized. I went over to the window and checked the radiator. It was scalding to the touch.

I went back to the front room. 'Wonder where she is,' I said. 'Heating's on.'

Brownie sat on the two-seater sofa, licking cigarette papers. He didn't seem to notice my presence.

'I need you clean,' I said. 'What've you got?' I moved towards him.

'Relax. It's only resin.'

I saw the chunk of dope and let him get on with it, thinking it might help with his shakes. Watching him warm the dope reminded me again of Jo and another bolt of dread hit me.

What next? We were running out of options. I thought again about whether we should go to the offices, get the cash, and hand it over. More and more it appeared like that was my only option. It was Martha's money, according to Brownie. And she'd given it to Brownie, or at least she thought she'd given it to Brownie, so he could pay his debt. So perhaps that was the right thing to do. Something held me back, and as I glanced around the front room, I knew what it was. Martha's flat didn't look like the home of someone with twenty-four grand to burn. Where had Martha got that much money from?

But I had to get Jo back. And if that meant handing over the cash, that's what I was going to have to do, even if it felt like giving in.

A silence fell until I realized it wasn't a silence. Beyond the rustle of Brownie's cigarette papers, there was a noise. A gentle humming. It tugged at my memory. A moment's pause as I worked to place it and recognition dawned. The sound of speakers when there's nothing left to play. I've woken up to that sound often enough. I saw the iPod dock on the shelves and crossed the room. Sure enough, the speakers were on. I tried to fire up the screen of the iPod, but it needed a code. I turned the volume control knob on the speakers until they clicked off and the hum died away.

Dread pricked my skin.

'Something's not right,' I said.

Brownie didn't speak. His eyes scrunched up against the smoke, inhaling his first lungful.

I crossed back into the hall. One last door. I'd dismissed it as a broom closet or something, but of course there was a room I hadn't discovered yet. Even in flats this small, there has to be a bathroom.

The door wasn't locked. As soon as I pushed against it, it opened, and the dampness of the air hit me.

I took a step inside.

Cold steam, the heat long gone, the hot air turned back to water, condensation dripping down the tiles. Tendrils of damp. Wet cold.

And there she was.

In the bath.

Naked.

Eyes open. Or at least one eye open. I could only see her left eye; her right was submerged under the waterline. Her left shoulder was caught against the side of the bath, her skin pruned and bloated. Her hair floated around her like seaweed.

Our first client.

Mrs Wilkins.

Martha.

Whatever her name was no longer mattered. She didn't need it anymore.

Chapter Twenty-Two

I opened my mouth to scream, but before my vocal chords had time to get their shit together, my brain clamped them down. I stood burned to the spot. My mind flashed to Brownie, skinning up in the front room. Then Jo. Jesus, Jo. Fear flushed through me. I crouched low on the floor, put my hand on the damp lino to steady myself. I tasted vomit at the back of my throat and forced myself to swallow it down. How long since we'd watched Martha climb the stairs of the Students' Union? How did she get from there, from moving, alive, to here, a bloated, lifeless mannequin? There was so much I didn't know, couldn't understand. What happened? What had she done? I hated myself for not recognizing how deep her pain had been. If I'd been less angry with her, could I have stopped this?

How?

When I felt steadier, I edged closer and forced myself to dip my hand in the bath. My fingers disturbed the water, made a small ripple in its surface. The shoulder nearest to me moved on the wave and it was all I could do to keep my feet planted on the floor. The water was cold as stone. Martha's dark hair splayed around the shoulder, covering the side of her face.

'I'm sorry,' I whispered. Hot tears.

I straightened my legs and stood up. It took a moment for my knees to lock. Suicide. But I dismissed it almost as soon as the thought became a word, fully formed. You don't pay a firm of private investigators double rates to find a missing person and then top yourself before finding out whether they've succeeded.

When?

I forced myself to imagine her alive, her hair clipped to the side of her head. I pictured us in the university, the tremble in her fingers as she'd stirred her coffee. She'd told us not to ring. Told us she was going out.

Had she been and come back, or did she die before she'd had the chance to go? Where had she gone when she'd left us? I'd assumed she'd been going home, but I don't know why.

She wasn't the suicidal type. I felt on stronger ground. I know the type, or, let's say, I know the signs. She still had hope. She had something to live for. She loved someone.

I glanced around the room. A bottle of shampoo lay on the floor by the bath, and another under the sink. I had the sense that something was missing but couldn't put my finger on it. What wasn't here? No drugs, no drugs paraphernalia, no electrical appliances. No cut wrists. My mind flitted around trying to make sense of the scene in front of me. A voice in my head said no woman intends to die naked.

Clothes. I glanced around the room. No clothes. The chair in the bedroom, the shirt hanging over the back of it. The shirt was the shirt she'd been wearing earlier.

Why?

I wanted to roll back time. I thought of Jo and I couldn't stop the tears. My body wanted to empty itself, but I tried to contain it. To hold it. Martha had said someone was watching her. She'd had the feeling of being watched. I forced myself to look at her again, to make my brain accept the series of unacceptable facts before it. Martha was dead. Someone had killed her. You don't just die in the bath. Someone must have killed her. I flinched at the sight of her left eye, how it bulged from its socket. Somebody had been here, in the flat, and they'd killed her. They'd killed her because of Jack, because of the missing money, because she knew something I was on the edge of discovering.

I wiped my nose on the back of my sleeve and tried to get a grip. A dressing gown hung on the back of the bathroom door. I touched it and felt its clammy dampness, the collar properly wet. She'd got out of the bath and put on the dressing gown. Her wet hair had soaked the collar. She'd taken it off and got back in the bath. Or someone had put her in the bath.

No sign of a struggle.

I forced myself to turn her head, to look into her wide-open eyes, see if I could decode the message there. Her last thought. Her unseeing pupils, her irises darker blue than I remembered, bore past me, to an indefinable point somewhere in the next life.

I breathed through my options. I swear I thought about ringing the police, but as soon as I got past the 'I've found a dead woman in a bath' line, I ran into trouble. How did I get into the flat? How did I know said dead woman? When did you last see her alive? What's her name? None of these were questions I could, or wanted to, answer.

And besides, I was a woman on a tight timescale. Was the person who killed Martha the same person who now had Jo? I could hardly tell the police that I was waiting for drug dealers to phone. Dealers who were going to give me the ransom details for my best mate so I could hand over twenty-four grand and a tin of smack we'd got stashed at our office. There's no way the police would let that happen, and I couldn't let them endanger Jo.

All these thoughts passed through my mind in the time it takes to look around a small bathroom. I noticed without noticing two bottles of mouthwash on the windowsill, a woman's Bic razor, pink-edged, cotton wool buds. I stored the images in my brain, all the time thinking what to do about Brownie. I hadn't heard him move, could smell the sweet aroma of resin and tobacco mixed. Martha turned in the water in front of me, her head pulling her downwards, but her shoulder preventing the twist. How would Brownie take this? Should I even tell him? Could I get him out of the flat without him noticing?

I was saved from answering any of these questions by a voice behind me.

'What …?'

I turned to see Brownie standing in the hallway. He held out a spliff towards me. My jacket was about four inches too short for him in the arms and didn't reach down far enough to cover his grey underpants. The small amount of colour he'd had drained completely from his skin, so he looked like a ghost, a greasy ghost.

'Jesus.' He put a hand to his hair and tugged at it as if he were trying to wake himself up. The spliff fell to the floor. 'What …?'

'Brownie.' I straightened and tried to position myself between him and the body in the bath behind me, but I wasn't big enough.

'Martha?' he said in a voice that almost broke my heart.

'She's dead,' I said, never shy of stating the obvious.

His knees went first, and he crashed to the ground like he'd been felled. He dropped, all six foot of him, right in front of me, landing on my Docs with such force I thought he'd broken my toes. I prised my feet from under him. He didn't flinch, didn't move at all, his arms and bare legs splayed at odd angles. My first thought was he'd had some kind of massive heart attack and I was now stuck in a flat with two dead bodies, but when I put my hand on his back I felt the rise and fall of his breath, shallow and fast.

I took the crushed spliff from under his arm and stuffed it down the plughole in the bathroom sink. I left the tap running, jumped over him and ran down the hall to the bedroom. I opened the drawers and rummaged until I found a pair of dark blue tracksuit bottoms. I ran back to the bathroom and dropped them on top of Brownie.

We had to get out of there. I had to find Jo. Every time I thought of her another burst of acid hit my veins. I put the cold tap on in the bath. Martha's body bobbed with the movement of the water, making her seem alive. I shuddered and headed for the kitchen, looking for a clock. The one on the cooker showed nearly midnight, which meant it was almost time for my ransom phone call. I grabbed the resin and the Rizla papers that Brownie had left on the table and shoved them in my pocket. We had to get out. I had to find Jo. I couldn't do anything else until I'd found Jo. I ran back to the bathroom, turned off the sink tap, making sure there was nothing left of the spliff. I squatted down next to Brownie, grabbed his right arm and dragged him up to sitting.

'Brownie? Listen to me.'

His pupils did their best to focus, but I wasn't certain he was seeing me. I waved my hand in front of his face. His gaze didn't change. I didn't have time to spare. I snatched my hand back and smacked him as hard as I could across the face. His throat bulged. He made a noise, something between a burp and a cough. I grabbed his hair and yanked his head as hard as I could in the direction of the toilet, just as thin, yellow liquid erupted from his mouth.

Some of it made it into the white porcelain. Some of it didn't. I wiped my hand on the jacket he was wearing before I remembered it was mine. He retched another two or three times, each time the splash of his piss-like vomit hit the back of the toilet. When I was sure he had finished I flushed the chain.

The water in the bath was nearing the top.

'Put these on,' I said to Brownie. He'd collapsed into a heap on the floor. I hit him with the tracksuit bottoms on his calf muscle. 'Brownie. Focus. I have to go. I've got to find Jo.'

'Can't leave,' he said, trying to sit up, his voice high-pitched.

'I haven't got time to answer questions.'

'Questions.'

173

'The police.' I thought about my fingerprints, probably splattered all around the flat by now. I calmed myself with the thought I'd never been arrested.

'Police.' He repeated everything I said, like he was learning language for the first time.

'The police are going to want answers.' I spoke as slowly as my pulse rate would allow. I didn't know about Brownie. Maybe his prints were on file somewhere. He struck me as a likely candidate for police attention. But then his prints had a reason for being here. He'd been here before.

'Right.'

'Martha is dead. The police will want to know why. How. When. Those kinds of questions.'

Finally, something seemed to register. He frowned, rubbed his eyes, shook his head like a dog might after a river swim. I got to my feet. It was time to get the hell out.

Brownie struggled to get to his. I threw him the tracksuit bottoms for a second time. He caught them in one hand and then stared at them like he didn't know how they'd got there.

'Put them on,' I said.

'Martha.'

'There's nothing we can do.' I knelt beside the bathtub and turned the tap so that the gush of water reduced to a trickle. I took the facecloth from the side and did my best to squash it up against the overflow, using Martha's left foot to hold it in place. I swallowed again. Forced myself to look at her face. Her pale, almost translucent body hunched over, the water milky white. 'I'll find out what happened,' I said to her. 'I swear they won't get away with it.'

After a moment or two, I stood up, turned my back on her and stepped out of the room, pulling Brownie with me. I closed the door.

'She's dead, Brownie. No matter what we do, she's still going to be dead. I can't change that.'

Chapter Twenty-Three

Brownie tried to get his legs into the tracksuit bottoms. After two failed attempts I wrapped his arm around my shoulders and held him up while he got them on. We left the flat, almost falling down the stairs in our hurry to get away from there, out of the building, dreading bumping in to anyone. Through the main door, back to the car park, the night air cold, my senses heightened.

'Do you think she ... did she ...?'

'No,' I said as I unlocked the van.

'Top herself?'

'No,' I said again, trying to keep any trace of doubt from my voice. 'She couldn't have. Not as easy as you think.' Believe me, I've tried – got right up to this peaceful, white-light state – a moment that makes you believe in an afterlife. I shook the memory clear. 'You need a current,' I said to Brownie. 'Otherwise the survival instinct pops you up. Virginia Woolf filled her pockets with rocks. You need something to drag you down.'

He screwed up his eyes, wiped the snot from his nose. 'OD?'

'You checked the flat. Never heard of anyone ODing on pot.'

'Then—?'

'I don't know, Brownie, but we aren't going to figure it out standing here. Get in.'

'You think it was Duck and Bernie?'

'How come there's no fag ends in the ashtray?'

'She flushes everything.' He ducked his tall, gangly frame into the van. 'Paranoid about getting busted.'

I climbed into the driving seat, started the engine and crunched the gears. 'Let's get out of here.'

Brownie didn't answer. I glanced at him. He was bent over, holding his head in his hands, his shoulders juddering so much the van rocked.

'Seatbelt,' I said.

'Fucked it all up.'

I strapped myself in. 'You didn't kill her.'

'She lied,' he said.

'Come on, seatbelt. I really don't want to get pulled over now.'

'Why? Why do women just mash your mind?' He nutted the dashboard of my van so hard it dented.

The noise made me jump and a flash of anger zapped my veins. 'All right, steady on. Let's get out of here, think what to do.'

I released the handbrake, let the clutch up and we lurched towards the car park entrance. I hesitated, not sure whether to turn left or right. Shock had wiped the contents of my brain and in the vacuum a plan formed. Maybe my subconscious had been mulling it over while the rest of me had come to terms with the horror of Martha's flat, I don't know. But suddenly I had a fully formed plan in my head.

We had to get out of Leeds.

I had to get Jo.

And we needed a safe house.

But first, we had to swoop by the office. I needed envelopes.

It was only a five-minute drive from Martha's flat to our office. I parked the van a couple of streets away, down the hill. 'You stay here,' I said to Brownie. 'I'll only be ten minutes.'

176

He threw open the van door and vaulted onto the pavement faster than Usain Bolt.

'No chance.'

He kept close to me as we walked round the block and didn't say anything as I undid the padlocks and we squeezed through the makeshift door. His eyebrows knotted at the 'Be scarred' spray paint on the wall, but I didn't give him time to ask questions.

'OK, make us a brew. I have to sort a few things.' I steered him through to the back and pointed him in the direction of the kitchenette. 'Hot, sweet tea.'

I had no intention of drinking it, but he needed a focus. While he was occupied I snuck into the back room and opened the broom cupboard door. I took down the poster to reveal the safe, entered the combination and tugged the door open. A scattering of thick brown envelopes fell at my feet. I picked them up, scooped the notes out and shoved the cash in an old money belt that was hanging among the bags on the wall. I clipped the belt around my middle and stuffed the empty envelopes into a knapsack.

The Old Holborn tin lay at the back of the safe. I shoved it into the bag. I relocked the safe, even though it was empty, put the poster back and closed the broom cupboard door.

Brownie was in the main office. 'Here,' he said, holding out a mug with steam coming off the top of it.

'We'll have to take them with us,' I said, glancing around the office. I pulled open the bottom drawer of the desk and scooped out a handful of compliment slips. 'They're going to be ringing any minute.'

I checked Jo's phone again, made sure the ringer was on.

He stood my mug on the desk and sat down on the floor, his legs crossed in front of him, bare chest visible although he was still wearing my jacket. He was scrawny thin, even by my standards.

'I don't know anyone,' he said.

I stuffed handfuls of compliment slips into the envelopes in my knapsack. 'Come again?' I said.

He cradled his mug of tea, his gaze fixed on the carpet tiles in front of him. 'I don't know anyone to ring, anyone to tell.'

I found a roll of Sellotape in the top drawer and sealed each envelope with a strip before returning them to the knapsack.

'Who am I going to tell?' asked Brownie again.

'Not your problem,' I said. 'The police will notify next of kin.'

'We've been … you know … for months, and I can't think of one single person to tell.'

'What about mates?' I pulled the strings on the knapsack and slung it over my shoulder.

'Didn't have any.'

'She must have had one.'

'That's what I mean.' Brownie gulped some tea. 'Something's not right.'

I considered this. I'm hardly the world's most sociable person, but I have Jo. And there's other people I could call acquaintances, if not mates. To have no mates at all takes some doing.

'She said she'd just moved down. From Newcastle.'

I knew nothing about our first ever client. Everything I thought I'd known was a lie. 'What was she doing in Leeds?'

'PhD.'

'So, she'd have mates on her course, wouldn't she?'

'Wasn't a course. It was research.'

'On what?'

'Politics. Social movements, she said. Never really got it.'

'Come on, we're on a timescale.'

He didn't budge. 'I didn't get it, because I didn't ask.'

I put the knapsack down on the desk and sat on the floor next to him. I lit a fag and passed it to Brownie. 'It's not your fault.'

'My fault I don't know who to tell.'

'Hindsight is awful,' I said. Which is true. The present lacks the clarity hindsight offers. Hindsight is just a shortcut to guilt.

178

'If we knew what was going to happen we'd all do stuff differently. Point is, you didn't know.'

'Didn't care.'

'I don't believe that.'

He tried to smile and for an awful moment I thought he might cry. 'Typical bloke,' he said. 'Just looking to get my rocks off.'

He shivered in front of me. I made myself make eye contact. 'Don't believe that either.'

'Five seconds where the voices can't get you.'

I couldn't think of anything to say to that. Let her who is without voices cast the first stone. I put my hand on his knee. Even through the jogging bottoms I could feel the cold of his skin. I checked the clock on the wall. Almost twenty past twelve. 'We need to keep moving.'

He looked up at me and seemed to understand my point.

I hammered it home. 'They've got my best mate. If they do anything to her—'

'They won't hurt her. They want the cash, not your mate.'

'They hurt you.'

'I kind of had it coming.'

I put a hand on the belt round my waist. They could have the money, just don't let them hurt Jo. I couldn't bear it. 'You think it was them? I mean, Martha?'

He wrinkled his nose but didn't say anything, and I didn't have time to push it. I gave him the pair of old flip-flops I'd left at the offices when we'd been decorating. They were too small but better than nothing. We locked up the makeshift door, and I linked arms with Brownie as we walked towards the van, trying to make us look like a student couple returning from a night out, which wasn't easy considering his tracksuit bottoms only came to mid-calf and his chest was bare. I needed to get him properly dressed, I thought, but then we passed three lads dressed as Teenage Mutant Ninja Turtles and I stopped stressing about it.

The streets were pretty empty save for a couple of minicabs

bringing the wounded home. Brownie pulled me into his body. He was trembling skin and bone. I put my arm around his waist, tried to radiate body warmth his way.

We got to the van and I opened his door first, before running round to the driver's side. I got in, stashed the knapsack under my seat and turned the key in the ignition. I checked Jo's phone again before setting off. Why hadn't they rung? It was past time. I drove back the way we'd come. I wanted to get out of Leeds, but first I had to get Jo. As I pulled out onto Cardigan Road and headed for the traffic lights, we passed a dark-coloured car parked up on the left-hand side.

'There it is,' said Brownie, resignation in his voice.

'What?' My nerves were shot.

'Knew it.'

I watched in the wing mirror and sure enough the car slunk into the road behind us.

'Who is it?'

'They're after us.' Sweat ran down the sides of his face, glistening every time we passed under a streetlight. He moaned like he was in pain. And I know, believe me, I know that it is painful when you can't get what you need.

My eyes stung as I tracked the car behind us in the rear-view mirror. Was it the same car that had followed us to Moss Side? And if so, who the fuck was driving it? Was it following us or were we just being paranoid? No sleep the night before was messing with my mind. My bones ached, but my brain was wired. 'Is it Duck and Bernie?'

'It's not their car.'

'If they hurt her, I swear to God …'

'It's not Duck and Bernie you've got to worry about.' Brownie raised his voice to be heard over the roar of the van's engine.

'What?'

'It's a food chain.'

My stomach flipped. 'What?'

'Works on the same principle.'

'Who?' I glanced in my wing mirror.

'Dunno.'

'For fucks' sake.' In that moment I could have punched him. I mean like really punched him.

I think he sensed it. He picked at the skin on the side of his thumb. 'A guy called T. That's all I know. You cross him, you go for a swim in the canal. He broke Duck's thumbs once. Saw the bandages. Whole thing runs on fear.'

Fear. I remembered a line I'd been told, a long time ago. Courage is not the absence of fear, but the mastery of it. I tried to allow the adrenaline to run through to my fingertips, to power my body like petrol does a car. 'You think it's him? Is that T's car?'

'Dunno.'

Why hadn't they rung? It had been way over an hour. What had happened? I checked the screen of Jo's phone again. Nothing. I kept my foot pressed hard to the floor all the way in to the city. The van growled and barked and spat but I had the sense it loved this kind of driving. The only other traffic was minicabs, not known for their strict adherence to the Highway Code, so I kept throwing last minute turns in the hope I could shake the car behind. Once we got to the City Hall, my spirits lifted. The great thing about Leeds is the one-way system. I've lived here years now and still can't get my head around it. I ducked the van one way, twisted us through various dark little side streets, driving us round in circles. The car behind me clung on.

I crossed two lanes of cars by the Grand Theatre, threw a sharp right, followed by another down a back alley. I checked the mirror. 'Have I lost them?'

Brownie opened his window and stuck his head out. The focus seemed good for him. He clung to the headrest, didn't speak for a moment or two. Then he said: 'Think so.'

Silence descended. Too quiet. We drove in a suspicious silence for a few minutes, Brownie sticking his head out every few seconds or so. Nothing. I actually think I preferred it when they were behind me. The not knowing was worse – every set of headlights the potential enemy.

Jo's phone rang, and I leaped in my seat. The clock on the dashboard showed five to one. I glanced at Brownie, swallowed my spit and swiped the screen.

'Where the fuck have you been?' I yelled.

'Keep your hair on,' said the voice on the phone.

'You said you'd ring in an hour.' Driving's hard enough. Driving while speaking on the phone was a whole new kettle of fish. I held the wheel with my knees while I searched for the hands-free function.

'Chill out. Did you get the cash?'

'If you've done anything—'

Brownie grabbed the wheel as we caught a kerb. I dropped the phone into my lap.

'Yes,' I shouted. 'I got the cash.'

'All the cash?' asked the voice on the speaker-phone.

'Yes, yes, it's all here.' The traffic lights ahead turned red, so I took a last minute right turn and swung us round the corner, tyres screeching.

'OK. We need to meet.'

'Put Jo on first,' I said.

'She's here. She's fine.'

'I want to speak to her.' I fought to straighten the steering wheel with just my right hand. 'You said I'd speak to her.'

'Ask a question. One that only she knows the answer to.'

I thought for a moment. 'When's her birthday?'

The phone went quiet. Then the man's voice came back. 'The fourth of July.'

I exhaled. Closed my eyes for the briefest moment. 'OK.'

'So we need to meet.'

'I'm ready,' I lied. I took a left turn down Greek Street, hit a traffic cone that someone had left in the middle of the road. It made a hell of a bang, but the van kept going.

'There's a car park—'

'No.' I'd had enough of dancing to someone else's tune. For my plan to work, it had to be on my terms.

My knuckles glistened white on the steering wheel, reflecting the glare of the streetlights. 'Listen. I'll meet you at Dewsbury train station. Platform Two. There's a waiting room. You'd better be in there. You've got thirty minutes or I'm off and you'll never see your cash.'

'Don't m—'

'And if you've touched so much as one hair on her head, I'll fucking kill you. And your mother.'

'Let—'

'You want your cash, and your dope, you'd better be there. Thirty minutes. That's it.' I leaned across Brownie and, as hard as I could, I threw Jo's phone out of the open window next to him.

No more dancing.

I screamed. I screamed so loud and so long that I took myself by surprise. Brownie put his hands over his ears. I grinned at him. He stared back at me like I'd gone crazy. Maybe I had. But the feeling was amazing. The high better than any drug I'd ever taken. My scalp tingled.

Up until that moment I'd harboured a dark, unspoken fear that maybe I wasn't up to this, the business, the job. But right then, right there in the van, I knew. This is what I was born for.

'What the fuck did you do that for?' said Brownie.

The here and the now. There is nothing else. Learn that and the world is your lobster.

'Fucking hell,' I said. 'Fucking hell.'

'Your phone.'

'Electronic fucking tagging device. Now we're free. They've got no way of contacting us. They have to come to Dewsbury.'

But Brownie wasn't listening. He was watching the passenger wing mirror. 'They're back,' he said.

I glanced over my shoulder. Caught a glimpse of the square yellow lights. Shit. I wanted somewhere dark, somewhere we could leave the car and hit the ground running. Somewhere we could get lost. As we screeched around the north of the city, a thought came to me.

'Brownie?'

He looked at me like he'd never seen me before. I gripped his arm.

'I'm going to drive us to the Dark Arches. We need to ditch the van.'

I knew he wasn't seeing me. I raised my voice. 'When we get there, Brownie, we're going to need to leg it. You ready?'

He didn't look ready, but he didn't want to get caught any more than I did. The Dark Arches are, as their name implies, dark. They're the subterranean world under Leeds train station. Built in Victorian times to channel the River Aire, now they house a few bars and underground car parks for the tenants of the flats that are forever springing up around the city centre. The river rages alongside.

I headed south through the city, breaking every speed limit, praying the police were all busy dealing with the usual city centre fights as club kicking-out time approached. I drove the wrong way through the one-way system around Queens Square and pulled up at the traffic lights. A taxi driver in the next lane tapped his forefinger to the side of his head to indicate what he thought of me.

'You've lost them,' said Brownie.

I glanced left and right and, without waiting for the lights to go green, set off. I drove past the entrance to the Dark Arches, decided to do one more lap of the city. We had time to kill. I drove out to the south, down to the M1, then did a 360-degree turn around the roundabout, the back wheels spinning out, and headed north. Laughter bubbled in my stomach.

'Jesus, where'd you learn to drive?' Brownie grabbed my arm as I rounded the next corner.

'You should see Jo,' I said. I checked the rear-view mirror. Nothing. 'Right, I'll do a last loop and then with a bit of luck we'll have time to get a coffee before the train.'

'What train?'

'The Manchester one.' I was fairly familiar with the route – it was the same train we caught whenever we went to back to Liverpool to see Jo's mum. We'd caught it a couple of times at this time of night, when Jo had got the idea of her mum's breakfast fixed in her head after we'd been clubbing. As I skirted the north of the city, I remember thinking I had to find Jo, because her mum would flay me alive if I let anything happen to her only daughter.

I drove along Wellington Street and was just congratulating myself on a job well done when I saw it. The same car, I was almost certain, dark and square, parked up on double yellow lines, across the road from the railway station.

'Bollocks. How did they do that?' I didn't have to time to think about it. We didn't have time for another lap. I needed to get out of the city. I needed to get to Jo. 'Hold on, Brownie.'

I pushed the van to almost sixty as we looped round the station. I jumped the red lights and hung a hard left into the entrance to the Dark Arches. There's only one way in and out of the Dark Arches, and we were on it – a narrow road, only one car wide, that crosses the river. I knew as I drove across the bridge that it was a dead end ahead. Whoever was driving the car behind must have had the same thought, because it stopped on the bridge, blocking our exit. The only way out now would be on foot. I watched in the rear-view mirror and saw a figure climb out.

I kept driving forward. There's a rough patch of car park on the left, outside by the canal, so I pulled in there, threw open my driver's door and turned to grab the knapsack from the backseat.

'Run,' I shouted to Brownie.

He fell out of the left side of the van and I went round to catch him. He was a chain round my neck, really, and if I'd had any sense I would have just left him there, but I can never pass by an underdog. It's in my genes – I'm duty-bound. I knew we had a few hundred yards on whoever was behind us.

I hoped it was enough.

Chapter Twenty-Four

I could tell by the way Brownie leaned on me that his legs weren't functioning. His knees weren't locking, his entire body trembled. I pulled his arm tight around my neck.

'Hold me. Shut up.'

I put the knapsack on my back and half-dragged Brownie out of the car park and up against the wall. I thought about which way the driver of the car would expect us to go and turned the other, keeping us up close against the brickwork. The water rushed past, creating enough noise to mask the sounds of our feet. A positive, but one that worked both ways – I couldn't hear whoever was following us either.

Intermittent, low-level security lighting lit up some of the arches. As we entered the maze of tunnels, I could see the headlights of the car to the right of us, still blocking the entrance.

I pulled Brownie close to me as I heard the scuttle of a tin can. Brownie's breathing in my ear reminded me of the film *Jaws*. Fear prickled my neck. Not the absence of fear, the mastery of it. Channel the energy, make it work for you.

We went deeper into the tunnels. There's loads of small rooms, like mini brick caves, all with arched ceilings, that have been turned into lock-ups – each housing ten or so cars. Plenty of places to hide. I didn't want to hide. I didn't have time to hide. I needed to escape.

The River Aire is huge – it crashes through four parallel tunnels, the noise echoing off the walls. Was there someone waiting in the car, as well as someone following us?

'We're going that way,' I whispered to Brownie, pointing to the nearest tunnel. He stared at the river cascading through.

'You're taking the piss?'

The current was strong enough to wash away elephants. 'There's a ledge.' I pointed over the side of the bridge. I slipped my hand into Brownie's. His was colder than ice. An old metal gate blocked the pedestrian entrance to the bridge. The car was still parked across the road side, its headlights off. No one was in it, at least not that I could see. I pulled the gate open, cursing the squeaking noise it made. A train rumbled overhead, and I hoped it masked the noise. We climbed over the metal railings, down onto the thin stone ledge that ran alongside the inky blackness of the water. I prayed Brownie was stable enough to walk along the thin strip without falling in. If he did, I doubted I'd be able to save him. The water looked freezing, smelled cold and dark. At the end of the tunnel, a few hundred yards away, I could see the first light of dawn.

We crept along the ledge. A rat ran out of the shadows, more alarmed by us than we were of him, but I saw Brownie react, jerk. He called out, 'Shit,' and something else but his words got lost in the rush of the river.

We'd got halfway along when something made me turn around. I'm not sure whether it was a faint shout, a noise of some kind. I turned in time to see the outline of someone climbing over the railings of the bridge. He had a torch – a really powerful one, and the beam snaked its way towards us. I prodded Brownie in the back.

'Faster. He's seen us.'

Brownie speeded up, but this made progress more frightening.

At one point his right foot slipped over the side and I had to grab his left wrist. The ledge was uneven and slippy and the rush of the water meant I couldn't hear the guy behind me. I didn't want to waste time by keeping on turning round but the temptation was awful. By the time the tunnel opened out, I glanced back to see a hooded figure only a hundred or so yards behind us.

'Is that him? Is that T?'

'Dunno. Never met him.'

The path widened, became like a towpath outside the tunnel. I spotted a half brick on the floor. A metal set of steps up to the road. I pushed Brownie towards the metal frame and up the first few steps.

'Wait for me at the top. Stay out of sight.'

I turned back towards the man following us and yelled: 'Stop.'

I held the brick up in one hand. He was caught, still too far away for me to make out much, except that he wore a hooded top. I was willing to bet he wasn't a policeman, which meant that if he wasn't a force for good, then he was probably a force for bad. Whatever, he was caught between a rock and a hard place. I mean literally, and I think he knew it. The stone wall of the tunnel to his left, the river to his right. The ledge only a couple of feet wide. He held up his hands in surrender as I threw the brick with all my strength towards him, the hatred of a dozen fascist PE teachers infused in my arm. He ducked, and the brick hit the water. There was nothing for him to grab hold of, nothing to steady himself against. He squatted low, too far away for me to get any clear idea what he looked like. I was fairly sure it was a man, from the way he held himself, the curve of his shoulders. He remained squatted, eighty, maybe ninety yards inside the tunnel. I turned round. Brownie had made it to the road.

'Turn back,' I shouted down the tunnel again.

He didn't move. I found a glass bottle on the floor and lobbed that at him as well. Anything to keep him off balance. Anything to keep him crouched and trying to cling to the ground for safety.

'Turn round,' I yelled again.

Someone or something was on my side – I had what looked like an entire junkyard at my disposal. I threw another couple of half bricks, a tin can full of water. My hand lit on a piece of rock that had a piece of metal bar embedded in it. I balanced myself and threw it as hard as I could. It pirouetted in the air, two or three complete turns, before arching up and catching the guy on his shoulder. He yelled out and I felt a momentary rush of pride. I was always shit at rounders. And that was some distance. But my pride turned quickly to worry as he stumbled backwards, tried to stand and his left leg slipped from under him and went over the side. He grabbed at the ledge. I watched for a moment to see whether he could hold on. I didn't fancy his chances if he went over. The river raged beside us. Cold and inky. He clung to the rocky ledge, gathering the strength to pull himself back up.

Could I leave him there? If he fell in he had no chance. The water battered the tunnel walls, smashing anything that got in its way. I thought of Jo, of what they might be doing to her while I stood wondering whether to save a man who wished me harm. I took a step towards him, then another.

'Leave him,' Brownie yelled from the top of the metal staircase. 'You think he'll make it?'

'Not our problem,' Brownie said.

I glanced back at the man. He'd managed to get his right knee up on the ledge and was hauling the rest of his body up. I turned and ran, threw myself at the metal stairs as Brownie reached an arm down and yanked me up.

Together, we legged it to the station entrance. Sweat beaded on Brownie's forehead as we ran, and I knew exercise wasn't part of his daily routine. My lungs were bursting by the time we reached the departure boards, and I swore I'd give up smoking if we got out of this alive. I scanned the information in front of us. There weren't that many trains at this time of night, only the sleepers going up to Stirling and down to London, so it didn't take me long to find what I was looking for. The Manchester airport train. On time. I checked the clock on the board. Three minutes.

I raced Brownie across the station towards the entrance to the platforms.

'We're getting a ticket on the train,' I yelled to the disinterested guard, who was reading his paper in the booth.

We pegged it across the station forecourt and I dragged Brownie up the stairs. The Manchester train always went from the far end. My legs burned as I yanked us onwards over the bridge. As we crossed the tracks I saw our train at the platform.

'Faster,' I shouted to Brownie.

'Leave me,' he said, his legs crumbling under him.

'No fucking chance.'

The guard stood by the train, whistle in mouth as we fell down the stairs. 'We want that one,' I yelled, somewhat unnecessarily. He nodded, held up a hand and we threw ourselves through the open door and into a carriage. A second later the doors closed, and the train's engines fired up.

I pushed Brownie into a seat. 'Keep your head down.'

The train rolled off a moment later. I sat down and kept my eyes fixed on the window. As we pulled out west of the station, I saw a figure burst through the entrance gates, running as fast as we had. The train lurched forward, gathering speed. I peered as hard as I could through the window, but it was no good. He was too far away. His hooded top was grey, and he wore boots the colour of sand. I saw him yell something, but the train gained momentum and I knew enough to know it wouldn't stop now.

I got up and flopped into the seat next to Brownie. 'It's OK. We made it,' I said. I checked the time. I felt Brownie lean his head on my shoulder, and as the adrenaline seeped from my body with every chug of the wheels, I felt giddy, high with relief.

191

'I'm starving,' said Brownie. He checked the timetable on the wall. 'Twenty minutes till Huddersfield.'

I hitched the knapsack higher over my shoulder. 'We're not going as far as Huddersfield.'

He turned and checked the timetable again. Then frowned at me. 'That's the first stop.'

'Not tonight it isn't.'

Chapter Twenty-Five

I pushed Brownie down the train, trying to find an empty carriage. It was just past one o'clock on Sunday morning and we were conspicuously different to the rest of the passengers, all of whom were dressed for their holidays. Nearly everyone wore sunglasses, and suitcases the size of small houses hung from the luggage racks. A crowd of young women, obviously a hen party or something, occupied half the next carriage. I glanced at Brownie. His skin was grey and kind of shiny and he smelled, a salty, acrid smell. I did the maths, at least forty hours since his last hit.

We settled ourselves at the far end of an almost empty carriage, where no one could hear us. I sat back in my seat, closed my eyes and visualized Dewsbury station. I'd passed through it enough times – on the way to visit Jo's mum, and me and Jo had unintentionally spent some time there just before Christmas. We'd been to see Arcade Fire in Manchester and got so pissed we'd been thrown off the train at Dewsbury by a guard with no sense of humour. It had taken hours to find a taxi willing to drive us back to Leeds.

I focused my mind. Eliminated everything except the next ten minutes. I visualized the station, what I remembered of it. Duck and Bernie would have to leave their Escort in the car park beyond the station entrance. Then they'd have to go on foot through the station to Platform Two. I pictured the small waiting room, like a Perspex bus stop. We'd thought about kipping there at one point.

I opened my eyes again, felt sweat trickle down my stomach, the money belt feeling like a bandage wrapped around my torso. Nine minutes.

I spent three of them outlining the plan to Brownie. His eyes blurred, and I knew he was a weak link, my Achilles heel, but there was nothing I could do about that. He didn't have much to do. I had to hope for the best.

'If they see me, they'll kill me,' he said.

'They won't, because I've got this.' I patted the knapsack on my back. 'This is what they're after.'

I stopped talking and left Brownie, spent two minutes walking from one end of the train to the other, trying to keep a count of who was in each carriage. I took a quick peek inside the guard's van at the far end. Unoccupied.

When I got back to Brownie he seemed resigned to his fate. I used the next two minutes to centre myself, breathing in and out, slow as I could. This was going to take confidence, authority. I had to compel them to do what I said. There wouldn't be any time for persuasion.

I opened my eyes. Almost time. I stood up, pushed Brownie all the way down the train to the doorway in the last carriage. I held up two fingers, one at a time with each instruction.

'One. Get off the train,' I said, my eyes boring into his. 'Two. Say sorry to the guard.'

I left Brownie standing by the door and made my way back towards the front of the train. I'd got as far as the middle when the first signs of civilization appeared through the window. Houses poking out among the trees, then a factory, a mill chimney, streetlights. I took five twenty-pound notes out of my money belt and zipped it back up. Held onto the cash with my right hand and, with my left, reached for the emergency pull cord. I licked my lips, counted to three and then yanked.

Nothing happened for a second. Then a jolt and I was thrown forward. The wheels screeched, metal on raw metal, awful sound. I glanced to see whether anyone had seen me pull the cord, but the grown-ups in the one family in the next carriage both had their backs to me. I walked as calmly as I could past them, stopping only to place my knapsack in the overhead luggage rack.

The train slowed. I continued walking down it. I saw a church tower. I had no idea how long a train took to stop but we were rapidly losing speed. I stumbled into the back of another seat as the carriage juddered. Dewsbury station came into view.

'Please be there,' I heard myself whisper.

Two men, one in a leather jacket, hovered by the waiting room, illuminated by two globe-like lamps on the waiting room wall. The next thing I saw made my heart bounce. Jo, sitting inside, arms folded, facing out. I know she saw me too because she grinned. I turned and set off towards the rear of the train, jogging now, as the train slowed to a crawl. I fought the urge to sprint. On the platform, the guy in the hooded top noticed my sudden movement and frowned. I carried on running. There was no one else on the platform, no one standing waiting to get on. No one waited at a station where the train wasn't scheduled to stop.

We ground to a halt and I heard a shout from somewhere further back down the train. I looked back out of the window and saw the guy in the leather jacket moving diagonally across the platform, heading towards me. No sign of Brownie.

'Get off the fucking train, Brownie.'

I reached the doors just as the train hit a standstill. I pressed the button and shoulder charged the door. It flung open.

'Your money's here,' I shouted.

The man in the jacket was white, mid-twenties, overweight. He wore a gold signet ring on the middle finger of his right hand.

I drank in the details of him, committed them to memory. The second guy was on his way over. Twenty paces behind.

'Everything you want.' I opened the palm of my hand. Showed him the clutch of twenty-pound notes.

The train driver had got off the train. 'What's happened?' he shouted. I swallowed as I caught a glimpse of Brownie at the far end of the platform.

I returned my stare to the bloke in front of me. 'The rest of your cash, all of it, is in a blue knapsack, in the luggage rack, third carriage down. You need to get on the train.'

Brownie had reached the train driver. He positioned himself, as instructed, so that the driver had his back to us.

'Get on, Bernie,' I said to the man in the leather jacket. 'Tell Duck to get on the train.'

Duck reached his mate, so they both stood in front of me. The train driver shouted something at Brownie. Something along the lines of, 'You stupid fucking idiot,' I'd guess.

Duck turned, caught sight of Brownie. Duck clenched his fists.

I spoke to Bernie. 'Leave Jo and leave him.' I gestured towards Brownie. 'Everything you want, the cash, everything, is on this train.'

I watched the driver climb back on board, shaking his head. I turned back to Bernie and Duck. 'It's going to go. The train is going to go. You've got to get on.'

No time to make an informed decision. Bernie grabbed Duck's arm.

I stepped aside, still holding out the twenty-pound notes. Bernie stepped on the train. He went to grab the money from my palm, at least I thought he did, but instead of taking the cash, he held onto my wrist. Duck jumped on board. The engines started up again. I tried to move forward, towards the door, towards the station platform, but Bernie's grip was strong.

'You're with us,' he said.

He slammed the door shut. Through the window I saw Brownie with Jo. The train inched into gear.

196

'OK, come with me,' I said, in as normal a voice as I could, like this was always the plan. I wiped the palms of my hands on my trousers.

I walked them into the first carriage. 'I've got us a good seat.' They followed me through the first, into the second carriage. Holidaymakers stared up at us. I kept smiling at everyone. 'Wonder what that was all about,' I said to no one in particular.

The third carriage had the family with the two young girls in it.

I stopped at the seats opposite them and slipped into the row. Bernie and Duck followed me.

I raised my eyebrows and nodded at the family opposite. My cheeks ached from the size of my grin. 'Fancy bumping in to you two,' I said to Duck and Bernie. 'Sit down, you're making the place look untidy.' I pulled a face at the mother and laughed.

Duck and Bernie frowned but did as I said. As they sat down, I stood up again. 'Oh, I nearly forgot. I brought your stuff.'

I reached up to the overhead luggage rack and tugged the knapsack down. I held it by the straps. 'It's been ages. How've you been?'

'What's going on?' asked Duck. 'What about—?'

'Don't worry about them,' I said. 'They'll be fine. Probably go for a picnic. Forecast is great.'

The train gathered speed and I watched the platform move past the windows. I dropped the rucksack onto Bernie's lap. His fingers closed around the straps. 'This everything?'

'Yes. Thanks for lending. Really enjoyed *Toy Story 2*. So funny.' I made as if to sit down, but before my bum hit the seat, I jumped back up. 'I'll just nip to the loo. Sorry, bursting.' I threw a smile at the two girls, who grinned back. 'Won't be a sec.'

I turned and made my way down the train, towards the rear. I heard Bernie say, 'Hang on a minute,' but I didn't stop to hear more. I ran through the next carriage. The train picked up speed, the clackety clack noise rhythmic. I sprinted on till I reached the guard's van. Still empty. I unclipped the sash window. My stomach heaved as I skipped one leg up onto the windowsill, then the other. I paused for a millisecond, then pushed myself out and dropped onto the moving track below.

I stumbled as I hit the ground but didn't fall. My knees hesitated, trying to decide whether to collapse or hold firm. The train rushed on past me. It took me a couple of seconds to assess myself as capable of movement and then I ran, in the opposite direction to the train, down the centre of the right-hand track, back towards the station. Three maybe four hundred yards. It took me eighty-seven seconds but it felt like twenty minutes, and I prayed there were no goods trains on their way. My lungs screamed as I sprinted straight for Platform One. The station was deserted, no sign of Brownie or Jo as I hauled myself up the wall, onto the stone platform.

I found them at the front of the station, on the steps. I threw myself into the back of both of them, feeling like my lungs were bleeding. Jo turned and grabbed hold of me. I almost collapsed in her arms.

'OK?' I asked, checking her face, her arms for bruises, any signs of maltreatment.

She pushed me away and pulled a face. 'You took your bleeding time.'

'Soz. Not easy, this Wonder Woman stuff.'

Jo punched me on the arm. 'You didn't give them the cash, did you?'

I grinned. 'You're back.'

'Thanks to you.' She punched me again.

'Got to make a phone call,' I managed, my breath still on the railway track. 'I'll have to find a payphone.'

'Where's my phone?' asked Jo. 'You've got my phone.'

'Oh. About that.'

'You lost my phone? How did you lose my phone?'

I stared at her. 'Well, fucking shoot me. It's been a difficult night.'

'That's two phones in two days.'

'Dock it from my wages. If we make it out of this alive.'

I found a public phone, to the right of the ticket office. I dialled 999 and in as low a voice as possible told the operator I thought there were terrorists on the 4.01 Leeds to Manchester airport train. Due to arrive in Huddersfield in twelve minutes. I said I'd heard them mention bombs and one of them was Asian. I know. Playing to racist stereotypes, but if that didn't bring the rapid response unit out, nothing would.

I hung up the call and picked a card for a cab firm from the hundreds pinned to the wall. Once I'd ordered a taxi I re-joined Brownie and Jo on the steps.

'Can't believe you gave them the cash,' said Jo. 'Low-life, dirty—'

'Relax,' I said as I steered them into the car park. 'I didn't give them the cash.'

'He said you did.' Jo gestured to Brownie.

'I gave them a bagful of envelopes stuffed with compliment slips. The money's here.' I lifted my jumper to reveal the money belt.

'No shit,' said Brownie.

'How did you get here?' I asked Jo.

Jo pointed at the only red Escort in the station car park.

'Now they're going to kill me,' Brownie muttered.

I linked arms with Brownie. 'Time to move.'

'Where're we going?' asked Jo.

I grabbed hold of Jo with my other arm and steered them down the steps as a taxi turned the corner and pulled up in front of us. We needed to hide, we needed breathing space. Brownie needed taking care of. The answer was obvious.

'To the safest house I know.'

Chapter Twenty-Six

We clambered into the taxi, Brownie in the front seat next to the driver, me and Jo in the back. The driver couldn't believe his luck when I gave him our destination, at least not after he'd asked for payment up front and I'd handed over a couple of twenties. I didn't blame his suspicion. It had to be said, we weren't looking great. Brownie's whole body twitched, and Jo's hair had frizzed to the point she looked like she'd had electric shock therapy. We stayed silent, lost in our own thoughts, as we hurtled along the M62.

I got the taxi driver to drop us at the first service station we came to. 'Come on, we all need coffee.'

'Starbucks is the safest place you know?' asked Jo, as we climbed out the taxi.

'We're not there yet,' I said. 'Want to make sure there's no one following us.'

I sent Jo and Brownie to get the drinks while I found another payphone and ordered us a second cab. They told me it would be twenty minutes. I checked the time and grimaced. She's always been an early riser, but, even so, we were going to be pushing it. I replaced the receiver and went to find Brownie and Jo.

Despite the fact it was still the middle of the night, we weren't the only ones in Starbucks. Jo had got us a table in the corner, and Brownie looked like he'd fallen asleep. He was curled in a ball on the settee.

'Where'd you find him?' asked Jo.

'He was locked in the toilet at Duck and Bernie's.'

'Why's he wearing girls' trousers?'

'It's a long story.' I nodded to the truck driver sitting a couple of tables away. He didn't notice me, his eyes fixed as they were on Jo. 'Wait till we get there.'

'Are we going where I think we're going?'

Aunt Edie lives in a maze of identical terraced houses in Accrington. She's lived in this house as long as I can remember, and I still find it hard to tell the streets apart. No one would find us here, but I got the taxi to drop us three streets down, just to be certain. As we passed the corner shop, a van driver threw a bundle of *The Sun* newspapers onto the pavement where the newsagent was waiting in his slippers.

I weaved Jo and Brownie past umpteen doorsteps and front room windows, the curtains all closed, and down one of the narrow alleyways that criss-cross the streets, until we got to the right road. Aunt Edie answered the door wearing a floral dress that was pulled to bursting point across her bust.

'What the Dickens?' she said.

I raised my hands, like she might shoot me. 'You're up.'

'I'm always up. What with my knees.'

'I lost my phone. Can—?'

'Don't think you know how to use a phone. What the devil? You look like something the cat dragged in. Is this your fella?' She eyed Brownie hopefully, despite the blueish tinge around his lips and the fact he was wearing girls' trousers and flip-flops. Honestly, Aunt Edie'll try and marry you off to anyone.

'This is Brownie. He needs …' I tailed off. Where to start?

'Well,' said Aunt Edie, cuffing the back of my head, 'what you standing there for? Kettle's on. You look like you could do with something warm and wet inside you. Well I never. The lot of you.'

She took a quick look up and down the street before bustling us into the front room. The aroma of freshly baked parkin wafted down the hallways. I've never once been to this house when that smell hasn't been there, warm and earthy. My eyes ached at the memories.

'Sit tight. Let me go and tell Flora I'll ring her back,' Aunt Edie said as she disappeared out of the door.

'It's not five o'clock yet,' said Jo as she collapsed into the armchair by the fire.

I felt my shoulders sag. Crossing the threshold to Aunt Edie's is like stepping back in time to a world that is safe and simple. The furniture has been polished daily for the last forty odd years. And not with spray polish. I can still remember the feel of the soft wax against the ripped-up squares of cloth she uses for dusters.

'God, what a night.' I tried to roll my shoulders to get rid of the cricks.

Brownie crossed to the window and pulled the curtains closed.

'We were set up,' said Jo.

'I came looking for you—'

Jo shook her head. 'The door opened.' She raised two fingers, gave us the peace sign. 'Two guys. One grabbed me, the other put a bag over my head. They walked me straight through the house and out the back door. I swear to God they were waiting for me. Martha set us up.'

'Jo—'

'Shut up,' said Brownie, wheeling round from the curtains to face Jo.

'They rang her,' she said. 'When we were in the car. I heard them say "We've got her".'

'How do you know it was Martha?' I asked.

'Who else could it've been?' Jo kept her gaze on me. 'She's the one that sent us round there. She gave us the bloody address.'

'She didn't,' said Brownie.

Jo stood up. She was about two feet shorter than Brownie but there's something about the way that Jo stands that always seems to give her the height advantage. She put her hands on her hips, stared right at Brownie, unflinching. 'She fucking did.'

'She wanted you to find me.'

Jo's brow furrowed, like she didn't quite understand why anyone would want to find Brownie. In his current attire, it had to be said, he wasn't much of a catch. 'So why'd she tell them I was coming?'

'She didn't,' said Brownie, again. We waited for him to expand, to give us the proof that underpinned his assertions. He continued with less confidence. 'She's not like that. She's loyal.'

I frowned at Brownie. I knew it wasn't the time to challenge him, but he'd changed his tune. I put a hand on Jo's arm. 'Jo,' I began.

She shook me off. 'I'm not buying it,' she said. 'Martha gives us the address, we go round and they're waiting for me. There's a car out back, engine running. I'm telling you, they knew I was coming.' She picked at a fingernail, and I noticed that only a few flecks of red nail varnish remained. 'Can't wait to hear her side of the story, the next instalment of total bullshit.'

'Jo.' I watched Brownie collapse into an armchair.

'She's a lying, conniving—'

'Jo.' I raised my voice to gain her attention. When I got it, I didn't know what to say, so I blurted the words. 'Martha's dead.'

'Two-faced ... What?'

'She's dead.' My stomach swirled as I said the words aloud for the second time. I could still taste the wet damp of the bathroom.

'Dead?'

'Murdered, I'm pretty certain. Saw it with my own eyes.' I glanced across at Brownie. 'We both did.'

Jo sank into Aunt Edie's sofa. Well, as much as you can sink into something that feels like it's made out of breeze blocks. 'Jesus Christ.'

'Now then, pottymouth, I'll have less of that language,' said Aunt Edie as she bustled back into the room, having covered up with her trademark pink nylon housecoat. 'You know what day it is.'

Jo frowned.

I mouthed, 'Sunday' at her before turning to Aunt Edie. 'Sorry, Aunt Edie,' I said.

She crossed the rooms and opened the curtains. 'Now, look at the state of the lot of you. Tea's brewing and then it's breakfast. No arguments.'

Jo frowned again. For the first time since I'd seen her at the train station I realized how knackered she looked. Bewildered. I wanted to hug her, but I have to wait for Jo to initiate that kind of thing.

Aunt Edie settled herself in the armchair by the fire. 'So,' she said, 'what've you got fresh?'

We stared at each other and silence mushroomed. 'Well,' I said, 'I told you we were starting our own business.'

'Finding people.' Aunt Edie tutted. 'In my experience, people that disappear should be left to disappear. No sense raking over old coals.'

'What if someone's disappeared because someone's made them disappear?' asked Jo. 'What if they want to come home but they're too scared?'

'We could all use the chance to start over.' Aunt Edie glanced at Brownie.

'Really?' I asked. 'But—'

'You disappeared,' she said to me. 'You left to go and study at university. Start again. Not everyone has that opportunity. Some people have to slink off.'

I was saved from replying by a knock on the front door. My heart thudded at the sudden noise. 'Who's that?'

'It'll be Gordon,' said Aunt Edie.

'At five in the morning?'

'Welcome to Insomniacs Anonymous. I'll tell him he'll have to come back.'

She hauled herself up from the armchair.

'Who's Gordon?' asked Jo.

'Never heard of him,' I said. I crossed to the window and peered out, but the angle was too tight, and I couldn't see anyone.

'It's my fault,' said Brownie, and I turned back round to see him pacing the lounge. His lanky frame nearly reached the ceiling. It's not often I get this close to men. I grew up in a woman-only household. The only man I had any contact with was Bert the Perv, my mum's next-door neighbour, and I spent much of my adolescence making sure I was never alone in a room with him. His heart was in the right place, but his brain wasn't.

Men are big, take up too much air space. I flinched at Brownie's proximity, glanced at the door.

He spoke to Jo. 'She was straight, so let's get that sorted. I'm the fuck-up.'

'Listen, Brownie,' I said, guiding him to the armchair Aunt Edie had just vacated. 'The person whose fault this is – is the person who killed her. You have to be tough.' I handed him my packet of tobacco. 'Make me a fag.'

'I can't believe she's dead,' said Jo.

'Trust me. She is,' I said. I saw the dark tendrils floating around her face, the white bloated face, the unseeing eyes. I blinked.

'You actually saw her?'

'Yeah. We both did. That's why …' I tilted my head in Brownie's direction. His attention was on the cigarette papers in his hand.

Jo seemed to get my point. She lowered her voice as I took a seat on the settee next to her. 'How?'

'We went to her flat. He's got a key. She was in the bath.'

'Dead?'

'Stone cold.'

'How d'you know she was murdered?'

'People don't just die in the bath.'

'Er, Whitney Houston? Bobby Kristina Brown?'

'The flat was clean.'

'Your Bollywood woman,' Jo continued. 'What's her name? Something Kapoor?'

'Martha got into the bath of her own free will. She'd had half a glass of wine. Left her clothes neatly folded in the bedroom. There was a dressing gown hanging on the back of the door. It was damp, all round the neck.'

'So?'

'I figure she got out of the bath to answer the door, and whoever it was killed her, then dumped her body back in the bath.'

'And hung up her dressing gown?'

'She left us, went home, got a bath. Getting ready to go out. It was six when we left her.' I glanced across at Brownie and whispered to Jo. 'We could have been the last people to see her alive.'

'When did you, you know, find her?'

Brownie passed me a roll-up. It was damp with his sweat.

'We got to hers about eleven,' I said. 'It couldn't have been her that Bernie rang.'

'She might have been out, come back, got a bath before bed.'

'The water was freezing. She'd been in there ages.'

'Would you get out of the bath to answer the door?' asked Jo.

We don't get many visitors, me and Jo, so that was a difficult question to answer. We often don't get off the couch to answer the phone, and that's in the same room. 'Maybe she thought it was Brownie,' I said.

Brownie lit his fag. I handed him the ashtray from beside the gas fire. It gleamed in the light of the fire.

'I thought he had a key,' said Jo.

'You don't die taking a bath,' I said, keeping my eye on Brownie. His knuckles looked white as he pulled on his thin roll-up.

'Maybe she topped herself,' said Jo. 'She was broken-hearted.'

Brownie jumped up and moved across the room to Jo. She made to get up out of the seat, but he shoved her, tipping her backwards into the settee. He loomed over her. 'Shut up. Shut the fuck up.'

'No drugs, no blades, no electrical appliances,' I said, standing up to grab Brownie by the arm and pulling him away from Jo, back to the armchair. 'No note.'

Jo glowered at Brownie but did nothing. 'You didn't call the police?'

'I was focused on getting you back.' My voice rose in my defence as Brownie allowed himself to be seated. 'And we need to work out what we're going to do with this,' I said, pulling the fat money belt of cash from around my waist. I dropped it down onto the coffee table. 'How we going to explain that to the cops?'

Brownie made a noise that sounded like puppies being run over. Jo and me both stared at him.

'She gave you the cash?'

I nodded. 'How do you think she got it?' I asked.

'She's a student, for fuck's sake,' said Brownie. 'How'm I supposed to believe she's got that kind of cash lying around?'

He'd stood up again and I felt dwarfed. 'Brownie. That's my point. Where did she get it from?'

'How the fuck would I know?'

Aunt Edie barged back in with the tea tray. I noticed she'd applied lipstick since we'd arrived. 'I didn't know if you wanted milk, so I brought the jug.'

'That's great, Aunt Edie. You're a superstar.'

'You kids.' She grinned. 'And that's a bad habit, young man.' She nodded at Brownie's roll-up. 'No wonder there's no meat on any of you.' She hesitated and glanced at Jo.

'Who's Gordon?' I asked.

'Does my hair. And records things for me.' She held up a plastic wallet with a DVD inside.

'Does your hair on a Sunday?'

'No. On a Sunday we do the crossword together.'

'Ah.'

My thoughts must have been obvious from my tone, because Aunt Edie rapped me on the knuckles with the disc. 'Don't get any funny ideas. He's not that way inclined. Camp as Christmas. Not much good at the cryptic, either.' She sniffed.

'Are you sure about breakfast?' Jo asked. 'We don't want to put you to any trouble.'

I marvelled again at Jo's ability to read a person. Aunt Edie grinned. 'Let me get the frying pan on.'

When Aunt Edie left the room, I turned back to Brownie. 'Brownie, it's really important. If we knew where she got the money, we might find out who killed her.'

'You think it's about the money?' asked Jo.

'She gets twenty-four grand, stashes it in Brownie's room.'

Brownie hit the arm of his chair so hard the ashtray fell off and clattered to the floor. 'She bleeding didn't.'

'You'd swapped rooms with Jack. Martha didn't know that.'

He stared at me, but right through me, like I was a ghost.

I carried on. 'The money disappears. She's desperate to get it back. She thinks Jack's taken it. She hires us to find him.' I turned to Brownie. 'She must have said something about where she got it.'

Brownie picked up the ashtray from the floor and flicked his ash into it. He examined the roll-up in his hand and then stubbed it out. 'We talked about all kinds of shit, never thought she was serious.'

'Tell us everything you can remember,' said Jo. 'Maybe we'll see something you can't.'

He raised his eyebrows at me. I tried to help him.

'You said you told her you were in debt.'

'Yeah.'

'The night you got her to smoke heroin,' I prompted.

208

'You got Martha into smack?' The disgust in Jo's voice was obvious.

I glared at her. 'Go on, Brownie. Tell us what happened that night. Anything you can remember.'

'I did, I kind of told her everything, about the dealing, about how I owe money.'

'What did she say?' I asked.

'Lots. Ranting about how I should have told her from the beginning. Saying it was stupid to owe people like that money. Worried they'd hurt me.'

Jo tucked her legs up under her. 'Women.'

'She said I needed to pay them off. I said, no shit, Sherlock.'

'Did she have any ideas?'

'I remember asking her if she had any rich relatives about to pop their clogs.' He paused, glancing up at me. His eyes where rheumy like an old man, and I was struck by how worn out he looked. 'She didn't.'

'Shame,' said Jo. She turned to the tray that Aunt Edie had left on the small table by the side of the settee and poured the tea.

'Shit,' Brownie said. From the tone of his voice I knew he'd just remembered something. Something important.

'What?'

He rubbed his face and a look crossed it that made me think he was in pain.

'I told her Jack's dad was wadded.'

Jo passed the first cup to Brownie. Aunt Edie had got out the Sunday best. Proper teacups and saucers. Brownie's rattled as he held it. I took the saucer from him and he cradled the cup in his hands like it was a pot of frankincense, or myrrh or whatever it was the three kings carried. I wondered why it wasn't burning the skin off his palms.

'So?' I said.

'He is wadded,' Brownie said.

'I know. We met him.'

209

He put his cup on the table, stood up, ran a hand through his hair. He bent slightly at the middle, hunched over. 'Fucking hell, I think I told her.'

'Told her what?'

He lunged towards to the door.

'Brownie.'

'I need to … Shit.'

I followed him into the hallway. He scrambled up the stairs but, from the smell, I guessed it was too late.

I called to Jo. 'Go stand outside the bathroom window, case he tries to do a runner again.'

She didn't look best pleased, but she did it. Aunt Edie appeared in the hallway, wearing her pinny.

'Everything OK?'

'Have you got any spare trousers? Men's trousers?'

She pulled a face.

'Sorry, Aunt Edie.' I pointed up the stairs. 'He's not been very well.'

'I still have some of our Arthur's clothes. I'll have a look. The poor sausage.'

I wasn't sure whether she was referring to Brownie, Arthur or the breakfast she was frying up, but she returned with a pair of men's suit trousers, a shirt and a pair of Y-fronts that weren't new, but they were clean. I took them from her, climbed the stairs and knocked on the bathroom door.

'Brownie, there's some pants here.'

The door opened a fraction, and I held out the articles of clothing. He snatched them from me, and the door closed again.

When he came out, he looked beaten. The clothes hung from his skinny frame and made his piercings seem totally out of place. The trousers were soft brown fabric and they'd gathered round the waist, held up by a belt. The shirt was old and ironed to the point I could see Brownie's nipples through the thin fabric. I helped him back down the stairs and onto the sofa like he was

210

an old man. Jo must have heard us because she came back into the front room.

'Come on, Brownie,' she said, and her voice was softer. 'You need to get it off your chest.'

He scratched at the dog bite on his ankle, reopening the wound. A trickle of blood ran down his foot. 'Can't remember how we got to it now. I think she was trying to think up ways we could pay off the debt, and she was coming up with all kinds of scams and then one of us, can't remember who, said if we knew something about someone, something they didn't want known, then that might be a thing. And that's when I told her about Jack.'

'What about Jack?'

'You know. About his family and stuff.'

'Tell us everything, Brownie. We need to know everything.'

'I told her about Jack's dad.'

I thought back to Mr Wilkins, the look in his eyes when I'd mentioned his son. 'What about him?'

Brownie wiped his eyes on the back of my jacket sleeve. 'He only ever mentioned it once.'

'Who did?'

He paused.

'Come on, Brownie. Better out than in.'

'We were both shit-faced.'

'And?'

'Jack told me his dad killed his mum.'

A feeling ran through my body, like coming up, alarming the hair follicles on my scalp right down through my spine.

'I laughed,' said Brownie. 'Thought he was taking the piss, but he wasn't, he was deadly serious. And I knew, straight up, there was something in it.'

'She died in a car crash,' I said. I glanced at Jo. 'That's what Carly said.'

Brownie shrugged. 'Maybe he fixed the brakes.'

I watched Jo's reaction, and I knew we were both thinking the

211

same thing. Jack's dad worked with cars. If anyone knew how to fix the brakes, he did.

Jo spoke to Brownie. 'And you told Martha this?'

'Yeah. Jack never said, but it's obvious. Must be wadded. He got sent to boarding school when he was seven. We had that in common.'

'You didn't go to boarding school,' I said, unable to keep the disbelief from my voice.

'Boarding school. Care.' He shrugged. 'Same difference.'

'So, Martha blackmailed Jack's dad for the cash?' That wasn't beyond the bounds of plausibility. I chewed it over. It would explain why Mr Wilkins had flipped out when he heard I was looking for Jack.

'Maybe. I told Jack, once, to ask his dad for a lend. Wouldn't have any of it. I was like, "Jack, they're going to break our legs", but he wouldn't listen. Stubborn sod.'

'But why? Why would he kill her? Martha, I mean. If he'd already paid up?'

Jo turned to me and pulled a face. 'To punish her. Men like that need to show who's boss.'

'Jack idolizes his mum. He's got this picture of her, carries it everywhere. She's cracking looking.' Brownie grinned, and, for a brief, fleeting second, I saw what Martha saw in him.

'Carly said she died when he was 5,' Jo said.

'It's possible,' I said, thinking aloud. 'Martha blackmails Jack's dad, gets the cash, but before she can give it to you or to Jack, maybe Jack's dad comes looking for him. Realizes he's told the family secret.' I stared at Jo as a prickle ran down my spine. 'That must have been his mate following us, the guy with the gun. Must be his bodyguard or something.'

Jo finished the thought I was trying not to have. 'You think Nick Wilkins has killed his own son?'

Chapter Twenty-Seven

Brownie shot up off the settee. He made for the door. I grabbed his arm and pulled him back. His eyes pleaded with me. 'I can't handle this,' he said.

'You don't have to, Brownie. Jo and me, we'll sort it. I promise.'

He stared at a spot on the green paisley carpet, his skinny shoulders hunched around his ears. 'I need Jack,' he said, his voice barely a whisper.

When you don't have a family, friends matter. I know this. I met Jo the first week I moved to Leeds – in Freshers' Week. I was wandering around the stalls, feeling like a fish out of water. She cadged a fag off me, and we realized we were on the same course. Four days after that, I was taken out of a lecture, on the invitation of the welfare state, to be told my mum was dead. I don't remember much about that day, I mean after. But I know Jo was by my side every minute of it, and I know I wouldn't have got through without her. I went to touch Brownie's arm but didn't quite connect.

'I know you do.'

'Who wants black pudding?' said Aunt Edie, barrelling through the door. Brownie turned away from her, buried his head in his hands.

Aunt Edie looked at me.

'Ah. Er, Brownie's vegan,' I said. 'That means—'

'I know what it means. I'm not completely cabbage looking. Right. Bear with me. In fact, you, young man, come and give us a hand. I need someone tall to reach down my big plates.'

Aunt Edie put up the drop-down leaf on the table in the front room window. The wood on the side panel was a completely different colour to that on the top, a dark rich mahogany compared to bleached yellow. After a rummage through her cupboards, which are stocked in preparation for the next world war, she'd rustled up some kind of vegan hash, made with sweet potato and kidney beans, as well as a full English. She fussed around us while we ate, and I wasn't surprised to see three empty plates at the end of the meal. Aunt Edie's bosom swelled but she tried not to show it.

When we'd all finished, she poured us a cup of tea from the fresh pot and took a seat at the table. 'So, what trouble are you in this time? And remember, I'm too old for fairy tales.'

I glanced across at Jo. She licked her fingers first, then nodded at me.

'We're on our first case,' I said. 'And we've run into a bit of difficulty.'

'I know your problem, young man.' Aunt Edie put a hand on Brownie's arm to take the fierceness from her tone. 'See it round here all the time.'

Brownie blinked and tried to move his arm, but Aunt Edie's grip must have been stronger than I thought.

'Life is hard,' she said. 'I know that. But you can't numb your way out of it. You have to face it down.'

Brownie looked like he might cry. Aunt Edie patted his arm, and he grabbed her hand in his. Held on to it like a child would. Her voice was softer than I'd ever heard it. 'Where's your mother, pet?'

'She's not well,' Brownie managed. I felt a lump at the back of my throat and pushed my chair back.

214

'You'll feel better after a nap,' Aunt Edie said. 'You look shattered, the lot of you.'

'That would be ace, Aunt Edie. Don't think he's slept the last two nights.'

Brownie's eyelids were thick.

'There's a bed made up in the spare room,' said Aunt Edie, holding his hand to pull him out of the chair. 'Come with me, pet. Let's get you settled.'

She was back ten minutes later, telling us he was fast asleep. 'I read the financial section to him. If that doesn't put you to sleep, nothing will.'

'We need to keep an eye on him,' I said, unsure of how much to say.

'Don't worry, the windows are too small to climb out of and I've put a chair under the door handle. He's not going anywhere.'

'Right.'

Aunt Edie busied herself collecting the empty plates. 'So, that's one of you out of harm's way for the while. Now, let's hear about you. How're you keeping?'

'I'm doing OK.'

'Don't kid a kidder, kid. You've lost half a stone since I saw you last, and it's not like you had it to spare.'

'I've taken up running. I think that keeps me—'

'If you don't take care of yourself, no one else will.'

'I am taking care.'

'She's quit drinking, Edie,' said Jo. 'And I keep my eye on her. Give me those.' Jo took the plates and went through to the kitchen. I heard the splash as she put them in the sink.

'And what about the rest?' Aunt Edie said to me, her voice lowered.

'There wasn't really a rest,' I said, feeling the burn in my cheeks spread down to my chest.

'You forget, I sat by your bed in that hospital, four nights, wondering if each breath was going to be your last. As God is

215

my witness. She can vouch for me.' She nodded at Jo as she came back into the room.

I helped Aunt Edie pull the leg of the table out so that the drop leaf fell back into place.

'That wasn't anything. Just ... anyway, I don't do that kind of thing anymore.'

Edie picked up her cup of tea, saucer and all, and lowered herself into the armchair. 'No one's saying it's easy. You've had it as worse as anyone. Losing your mum at such a young age and then all that business—'

'I know, Aunt Edie. And honest, I'm dealing with it. It helps if we don't talk about it.'

'Just like my mother, God keep her soul. That was her motto. "Least said, soonest mended".'

I took a seat on the settee. 'See.' I liked the sound of Aunt Edie's mother. Stoical.

Aunt Edie rapped my knuckles with the teaspoon she was holding. 'And look what happened to her. She didn't see 50. Cancer. Eating away her insides. You want to end up like that? Better out than in. You have to talk to people.'

'I do.'

'You don't,' said Jo. 'You beat the shit out of a punchbag, that's what you do.'

I glared at Jo. 'Better than drinking.'

'I know,' said Jo. 'But is it as good as talking about it?'

'You're ganging up on me now?'

'Don't be daft. We're on your side.' Aunt Edie hauled herself up from the armchair and stepped into the hall. 'We're your family,' she called through.

'Traitor,' I said to Jo.

'And pick up the phone once in a blue moon, would you?' said Edie, coming back into the room with a carpet sweeper. 'Then I know not to worry.'

'And you'll stop with the lecture?'

216

'Deal,' said Edie. 'Now get the telly on while I see to those crumbs. Gordon's brought last week's *Songs of Praise.*'

I don't think either Jo or I made it to the end of the first hymn. We both crashed on the sofa, didn't wake up till lunchtime. When I staggered into the kitchen to get a glass of water I found that Aunt Edie had spent the morning making soups, hundreds of Tupperware boxes covered every inch of worktop.

'You can put them in your freezer.'

I didn't have the heart to tell her we didn't have a freezer. Aunt Edie heated us both up a bowl of French onion, while Jo flinched at the ox's tailbone poking out of a pan on the stove.

'Now, what's the plan?' asked Aunt Edie.

'We have to find Jack,' I said. Our client might be dead, but Jack was still our missing person. I felt strangely proprietorial considering I'd never met the guy. 'We have to see it through.'

'Tenner says he's dead,' said Jo.

Aunt Edie flicked her with the tea towel. 'Don't say that. That lad up there' – she pointed towards the ceiling – 'needs him.'

'How do you know that?' I asked. I'm always amazed at the way she can pick up on stuff. She can spend five minutes with a complete stranger and come away knowing their entire life story.

'He's never going to get round this on his own. You have to find Jack, for Brownie's sake.'

217

Chapter Twenty-Eight

We left Brownie at Aunt Edie's. He needed someone to keep an eye on him. He needed sleep and feeding up. Music to Aunt Edie's ears. She even kept the soup.

We caught a taxi back to Leeds, which was extravagant, but I did have twenty-four grand burning a hole in the belt round my belly, and Jo pointed out we could claim the whole fare as expenses. It dropped us in town so that Jo could buy two new phones for us. I pretended to be pleased with mine, although I couldn't help noticing I'd been downgraded a model. Once the teenager in the shop had set them up for us, we looped back to the Dark Arches to collect the van. Jo drove us up through the city.

'Home?'

'No, the office,' I said. 'I want to put the cash back in the safe.'

I was just putting my key in the padlock on the front door when a low voice behind me said: 'We need to talk.'

Even though it was broad daylight, my first instinct was to shout at Jo to run. I turned, saw a tall man with long hair standing in front of me. I lifted myself up onto the balls of my feet, kept my body light, my fists coiled. I kept my voice level, spoke slow.

'Leave us alone.'

He reached inside his jacket. One second split into twenty and it took me five of those units to realize there was no decision to be made. I kicked out, first with my knee then with my boot, connected with his gullet. A quick one-two, followed it up with a decent right cross.

He doubled over.

'Stop,' he yelled. I saw his hand withdraw. It wasn't holding a gun, but a wallet. He flicked it open. 'Police.'

Jo turned, and we stared at each other. I wasn't sure whether I felt relieved or more frightened. He clutched his stomach and tried to straighten up.

'You're going to need to come with me,' he said.

I haven't had the best relationship with the police, but I'm trying to put my prejudices to one side. If I'm fighting for truth and justice, I have to stop seeing the police as the enemy. Not easy when you've a soft drugs habit to support.

'Police? What the hell do you want?'

He glanced around. 'Not here.'

'Don't look like a copper,' said Jo. He had brown hair streaked with grey tied back in a loose ponytail. He wore a silver sleeper in his right ear and his jeans were ripped at the knees.

'Undercover,' he said. 'Col.' He exhaled and rubbed his belly.

'Give me that,' said Jo. She took the ID wallet off him, examined it closely. She nodded at me before handing it back to him.

I waited for him to get his cuffs out. Instead, he surprised me by saying: 'Could I buy you both a drink?'

'We'd rather just hear what you've got to say,' I said. 'We're tired, need to get home. Feed the cat.'

Jo frowned. We don't have a cat, but I was knackered and ready for this day to end. 'What's it about?' she asked.

'I don't want to discuss it out here.' As he said the words a couple of students, one in a dressing gown, sauntered down the middle of the road. 'Is there somewhere we could go?'

'There's the Royal Park,' said Jo. She shrugged her shoulders at me. 'A quick one,' she said to Col.

They started off down the hill together. She was right, he didn't look the least bit like a policeman. I sighed and followed on behind, running over the events of the last twenty-four hours. What did he want to talk to us about? Did he know I'd been in Martha's flat? Would forensics be back that quick? Had they traced the phone call I'd made at Dewsbury station? A thousand paranoias ran through my mind as Jo led the way to our local – the Royal Park pub. Another student favourite, a huge red-brick building squashed between the terraced houses. We got inside, and Jo asked Col for a half a pint. I shook my head.

Jo and I went through the pub and sat outside under the wooden awning at the back, while Col went to the bar. Patio heaters glowed above our heads, but it didn't make much difference to the actual temperature. Jo lit two cigarettes and passed one to me.

'What's he want with us?' I asked.

'Only one way to find out,' she said.

He joined us a moment later. Up close I noticed the deep lines round his eyes. He wore a silver ring on the third finger of his left hand and had a small tattoo of a swallow on the back of his right, between the base of his thumb and forefinger.

As soon as he set the drinks down on the table he rubbed his ribs again and said: 'That's a hell of a punch. Where did you learn to fight like that?'

I felt a flush of pride, despite the circumstances. 'Thailand. Yuki taught me.' As soon as I'd said the words my cheeks warmed. For starters he'd have no idea who Yuki was and, secondly, Thailand was something I didn't want to talk about. Thailand gave us the idea for No Stone Unturned, but that's another story. One I'm not planning on telling, especially not to undercover police officers.

I think Jo sensed my discomfort because she wiped the beer

220

froth from her lips with the back of her sleeve and said: 'What do you want?'

Col turned his gaze to her. 'What do you know about Megan Parsons?'

Of all the questions I was prepped for him asking, that wasn't one of them. 'Who?' I asked as Jo had her glass to her lips.

'You may know her as Martha.'

Jo swallowed, put down her glass. 'Mrs Wilkins?'

'Eh?' he said.

'Martha?' I said, pressing on Jo's foot under the table. Technically our client was dead, but my feelings of loyalty were increasing by the minute. Having pocketed her fee, we owed her something, and until this man proved he was a force for good I was proceeding on the basis he was a force for bad. I leaned across the table towards him. 'What do you know about her?'

'You know she's dead?' He watched my face for a reaction. I fought to control any flicker of emotion.

'No,' said Jo, her voice too loud. The students at the next table glanced across at us.

Col lowered his voice. 'So you know … knew her?'

I shook my head as Jo asked: 'What happened?'

'She was murdered,' said Col. He squeezed the flesh at the top of his nose between his thumb and forefinger. 'Last night.'

'Murdered?' said Jo. 'God, that's dreadful. In Leeds?'

I worried Jo was in danger of overdoing it. I was so tired it was hard to gauge normal human interaction. 'Murdered how?' I asked.

Jo blew her nose.

I suspected our undercover friend wasn't buying any of it. 'Look,' he said. 'We need to level with each other.'

'What's your name again?' I asked.

To give him his due, he did kind of acknowledge my pointed question. He held up his hands. 'Col.'

'Col what?'

221

He didn't answer, just looked at me like I was vaguely stupid. I crossed my arms and stared back, making sure not to blink. 'What makes you think we know this woman?' I asked.

'She told me she'd been to see you.'

'She told you "she'd been to see us",' I repeated, because I didn't really know what else to say. 'I've never heard of Megan Parsons. Who is she?'

'I think you're in danger,' he said.

'No need to worry about us,' Jo said, as I thought back to the hooded figure who'd chased me and Brownie through the Dark Arches. The hairs on the back of my neck pricked up as fear trickled through me. 'We can take care of ourselves.'

'What happened to your offices?'

'Kids.'

'Bollocks.' He ran his fingers through his hair, as I tried to place his accent. It wasn't Leeds, or Lancashire. Somewhere more to the south, Nottingham maybe.

'This is LS6,' Jo said. 'Well known for being the most burgled area in the country. Police don't seem to want to do anything.'

'I'm trying to help.'

'Thought you wanted us to help you,' Jo fired back.

'You're in way over your heads. I need to know what Megan told you.'

'We don't know anyone called Megan,' Jo said.

'Martha. Tell me what Martha told you.'

'No chance.' Jo folded her arms across her chest, and I knew that posture well enough to know he wasn't going to get anything further from her.

I tried to take a more conciliatory tone. I knew we didn't want to get on the wrong side of the police, or we'd be fending off speeding tickets for the rest of our lives. 'Why don't you go first?' I said. 'Tell us what you know about her.'

He took a mouthful of his pint, wiped his lips on the back of his sleeve. He glanced from me to Jo and back again. He had

222

grey-green eyes, piercing. We held each other's gaze a moment longer than necessary, and I knew what he was going to say before he said it.

He opened his mouth, paused and then said: 'She was one of ours.'

Brownie's words had been haunting me most of the day. It was the quality of her disguise as Mrs Wilkins that I hadn't been able to square. She'd managed to make herself look ten years older. The blonde hair must have been a wig, but it was totally convincing. It had to be professional.

Jo wasn't as easily convinced. 'A copper?' she said, in a too-loud voice. Col gestured at her to keep her voice down. 'No way.'

Jo stared at me like *why aren't you surprised* and I found myself shrugging.

'Undercover,' said Col.

'You were working together?' I asked.

'She was trying to infiltrate a known drug-dealing gang.'

'If they were known, why would they need infiltrating?' asked Jo.

'Difference between knowing and proving.'

'She was an undercover copper?' said Jo. She sat back in her seat. 'Well, fuck me.'

'Who killed her?' I asked.

'When I find that out …' He let the rest of his sentence trail off.

'How?' asked Jo. 'How did they kill her?'

'I had her back,' said Col, if that was his name. I suspected not. He looked so unlike a copper I suspected he didn't know his own name by then. His voice wavered, became husky. He took another mouthful of his pint, and I caught a glimpse of what a dangerous life he led. 'She had mine.'

'That's tough,' I said. I knew what that felt like: when you're supposed to be watching out for someone, and something terrible happens. Something you should have seen coming, but you didn't.

223

I sat still, forcing myself not to reach across the table for Jo's lager, the voice in my head telling me the feeling would pass, to ride it out, let it through. The pain spread from my heart to my lungs, pushing through my body like ice.

'I wasn't watching close enough.'

I wasn't either.

He stared over my shoulder, over to the door to the pub. He stared so hard I turned around in my seat to see what was happening. I saw one of my old lecturers huddling by the back door, smoking a fag with a bunch of what looked like students. We caught each other's eyes, and he smiled at me. I hadn't seen him since I'd left my course. I took it as a sign and emptied my mind of the past. The things I cannot change.

Col focused his gaze on me. 'I didn't expect this,' he said.

'How come you're both undercover?' Jo asked.

'I can't say. I shouldn't be here.'

'So Martha's real name is Megan?' I asked. 'And she was investigating a drugs ring?' There was something about the whole conversation that made my skin itch. 'What kind of drugs?'

'The worst kind.'

'Heroin?' said Jo.

'That too, but that's not what they're worried about. The latest thing is Flakka. It's—'

'I know,' said Jo, holding her hands up. 'Alpha-Pyrrolidinopentiophenone.'

'What?' I frowned at Jo.

'Alpha-PVP for short. An upper, produces feelings of euphoria. Excessive use can lead to paranoia, hallucinations and even flesh eating. Hence, it's nickname, the zombie drug.'

'You know a lot about it,' Col observed.

'I know a lot about the Conservative Party,' said Jo. 'Doesn't mean I ever voted Tory.'

'There was a raid in Leeds a few weeks ago. Flakka was seized. Now everyone's terrified the same epidemic as the States is going to happen here. That's why the guys at the top decided we needed to go in.'

'Go on.'

'Megan had started to make contacts.'

'Meaning?'

'She was establishing herself. That's all I know. But,' he paused, and I knew he was wondering how much to tell us. 'But, the last time I spoke to her, I thought she was holding something back.'

'What do you mean?'

'Listen, it's bloody hard, undercover work.' He glanced around. 'We all know it's not a case of good guys, bad guys. There's all kinds of shades in-between.'

'I'm guessing that's not the official line,' said Jo.

'She told me she was coming to see you two. She said you were local, well connected round here.'

I felt an inappropriate flush of pride. I know Jo felt the same because she grinned at me.

Col didn't notice. 'I was meant to keep an eye on her,' he said. 'I screwed up.'

'Not your fault,' I said. 'You didn't know what she was getting into.'

'I owe her,' he said. He spoke directly to me, and I recognized the look in his eyes. It's the same one I see whenever I catch a glimpse of myself in a mirror. 'I owe her the truth – to find out who did what they did to her.'

This made things tricky. Because I know what that kind of responsibility feels like – to make a mistake that you'll spend the rest of your life trying to correct, at the same time as knowing that nothing you do will ever make it right.

'You want us to help you find her killer?' I asked. My stomach flipped at the thought.

'We'll find her killer, don't worry about that. There's a top team on this, the best. They won't stop until that bastard is caught.' His knuckles tightened.

225

'Oh.' I admit, I was disappointed. Working with the police to track down a murderer, less than three months after we'd opened for business, would have been quite something. Not that I wanted to work with the police. Jo narrowed her eyes at me. I ignored her. 'So what do you want?' I asked Col.

'I want you to make sure there's nothing that's going to come up in this investigation that would show Megan in a bad light.'

I glanced across to Jo. She gave an almost imperceptible shake of her head. 'We don't have to tell you anything,' she said.

'Not true. If I think you're perverting the course of justice I can get a warrant, seize your files.'

'You'll have a job. Our files were trashed.'

I frowned at Jo. We didn't want to make enemies of the police, and I couldn't see how giving him the basics would hurt. 'We're a missing persons' bureau,' I said.

'Who's missing?' Col asked.

Jo sat back in her seat and folded her arms across her chest.

'An ex-student called Jack Wilkins,' I said.

Col nodded with recognition. 'Heard the name. One of the blokes from the squat in Woodhouse? Why would Megan pay private investigators to find a junkie?'

'You see. This is why people don't like helping the police,' said Jo. 'Junkies are people too. Just like policemen. They have families, people who love them.'

'We're on the same side,' said Col.

I could feel Jo glaring at me as I tried to think of the best way to answer Col's question. 'Perhaps she thought he'd taken some money with him.'

'What money?'

'I don't know.'

'How much we talking?'

I glanced at Jo. If looks could kill, I don't think I'd have got the next sentence out. 'Don't know. But let's say a significant amount.'

226

'I'll get another round in,' said Jo. 'Same again?' Col nodded, and Jo headed for the bar.

Once she'd gone he lowered his voice and said: 'I can't work with you if you're committing any kind of crime.'

I smarted at that. 'We're totally legitimate. Members of the Professional Institute of Private Investigators.' I felt in both my back pockets and tugged out a business card.

He read the front of it as he sank the remainder of his pint. 'Which one are you?'

'Lee.'

'Lee. Nice. So, Lee, who does the cash belong to?'

'I honestly don't know.'

'Listen,' said Col. He moved his empty pint glass to one side. 'I'm going to ask you straight out. Have you found out anything in the course of your enquiries that might suggest Megan crossed the line?'

In my mind, I ran through the list of what I knew about Megan. Had she crossed the line? Besides having a sexual relationship with a suspect, blackmail, breaking and entering, possession of hash, smoking heroin and impersonating someone's mother? I tried to think of anything I knew about her that didn't involve her in illegal activity. I tried to find the right words. 'She always struck me as someone who was trying their best.'

'That's not what I asked.' He leaned back in his seat, ran his arms along the edge of the bench seating. His jeans were faded, bleached to the palest blue, and they fitted like they'd been made for him. 'How long have you been in the business?'

Jo came back from the bar with three pints in her hand. She put one in front of Col and put the other two on the table as she sat back down. I sensed things might be about to get colourful.

'Long enough,' she said.

'You don't seem to have found out a right lot.'

'We're not the ones begging for information,' said Jo. She swigged from the first pint.

227

Col gave up talking to Jo. He faced me. 'Did you find Jack?'

'No.'

Col sighed, and I could tell he was having trouble remaining patient. 'OK. Say for example, Megan had had a relationship with someone she shouldn't.' He stared at us both, and I knew he was looking for the slightest hint of recognition. I worked hard to maintain a completely neutral expression. 'She'd get into a whole heap of trouble—'

'Can't get into any more trouble than she already did,' Jo pointed out.

He didn't take his eyes from my face, and I wondered how much he already knew.

'She's got a kid, did you know?'

I flinched, swallowed down hard. 'No.'

He leaned closer to me. 'I want her remembered for who she was. She believed in what she did.'

'How old's the kid?' I asked, not wanting to hear the answer.

Luckily for me, Jo stepped in. 'How far are you willing to go to protect her reputation?'

'My hands are tied. There's going to be a full-scale investigation.'

'And you're worried about what they're going to find,' said Jo, like she was stating a fact.

He nodded.

I raised my eyebrows at Jo. She calls it my "owl eyes" look. She frowned at me. We remained like that for a few moments, unblinking. 'We need to discuss this,' said Jo, standing up. 'Excuse us a moment.'

I followed her inside the pub and straight to the women's toilets. No one else was in there, so I let myself into the nearest cubicle and went for a wee. 'What do you think?' I asked through the cubicle walls.

'He's a fucking copper, that's what I think.'

'Meaning?'

'Can't be trusted.'

'What, none of them?'

'School prefects on speed.'

'Might be useful having a policeman for a client. We'd get access to their information.'

'I'm not working for the police. It's a corrupt, institutionally racist organization. Might as well work for Britain First. We didn't set up No Stone Unturned so we could get in bed with those bastards. We're supposed to be redressing the balance.'

I flushed the toilet and came out, trying to find the best words for what I wanted to say. 'You don't think you're letting …' I coughed, tried to clear the frog in my throat that was making my voice sound strained, '… past experiences cloud your judgement a little bit here?'

Jo's blue eyes went dark. She folded her arms across her chest. 'Don't you fucking dare,' she said.

'OK, OK.' I held up my hands in a gesture of complete surrender. 'But he's a client. We don't have a case without him.'

I withered under her stare. I crossed over to the sinks, flicked my hands under the cold tap and wiped them dry on my trouser legs. 'I don't think we can say no,' I said. 'Not without looking like we're dodgy.'

I turned round and realized Jo had gone.

I took a deep breath and made my way back to the table outside. Jo was already sitting down. The first pint glass was empty. She didn't look at me as I took my seat with them.

'What if we find out Megan had crossed the line?' Jo asked.

'I'll do what I can to keep it from coming out. Bearing in mind I've a duty to uphold the law,' said Col. 'And you can't tell anyone but me. Whatever you find out.'

'We charge,' said Jo.

He nodded. 'I can live with that.'

'Cash up front,' said Jo.

He took an envelope out of his jacket pocket. 'Consider that a deposit. You find out who killed Megan, I'll treble it.'

'What about her kid?' I picked at the beer mat on the table.

'That's my next job,' said Col. 'To go and see him, tell him he isn't ever going to see his mother again.'

My stomach churned on his behalf. I watched Jo make a start on the second pint of lager. I could almost taste it.

'Where is he?' I asked. I thought back to Martha's flat. There had been no sign of anyone in her life. No photos, nothing.

'Lives with his dad.'

'Right,' I said.

There was a pause as we digested this. No matter how far feminism has come, it's almost impossible not to judge a woman who doesn't have custody of her own child.

Col seemed to sense this. 'Losing her kid was what drove Megan to turn her life around. That's why she joined up. She cleaned up her act, got the force to accept her, despite her past.'

'What past?'

'Nothing major. But when her and the kid's dad split up, he dragged her name through the mud. Accused her of taking drugs, shoplifting, that kind of thing. Nothing he could prove, but mud sticks. They took a risk on her, and I don't want anyone saying the risk backfired. She is … was, a great copper. Doesn't deserve to be remembered any other way.'

We left the Royal Park not long afterwards. 'Where's your car?' I asked as we crossed the road.

'Don't have one. Anything you come up with, anything you remember, no matter how insignificant it might seem, call me, OK?' He gave me his number scribbled on a piece of paper. Col put a hand on my arm, just for a second, and I felt the warmth of his fingers, even through my jacket. He gave me the briefest of smiles, and I was struck by the crow's feet around his eyes. He looked completely different when he smiled. Lighter. As he headed off in the direction of the city, I stood next to Jo, watching him go until he was a dot in the distance.

'Sorry,' said Jo.

I braced myself for the punch line. Or the punch. 'Sorry?'

'You're right,' she said. 'Having a copper for a client is good for the business. We can use him.'

'Really?'

'Really.' She set off up the hill to our office. 'And,' she said, looking back at me over her shoulder. 'Two clients in two days. Not bad. Business is looking up.'

'Let's hope we can keep this one alive,' I muttered as I tagged along behind her.

Chapter Twenty-Nine

Despite the fact I'd spent four or five hours asleep on Aunt Edie's sofa, I fell into bed on Sunday evening and don't remember a thing until the sun was in my eyes on Monday morning. I woke not knowing where I was, or what day it was, or who I was. I love those moments – can probably count them on the fingers of one hand – when it feels like the entire contents of your brain have been erased by sleep. I want to die like that. Empty.

It didn't last. A few seconds later, it all came tumbling back. Martha's blank-eyed stare, the smell of Brownie's vomit, the fact we were no closer to knowing where Jack was. I lay in bed and tried to concentrate on the positives. Bernie and Duck were hopefully in police custody, the heroin was off the streets. We'd got Brownie to the nearest thing to a detox clinic I could think of. We had a new client, a new income stream.

But my thoughts all ran back to Martha. Now Megan, I reminded myself. A woman with more names than a member of the royal family. An undercover policewoman, a mother, Col's friend. I knew nothing about her and yet still felt like I owed her, despite her lies. We now had two missing people: Jack, and the person who killed Megan. I was going to find both of them, no matter what it took. I sat up in bed, rolled a fag and thought about whether our new client changed the nature of our investigation. Col wanted to know what Megan was up to. Megan had wanted us to find Jack. The more I thought about it, the clearer it was. I owed it to Megan, and to Brownie, to find Jack, find out what happened to him. It was like unknotting a tangled ball of string – each tangled thread led me to the same conclusion. And in order to find out what had happened to Jack, I needed to find out what had happened to his mother. Those two strings were knotted together.

I threw on some clean clothes and knocked on Jo's bedroom door. 'Come on.'

'Where we going?' she shouted back.

'Alderley Edge. Back to the old fella's house.' He knew more than he was letting on, I was sure of it. 'Five minutes,' I shouted through the door. 'I want to get there before he's pissed.'

We were back outside his house in Alderley Edge before nine on Monday morning. I used my fist to bang on the solid oak front door. He opened it wearing the same dressing gown he'd been wearing the last time we'd seen him.

'Knew you'd be trouble,' he said. He licked a finger and ran it over his right eyebrow.

I gave him my best don't mess with me smile. 'We're investigating the death of Mrs Wilkins. We think you can help.'

'How do you know she's dead?'

'Give us a break,' said Jo. 'We know she's dead.'

'No body.'

'Nobody what?'

'Never found a body.'

'In a car crash?' I had visions of a high-speed collision, Mrs Wilkins being catapulted through the air. Surely her body would be impossible to miss.

'Car crash?'

Jo put a hand against the front door and pushed it open wider. 'I think we better come in.'

He shrugged and stood aside to let us into the entrance hall. 'Is that what Wilkins told you? Don't trust that slimy bugger. All points to him.'

'Let's start at the beginning,' I said, leading the way through to the kitchen. 'What's your name?'

'Professor Peter Partingdon.' He bowed. 'Delighted to be of service.'

'How did Mrs Wilkins die, Professor Partingdon?'

'She didn't. Well, she probably did, but no one knows for certain. She disappeared.'

'And they never found her body?' asked Jo.

'One day she was here, the next gone.' He clapped his hands together.

'And she's never been found?' I wanted to be clear.

'I'll have the newspaper cutting somewhere.' He inched up his dressing gown sleeves like he was a doctor about to perform surgery. 'Give me a minute.'

He disappeared into another room. Jo pulled a face at me.

'I'll stick the kettle on,' she said.

We heard bangs and muffled cursing coming from the other room. Jo brewed up, we drank a mug of tea, then let ourselves out of the back door and smoked a cigarette in the vast overgrown garden.

'Do you need any help?' I shouted through when we heard a noise that sounded like him falling off a chair or a set of ladders or something.

'Not necessary, thank you.' He popped his head around the door, his arms full of newspapers. 'System's shot to hell, but it's all in here. Somewhere.'

He disappeared again and came back almost fifteen minutes later, holding a single newspaper above his head like it was the FA Cup. 'Told you. Never lost a thing. Just a question of searching long enough.'

He handed me a copy of the *Manchester Evening News*, dated

15 September 2000. The story was on page two and the headline had been circled with marker pen.

'Police question millionaire in wife's disappearance.'

I felt my pulse quicken, a wave of something akin to excitement flooded my system. We'd found the source of the river.

I took a seat in the armchair, and Jo peered over my shoulder as I read the article, whispering the words to myself, careful because I didn't want to miss anything, any slight clue that might have been left for us, all these years later. '"The husband of missing housewife Jayne Wilkins has been called in for questioning, according to sources close to the investigation, writes Martin Blink"; Martin Blink. Write that down,' I said to Jo. She rummaged for a pen while I read the article aloud.

'"Nick Wilkins was the last person to see his wife alive, in the early evening of Friday, 8 September. He told police she was going to the cinema with a friend. Police have been unable to locate the friend and checks with local cinemas have failed to confirm Mrs Wilkins attended on the night in question. Police are keen to speak to anyone with information, particularly from members of the public who visited the Odeon cinema on Oxford Street on the night of Friday, 8 September"'.

'Wow,' said Jo.

'And they never found her?' I asked the professor. I turned to see he'd poured himself a drink.

'Not a single trace.'

'And Nick Wilkins wasn't charged?'

'No evidence. Either he didn't do it, or he covered his tracks well. That journalist tried – buying beers for anyone who might want to talk about it.'

'Can we take this?' I held up the newspaper.

'You most certainly cannot.' He snatched it from my fingers, and for a moment I thought he was going to hit me round the head with it. 'Not much point in keeping records if I'm to hand them over to any Tom, Dick or Harry who turns up on the doorstep.'

'OK, no worries. You've been very helpful.'

Jo and I left the house. 'Why did Jack tell Carly his mother died in a car crash?'

'Maybe that was what he was told.'

'But he said he was in the car.'

'Survivor guilt. He blames himself, so he puts himself in there. He was only 5.'

'Do you get survivor guilt if no one died?'

'She died, Lee.' Jo climbed into the driver's seat and slammed her door shut.

I got in the passenger side. 'There's no proof.'

'He paid Martha, Megan twenty-four grand to keep quiet.'

'We don't know that for a fact.'

'Why would he tell Jack his mother's dead if she wasn't?'

I buckled up my seatbelt. 'I don't know.'

Jo turned the key in the ignition and pressed the accelerator down so that the engine revved. 'Let's see if Martin Blink can shed any light,' she said. 'Bet you a tenner that's a made-up name.'

Martin Blink wasn't a made-up name. I fired up my new phone and googled 'Manchester Evening News'. When I rang the news desk I was told Martin Blink didn't work there anymore. 'Is there any chance we can get a message to him,' I asked, using my best professional voice. 'We want to talk to him about a story he worked on.'

The woman promised she'd try and reach him. 'He'll be happy to hear from you. Too much time on his hands now he's retired.'

I put the phone down and we drove in silence for a while, no real plan as to where we were headed, but my mind chewed over the new information. 'You think I should give Col a ring? He might be able to find out what happened in the original investigation.'

'I guess. Make the most of working for a fascist pig.'

I pulled a face.

'Joke,' said Jo. She didn't laugh.

Col had given us a telephone number but warned that he wouldn't always be able to access it. I left a message on his voicemail and hung up. I was just about to switch my phone off when it rang, making me jump.

'Hello?'

'Lee Winters, please.'

'Who's calling?'

'Name's Blink, Martin Blink. Is Lee available?'

'You're speaking to her,' I said. I explained we were private investigators and that we'd like to arrange a meeting because a case he'd reported on might have some relevance to a missing person case we were working today.

'In 2000?'

'I know. It's a long time ago.'

'Ha, might be to you. When you get to my age, seventeen years feels like yesterday. What's the name?'

'Lee.'

'Not your name. The vic.'

'The vic.?'

'The victim. The story.'

'Oh. Jayne, Jayne Wil—'

'Wilkins.' He finished my sentence for me. There was a pause and I thought I heard him whistle down the phone, but it might have been wheezing. He sounded pretty old. 'When were you thinking?'

'Sooner the better.'

'Well, I'm retired. Don't have a right lot to do any day. Where are you now?'

'The city centre, trying to find somewhere to eat.'

'Then meet me at the café on John Dalton Street. Be there as soon as I can.'

The café was painted green, and Jo ordered pie, chips and gravy. I was still full from Aunt Edie's breakfast the day before. I've never had that big an appetite, but it's got worse since I gave up drinking. Jo keeps telling me heroin chic is out of style but it's not that I don't want to eat. It's just I'm not as hungry as I once was.

We'd been there forty minutes when Martin Blink arrived, dressed in a tweed jacket. He carried a briefcase and walked with a limp, his right knee twisted out to the side so that it looked like his leg might buckle any moment. You could feel his pain as he made his way across the café, but he didn't look that old once he'd sat down. Loads of life in the old dog yet, I caught myself thinking.

'Funny name for a girl.' We shook hands, and Martin Blink gestured over to the woman behind the counter.

'The usual?' she shouted across.

'Aye.'

By the time Jo had soaked up the last smear of gravy with her chips, Martin had had a cup of coffee and a currant teacake delivered to him. Jo put down her knife and fork and held her finger and thumb together to form a circle to the waitress.

'Jayne Wilkins. Always hoped someone would show up one day, have another crack at this one. Lovely looking woman.'

I didn't have to look at Jo to know that her hackles would be rising. I knew what she was thinking and, of course, she's right. It's a disease, but one we all catch. People are more interested in good-looking people. Fact.

'Lovely looking dead woman,' said Jo, leaning back in her chair and cracking her knuckles.

'Unproven,' said Martin.

'Her son thinks she's dead.'

Martin took off his glasses and polished the lenses with a napkin. 'Must be all grown up now. Early twenties. What does he say?'

'We haven't spoken to him,' I felt obliged to point out.

'What was his name now? James? No. Jake?'

'Jack,' I said, stacking Martin's empty plate on top of Jo's and pushing both to the side.

'You haven't spoken to him?'

'No.'

'Then how do you know what he thinks about anything?'

'Girlfriend,' said Jo.

'His girlfriend told you Jack thinks his mother's dead?' He replaced his glasses. 'Bit tenuous. What's your interest?'

We'd talked about this on the way to the café. How much to tell Martin Blink? The fact he was a newspaper reporter, albeit retired, meant he was surely a safe bet when it came to protecting sources. And we didn't have a lot to protect at that moment. Does client confidentiality matter when your client's dead? We'd decided to stick close to the original story – Martha hiring us to find Jack. No need to complicate it by mentioning Martha's death or Col's involvement.

'Jack's missing. We're trying to find him.'

'Any leads?'

'Not much.'

'Who wants him found? The father?'

'A friend of his, a woman called Martha. She's worried about him.'

He sat back in his chair and pulled a packet of Fisherman's Friends from his pocket. He popped one in his mouth. I could see the cogs in his brain whirring. He licked his lips and lowered his voice. 'Missing, like his mother. Interesting. I can tell you something – Jayne Wilkins loved that kiddie. Spoke to the neighbours, her brother. Everyone said the same thing. Inseparable. 'Course, you don't get that so much these days. Women more focused on careers. They'd see her in the mornings, picnic basket on her arm.'

'Jesus, a regular, real-life Mary Poppins,' said Jo.

'Took him all over – art galleries, museums, libraries.'

Jealousy made my nose wrinkle – not something I'm proud to admit. Jealous of a smack addict who was either on the run or dead, whose mother disappeared when he was 5, his father chief suspect in her probable murder. Doesn't make sense when you write it like that, but the image of a mother skipping down the road with a picnic basket? I've never even watched the movie. It was hard enough to get my mother to leave the house. Fact is, she didn't, not for the last few years. She stayed in, mouldering to the settee.

'He was only 5 when she left,' I pointed out.

'She didn't leave.' Martin banged the table with his fist, shocking both of us and making the builders on the table in the corner turn and stare. I wondered whether the journalist's interest was purely professional. 'Not of her own free will.'

'You think she was killed?' asked Jo.

'No body, no proof, no crime. But a woman like that doesn't walk out on her kid. I'd stake my pension on it.'

'Where was Jack?' asked Jo. 'At the time?'

'Friend's house. Gone for a sleepover. Which also makes the father's statement a bit of a lie. What happily married couple gets a kid-free night and decides not to spend it together? According to him they were the most loved-up couple since Taylor and Burton.' He flashed me a grin of brownish teeth. I wondered if it was the Fisherman's Friends. 'Before the divorce, obviously.'

'So, there was no car crash?'

'"Car crash"?' He frowned. 'Where've you got that from?'

'Jack's girlfriend,' I said. 'She thinks Jayne might have been involved in a car crash.'

'Not that I heard. Nick Wilkins had a bit of a chequered history when it came to cars. Drunk driving, I think. Not connected though.'

'They arrested him?'

'No. Questioned, never arrested or charged. He was always just "helping the police with their enquiries".' He made the quote signs with his fingers in the air. 'They never proved anything. No body. No crime.'

'But he was under suspicion?'

'Aye.'

'How do you know?' asked Jo.

'It's my job to know.' He paused, corrected himself. 'Was my job.'

A man and woman walked into the café with their arms around each other. The man laughed at something his girlfriend said. I felt a pang of something and turned back to Martin Blink. 'How?' I said.

He tapped the side of his nose. 'Sources. Close to the investigation.'

I glanced at Jo, tried to gauge what she was thinking. There's times we're so close I could swear we're telepathic, but right now her face was giving nothing away.

'Listen,' Blink said. He leaned towards us. 'Everyone thought he'd done it, just no one could prove it.'

'Innocent till proven guilty,' I murmured. 'Why did everyone think it was him?'

'Because forty per cent of murdered women are murdered by their partners.'

'Means there's a sixty per cent chance it was someone else.'

Martin Blink puffed out his chest. 'He was caught out. Over and over. Lies. His version of their relationship turned out to be a fairy tale. He was having an affair.'

Jo sighed. '*Quelle* fucking *surprise*.'

'Who with?'

'More than one, by all accounts.'

'Any names?' I couldn't help the feeling Martin Blink had an axe to grind.

'Karen Carpenter, like the singer.'

'This is fact?'

The retired journalist leaned in to me so I smelled his liquorice menthol breath on my face. 'It's gospel.'

Chapter Thirty

I pride myself on being a good judge of character and, having met Nick Wilkins, I had no trouble believing him capable of an extramarital affair. Jo, I knew, had no trouble believing any man guilty of sexual infidelity. Fact is she'd have trouble believing in a man who didn't put it about. Still, I reminded myself, I was an investigator. Investigators require proof.

'How do you know?' I asked Martin.

'Tip-off.'

We all started when my phone rang. I tugged it out of my pocket and gave it to Jo.

'No one's got this number.'

She checked the screen and got up from the table. 'I'll take it,' she said.

'Who is it?' asked Martin.

I frowned at him. Like I would know. 'Tip-off from?'

'Can't reveal my sources, you should know that, lassie.'

'Did they give you a name?'

'Several names.'

'You checked them out?'

'I was the best investigative journalist north of Watford. Got more commendations hanging on my walls than you've got text-books. 'Course I checked them out.'

'And?' I couldn't help sensing that Martin Blink was playing us like bass guitars. His blue eyes had a glint to them. The more time we spent with him, the younger he looked. 'What happened?'

'Found two of them. Both denied it, of course. And you can't blame them. Finding out the man you're having a fling with not only has a wife but has a wife who's disappeared in very mysterious circumstances – 'course you're not going to admit to it. But I'm not daft.'

'"Not daft"?'

'They were frightened.'

'Of?'

'Frightened the same thing might happen to them. He's a powerful man, Nick Wilkins. Powerful and sailing too close to the wind.'

'What wind?' I asked.

Blink didn't answer.

'This all sounds like myth and rumour to me,' I said. I leaned back in my seat and pretended to examine my fingernails.

'Her brother thought he'd done it. What was his name? Tom, Tom Smith. That's it.'

'And what did he say?'

'He knew she kept a diary. Always had done, since she was a kid. He told the police, but Wilkins swore blind she didn't keep one. So, the brother went looking for it himself.'

'And?'

'And he found some of it.'

'"Some of it"? What did it say?'

'He talked to Wilkins's neighbour – there'd been a bonfire. The day she disappeared. Tom took a look around. Found a fire pit at the bottom of the garden.'

'When was this?'

'Soon after she'd disappeared.'

'And he found her diary in the fire pit?'

He nodded. 'Well, he found a scrap of paper no bigger than fifteen centimetres square.'

'He told the police?'

'They made out three words.' He paused, let the tension build.

'Let me guess.' I leaned closer to him, dropped my voice to a whisper. 'Nick killed me.'

Martin had the good grace to smile, even though I could tell he was annoyed. He shook his head. '"Friends take me".'

'*Friends take me*? What does that mean?'

'No idea, but they proved it was her handwriting. Why would you burn a person's diary unless you had something to hide?'

'Maybe *she* burned the diaries?'

'The neighbour said it was definitely Nick having the bonfire.'

Jo came back to the table and passed my phone back to me. 'Did I miss anything?'

'Not really,' I said. I turned back to Martin. 'How come the police didn't arrest him?'

'Tom, Jayne's brother,' he added for Jo's benefit, 'believed Nick had bought them off, or put the frighteners on them. Something. He's a big fish in a small pond. Thinks he's Al Capone.'

I thought back to the Mr Wilkins I'd met. The look in his eyes when I'd mentioned Jack.

'They're all the same,' said Martin. 'They're the ones who've destroyed this country, turned greed into a virtue.'

'Any idea where Karen Carpenter is now? Or any of the other women?' I tried to bring the conversation back to the point. Inside I was thinking that maybe they'd be willing to speak to us now. Surely they didn't still live in fear of Nick Wilkins?

Martin Blink ducked down and picked up his briefcase, a battered leather affair. He pulled out a notebook, a black, leather-bound book with an elastic band round its centre. On the front was a rectangular sticker. On that was written:

'Jayne Wilkins. Disappeared: 8/9/00'

My heart thumped out an extra beat. 'You've still got your notes?'

'Every case I ever worked. All at home.' He raised his eyebrows at me, like I'd made a comment, challenged him in some way. 'Wasn't going to leave them at work. They're my notes.'

He turned over the front cover, cast his eyes down the first page. I strained to read his writing upside down, but when he caught what I was doing, he pulled the notebook closer to his chest. 'Didn't give me a backwards glance. Day I turned 65, it was: thank you and goodnight. Management tools, think they know it all. Don't know how to wipe their own backsides, half of them. Wouldn't know investigative journalism if it jumped up and bit them on the—'

'Can I see?' asked Jo.

He held the notebook against his chest and took a slug of tea. He stared at me, and I didn't flinch. Stared at him right back. 'I'll do you a deal,' he said.

'What kind of deal?' Jo narrowed her eyes.

'I give you my information, you give me yours. First dibs.'

'What?'

'I get the story. Before anyone else.'

'Thought you'd retired,' said Jo.

I hesitated. Thought of Col. We'd promised him almost the exact same thing. 'We can't promise that.'

'Come on, who else you going to tell?'

'The police?' I tried to make it sound theoretical rather than a prearranged contract.

'Rubbish. They weren't that interested at the time, they're hardly likely to be interested seventeen years later.'

'They might be if Jack doesn't turn up.'

'Police aren't interested in young men who've taken off. Unless there's evidence a crime's been committed.' His voice rose at the end of the sentence, like he was asking a question.

246

I shook my head.

The waitress meandered over and cleared our plates away. We all watched her cross the room back to the counter. I don't know whether she sensed our attention because she turned and said: 'Anything else?'

'Another cup of tea would be nice,' said Jo. 'Thanks.'

'All right,' said Martin, leaning across the table, 'first dibs on the story, unless the police show up demanding answers.'

Jo and I met eyes across the table. Jo stuck out her bottom lip, gently shaking her head from side to side. 'We could live with that,' she said, and I found myself nodding in agreement.

I reached over for the notebook, but he clutched it tighter to his chest. 'I want to be kept in the loop.'

'Deal.'

'Any developments, no matter how small.'

'We're not going to ring you every five minutes,' said Jo.

'Twice a day. Morning and evening. Give me an update. And if anything major happens.'

I shrugged. 'All right. Hand it over.'

He hesitated, looked me in the eyes and I knew he was working out whether he could trust me. I was struck by the eagerness in his eyes, how much he clearly wanted to be a part of this.

'Scouts honour,' I said, tapping two fingers to my forehead.

He released his grip on the notebook, and Jo took it off him. I watched her nod her head, impressed.

'This is great,' she said. She passed the notebook across the table to me. 'I'm going for a piss,' she said, pulling herself up from the table. She made her way to the back of the room.

'Ladylike, your mate,' said Martin.

I grinned. 'Ladylike don't get the job done.'

'A woman after my own heart.'

'You married?' I asked Martin.

'Divorced.'

'Children?'

247

'Me? No. I'm just your regular standard hack cliché. Thought kids'd cramp my style. Hah. That's probably why the wife left. Didn't even care at the time. Thought it was less complicated. You don't think you're going to get old. Or lonely.'

'It's never too late,' I said in what I hoped was an encouraging voice.

'You know what, lassie? That's another lie. That's a lie they tell you to keep your nose glued to the grindstone. So that you don't notice that your life is passing by, and that you'll never get it back.'

I pulled my tobacco packet from my pocket and rolled myself a fag. I noticed him staring so I offered it to him. He shook his head.

'Gave up.'

'Oh.'

'Yes. Nineteen days.' He popped another Fisherman's Friend and crunched it. 'Bloody killing me.'

I slipped the packet of tobacco and the roll-up back into my pocket.

'Mind you don't just think about business,' said Martin.

'Business is the wrong word. It's a mission.' I grinned to take the intensity out of my words, even though I meant every one of them.

'What about the other?'

I frowned, not following him.

'Boyfriend?'

'Oh, no.' I shook my head. I glanced over at the young couple who were holding each other's hands across their table. 'Not interested.'

'Girlfriend?'

I pulled a face.

'Well, take my advice, while you're young, and good-looking, find yourself a bloke. Make sure you treat him like he's the best thing since sliced bread. Because one day you're going to wake up old, and being old and alone is the worst thing ever.'

I shrugged and put my feet up on the seat Jo had vacated. 'Who knows how the cookie's going to crumble?' I said. 'People spend forty years putting up with each other's bad habits, then one of them drops dead of a heart attack. You're still alone.'

'Maybe.'

'No guarantees, whichever path you choose. Maybe it's about learning to live with solitude.'

He brushed the crumbs off his jacket lapels and shook his head. 'It's called stacking the odds. If I'd had kids, I might have grandchildren now. Could have four or five of the buggers running around the place.'

'Or they might have emigrated to Australia.'

He gripped my arm across the table. 'I focused on myself. My career. Me, me, me. Thought the job was enough, thought it would last forever. Conned into believing my own bullshit. We all need someone. Even if it's just someone to argue with over which TV channel to watch.'

Jo came back to the table, adjusting the waistband on her miniskirt, which she wore over the top of a pair of red-and-black striped leggings.

'I don't care,' she said. 'They're all crap.'

Martin pointed a bony finger at me. He looked like he was about to say something more but then his shoulders shrugged, and he closed his eyes as he downed the rest of his coffee.

Jo slipped back into the seat next to me, pushing my feet to the floor. 'Anyone else we should talk to?'

Martin called over to the woman at the counter for a glass of water. He waited till she'd brought it to our table and took a sip, before replying to Jo's question. When he next spoke, it was like he'd slipped back into his journalist role. Clipped and professional.

'There's nothing like the feeling,' he said, and you could see it in his eyes. 'When you're on to something. The best drug.'

I looked at Jo and we both grinned. Happiness bloomed inside of me and I had this flash of feeling, this knowing, for the first time in my life. I knew I was lucky. Doing the thing I loved doing most, with my best mate, who was the best mate in the world.

'I hope you crack this one. I'd like to see Nick Wilkins get what's coming to him. 'Bout time someone brought him to book.'

We left Martin Blink in the café and went back out onto the street. The clouds had dissipated, and the afternoon felt warm. Spring was coming, and it made me want to find a pub and sit outside drinking pints of lager top. I gripped my thumbs tight in my palms.

'Boy, have we got leads,' said Jo. She surveyed the street and nodded her head approvingly, her lips pursed. 'We're investigators on the trail of a murderer and we have leads. How good is that?'

I tried to wipe the picture of floating Martha from my mind. 'Who was on the phone?'

'Oh, yeah. Col.'

'What did he say?'

'Not much. They're waiting on the autopsy. It's being rushed through, apparently.'

'Did you tell him about Wilkins?'

'Yeah. You're right – having a fascist pig for a client is useful.'

I pulled a face at her, and she gave me a grin to take the sting out of her words.

'He's going to try and find out what the original investigative team thought – if they're still around. We're getting close, I can feel it.'

'Yeah, I guess. What next?'

'See if we can find the women he was having affairs with? They might be willing to talk after all this time.'

'It's a bit …'

'What?'

'Dunno – clichéd. Don't you think?'

'What is?'

250

'Cut-throat businessman, having affair with not one but several blonde bimbos, kills devoted wife and mother ...'

'We don't know they're blonde. Or bimbos.'

'Still ...'

'Yeah, well clichés come about for a reason,' said Jo. She linked arms with me, and we set off in the warm sunshine towards the van. 'Because that shit happens a lot.'

Chapter Thirty-One

I read Martin's notebook aloud to Jo as she drove us back to Leeds. It contained the names of three possible women Wilkins might have been involved with. Blink had spoken to one of them, the one he'd mentioned in the café – Karen Carpenter. She'd denied it, according to his scribbled notes. Claimed they were just friends and that Wilkins had confided in her about his wife being troubled. The second woman, Alison Williams, had refused to speak to him and the third, known only as Sue, he hadn't managed to find.

We were back in Leeds by teatime. As we drove back through the city centre we passed The Warehouse, and I caught sight of Bill, standing on the pavement, talking to the driver of a truck piled high with beer barrels.

'Pull over,' I said to Jo. 'Let's see if Carly's in tonight. I want to ask her more about the car crash – find out where Jack got that idea from.'

Bill didn't look that pleased to see me.

'Is Carly around?' I asked.

'Carly hasn't been around since the last time you were here.'

'Where is she?'

'Your guess is as good as mine.' He waved a hand as the truck pulled away from the kerbside. 'And no talking to anyone else. I can't afford to lose any more staff.'

I jumped back in the van and slammed the door closed. 'We're losing more people than we're finding.'

'Not really.' Jo started the engine. 'Who've we lost so far?'

'Jack.'

'He was already missing.'

'Our first client.'

'Megan? She's not missing. She's dead.'

'So we lost her big time.'

'Not our fault.'

'Brownie.'

'We found him,' said Jo, frowning at me as she made her way up the hill towards Woodhouse Street. 'That's the opposite of losing someone.'

I made a mental note to give Aunt Edie a call, make sure he was still there. 'Bill said Carly's not been in since we were last here.'

'Maybe she's gone to see her folks.'

'Without telling work?'

'I need to go home and get Tampax,' said Jo.

'Then what?'

'Then let's go to the office and do a review of everything we've got so far. You can do one of your wall charts.'

I cheered up a bit at that. Jo was right, a wall chart was just what we needed. She drove back up to Hyde Park Road and I sat outside in the van while Jo ran into the house. I closed my eyes. *Switch off the brain. I am above thought. I am the watcher of my thoughts.* It's in the moments when the brain is quiet that deep realization occurs. Almost impossible to achieve when squashed in a Vauxhall Combo on Hyde Park Road, but I crossed my legs on the seat, breathed from my belly and tried to still my mind. We live in our brains when really they are just another organ of the body, like the liver. Switching off the mind means being in the body.

I was pulled out of my non-thoughts by a knock on the window.

I opened my eyes. Shut them again. Opened them. Wished I hadn't. Wished I could erase the scene in front of me. I froze.

The man stood on the pavement to my left, his collar turned up, making a winding motion with his fingers. I can't remember how long it took me to realize he was telling me to put the window down, but it was probably minutes. I fixed my gaze forward, stared out of the windscreen, like I could imagine myself out of there. Teleported. Anywhere but there. He opened the passenger door, and I half-fell out of the van and onto the pavement at his feet.

'Hi,' he said.

I straightened myself up. Didn't know whether to stand, or stay seated, so I chose a kind of in-between option where I was half-crouched by the side of the van. I put a hand on the door-frame to steady myself.

'It's so good to see you,' he said.

I glanced along the street half expecting to see a horde of police officers bearing down. For the first time in living memory, there wasn't a single person in sight. Where the fuck was everyone? The nuclear holocaust had happened without my knowledge.

'Aren't they looking for you?' I said.

He held out his hand and, for some reason I will never be able to understand, I took it and allowed him to pull me up from my crouch, so that I was upright in front of him. For one awful, bone-melting moment I thought he was going to hug me. He stared at me like I might have grown horns in the years since I'd seen him. How many years? Only three. Lifetimes.

'How've you been?' he said.

Jo. I needed Jo. I looked up at the house, at our first- and second-floor flat windows, mentally screaming for her to come down, come out, to save me.

'There's a café round the corner,' he said.

The thing I love most about living on Hyde Park Road is the fact that there's a park on the other side of the street. When I'm in my bedroom, up in the attic, all I see is trees. I thought about running, but my legs didn't work.

His hand hot on my elbow. The next thing I remember we were sitting in the small Turkish café next door to the Asian supermarket. I have no idea how we got there. It freaks me out now, thinking about the blank spots. I've got flashes of memory – like postcards. Sitting at the table with a cup of mint tea in front of me. His hollowed-out cheeks. The flock wallpaper. I remember I asked him: 'How did you get out?'

I remember that because I had pictures in my head of the poster in *Shawshank Redemption*, whatshisface in *Escape from Alcatraz*, the army guys with the tunnel in the black-and-white concentration camp film.

He shook his head, like he could see what I saw, and he said: 'I was released.'

I couldn't look at him, couldn't bear to see the eyes that are the exact same muddy green as mine.

'You can't have. I mean, that's not fair.'

He closed his eyes, and I wished he would stay that way. So I could stare at him without being seen. So I could spend some time assessing, to take in the paleness of his skin, the shadow of his stubble, the heaviness in his forehead. But he opened them again, and I had to look away.

'I'll never finish paying for what I did,' he said.

'Don't.' I took a sip of tea and a layer off the skin on the roof of my mouth at the same time.

'No one knows more—'

'I said don't.'

He stopped talking, and I became aware of a table of students at the front of the café, laughing. I had to fight the urge to fling my cup of tea over their heads.

'How've you been?'

'Fine.'

We both knew I was lying. In that moment I realized I was so far from fine – everything was, had been, a sham, a pretence. I'd thought I was coping, when actually coping was the furthest thing from me. I was out of coping's reach, miles out, adrift, alone, lost, at sea.

I closed the voices down. 'Why are you here?'

'To see you.'

'Why?'

'We have to … to make sense of what's happened.'

'Fuck off.'

'I've lost one daughter.' He leaned over the table, put his hand under my chin and tilted my head so that I was forced to look at him. 'You're all I've got left.'

'You didn't *lose* a daughter.' I couldn't keep the venom from my voice. I pushed his arm away.

'Please, Lily.'

'That's not my name.'

'I understand, you need a new start. Christ, I know.'

'You don't know. You don't know anything about me.'

'I know more than you thi—'

'You killed her.' I shouted the words, spit flecked his face, and everything stopped.

Silence.

He stared at me and for the first time I stared back.

'Yes,' he said.

'You killed her,' I said, my voice quieter, 'and her baby, and now you want us to play happy families?'

'I didn't mean … You must know. I would never have wanted that to happen. I loved her, I still do, always will. You can't begin to imagine how it feels to live with what I've done.'

The most awful part of this was that I could imagine. 'You want sympathy?'

256

'We're all each other has.'

'Not true.'

'We have to forgive each other, before we can forgive ourselves.'

'*Forgive each other*?' My voice came out high-pitched, like a shriek. Even the students stopped talking.

He kept his voice low. 'You know what I mean.'

I didn't care who heard. 'I didn't kill her.'

'You don't have to feel guilty.'

I jumped up from the table, knocking over both cups of tea. The crockery spilled, clattered to the floor. One smashed. Two men appeared from the rear of the café.

'Leave me alone,' I said. 'Don't come anywhere near me, ever. If you do, I'll call the police.'

He got to his feet. I turned and barged past the table of students on my way to the door.

'You know as well as I do, you can't run,' he said.

By the time I hit the outside he had raised his voice so he was shouting after me.

'Whatever happens, Lily, I'm still your dad.'

257

Chapter Thirty-Two

I sprinted back round to our house, my body moving faster than my legs so that I stumbled forward, tripping over my feet. Jo was sitting in the van, still parked outside our flat. I flung myself through the passenger door and screamed: 'Drive, drive.'

To give Jo her due, she didn't hesitate. She flicked her reefer out of the window, turned the keys in the ignition and lurched the van forward. A car sounded its horn as she pulled onto the road. She threw the gearstick to second and we gathered momentum. I scanned the pavements.

'What?' asked Jo.

'Drive.' Sweat ran down my forehead, dripped into my eyes. I wiped my face on the bottom of my T-shirt. 'Down the hill.'

'What's happened?'

'Oh my God.' It came out as a moan.

The van hit thirty. Jo pushed it on. We cleared the park. I kept my gaze fixed on the wing mirror.

'Thought you'd been abducted by aliens.'

'I wish.'

'Where we going?'

'Anywhere. Anywhere that's not here.'

She threw me a glance. 'You look like you've seen a ghost.'

'Yes.'

'You've seen a ghost?'

'Worse.'

'What?'

'David.'

Jo crunched the gears into fourth. 'David who?'

I didn't answer, waited for her to catch up. Knew she'd get there.

I felt her stare on me.

'Shit, David David?'

'Watch out!'

She threw the steering wheel to the right and narrowly avoided the parked car outside the newsagents.

'Jesus,' she said a minute or so later, when we'd got to the bottom of the hill and pulled out left onto the main road into town. 'How the fuck?'

'Released, he said.'

'Released? He got seven years.'

'It's been three.' I stared out of the passenger window. 'I don't know. I don't want to know.'

'What does he want?'

'Me,' I said, the dull realization flooding my system, making my arms ache. 'He wants me to take her place, to fill the void.'

'Fuck off.'

'That's what I said.'

'Where's he living? What's he—'

'I don't want to talk about it. Just drive.'

She didn't say a word, and the buildings blurred past the window. We got to the edge of the city, then looped round and joined Kirkstall Road heading us back out to the west again. The road widened, and the traffic thinned. Jo picked up speed, and I thought about the places we could go. I didn't have my passport. I couldn't go home. We got as far as Horsforth, to the outer ring road, before Jo spoke. 'Was he in a car?'

'I don't know. I didn't ask.'

'Does—'

'What bit of "I don't want to talk about it" don't you understand?'

'Jesus, Lee. I'm just trying—'

'Well, don't. Stop here.'

I pointed to a corner shop a couple of hundred yards ahead. She pulled up outside it.

'Where you going?'

'To get fags.' I slammed the van door behind me.

I was carrying a white plastic bag when I got back to the van. Jo said: 'Don't, Lee. He's not worth it.'

'Chill the fuck out, would you?' I said. I flung the carrier bag into the footwell. 'It's Red Bull.'

We found a park, with a fish and chip shop opposite. Jo ordered for the both of us and we sat on a low stone wall bordering a rose bed. I had chips and mushy peas, in a polystyrene tray, the vinegar forming puddles. Maybe I ate some, I don't think I did. Mainly I just dipped my fingers in the vinegar. We found a deserted playground within the park and sat in the sandpit. Jo had brought the hash tin and we smoked until conscious, rational thought was off the menu.

It got cold.

And dark.

I know Aunt Edie would say I should have talked it over with Jo, but I don't like talking until I know what I'm going to say. I couldn't sort out the overload. Everything I'd hidden from for the past three years had caught up with me. He'd reopened a book I thought I'd closed, a storage container I'd thought I could keep the lid on. I didn't want to talk about him, because talking about him would make me remember her. And I didn't want to remember her, because whenever she flashed onto the screen of my brain she brought only pain and its harder, less forgiving cousin, guilt.

'Wonder how Brownie's getting on with Aunt Edie?' said Jo. She lay on her back in the sand, staring up at the stars. She propped herself up on one elbow and passed me the spliff.

I wiped my palms on the front of my jacket, decided to give up on my sand lion, which looked more like a sand hillock. It was getting hard to see in the dark. 'This sand isn't sticky enough.'

'Should be. It's full of melted ice cream and kid pee.'

'Nice.'

Jo shivered. I crouched next to her, trying to share what little body warmth I had.

'We can't stay here all night,' she said.

'OK.' I was frozen, my shoulders trying to act like a scarf, hunched up around my neck.

'You want to go home?'

I couldn't miss the hopefulness of Jo's tone. I stubbed it out. 'No.'

'Where then?'

'The office. There isn't anywhere else.'

It was getting on for half past eight. Monday night, not exactly quiet, but quiet by LS6 standards. I made Jo park the van a few streets away, and we looped back round to the office on foot. There was no way David could know about the business; I repeated the thought over and over like a mantra. We'd rented it in the name of the agency, and the agency was set up in my new name. I cursed myself for telling him I'd changed my name, but I didn't think I'd told him my new one. The whole conversation felt like a scene from a movie I'd watched years ago. I couldn't separate fact from fiction. The things he said, the things I wish I'd said, the things we didn't say.

We'd have to move. I'd have to tell Jo, we couldn't stay at the

261

flat. Shame, because we'd lived there for four years and it had started to feel more like home than any other place I'd ever lived. We rented it from a landlady who was about ninety and never bothered us. But I couldn't live there now, not knowing he could turn up at any second. It took me a few minutes to get the key into the padlock of the office door, which made me realize how battered I was.

'Hurry up,' said Jo. 'I need a wazz.'

That made us both laugh. Tension release. Jo cross-legged, jigging about, clutching her bits.

I finally managed to turn the key, the clasp released and a voice behind me said: 'Hi.'

I whipped round ready to kick out, but stumbled and found myself face to face with Col. He had his hands up, ready to parry any punch I might throw at him.

He was lucky. I doubt I'd have been able to slap my own thigh. Thank God it was dark because I knew blood was rushing to my cheeks. It crossed my mind to confess, hand him the dope tin, get it over with, but I didn't get the chance, because Jo gave him a punch on the shoulder, which nearly sent him into the poor excuse for a privet hedge that divides our office from the house next door.

'Anyone ever tell you not to sneak up on women?' she said.

'Sorry. Everyone's jittery. Trying to maintain a low profile.'

'Next time,' said Jo, rubbing her knuckles, 'it'll be a stiletto, right through the eyes.'

He glanced at me. 'You OK?'

'Yeah. Come in, I'll get the kettle on,' I said, standing aside to let him in. I smelled Paco Rabanne as he passed.

Despite our best efforts the place still was trashed.

'Christ, you really got done over. You got insurance?'

'Don't be funny,' said Jo, taking off her jacket and switching the heating on. 'Cheaper to buy new stuff than it is to pay the insurance premiums round here.'

'What did they take?'

I pictured our small safe, dented but proud. 'Nothing much,' I said. 'Not really. What you doing here?'

'There's been an arrest.'

'For Megan's murder?'

'Two people connected to the investigation. That's all I can say. Anonymous tip-off. Caught getting off a train in Huddersfield yesterday. The person who called it in thought they were armed.' He picked up a penholder that had rolled under the low window at the front of the office and stood it on the one desk we'd managed to salvage.

'You think it's them?'

'Don't know. Not my case, so I've not had a chance to talk to them. Apparently, they say they've got an alibi but it's a weird one.'

'Weird?'

'They reckon they kidnapped a junkie, Friday night. They said they were with him all day. Said he was tied up in their house, but when uniform went round to have a look there was no one there.'

'Oh.' I pretended to be tidying up my desk. 'You believe them?' I glanced at Jo.

Col shrugged his shoulders. 'Who knows? Powers that be aren't convinced. But they've been charged with possession and intent to supply. Least that gives the lads time to see if they can get a confession.'

Jo flinched and put her hands over her ears. 'Spare me the details.'

I pulled a face at Jo, but Col didn't seem to mind. To be honest I'm not sure at that moment in time Jo was that concerned about how Bernie and Duck were being treated by the boys in blue. Made me realize it's easier to be righteous when you haven't been wronged.

'Coroner's put the time of death between 6 p.m. and 8 p.m. She was strangled. Then put in the bath.'

We'd waved Megan off at 6.15 p.m. and I'd assumed she'd been walking. I guessed it would take twenty, thirty minutes to walk to the flats on Cardigan Road, which meant she must have been murdered almost as soon as she got home. Was someone waiting for her? Bushes and shrubs – ample hiding places – surrounded the car park to her flats. Perhaps someone was hiding there, biding time. Perhaps they watched her go in, gave her time to get settled, have a glass of wine, put some music on, undress, climb into the bath. I moved to stand by the radiator, but the heat hadn't seeped into it yet.

'Who found her?'

'Downstairs neighbour called the police. Tap was dripping, the bath overflowed.'

Col took a seat and put his feet up on the desk. I went through to the kitchenette and took some deep breaths while the kettle boiled. Col shouted through from the front office.

'I checked out the Wilkins case you gave me.'

I re-joined them in the outer office.

'And?' said Jo.

'You're right. There were rumours of an affair. More than one by all accounts.'

It hit me that I hadn't thought about David for the past three minutes and my spirits rose at the realization. Maybe I wasn't condemned to drown in dysfunctionality. Maybe work would save me.

'Let's go through to the back,' I said. I picked up my notebook. 'No one can see us in there.'

Col frowned but got up and followed me through. Our clear up efforts had had more of an impact here, we'd managed to get all the broken furniture out of the room, and the punchbag still hung in the corner.

'So I checked them out. And guess what?' said Col as he glanced around the room for a chair then took a seat on the floor.

'You found them?' I said.

'We get first dibs,' Jo said. 'We gave you the tip.'

Col held up a hand. 'No one's going to speak to them.'

He didn't need to say the rest of the sentence. From the heaviness of his tone, we knew what was coming. He paused, allowed us to reach our own conclusions.

'They're dead?' I said.

He paused. 'I don't know they're all dead. One emigrated, never to be seen again. The other …' He pursed his lip and nodded.

'How?' I asked.

He stretched his legs out in front of him and leaned his back against the wall. 'Car crash.'

'When?' said Jo.

'Another car crash?' I said, before I remembered Jayne Wilkins didn't die in a car accident. At least not one that anyone could prove. My brain ached, and I cursed the number of spliffs we'd smoked. It was like trying to do the hurdles after a drinking session.

'December 2000,' Col said. 'Three months after Jayne disappeared.'

'Balls,' said Jo.

'She was 23.'

'There goes our witness,' said Jo. 'What happened, brake failure?'

'DUI.'

'Who was?'

I marvelled at Jo's ability to keep up. My brain scrambled to get a hold of the conversation. 'What's DUI?'

'Drunk driving,' said Jo.

'She was called Karen,' Col said.

'Karen Carpenter?' I thought back to Martin's notes.

'That's the one. They found her behind the wheel, at the bottom of a lake, out east. The coroner reckoned she took the bend too quickly. Water would have been freezing. Drowned before anyone could get to her.'

'There goes our witness,' said Jo again. 'Conveniently.'

'I pulled the file,' said Col.

'Bleeding typical,' Jo muttered. She jumped up from the floor and left the room. We heard the sounds of her relieving herself from the toilet next door. I told you, the walls are plasterboard thin.

I turned back to Col. 'How does that help us?'

'It doesn't. Not really. Apart from ...'

'"Apart from" what?' I sat cross-legged on the floor, a distance away from him. I didn't want him to smell the smoke in my hair, on my clothes.

'I don't know. Might be nothing.' He lit a cigarette, and I pushed the ashtray across the floor to him.

'Go on.'

He held the cigarette between his thumb and his first two fingers, his hand curled, like he was used to smoking outside in strong winds. 'She was pregnant.'

'*Pregnant*?' The word was like a slap across the face.

'The autopsy put it at seven weeks.'

'The baby died?' Stupid question. A seven-week old foetus inside a dead mother. I had to look away. I could feel his stare on me, but I kept my gaze on the floor until I'd got control.

'You think she didn't want to be pregnant? Killed herself?' asked Jo, coming back into the room, fastening her belt.

'Impossible to know. But,' he held up one finger, 'according to her mother, Karen had been told it was highly unlikely she would ever be able to have children. She'd got some condition. Getting pregnant was a miracle for her.'

'So, not suicide.'

'Her mother swore Karen wouldn't have done anything to harm the baby. Refused point blank to believe she'd have had a drink if she'd been pregnant. And even if she hadn't been pregnant, her mother was adamant she'd never drink and drive.'

'Bet he fixed the brakes,' said Jo. 'And spiked her drinks.'

'There's a question mark over whether she was driving. When they got to her she was in the back seat. Whether she climbed there trying to escape, or whether she was there when the car entered the water, we'll never know.'

Not for the first time I thought about how it must feel to die with a baby growing inside you. To die when you're responsible for creating, nurturing life. You must die with the belief that you've failed on a fundamental, catastrophic level.

'He's got away with murder,' said Jo. 'Twice.'

'No proof,' I said. 'They never arrested him.'

'Lee's right,' said Col. 'It's just interesting in light of the fact she's connected.'

'More than interesting,' said Jo.

Col leaned across towards me and stubbed his cigarette out in the ashtray. His fingers brushed mine, and I shrank my hand away.

'I had a look at Wilkins.'

'Anything?'

'Couple of minor things, but not for years. All traffic related. A drunk driving conviction, failure to report an accident. Likes his fast cars. But nothing in the last ten years. I even looked at his tax returns. All filed. Not worth as much on paper as you might think, but not declaring the odd car sale isn't the crime of the century.'

'It's him,' said Jo. 'I know it is.'

'We've got no proof,' I said.

'There was one thing that caught my eye,' Col said.

'What?'

'I got a mate of mine to have a look at his bank account. Strictly off the record. Ten days ago, Nick Wilkins withdrew £25K, in cash.'

I couldn't help it. I caught my breath and the sound carried in the room.

'What?' asked Col, looking at Jo then turning his gaze to me. 'What?'

267

'That means it's true,' said Jo. 'It's him.'

I glanced at Jo. We couldn't help ourselves. The words spilled out the both of us, fast as anything. I think Jo started the sentence, but I finished it. 'That's the exact amount Jack and his mate owe their dealers.'

Col pulled a face like he didn't believe us. 'You sure?'

'Absolutely.'

'And you think Wilkins paid Jack's debts for him? Thought they weren't speaking to each other?'

I looked at Jo. 'I don't think he paid it willingly.'

'Come again?'

'We think they blackmailed him.' Jo sat on the floor, her legs outstretched in front of her.

'*Blackmail?* What have they got to blackmail him about?'

I glanced at Jo. 'Jack thinks his dad killed his mum.'

'Why didn't you tell me this before?'

'We weren't sure it was relevant.'

'Listen.' He jumped up and his keys fell out of his pocket. I picked them up and handed them to him. He took them from my hand and again I felt my skin tingle. 'You've got to be straight with me. If you don't tell me what's going on, I can't protect you. This isn't a game.'

My cheeks burned. 'I'm—'

'Look what happened to Megan. You have to trust me. We have to trust each other. If you don't, I can't help you.'

My thoughts came at me in random bursts. 'We think they blackmailed Jack's dad to get the money to pay the dealers.'

'Where's the money now?'

Despite his plea for truth, I daren't admit we had it in the safe. We'd have to hand it over. I didn't want to hand it over. It was our trump card, the one thing we had that no one else did. I stood up. 'That's the question everyone's asking.'

'But,' said Jo, her eyes shining, 'if Wilkins paid the blackmail demand, that means he's guilty.'

I made my way to the kitchenette. I could still hear them both speaking, and I'd just remembered the tea. I guess, if I'm honest, I didn't like the fact Col was dressing us down like we were school kids. My head was too hot. I splashed cold water on my face.

'You can't jump to those kinds of conclusions,' I heard him say to Jo. 'Maybe he paid because he wanted to help his son out of trouble.'

'They're estranged,' Jo said. 'He told Lee he hadn't heard from Jack for years.'

'That's not proof,' said Col. 'I can't go to my boss with that.'

I took a deep breath and carried the mugs into the back room. Tea sploshed over the sides as I walked across the room, scalding my knuckles. 'Megan might have been involved in the blackmail.'

He turned to me and the room fell silent. 'What makes you think that?'

'I just know,' I said.

Col didn't stop staring. His oversized woollen jumper had holes in the sleeves. 'That would be a serious breach of judgement. A criminal offence.'

'Yes,' I said. I handed him a mug of tea. 'I'm sorry.'

'Why would she do that? Doesn't make sense.'

I gave the other mug to Jo and then turned back round to Col. 'She'd fallen in love,' I said. 'With one of the guys she was supposed to be watching.'

I left the room to fetch my own mug and the chocolate Hobnobs Jo had bought.

'Which one?' asked Col when I stepped back into the room. 'The one who owes the money?'

I nodded.

'Jesus.' He ran a hand through his hair. 'You're accusing a senior police officer of … Do you know what that would do to her reputation? To her son? Don't throw accusations around, especially ones you can't prove.'

'It's true,' I said. 'Even if I can't prove it.'

269

'*Fallen in love*?' He looked at me and I knew he was willing me to say I'd made a mistake. I couldn't. He hit the panelled walls with the palms of his hand. 'I knew there was something wrong.'

'Don't judge,' I said. 'You said yourself there's no such thing as black and white.'

'It's my fault. She wasn't ready. They put her in too soon. I knew there was something wrong. Knew I should have pushed it.'

'Easy with hindsight,' I said.

'Chuck us a Hobnob,' said Jo.

I threw her the packet, and she took one and dunked it into her tea. When she'd bitten the melted segment, she licked her lips and said: 'You're both missing the point.'

'What?' Col had put his tea on the floor and was pacing the room.

'What's the likelihood of us having more than one murderer on our hands?' said Jo.

I still couldn't get my head straight, but even in the fog I knew where Jo was headed. I tried to put it into words, to get the order straight in my mind. 'Wilkins kills his wife but gets away with it because he's hidden the body somewhere no one can find it.'

Jo finished her biscuit and took over the narrative for me. 'Karen, his bit on the side, gets suspicious, so he kills her.'

'Or...' I reached for another Hobnob, '... maybe he kills her because she's pregnant with his child, and he knows it looks bad.'

Col added the final act, his voice flat and monotone. 'Then, seventeen years later, Megan shows up, saying she knows the truth.'

I think we collectively caught our breath, because the air seemed to get sucked from the room.

'Which means,' said Jo, 'Wilkins killed Megan too.'

Chapter Thirty-Three

We talked on into the night. I didn't feel tired – the opposite. I felt wired, like I could run up a mountain. I knew we were close and I had a sense of my role in what was coming. I had a purpose, a way of atoning. The anticipation of it was like a drug.

'We have to prove Wilkins killed Megan, without anyone finding out about the blackmail,' said Col, as we drank our mugs of tea and Jo and I munched our way through the rest of the Hobnobs. 'It's just a question of how.'

'He's got away with murder three times.' That made him an impressive adversary. We couldn't underestimate him. 'We'll have to get him to confess,' I said at last. 'We need another set of wires.'

'He doesn't strike me as the confessional type,' said Jo.

'Slow down. I need to think about this,' said Col. 'I should pass it up the chain. Jesus, they're going to go ape.'

I punched the bag in the corner of the room a couple of times. 'You can't. If you tell your boss about Wilkins, you drop Megan in it. They'll want to know why she blackmailed him.'

'And what about Jack? What if his dad's killed him too?' Jo added.

'What are you suggesting?' asked Col. 'Turn up and say we

know you killed Megan?' He put a hand on my arm, and I stopped punching. 'He's never going to play ball.'

I could see the concern in his eyes. 'This is our case. We owe it to Megan.' We owed it to her son.

'You should go,' I said to Col as Jo took the mugs through to the kitchenette. 'The less you know the better. Give us forty-eight hours. If we haven't come back to you with proof, you can go to your boss with what we've told you.'

'I can't. I—'

'All right, twenty-four hours. One more night – if we don't come back with something …'

He touched my arm, and my skin goose-bumped. 'If anyone ever told me the job would get this complicated I'd never have signed up.'

'Why did you?' asked Jo, as she came back into the room.

Col turned to her. 'Failed my A levels. Needed to get out of Luton. Poxy place. Basically, it was the police force or the Army, and I knew I'd never be able to kill anyone.'

It didn't take long for the plan to form. If I'm honest it wrote itself. There was only one way forward, one clear path ahead, and the prospect of walking it thrilled me.

'I've got something for you,' Col said.

He lifted his shirt, the flesh on his stomach white and taut. I caught a glimpse of a scar on the left-hand side of his ribcage. I wanted to press my fingers against it. I hadn't had sex for months. Desire flashed through me, muscle memory. The body holds on to things the brain tries to forget. I heard the sound of plasters peeling off skin.

'Here,' he said. He handed Jo a wire, so small and neat it made the one we'd got from The Spy Shop look like a child's toy.

'You've been recording us?' I mentally flicked back through all the things we'd discussed, trying to assess how much trouble we could get into if the recording fell into the wrong hands.

'I wear it all the time, force of habit. It's not switched on, see.'

He showed Jo how to use it. 'It records to a remote machine, back at mine.'

At ten o'clock, Col ran us through the plan one last time, tested us on every part of it and declared himself satisfied. 'Want me to walk you home?'

'No.' I knew the word came out too loud because Col frowned at me. 'I'm not going home,' I said.

'We'll kip here tonight,' said Jo. 'Give us more time to prepare.'

Col glanced around the bare room. 'Where?'

'On the floor.' Jo stood up, stretched her arms above her head and yawned. 'I'll go get duvets and stuff.'

We wrote a quick list, and Jo left to collect the things we needed from the flat. Col and I went through to the front office, watched her leave. The door closed behind her and silence descended. The central heating was on too high. I was still hungry.

'Why don't you want to go home?'

'Nothing to do with this,' I said.

'OK.' He paused, and he was so close to me I could feel his breath on my face. 'This whole thing turns on trust,' he said.

I have issues with trust in intimate relationships: I don't need a psychology degree to know that. He followed me through to the back room. I picked up the mugs from the floor, took them to the sink. Came back and he hadn't moved. He stood there, with his arms folded, and I knew he was waiting for me to say something. To answer a question I didn't remember him asking. He stared at me until I couldn't bear it any longer.

'Someone showed up at my house earlier, someone from my past.'

'Who?'

'No one you know.'

'A bloke?'

'An old story.'

273

'Giving you trouble?'

I knew Col had jumped to the wrong conclusion, but I let it slide. Couldn't face the idea of telling him the truth, giving him a glimpse of my family. I didn't want him to think I wasn't trustworthy. I didn't want him to think I was fucked up.

'If you need someone to have a word …'

'It's not a problem,' I lied. I glanced around the room, unsure where to put myself. Having no furniture didn't help. I didn't know what to do with my arms. 'I just don't want to deal with it now. That's all.'

'I wouldn't blame him for persistence,' Col said. I didn't know what he meant. My radar was still off, my nervous system in overdrive.

I twisted my neck from side to side, my body felt like one of those metal cages they used to hang criminals in, back in the Middle Ages. The cold of the park had got into my bones, and even though the room was too hot I couldn't get warm. I could feel the frayed ends of my nerves, like a cat-o'-nine-tails.

'If he becomes a problem, let me know.' He put his hand on my arm, just gently on the side of my bicep. 'Some men need another man to tell them where to get off.'

It was a tempting thought. I screwed up my eyes and imagined Col frog-marching David out of my life, Col with a truncheon, and a policeman's hat, like a scene from a Punch and Judy show, pulling David along by the collar. If only it were that simple. I wondered whether Col had a uniform somewhere. He didn't look anything like a copper, in his faded Levi's and orange Caterpillar boots.

'Do you have a real life?' I asked. 'Like a wife and two-point-four kids?'

He smiled and shook his head. 'Couldn't do this job if I did. You've got to live it, otherwise it would do your head in.'

'What about your parents?'

He held my gaze. 'Luckily, I come from a really fucked-up family. I don't feel the need to visit them too often.'

274

That made me smile. I'd never heard anyone express it that way before. I tried the words out in my head. *Luckily, I come from a really fucked-up family.* I'd have to practise.

'When I go in, I go all in. Then I go to the next place. No ties.'

'Where is the next place?'

He shrugged his shoulders. 'Don't know. Wherever they send me.'

'Oh.' I jabbed at the punchbag, just gently with my right fist. The rhythm soothed me.

Col crossed the room and held the punchbag steady, so I could hit it with a bit more force. 'I'm getting too old,' he said. 'It's all right when you're young, but now …'

'You're not old.' I jabbed harder, the tension in my shoulders easing a fraction. I breathed deeper and threw more force behind the punches. My sleeve rode up, and I saw him catch sight of the scars on my arms. I'm used to that look, when people catch a glimpse. There's nothing I can do, nothing I can say. The past is another country; one I don't visit anymore.

'Keep thinking about finding a place I can settle.' His body swayed to absorb the swing of the bag.

When the connection is right, energy expands. I hit the bag square in the middle at just the right moment in time. Its momentum met the force of my punch, creating its own synergy. I hit it again. Harder.

'Used to dream about owning a ranch, somewhere like Montana or Colorado. These days I'd settle for a smallholding, somewhere I could keep chickens. The odd goat.'

'Odd goats are great company, I've heard.'

He grinned. 'Got to beat humans. One thing I've learned in this job is mankind ain't kind.'

'You probably see the worst of it.'

He made no comment.

I continued hitting harder each time, my knuckles warming against the hessian. He stepped backwards to allow the bag more room to swing. Every punch knocked him off balance, and there was something about that that I liked.

'I've been here nearly nine months, longest I've been anywhere since I was about 6.'

A bead of sweat flew from my head and splattered on the bag.

'I like Leeds.' I could see from his face that I was making him work hard now. 'It's true what they say about northerners.'

Did I want to know what they said about northerners? Probably not, but I was about to ask when the phone rang, and I jumped out of my skin.

I stopped punching and stood still. 'Who the fuck is that?' I asked Col, like he might have some idea.

He looked at me funny and said: 'Want me to answer it?'

'No, no, it's OK.' I hurried through to the outer office, rubbing my knuckles. It was too late for calls about water coolers. I swallowed, my hand poised in mid-air over the receiver. It rang another time. Col was in the doorway, watching me. I picked it up.

'No Stone Unturned,' I said into the receiver, steeling myself for his voice. Poised to slam the phone straight back down.

'Morning and evening, you said. That was the deal.'

It took me a moment to place the voice, but it wasn't David. I couldn't think who it was, but it wasn't David. I slumped over the desk.

'In this business all you have is your word.'

Sweat ran in rivulets down the side of my face. I wiped my forehead on my sleeve. 'I'm sorry.'

Martin Blink harrumphed down the phone.

'I was just about to ring,' I said. 'Sorry, it's been a mental day.'

'Go on then, tell me about it.'

I glanced across at Col. He had that puzzled look on his face, wanting to know who I was speaking to, whether it was connected. The sight of him helped me form sentences.

'I can't right now, I'm afraid. I've got a client with me.'

'At this time of night? Pull the other one.'

276

'No, I swear.'

'What client?'

The front door burst open, which gave me another shot of adrenaline. A hillock of duvets pushed their way into the room.

'I'll ring you back,' I said to Martin. 'Jo's just here. Give me half an hour.'

Jo and I tried to have a conversation through facial expression, me still holding the phone to my ear. Had she encountered anything, anything that wasn't supposed to be there? She shook her head at my unspoken question. I put my hand over the receiver and mouthed, 'Aunt Edie.'

'That's a promise?' said the voice on the phone.

'I've got to go.'

I allowed myself to breathe. Maybe David had got the message and that was the last I'd ever see of him. I forced my brain to embrace the possibility.

'Thirty minutes,' said Martin.

'Absolutely. Jo says hi.'

'Hi, Aunt Edie,' Jo shouted into the receiver as she put her armful of duvets on the desk. Col stepped forward to catch the penholder she knocked over.

'Who the bloody hell is Aunt Edie?' asked Martin.

I watched Jo step back outside.

'Speak soon, Auntie.' I put the receiver down and hurried after Jo, to help unpack the van. I don't know why I pretended that Martin was Aunt Edie, just that I didn't fancy explaining to an undercover copper that we'd made a deal with a journalist. Their driving principles seemed at odds with each other – Col wanted to keep things hidden, Martin wanted to expose.

'You OK?' asked Jo as she pushed a cardboard box into my hands.

'Kind of.' I don't like lying, even white lies. I believe truth runs like a river, and it's not a good idea to try to stem the flow. It only backs up and overwhelms you further downstream. 'No sign then?'

'No. Nothing.' Jo banged the van doors shut and locked them. She had an armful of pillows and a couple of carrier bags. We took it all into the office and unpacked. She'd brought my alarm clock, a couple of Ginsters cheese and onion pasties from the fridge and a rucksack full of random clothes. Everything you need for a sleepover.

'Who's Aunt Edie?' Col asked.

'Closest thing I have to a mother. Mad as a stick. Don't worry about her.'

'OK, well, I'd better let you two settle in,' Col said. 'Get some rest. And, listen, if you decide you don't want to go through with it, just give me a ring. We can think of something else.'

'I won't,' I said as I walked out the door with him. Jo stayed in the office, munching her pasty.

'You're an amazing woman,' he said as we hit the pavement.

'I'm really not.'

'Do me a favour?'

'What?'

'Find someone who deserves your anger. Don't turn it on yourself, Lee. There are enough good people suffering out there.'

I tugged at my sleeves. 'They're nothing – I was a kid. Stupid.'

'Anger's fuel. Use it to make the world a better place, a cleaner place.'

We stopped walking. There were a million stars splattered across the sky. I felt peaceful, knowing how small we were. How none of this mattered to the cosmos. It would go on regardless of what happened.

He put his hands in his pockets. 'Would you fancy a drink some time? With me, I mean?'

'Aren't you off to the next place?'

'Maybe.'

'Well, you know where I am,' I said. I tried to clear the frog in my throat. 'I'm not going anywhere.' I realized as I said that, that I meant it. Leeds is my home, which is weird, because it's

278

the first time in my life I've felt like I've had one. I knew then that I'd have to find a way of getting rid of David. I'd done running.

He leaned forward and kissed me, just above my lips. I felt the warmth of his breath, smelled mint and tobacco. I didn't move.

He put his hand on my waist, gentle, hardly touching.

'Ring me if you need me,' he called after me as I headed back to the office. 'You've got my number.'

Jo was watching me, so I rang Martin and gave him an update on what had happened. In truth there wasn't much I could tell him, but I did let him know that Karen Carpenter had died in suspicious circumstances.

'I missed that,' he said, and I knew he was pissed off.

'Happened out east,' I said. I could still feel the warmth of Col's hand imprinted on my waist. 'Probably didn't make the national news. We're going to try and find the others – the one who refused to speak to you back then. Maybe she'll have something to say now.' I told him we might also try to talk to Jayne's brother.

Lies. More lies. My insides churned. 'So I won't ring you in the morning, but I'll try and call tomorrow night. Late. OK?'

'I knew this one would come around again,' he said. 'I bloody knew it.'

Jo had put the duvets and blankets on the floor in the back room, and we lay down and slept until almost lunchtime on Tuesday. A full twelve hours. My body seemed to know what was coming, that it needed to recharge. I woke up five minutes before the alarm. I switched it off and lay on my back, thinking about the day ahead.

Col had got us Wilkins's home address with just one phone call. I thought about the kiss he'd given me. I'm not good at the physical. I'm not used to it. Sometimes I think I'm allergic to other people. That some kind of chemical reaction goes off in my skin. But he'd kissed me, and it hadn't hurt. I usually need to be pissed for that to be the case. I kicked the duvet off and sat up, rolled two cigarettes and blew on Jo's face. She rubbed at her nose in her sleep. I blew again.

'Get lost,' she said.

We didn't talk much as we got dressed. I folded the duvets away and made us both a cup of tea while Jo went to get the items we'd put on the shopping list.

While she was out, I rang Aunt Edie to ask how Brownie was doing. I could hear *The Archers* on in the background.

'Just cooking up some bone broth.'

'Bone broth? But he's vegan.'

'Put lead in his pencil. He's at the allotments with Joyce from number twelve, helping her turn her compost heap. Flora, bless her cottons, she went down to Sue Ryder's and picked him out some clothes.'

'He's not giving you any trouble?'

'Meek as a lamb.' She lowered her voice. 'But you should have heard him last night. Shouting out, screaming, yelling. All kinds of carry on. I had to sedate him.'

'*Sedate* him? With what?'

'Breaks your heart. But I told him, you'll find his friend for him. He needs his friend, Lee. He's not going to make it without Jack.'

'We'll do our best,' I said, but my words felt heavy. Since the previous night, I hadn't been able to shake the feeling that we might be too late to help Jack Wilkins.

Chapter Thirty-Four

I put the phone down on Aunt Edie and when Jo came back with a couple of shopping bags we checked the equipment and then packed it into knapsacks.

We filled the van with petrol on our way out of Leeds, Jo driving, taking the route into Alderley Edge that led us past Wheels Motor Sales. The signs were out on the forecourt, the flag flying. The king was in his castle. We didn't say a word to each other as Jo pressed on towards the village, my fingers on the road map, tracing the route.

Wilkins's house was set back from the road. After driving past it twice, we parked the van a couple of streets away and looped back on foot, Jo carrying the knapsack. He'd got a *Beware of the Dog* sign on the gate but, like many people, it told a lie. The gravel crunched beneath our feet as we made our way up the drive. It was four o'clock in the afternoon.

Breaking in was easy, despite the wealth of the place. You'd think he'd have been more concerned with security, but there was none. Not even a burglar alarm. Round the back of the house was a conservatory, wooden-framed, the paint peeling from the frame like chalk dust. Ivy and other creepers covered most of the windows. We had a quick look under the biggest stones and the

281

couple of ceramic pots that stood on either side of the back door, but no joy. I unzipped the bag while it was still on Jo's back and pulled out the crowbar and bolt cutters that Bobats stocked as a matter of course. Jo kept watch while I climbed onto an old chimney pot that had probably once contained flowers. I tucked the metal edge of the bar under the small window frame and levered. The first two didn't give and I had to clamber down and heave the chimney pot a couple of feet to the right. I climbed back up and was rewarded for my efforts. The third window groaned and splintered before it buckled and gave. As I opened it wide, the interior catch fell off and clattered onto the tiled floor inside. Jo was back by my side in an instant. She gave me a shoulder to stand on and from there I slithered through the gap. Like I said – a natural affinity for it. I crouched in the semi-gloom, waiting, listening.

Nothing.

It was darker inside than it was outside because the ivy covered so much of the glass. I gave it a minute, waited for my eyes to readjust. It was obvious that the conservatory hadn't been used in years, at least not in any conventional sense. A large wickerwork settee and matching armchairs were only just visible under piles of newspapers and hundreds of carrier bags. On the floor were several pots that seemed to contain only dead plants. I turned around. Once upon a time this would have been a lovely space, light and airy, overlooking the huge back garden. I could almost see the three of them, Nick, Jayne and Jack. Jack running in and out from the back garden while his mother made sandwiches and homemade lemonade, like something out of the Enid Blyton stories I used to devour in school. I felt a breath on the back of my neck and shuddered, then jumped a foot in the air as Jo banged on the window.

'Get a sodding shift on,' she mouthed through the glass.

I manoeuvred my way through the piles of cardboard boxes towards the door that led from the conservatory to the garden.

I could see scuffmarks on the paintwork. I saw the set of keys hanging on a rack to the left-hand side of the door and grinned. Wouldn't need the bolt cutters. I helped myself to the ring, and the second key I tried found its niche and twisted gently. The door groaned as I pushed it open. Jo winked at me. I stood aside and let her in, closing the door behind her.

There was a second door inside the dusty conservatory, which the first key on the ring opened. It led into the kitchen, a huge room that could have catered for scores of guests without any trouble; although I sensed it had been a long time since any kind of dinner party had been held. In contrast to the conservatory, it looked like this room was cleaned regularly, but it had a forlorn air, as if nothing ever happened.

We crept our way through the kitchen and into the large hallway. It was gloomy inside, so I pulled the torch from the bag and used the beam to point out to Jo a framed photograph on the wall at the bottom of the wooden staircase. I assumed it to be a picture of Jack with his mother. They were on a beach. She was wearing a summer dress that was blowing in the breeze, and the boy was laughing, his little hands clapped together. He looked 3, maybe 4 years old. Her hair swirled around her shoulders, and as she smiled at her young son, I was struck by what a good-looking woman she was. Nothing about her gave any sign of the tragedy to come.

Jo and I didn't speak as we scoped out the house. We'd agreed we'd start with the upstairs. We split up – Jo checked out the first room on the left and I inched my way into what was obviously the master bedroom. The walls were lined with black-and-grey striped wallpaper, and the sheets on the bed were black. The bed was made, which surprised me, but then I remembered the state of the kitchen. The guy had a cleaner. I hoped she worked mornings.

The master bedroom had a small shower room attached, again spotless. The maid or whoever obviously didn't consider the conservatory part of her domain. I turned and checked out every inch of his bedroom, opened each of the three drawers in the cabinet next to his bed, ran my hands under the mattress. Everything that Col had told me to do. There were two dozen pairs of highly polished shoes on shelves in one of the cupboards. Must attend a lot of weddings. Or funerals.

I found what I was looking for in the bottom of the last wardrobe, in a shoebox. I opened the lid and lifted out the gun. Heavy, cold. The weight of it surprised me. I didn't want to use it, but more than that, I didn't want Wilkins to use it. I stuffed it into the waistband of my trousers.

I joined Jo in the room next door. It contained a bed and a wardrobe but nothing else. The other two rooms on the other side of the landing were bare. Faint imprints in the carpet gave away the fact that furniture had been there once upon a time, but no longer.

'Find it?' asked Jo.

I nodded, and we made our way back down to the ground floor. Downstairs was a study, which was dark and masculine, with a large desk and piles of papers covering the floor. Next door to that was a room that contained a full-sized snooker table, the walls papered with a dark purple, embossed wallpaper – the kind you'd expect to see in a pub. We were in a museum, a house trapped in time. The huge front room had a carpet that was cream and green swirls, threadbare in places, with an exposed brick fireplace that took up the whole of one wall. There were two armchairs, opposite each other, one on either side of the fireplace and then two settees at the far end of the room.

'Where's best?' asked Jo.

'He's going to come in through the front door – no one's been round the back for years.'

'The hall?' she said.

'No. Let's stay here. Let him get settled.' It was obvious that was the room he used, apart from his bedroom and the study. I

284

noticed the ashtray on the table next to the armchair, and the newspaper on the floor. It must be odd living in a house this size on your own, I thought. I wondered what he did for food. I couldn't imagine him cooking in the huge kitchen.

We took a settee each, and lay for what seemed like hours, fighting the urge to smoke. I watched daylight drain from the sky. I hated the waiting. Hated the space in my brain for thoughts to creep in. I tried to keep it occupied by running through the sequence of events that had led us here, starting with 8 September 2000 when Jayne Wilkins hadn't gone to the cinema with a friend. We're all dancing to a tune that someone else set, whether we know it or not. Jack Wilkins's future was mapped out that night, and he wasn't even there. I thought of the boy in the photograph in the hall, frozen in time. Captured by fate.

'Jesus, how late does this guy work?' Jo stretched her legs up into the air.

'He's probably in the pub,' I said. 'Professor what's-his-face seemed to think he spent a lot of time in there.'

'Do you think we can risk one? In the back garden?' Jo asked for the thirtieth time. I was saved from saying 'no' for the thirtieth time by the sound of tyres on gravel.

We slid like eels from our respective settees and crawled to our positions. A moment later, a key in the door, a click, and a beam of light appeared around the edges of the living room door.

I listened to the heavy thump of his footsteps as he made his way down the corridor towards the rear of the house – the kitchen, I guessed. We heard a cupboard door, a crash of something. I crawled across the living room carpet and pulled myself to standing behind the door. My knees clicked as I straightened. I put my back against the wall, trying to use its coolness to instil a sense of calm into me. I slowed my breathing, trying to trick my body into believing it was relaxed.

I strained to hear the noises, thought I heard the sound of

285

glass hitting glass. Bollocks, he was going to sit in the kitchen. I chewed my lip. I couldn't see Jo now, it was too dark, so I couldn't guess what she was thinking. Questions tumbled through my brain as I stood there, flexing my fingers. How long do we wait it out? Should we sneak upstairs to the bedroom, wait for him there? All the while, the thrill of being the stalker, of being the one that knew something the other didn't, made my nerves tingle. I felt more alive, more in control than ever before.

I ducked to my knees, ready to inch my way across the room to Jo, to formulate a new plan, when I heard his footsteps, back down the corridor, lighter than before. I held my breath as he opened the door and stepped into the front room, his back to me. A chunk of light from the hallway spilled in behind him. I watched him place a bottle on top of the piano, then duck to switch on the standard lamp.

As light flooded the room, Jo sat up straight in the armchair. I knew she was trying hard not to blink. With the back of my heel I closed the door behind him. It made a noise as it clicked shut, and he turned from Jo to me. I pulled the Glock I'd recovered from his wardrobe from the waistband of my trousers. I pointed it at him and gave a short wave with my left hand.

'Me again.'

He placed the glass he was carrying onto the table next to the armchair, a reaction I knew was instinctive. He wanted his hands free. He reminded me of the bare-knuckle fighters that hang out at my local gym, their hands twitching.

'The fuck are you doing here?' he said.

'I've a few more questions.' I licked my lips.

'You've a hell of a nerve.'

I considered this. Ran a full body check. I surprised myself, but my nerves were holding steady. I was fairly certain I could take him, even without the gun in my hands, whatever mode of combat he chose. His time had been and gone. I knew it and I knew he knew it too, although I guessed he'd rather die than admit it.

'Want to tell us about your wife?'

He didn't move. Stock still, staring at me like he wanted to tear me to pieces. 'Get out.'

I moved my left foot so that I was standing with my feet hip-width apart. I spread my weight, feeling my centre of balance ground down through the soles of my feet.

'Do you care that no one knows where your son is?'

'You've got five seconds,' he said. 'Get out.'

'Bit of a coincidence, wouldn't you say?'

'Yes,' said Jo, raising one eyebrow like she was Miss frigging Marple. Wilkins turned his head towards Jo, giving her the same stare he'd been giving me. Jo didn't flinch, and I knew she was feeling the same way I was. I can't really describe the atmosphere in the room. It was like someone had plugged the floorboards into an electrical current. I'd never felt so powerful in my whole life, and I know Jo felt it too.

Jo said: 'People might say a missing wife was unfortunate, but a missing wife AND a missing son. That smacks of something else.'

'Piss off,' Wilkins said, clenching his fists at his side. I kept the gun trained on his upper body.

'You don't care where your son is?' said Jo.

'Why should I?' he said. 'Only ever turns up when he wants something.'

'What about your wife?' asked Jo. 'Is she ever going to turn up?'

'Doubt it.'

'Because you killed her?'

'Because it's been a long time since she disappeared – seventeen years – probably about the same time you were born.'

'Funny man,' I said. I moved a step away from the door, so that I was standing directly behind him, four or five paces. He'd

287

turned his whole body to face Jo, and I kept the gun trained on the area between his shoulder blades. 'Glad you can joke about it.'

'The police think you've killed her.'

'Who told you that?'

'We've made extensive enquiries.'

'You've been talking to Peter bloody Partingdon.'

Jo glanced past Wilkins to make eye contact with me. Neither of us liked the fact he got it in one.

'Old queen,' Wilkins continued, and I know he liked the fact he'd got a bit of an edge on us. 'Came onto me, pissed as a coot. I told him where he could put it. He tells anyone that'll listen that I'm responsible for killing Jayne. Bullshit.'

'You were willing to pay twenty-four grand to stop people asking questions,' Jo reminded him.

The pendulum on the balance of power swung back towards us. I watched Wilkins struggle to work out how we'd found out that bit of information.

'You're playing with fire.'

'Why would someone with nothing to hide pay twenty-four grand to keep someone quiet? You've got to admit, that looks bad.'

I let Jo do the talking, wanted to keep myself focused on his reactions, his body language. I knew he was looking for the opportunity to bring us down, and I wasn't going to let him find it.

'I paid because I figured Jack was behind it, and I figured he must need the cash. If he needs cash that bad, he can have it.'

'You'd let your own son blackmail you?'

'Always knew he blamed me. Who else is going to come round here with that kind of a bullshit story?'

'Your son thinks you killed his mother.' Jo crossed her legs and adjusted her position in the chair. 'What does that say about you?'

'He never would talk about it.'

'How did you kill her?' Jo asked. 'Jack thinks it was a car crash. But it can't have been, because they never found the body.'

Nick's shoulders slumped, and he shook his head. He put an arm out, steadied himself against the back of the other armchair. He looked old, suddenly. Weak. 'Christ, I've let so much …' He didn't finish the sentence. Instead he picked up his glass and necked the contents.

Jo hadn't had a fag for over four hours and the lack of nicotine was making her cranky. 'Why don't you just do us all a favour and come clean?'

'I can't believe he can remember that. He can't have been more than three.'

'So there was a car crash? You fixed the brakes?' I raised my voice, remembering the wire taped inside Jo's bra. I wanted the confession, loud and clear and unequivocal.

Wilkins took a step towards Jo. 'By the time I realized he blamed me, it was too late.'

'Stay where you are,' I said. 'Don't go any closer. In fact, take a seat.' I gestured to the armchair opposite Jo.

Wilkins didn't appear to hear me. In fact, he seemed lost, trapped in a world we didn't inhabit. 'And he's right,' he said, his voice so quiet I had to strain to hear him. 'What the hell, he's going to get it sooner than he thinks. No one else to leave it to.'

'So you did kill her?' said Jo.

My arms were tiring of holding the gun, and I realized I hadn't considered how long I could stand in this position with my arms outstretched. I needed to rest my arms on something. I glanced around the room.

'I figured if I turned up with the cash, it would be a good chance for us to have a chat, clear the air.' Wilkins stood still. 'You know, the last seventeen years, that's all anyone's ever thought about me – there's the guy who got away with murdering his wife.'

'How did you kill her?' I asked. 'With this?'

He turned and looked at me like he'd forgotten I was in the room. 'What?'

I pulled a face and raised the point of the Glock so that it was aiming directly at his head. Power surged through my veins as my finger clenched against the trigger. I spoke slowly, made sure he knew that I was losing patience. 'Why have you got a gun?'

He showed me the palms of his hands. 'OK. I'm not Mother Theresa. In my line of business there are a lot of dodgy characters. I got robbed, four times in three months. Bought it for protection. Never used it.'

'You admit you have a gun?' I said for the benefit of the wire.

He frowned at me. His body language had changed, like some of the air had been let out of him. He looked like an old man, a tired, old man. When he spoke, his tone was more conciliatory, like he wanted us to start over. 'What's all this got to do with you two?'

I think Jo must have caught the change in atmosphere because she flipped him a business card. 'We're private investigators.'

He took it off her, read it and frowned at me. 'Investigating what?'

'Jack's disappearance.'

'He's really disappeared?'

'We were hired to find him.'

'By who?'

The muscles in my forearms burned. 'Sit,' I said. 'And that's the last time I'm going to ask nicely.'

He thought about it for a moment then lowered himself down into the armchair opposite Jo. 'If Jack's missing, how do you know he thinks his mother died in a car crash?'

'His girlfriend told us.'

'He has a girlfriend?' He sounded surprised, like the possibility had never occurred to him. 'The one who came for the cash?'

'No,' I said. 'Not her. Did you see her?'

'I didn't, but I got someone to watch the drop and then follow whoever picked up the money. Got as far as Leeds then lost her. I figured that proved it was Jack. Last I heard he was in Leeds.'

If Wilkins had had someone follow Megan to Leeds, it added weight to the theory that he had killed her.

'What's she like? This girlfriend?' he asked, like that was more important than the money. If I didn't know better, I'd have said he sounded pleased.

'Feisty, curly-haired, freckles.'

He paused to consider this for a moment. I took my chance to sneak a glance at Jo. She raised a questioning eyebrow and plucked her tobacco tin from the top pocket of her jacket.

'He's not gay.' Wilkins smiled for the first time, and when he did I caught a glimpse of the younger man, the ladies' man he'd once been. 'Think she'd meet me?'

'I'd advise against that,' I said, keeping the gun trained on him. 'Women have a habit of disappearing when they're with you.'

He smiled again, this time a tired smile. 'Steady, Eddie. One woman.' He held up his forefinger. 'One woman disappeared. But Jack's right. I'm to blame.'

I almost squealed. I pictured the smile on Col's face, back at his house, listening to this.

'What about Karen?' Jo asked as she sealed her cigarette. She tossed it across the room to me and I caught it with my left hand.

'Who?'

'Karen Carpenter.'

'What the hell has she got to do with this?'

Jo added another pinch of tobacco to a cigarette paper. 'You killed your wife and then you killed Karen.'

'I didn't kill my wife.'

'You just admitted it.'

'I said I was to blame, I didn't say I killed her.'

I frowned at Jo. She shrugged her shoulders like she didn't know what he was on about either.

'Come again?'

291

Wilkins sighed. 'Want a proper one?' He flicked a packet of Embassy Number 1s from his shirt pocket and patted a couple out. Jo shook her head and continued to roll her own. Wilkins lit one and drew heavily. 'Here's the truth,' he said. He paused, and we waited. He exhaled a cloud of smoke and then took another drag. 'My wife, may she rest in peace, killed herself.'

I didn't believe him.

'I came back from work and found her. She hanged herself, in the garage, left a note on the kitchen table.'

'Suicide?' Megan's body in the bath floated before my eyes. 'Yeah, right.'

'Because of your affairs?' asked Jo.

'She'd either be the happiest woman alive or the darkest. Never knew which one you'd get.'

Jo lit her own cigarette, and I prayed for her to toss the lighter over to me. She didn't, instead placing it on the coffee table in front of her. Wilkins continued, his words flat and monotone. I reminded myself to focus, to concentrate only on Wilkins. He was scrabbling for an exit.

'There was a car crash,' he said.

I must have made a sound because he looked over at me.

'Before Jayne died. A year or more before. She hit a motorbike, down on Princess Parkway. She didn't stop.'

'Why not?'

'Don't know. Panicked, I guess. Jack was with her, in the car. She could never deal with the bad stuff. Would go nuts if she trod on a snail.' He ran a hand through his hair, and I had the idea he wasn't talking to us anymore, was hardly aware we were in the room. 'I went to the police. Said I'd been driving, that I'd had a drink and that's why I hadn't stopped. Luckily the guy she hit wasn't seriously hurt. I got disqualified – six months.'

'Very big of you,' said Jo. 'But why should we believe you?'

'No reason to lie.'

'Everyone has a reason to lie.'

'I want to show you something,' he said. 'In my study.'

'No chance,' I said. 'You're staying right there.'

'OK. Well, you go,' he said to Jo. 'On the right-hand side of the desk is a green folder, bring it here.'

Jo glanced at me. I shrugged.

Jo pulled herself out of the armchair and made her way to the door. As soon as she'd vacated her chair, I lowered myself into it. I crossed one leg over the other and used them to balance the gun. My forearms weakened with relief. Jo returned less than thirty seconds later holding the file. She offered it to Wilkins, but he shook his head.

'You read it.'

Jo frowned at me in her chair and went to sit on the sofa. She held the file like an unexploded bomb in front of her. 'What is it?' she asked.

'Read it.'

Jo opened the file, scanned the first few pages. Impatience sandpapered me.

'What?' I said.

Jo didn't say anything. Wilkins was the one to speak. 'I've got cancer, not the good kind, diagnosed just before Christmas. It's all in there.'

I stared at Jo, but she had her head bent as she read, so she didn't see the questions I was trying to get her to answer. Where was he going with this? I felt sweat trickle down the gap between my shoulder blades.

'Nothing they can do,' Wilkins continued. 'All the money in the world don't help you if there's nothing to buy.'

Jo stopped reading and nodded across to me.

I turned to Wilkins, unsure of what to say. There's times when I've thought knowing you were going to die must be the most liberating feeling in the world. I didn't feel like that as Wilkins stared at me.

'I've nothing left to play for.'

293

'Does Jack know?' asked Jo.

'He's hardly likely to want to make up with the person who killed his mother,' I said.

'For the last bleeding time, I didn't kill her.'

'She committed suicide,' I said. I paused then shook my head. 'Bollocks.'

'If you didn't kill her, why didn't you tell Jack the truth?' asked Jo, her voice softer. 'Why didn't you tell everyone the truth?'

'He was 5 years old. You can't tell a 5-year-old kid their mother committed suicide.'

'Better than thinking—'

'She wanted to be the best. The best mother. Jack adored her. She lit up rooms, like sunshine had just walked in. I loved her, Christ knows I did, but I never knew her.'

'You contributed to the myth,' said Jo. 'Taking the blame in the car crash, not telling Jack the truth about her death.'

'Hang on,' I said.

'After she died, there's whole years I can't remember. Numbed the pain.' He gestured towards the bottle of whisky. 'Sent Jack away. Couldn't face him, couldn't face the lost, fucking haunted look in his eyes. It was like looking at her. I hated her for years after. If she could do that, take herself from me, from Jack, from the family ...'

No one spoke. Wilkins poured himself another measure of whisky. The light above swirled through it, making it look like honey.

'You're three times more likely to commit suicide if your mother did. You know that?'

I flinched but didn't answer. I've fought really hard not to believe in destiny, can't bear the thought we're all hapless hamsters on some monstrous wheel of life, pre-programmed to repeat the sins of our parents. I shook the words from my head and reached for the lighter that Jo had dropped on the coffee table.

'And now you want him to know the truth?' There was more

venom behind the words than I'd intended, but once I'd started I couldn't stop. 'So you can die with a clean conscience and he can spend the rest of his life trying to work out whether you're telling him a pack of complete lies in order to make yourself feel better?'

I don't know whether it was the smoke, but my eyes stung. Wilkins rubbed his face. When he spoke, his voice was quieter.

'I want to say goodbye.'

'I get that,' said Jo.

I glowered at her. She pulled a face at me, like what did I expect, and I knew she was falling for his bullshit.

'Oh, come on,' I said. 'You can't—'

Wilkins continued like I hadn't spoken. 'I always thought there'd be time to clear the air. One day. In the future. I tell you one thing, being told you're going to die brings the whole damned thing into focus.'

'You can prove she committed suicide?' I said.

'As a matter of fact,' he said, hauling himself up on the arms of his chair, 'I can.'

Chapter Thirty-Five

The room went quiet, and I became aware of the clock ticking on the mantelpiece. It was pitch-dark outside, and I knew we should pull the curtains, but I didn't want to take my eyes off Wilkins. Standing up he loomed over me in my armchair, but a gun in your hands makes you feel big, whatever the perspective. I comforted myself with the thought that the house was set so far back from the road that even if someone did walk past they wouldn't be able to see in.

'I kept the note,' he said. 'Insurance policy. Knew that if push ever came to shove, I wasn't going to prison. They were screwed, without a body – couldn't even say for certain she was dead.'

'Where is her body?' As I said the words, I realized we'd overlooked the garage. As soon as the thought hit me, I checked myself. Seventeen years, for God's sake. She couldn't still be there.

'I knew if they ever did find her, forensics would probably be able to establish how she died. If they didn't, I had her note.'

Jo stood up, Wilkins's medical file discarded on the settee. 'Let's see,' she said.

'This way.'

He led the way through to his study, Jo followed him, I brought up the rear. This time in his study I noticed the bookshelves that lined one long wall. As he took a key from a pot on the mantel-piece and opened a cabinet on the left-hand side of his desk, I saw Jo checking out the spines of some of his books. I kept my gaze on Wilkins, watched as he opened the cabinet. Over his shoulder I could see that it was stuffed, I mean completely stuffed, with files. He put armloads onto his desk and shuffled through them. It took him a few minutes to find what he was looking for, but when he did, he passed it to me without reading it, his hands trembling.

It was a sheet of paper, writing paper, the posh kind – thick with a watermark running through. I swallowed and forced myself to read the delicate, loopy writing.

My dear, darling Nick

I'm so sorry but I can't do this anymore. I've had a headache for what feels like forever, I can't sit still and I can't turn off the noise. I'm exhausted and I can't sleep. I'm doing what seems the best thing to do, for me, for you, for Jack, for everyone.

I can't hang around spoiling your life any longer. Please understand that I have to do this now, while he's still young enough to forget.

Darling, darling man, please, please make sure he always knows that I love him – more than life. Don't let him know about the end. I want him to remember me on my best days, not my worst.

All my love, always, all days

Jayne

I licked my lips and swallowed but there was no saliva in my mouth. I passed the note to Jo, but she'd already read it over my shoulder. Wilkins perched against his desk, his arms folded across his chest. Jo took a seat on the high-backed, black leather office chair.

297

'She'd planned it all,' said Wilkins. 'Arranged for Jack to go to a friend's house for the night. Took him to school then rang me. I drove home, hell for leather, found the note on the table. She hanged herself with a length of washing line.'

'Christ,' said Jo.

'Had scratch marks all round her neck. Like she'd been clawed by a tiger. If I'd found her … if I'd got there quicker, if I hadn't wasted time searching the house … It was pissing with rain. I remember sitting in the drive, soaked to the skin, bawling like a kid.'

I saw the glisten of tears in his eyes. I couldn't bring myself to say anything. I hadn't spoken to my mother for weeks before she died, and she didn't leave a note. At that moment, seeing the look on Wilkins's face, I didn't know whether to be angry or grateful.

'I had a boat, a little spot in North Wales,' said Wilkins. 'We'd go there for weekends, mostly before Jack was born. I cut her down with the garden shears, wrapped her in bed sheets, laid her down on the back seat of the car. Sailed out for the last time. I weighted her down and dropped her over the side.'

'And her body never washed up?' Jo asked.

'No.'

I hate people who commit suicide. In my eyes, it's the ultimate shirk of responsibility. Jo gives me hell for it, says it's an illness, not a choice, but I can't bring myself to see it that way.

'The thing is with hindsight,' Wilkins said. 'You look back and it seems like you had a plan. But I didn't. I just reacted to a series of off-the-wall events. I thought the police would realize what she'd done. I even thought they might agree to keep it secret, to not let Jack know. I had crazy ideas.'

'How come they didn't find the suicide note?' Jo said. 'They must have searched the house for her.'

'They did. Turned the place upside down. But it wasn't here. I left it in the boat. They never found out about the boat. They concentrated on the cars. And that was a weird thing: when they searched the lot, they found a note on my desk. "Ring the missus, at home". Billy, one of the lads that worked for me, had left it. And on it, he'd written "Friday, 4.15 p.m.". Now I don't know how that got there, cos obviously she was dead by then. Maybe it was from the week before, maybe he'd got the day wrong. But when the police spoke to him, he was convinced he'd spoken to her on that Friday. And that saved me because they decided that at 4.15 p.m. she was alive and at home.'

'Billy was covering for you.'

'I don't know. He never said a word about it. But it meant I had an alibi. I drove back to Manchester. Couldn't bear to be alone. Went to the pub with the lads, got pissed, ended up crashing on Billy's settee. Went straight from there the next morning to pick up Jack. So, the police decided that even if she was dead, I couldn't have killed her.'

Truth is a strange thing. You can be told a lie and not know whether it's true or not, but when the truth is spoken, it's impossible to avoid. It has a ring to it that can't be faked. I hated admitting it, but I knew in my heart that Wilkins was telling the truth.

'Shit,' said Jo, spinning her chair from side to side. 'We're back to the beginning.'

A man rich enough to buy anything but couldn't make his wife stay. My mother didn't choose to die, but she didn't choose to live either. She surrendered after my dad went, and I grew up with the knowledge I was never enough to make her happy. I never filled the gap. There was always something missing for her, a hurt she clung to.

'Didn't …' said Jo. It's not often Jo's lost for words. She kept opening her mouth to say something and then thinking better of it. 'Didn't Jack ever ask you what happened?'

'Not in so many words,' said Nick.

'"Not in so many words"?' said Jo. Jo has a great relationship with her mother, even though they argue from time to time. Jo doesn't really get how some families don't talk about stuff.

'I said maybe she'd had an accident, lost her memory.'

Jo's forehead creased, and she spun the chair harder.

'He was 5 years old.' Wilkins sounded defensive.

'But isn't keeping alive the idea she might come back worse than telling him she's dead?'

I felt sorry for Jo, for her inability to grasp how dysfunctional families operate. Wilkins sighed, the air rushing out of him. He looked old again, beaten by life.

'And you've not talked about it since?'

Even I wished Jo would quit with the questions. He'd told her they didn't talk about it. As if he sensed I was more of a kindred spirit, Wilkins turned to me and said: 'What would you have done?'

I couldn't answer that one. I put the gun down on the sideboard and checked whether the cupboard was strong enough to hold my weight. It was, so I sat myself on it. No one spoke. In the silence we heard a noise, a muffled bang, and Jo and I both started.

'The boiler,' said Wilkins. 'On its last legs.'

Jo and I stared at each other. I knew we were both thinking the same thing. What the fuck next? Wilkins turned his back to us, began scooping up his papers and stuffing them into the cabinet.

'Before Jack was born, we'd managed. She'd always been a bit off the wall, but nothing like the problems after. Christ, I was scared to come home.'

I knew what that felt like too. Memories of hanging around after school, making the walk home last as long as it possibly could, anything to avoid the heaviness of home.

'I didn't want people to point the finger at me,' Wilkins said. 'There's the guy who couldn't make his wife happy.' He stuffed another pile of paperwork back into the cupboard and then turned to face us. 'We didn't know as much about it in those days.'

'"It"?' I said.

Jo's always faster at getting this kind of stuff than me. 'Postnatal depression,' she said.

I didn't know much about that. Perhaps I didn't want to. I carry enough guilt about my mother, I don't need any more. Besides, postnatal depression has to wear off eventually, surely?

I dropped my own problems from my mind, focused on Wilkins's. 'Jack deserves to know what happened.'

Wilkins shook his head at me, like he felt sorry for my ignorance. 'You think truth is objective. That's because you're young.'

'What about Karen?' asked Jo.

'Karen?' He checked his watch. 'You mean Karen Calvert? What about her?'

'Karen Carpenter.'

'She's Karen Calvert now. Has been for—'

'Were you the father of her baby?'

'Karen's baby?' He finished stuffing papers into his cabinet and turned back to face us. 'Where did—?'

'She was pregnant when she died,' I said.

'Who told you that?'

I glanced over at Jo. Again, I had the feeling the facts were running away from us, sprinting from sight.

'Karen isn't dead,' Wilkins continued. 'Least not as far as I know, and I'm sure I would have heard.'

'She died in a lake,' said Jo, but I could tell by her voice she'd also lost the certainty we'd arrived with.

'When?'

Jo glanced at me. I shrugged my shoulders. 'Seventeen years ago.'

'Well, someone needs to tell Eric.'

'Eric?'

'Her husband. I saw him not that long ago. Never said anything

301

about her being dead.' His forehead scrunched as he tried to remember the details. 'They'd just got back from Spain. Andalusia, I think he said. All five of them.'

I shook my head. 'She died in a car crash, in East Yorkshire, years ago—'

'She married Eric Calvert, not long after Jayne died. I was invited to the wedding. Didn't go.'

A sick feeling hit my stomach. 'What about children? Did they—?'

'Three. All boys. Who told you she was dead? Peter bloody Partingdon? He's getting worse, certi-bloody-fiable.'

Jo did a 360-degree turn in the chair, then slapped her own leg. 'The tail.' She looked my way first, then back to Wilkins. 'What about the guy that followed us?'

'What guy?'

'When we left you, on Saturday, you followed us.'

He nodded at me. 'She mentioned Jack. I wanted to talk to you, that's all.'

'And you had someone else follow behind, a Volvo,' said Jo. I breathed a sigh of relief. His accomplice.

'Navy blue Volvo?'

'Yes.' We both shouted the word out. For one glorious moment it felt like we were all on the same page.

'Who's he and why was he carrying a gun?' asked Jo.

'No idea,' said Wilkins. 'Nothing to do with me.'

But he'd given himself away. I grabbed the realization, swung on it like Tarzan through the jungle. I couldn't keep the excitement from my voice. 'Then how did you know the Volvo was navy blue?'

But Wilkins's voice remained steady, even. 'Because I saw it. I've seen it a few times. It's been at the garage, here, followed me to the pub the other night. Thought it was something to do with you two.'

'It wasn't your gun?' I picked up the Glock and waved it in his direction.

'Where did you get that?' he asked, like he was seeing it for the first time.

'You know where. Your wardrobe.'

He frowned, and I knew either his confusion was genuine, or he was one of the best liars I'd ever come across, and I've come across a few.

'That's not my gun.'

'You admitted it,' I said. I looked to Jo for confirmation. She nodded. 'You admitted you'd got a gun. For protection, you said.' I wondered whether to tell him Jo was wearing a wire, that it was too late for him to start changing his story.

'I do have a gun. But it's not that one.' He turned back to his desk, ducked down to open the bottom drawer on the right-hand side, scooped out a pile of envelopes and a large wooden box. The top fell off the box and landed on the floor, and I caught a glimpse of jewellery inside. I jumped down off the sideboard and moved a step closer to him, my fingers tight on the trigger.

'Pull the other one,' Jo said but her voice sounded less full of bravado than it had before.

He emptied the contents of the box onto the desk. 'I swear to you. That's not my gun. Never seen it before.'

'So, where's your gun?'

'That's a funny thing,' he said. 'Not here.'

'What?'

He swivelled round to face us, holding the wooden box in his hands. He tipped it to towards us, to show us its green velvet lining and its lack of contents. 'It's not here. I keep it in this box. Someone's nicked my gun.'

Chapter Thirty-Six

As the three of us stood there, arranged in a triangle, each trying to make sense of the new facts that kept popping up like lottery balls, the study door pushed open. It took my brain a few seconds to work out what my eyes were seeing. My skin goose-bumped.

'Col.'

He was wearing the same clothes he'd been wearing the night before. I wondered whether he ever slept. He flashed his police badge at Wilkins. 'I can take over from here,' he said.

I tried to wipe the smile from my face. His baggy blue jumper was too long in the sleeve, so came down to his knuckles, leaving just his fingers exposed.

'What are you doing here? I thought ...'

He crossed the room towards me, kissed me on the cheek, like we were an old married couple and he'd just got in from work. He slipped the Glock from my fingers.

'I was worried,' he said. 'Wasn't fair of me to let the two of you handle this on your own.'

I shook my head, realized Col had some catching up to do. 'He didn't do it. He didn't kill his wife.' I turned to look at Wilkins who had returned to perching on the desk. The old man had his

304

arms folded again, his shirtsleeves pushed up his forearms. 'And if he didn't kill Jayne, why would he kill Megan?'

'Who's Megan?' Nick Wilkins asked.

Col ignored him and spoke to me. 'That can't be, Lee. He paid the ransom. Men like him don't hand over that kind of cash unless they've got something to hide.'

'He thought it was Jack.' I glanced over at Jo. Why wasn't she saying anything?

Col kept the Glock trained on Wilkins. 'Let's go into the front room. See if we can sort this out. It's comfier in there.'

Jo got up from her chair, still without speaking, and led the way across the hall. I followed, Nick behind me. We were like school children, allowing ourselves to be herded. Col brought up the rear, still holding the gun. Once we were all in the front room, he closed the door behind him.

'I don't buy it,' he said.

Jo retrieved her roll-up from the ashtray on the coffee table. She lit it again and retook her place on the settee. Wilkins returned to his armchair.

'What kind of car do you drive?' he asked Col.

'I don't,' said Col. 'Prefer public transport.'

'You lied about Karen,' Jo said. I hated her for pointing that out. I scrambled for explanations. Maybe there were two Karens. It was feasible. Col pulled at a stray piece of wool from the sleeve of his jumper.

'Where's the rest of the team?' asked Wilkins.

'He's dying,' I said. 'Jo's seen his medical notes.'

'Never known a copper come to a bust single-handed.' Nick crossed to the window and flicked back the curtain. I wondered who'd drawn them. They'd been open the last time we'd been in this room. I realized it must have been Col. 'Didn't hear any cars pull up.'

'I guess you could call me off-duty,' Col said.

'That a fact?'

'Wanted to keep an eye on these two. See, they thought they could handle you. Get a confession, get you behind bars, where you belong.'

'You're being set-up,' Nick said to me and Jo.

Still Jo didn't say anything, but from the expression on her face she didn't have to.

'I know a copper gone bad when I see one,' Wilkins continued.

I glanced at Col. 'You mean—?'

'Ignore him,' said Col. 'We're not listening to the word of a man who killed his own wife.'

'I can prove I didn't.'

'He's got her suicide note,' I said. The curtains made no sense. Why would Col draw the curtains?

'Faked.'

'I've got dozens of letters she wrote me, her signature on the deeds of the house, our marriage certificate, a couple of her diaries. Forensics will prove it's her handwriting.'

My mouth had gone so dry my teeth stuck to my lips. I tried to align myself with the new facts. Jayne killed herself, Karen wasn't dead. That left me with two pieces of jigsaw that didn't seem to fit with the new picture. I stared at Col, remembered standing so close to him last night.

'Who killed Megan?'

'You're looking at him,' said Jo.

I kept my eyes on Col. 'Am I?' I asked him.

Col sighed. 'I knew this was too good to be true.'

'What was?' asked Wilkins.

'Thought my luck had turned. If they could prove you'd killed your wife, this would be plain sailing. But you couldn't pull it off, could you?'

'Because he didn't kill his wife,' muttered Jo. She stood up, moved towards the coffee table; I think to flick the ash from her roll-up into the ashtray.

'It's true, isn't it?' I said. I sat down in the armchair, because

306

all of a sudden, I wasn't sure whether my knees would hold me up. 'You killed Megan.'

'Luckily, there is a plan B.' Col moved the Glock to his left hand and, with his right, pulled a second gun out of the inside of his jacket pocket.

'That's my gun,' said Nick.

'You can have it back, soon as I'm finished with it.' Col turned, raised his right arm, extended it forward and shot Jo.

That moment is preserved in slow motion in my brain, like a clip from a film. I can replay it over and over, a millisecond at a time. I can see everything. The confusion on Jo's face as Col points the gun at her. Her step backwards which knocks her into the coffee table. Her stumble, the bloom of red on her shoulder. Her fall to the ground. Nick's roar that reverberates as the scene plays out. I can see the whisky bottle on the coffee table. It tips but stays upright. I watch Nick catapult himself out of the armchair and across the room. He launches himself horizontally towards the gun, while my brain scrabbles to reclassify Col as bent cop. Cold-blooded killer.

Jo hit the floor, her body twisted at an angle that was just plain wrong. Nick was too slow, too old, but I was amazed by his fearlessness. He struck Col with all his body weight – charged him like a battering ram. Col toppled backwards, trying to keep Nick back with his right arm. He dropped the Glock, and it hit the carpet. I saw Col kick at it, and it disappeared under the sofa. I think I remained seated, frozen, my brain stretched with the effort of keeping up with the pictures in front of me, the two men grappling like sumo wrestlers. Nick had the size and height advantage, but Col was younger, fitter.

Then something snapped.

I fired from my chair. Rage, like rocket fuel, propelling me forward. I hit Col from the rear, kicked him in the ribs, low enough to hurt his liver. I saw Nick's gun drop to the floor, and I managed to get a foot to it, kicked it backwards along the carpet, out of the immediate area. Nick was on top of Col now and I crumpled with them, my left leg trapped under Col's body.

I think I took an elbow to the face. I shut my eyes to block the pain. I heard a shot, and I wondered how. I'd seen both guns leave Col's hands. Nick slumped, became a dead weight. The pain in my left leg got worse. I felt the warmth of wetness seep into my jeans.

I grabbed the armchair leg and tried to extricate myself, my mind only on Jo. I had to get to her, help her, make sure she was all right. But I wasn't quick enough, because Col grabbed me by the throat.

'Not so fast.'

'You fucking bastard,' I screamed. 'If you've—'

He pulled his arm back and slapped my face. So hard I felt my teeth move. He spoke slowly. One word at a time. 'Shut. The. Fuck. Up.'

He was on top of me, but the lower half of his body was still underneath Nick. He struggled to push Nick's body off him, and he crawled his way off me. He pulled himself up to standing, and I saw the gun in his hand. Another gun? I couldn't keep track. I sat up, the left-hand side of my face burning.

'You'll never get away with this.'

'Only one way to find out.' He grinned at me. In that moment he was the most beautiful ugly man I'd ever laid eyes on.

'You're going to kill me?' OK, I'd cottoned on to the fact he wasn't the man of my dreams. Hell, I'd even reconciled myself to it. It's not like he was the first man to not live up to expectations. But had I got last night that wrong?

'I didn't kill you,' said Col. 'He did.' He used his gun to point at Nick's lifeless form. 'I came to your rescue, soon as I got wind of your plan. But, sadly, I was too late.' He took one of the fags that Nick had left on the coffee table and lit it. I thought I noticed a tremble in his hands, but it may have been me. 'Tragic. But at least a murder got solved.'

'Which one?' I'd been right. Knowing you're about to die is liberating.

'Good question. Four murders got solved. Four for the price of one. Jayne, Megan, your good friend over there, and last but not least, you.'

'What about Jack?'

'Your guess is as good as mine. Who gives a shit? He's a junkie. No one cares.'

'Karen?'

'Sorry.' He paused to take a drag on his cigarette. 'I told a lie.'

'You're insane.'

'Thought you'd like it, given your history.'

I glared at him.

'I checked you out, Lee. Know all about your shitty family. You can run, Lee, but you'll never hide.'

'You utter bastard.'

'Not me, him.' He gestured at Nick's corpse. 'Brute of a man. Getting away with murder all this time. I'm the hero. Tragically a bit too late to actually save anyone, but still a hero for trying.'

'Why'd you kill her?'

'Why d'you think? Come on, you're the fucking investigator.'

'She was on to you. Knew you'd got involved in something.'

'There you go. Not just a pretty face.'

'She was going to turn you in.'

'And you are, Lee. You know, not pretty, a stunning face. Was looking forward to watching you suck my dick. Bet you're a fighter in the sack.'

'Now you'll never know.'

'That's the worst of it.' He half-laughed.

I felt my lips with my forefinger. 'Always had lousy taste when it comes to men. Can I have a fag?'

He sat down in the armchair and crossed his right leg over

his left. The gun pointed at me, resting on his knee. 'Get up off the floor.'

I did as he said. Hauled myself up, unsure whether my knees would obey the messages my brain was sending them.

'She found out you're bent. You're dealing.' I dropped myself into the second armchair, thought of Brownie and what he'd told me at Bernie and Duck's house. And the truth smacked into me. 'You're T.'

'You see, you go into the police force believing that crime doesn't pay, that the good guys always win. You start hanging out with the bad guys, and you realize they aren't so bad after all. They like the same things you like, football, having a laugh, a beer after work. Then you see the cash – more cash than I could earn in ten years as a cop. Ten years of putting my life on the line. No one gives a fuck. OK, they give you a decent funeral, but who really cares? After you're gone? They leave your wife with a pension and some vague notion that her husband was a hero. How does that help a 6-year-old kid?'

'"Six-year-old kid"?' I wasn't following the story. My eyes alighted on the whisky bottle Nick had brought with him when he first came through the living room door. Still holding its own on the coffee table. 'Fancy a drink?' I pointed. 'Bet it's the good stuff.'

'No chance.'

'Come on, live a little. I need to numb the pain. You need Dutch courage.'

I reached across for the bottle and retrieved Nick's glass from the floor. I crawled back to my armchair and filled the glass. 'So you are married.'

I held the glass out to him.

'No,' he said. 'Not me.'

'You said a 6-year-old kid?'

'Not mine.' He took the glass from my hand.

I didn't react, didn't move a single muscle, just kept staring at his green-brown eyes, the ones that reminded me of something, someone, some part of me.

'Who you talking about then?'

He drank the whisky down in one gulp and put the glass down on the coffee table. I hadn't had a drink for four months and twelve days. I sniffed the bottle that I still held in my right hand. My taste buds dampened. I swallowed the surplus saliva, put my lips to its neck. Stopped, made myself pause, inhaled first, drank second. The liquid burned the back of my throat, making my oesophagus come to life. I could feel every cell stir as the liquid seeped down my throat, telling me not to worry, reassuring me that everything would be OK, that the pain wouldn't last. I might have closed my eyes for a brief moment.

'A woman who appreciates her alcohol,' Col said.

'Jesus,' I said. 'That's the best ever.'

'See? Crime does pay,' said Col. 'He's living proof … Well, when I say living.' He trailed off for a moment as he glanced across at Nick's inert body on the carpet. I couldn't let myself look in Jo's direction. 'But you know, he lives in a mansion and drinks whisky that probably costs more for one bottle than I make in a month. How is that fair?'

'Maybe he worked hard.'

'Maybe he didn't.'

I shrugged. I learned a long time ago to let karma take care of what's fair and what isn't. 'He's got cancer.'

'We all die, Lee. Sooner or later.'

'Maybe it's about dying with a clear conscience.'

'Because?'

'Depends whether you believe in an afterlife.'

'I don't,' said Col.

I helped myself to another swig from the bottle. The alcohol didn't burn as much this time, leaving my taste buds to dance in the dusky taste. I leaned across and refilled his glass, despite him holding out his hand to say no.

'I believe in 6-year-old kids that don't deserve to have their dad taken from them before they're old enough to really know who their father was.'

'Whose kid?'

'Doesn't matter.'

'Matters to me.'

'My mate. Lewis.'

'A copper?'

He nodded and picked up the second glass.

'He died?'

'Car chase.'

'I'm sorry.' And I was.

'Stupid kids high on glue, nicked a car, and Lewis is the one that pays.'

'I'm sorry,' I said again.

'I've got to crack on,' he said. 'Time of death – they're shit-hot on that kind of thing.'

'You're forgetting something,' I said.

'I know, the wire. Don't worry. It's bust. Something wrong with the transmitter.'

Fucker. I kept my face neutral. 'Something else.'

'The suicide note. I'm going to go through this place—'

I shook my head.

'What?'

'That.' I nodded towards the piece he held pointed at me. 'It's not Wilkins's gun.'

He grinned. 'You could have been good.' He stood up, moved a step closer to my armchair, the one that Nick's gun was underneath.

I got to my feet and placed myself between him and the armchair.

'You can't kill me with that. Would really fuck-up the forensics, wouldn't it? Let me guess, you're going to say we came here looking for Jack. And because we're young and stupid, we brought

312

a gun with us, the Glock, that you planted here and told me where to find. So we tried to force Nick to confess to killing his wife—'

'Or his son.' Col shrugged.

'But because we're female and stupid, Nick overpowered us, grabbed his own gun,' – I waved towards the armchair Nick's gun lay under – 'which you stole at the same time as you planted the Glock.'

'Very good.'

'And then you burst through the doors to rescue everyone, kill Nick, but too late to save my life. Or Jo's.'

'I found out about your plan, drove here hell for leather, heard the first gunshot … I broke the window but by the time I got in he was standing over your body just about to fire a second shot. Jo was already dead. I fired, hoping the first shot hadn't killed you, but alas…'

'I'm truly moved,' I said. The whisky made me brave. 'But none of that stacks up if you kill me with your gun.'

I shifted my weight to the balls of my feet. Shook out my hands so that the alcohol bled to the ends of my fingers. I swear I could feel the heat radiate behind my fingernails.

'Don't be a dickhead,' he said.

I went to kick him, but he pulled his gun back and hit me across the face with it. Stars burst across my vision. He hit me again. I crashed to the floor. My vision blurred. I could just make out him ducking to his knees and putting an arm under the chair, feeling for Nick's gun. I closed my eyes. Earlier Nick had said there was nothing like knowing you were going to die to bring clarity and focus. And I had clarity.

I knew, in that moment, I'd been kidding myself.

I hadn't ever stopped drinking, I'd just been holding off, waiting. I love alcohol more than I love anything or anyone. Even as I waited for the shot that was going to kill me, the thing that fucked me off the most was that I couldn't finish the bottle.

313

The shot came. There was a warm wetness. My eardrums burst. Still the monster inside me demanded another drink. Just one more. More. The curse of the addict. There's never enough.

Time went funny. My vision went. I thought my eyes were open but all I could see was black. I don't know how long I lay there. I knew Col wouldn't be calling an ambulance and that I was destined to bleed to death, however long it took. Col was probably out the window by now.

Death. Funny how scared we all are to die and yet, in that moment, I didn't feel fear. I felt nothing but rage. Pure, white, blind rage.

'Lee?' I heard a voice that sounded like Jo's screech through my burst eardrums.

'More,' I said, but no words came out. 'More.'

I waited for the bright lights I'd read about but instead Jo appeared on my screen of vision. The once-white bits on her T-shirt were now blood red. She held the half-empty bottle of whisky to my lips. I felt it drip down the sides of my neck. The best anaesthetic in the world. No pain. They talk of my drinking but never my thirst.

Tears plopped down Jo's pale cheeks.

'I love you,' I said. At least I thought I said it, but I couldn't hear my own words.

'Shit. Shit. Shit.'

'Don't worry.' I felt peaceful. Like everything made sense and it was all OK. None of it mattered, not really, not at the end of the day.

'Help, Lee. Please. Shit. Shit.'

The pain in my leg lessened, which wasn't how I thought dying would go. Maybe it was the whisky. You see it's not all bad. People only tell you the bad stuff. But there's positives in everything. I kept closing my eyes thinking that this was my last moment, but the lights never went out. I replayed Jo's last words in my mind.

'What?'

314

'Oh my God,' said Jo. Her face was whiter than I've ever seen it, and that's saying something. I knew her during her Goth phase.

'I need another drink,' I said, but she wasn't listening to me. Her attention was elsewhere in the room. I pulled myself up by the arm of the chair and slouched against it. Jo was on her knees. I could see her flesh torn at the top of her left arm. It looked like raw liver: dark, blood red, almost black. I forced myself to look somewhere else. And it was then I saw the Glock hanging from her fingers.

Chapter Thirty-Seven

We had no time to think, no time to move, no time to plan a response. By the time I pieced together the noise of the police sirens from the road outside with the scene in front of me, the door was already being kicked down. After that all hell broke loose. I think Jo dropped the gun, but I don't know because someone yelled, 'Get down', and I did. Nose to the floor. We were ordered not to move until I felt my arms being fastened in handcuffs behind my back.

I was still trying to make sense of what had happened. I hadn't been shot. The warm wetness that spread down my leg when I heard the gun fire, that wasn't blood. That's all I'm going to say. Two policemen dragged me across the room, and I was stuffed into the back of a police car. A female officer sat in the front and ignored me. I saw an ambulance arrive, and then another one.

'I'm a private investigator,' I told anyone who would listen.

'We'll get to you in a minute,' the policewoman said.

One ambulance left with its lights flashing. The other stayed put on the drive.

'I want to speak to my partner.'

No one cared.

I was taken to the police station and locked in an interview room for over three hours. I hadn't seen Jo since the police had burst into Wilkins's front room. I told the story, over and over, just as it happened, except I didn't say I'd seen the gun in Jo's hand. They told me Nick and Col were both dead. I told them Col had given me whisky, too much whisky, and after that I didn't remember anything. I don't think they believed me but after three hours of my saying the same thing they let me call my lawyer. I didn't have a lawyer, so I called the next best person I could think of, the ex-journalist, Martin Blink. Despite the fact I must have woken him, he didn't need a single detail repeating. He told me not to say a word to anyone until he got there. He was at the station twenty minutes later, complete with a bleary-eyed criminal defence guy.

'It's not me that needs the lawyer,' I said. 'It's Jo.'

Simon, the lawyer, insisted on running over everything with me first before we had to repeat the whole process again with the detective, but an hour and a half later, after giving a full written statement, I was free to leave.

Martin Blink sat in the reception area, waiting for me, as I made my way out of the warren of interview rooms. He stood up as he saw me approach.

'I'm waiting for Jo,' I said.

'You'll be waiting a long time,' the desk sergeant cut in. 'She's not back from the hospital yet. They're waiting till she's discharged before they charge her.'

I glared at him. '"Charge her"? With what?'

He didn't say any more, but, what felt like a few minutes later, Simon appeared out of another room down the corridor. I could tell by the slope of his shoulders that the news wasn't great.

'They're not buying it,' he said.

'Morons,' I said.

'What?' Martin asked Simon.

'Murder.'

'"Murder"? Where's the intention?'

'They say she went equipped. And that she had the gun in her hand when the undercover entered the room. They think she panicked – thought it was a mate of Nick's, shot first, asked questions later.'

'Bullshit,' I said.

'They're saying there was no immediate threat.'

'"No immediate threat"? Are they serious?' I said. 'What about her arm? He shot her. He was about to shoot me.'

'Let's hope forensics back you up.'

'He shot her with Nick's gun. He nicked it. He set us up, right from the start.'

'Come on,' said Martin. He put an arm around the small of my back and pushed me towards the door, his limp causing us to bump into each other as we moved. 'We're no use here. Let's go grab a coffee and see what we can do for your mate. Simon will stay – he's the best there is.'

'I can't leave.'

'You can't help Jo while you're still in the lion's den,' said Martin, nodding his head in the direction of the desk sergeant. 'We need to talk where the walls don't have ears.'

There was a cheap transport café two streets away that was either a twenty-four-hour number or had opened before dawn. I checked my mug of orange tea to make sure the waitress's missing false fingernail wasn't floating in it. We sat in the far corner even though we were the only people in the place. Martin patted my arm, and said: 'Take it from the beginning, kiddo.'

The whisky hangover pounded my skull. 'I fucked up.'

'How?'

I thought back over the last twenty-four hours, which felt more like 124 hours. So much had happened, so much to process. I didn't know where to start.

'My dad showed up.'

From the look on Martin's face I know that was about the last thing he expected me to say. He frowned. 'At Wilkins's house?'

'No, before. The day before.' I wondered for a moment whether I was going to totally embarrass myself and cry my eyes out, sat there in the flickering neon gloom of the most dismal café in the world, while my best mate got charged with the murder of a policeman. 'It's all my fault.'

'From the beginning.'

I told Martin Blink everything I knew, from the moment Mrs Wilkins stepped into our office. Once I started, I couldn't stop. The words gushed out of me as the story took shape. I told him about Brownie, about Duck and Bernie, about Col telling us our first client had actually been an undercover policewoman. 'He was behind the break-in. I should have thought – why would anyone steal a client form?'

'He recognized Megan's handwriting?'

I let this statement sink in. 'Which means we're responsible for blowing her cover.' Another death on my hands.

'Could be he already suspected. Maybe he followed her to your offices. You'll never know.'

'I blew it. Really blew it.'

'Tell me about your dad.'

'He's not my dad. Well, technically, I suppose, he is.'

Martin frowned, and I knew I wasn't making sense. I breathed. Three times. 'He's my biological father. I never met him. Not till a few years back. He left home the day I was born, and I never saw him. Not when I was growing up.' Not when I really needed a dad, I wanted to say, but didn't, because it was hard enough not to cry as it was. 'Not one single time. My mum hated him, would never have his name mentioned. Then she died and that's when I decided. I went looking for him.'

The theory of chaos. That one small, single, unremarkable event sets off a chain of events that leads to total fucking global

319

melt down. Those moments when life fractures and goes off in a different direction to the one you thought you were heading. That one single moment in time, when life becomes two separate parts, the time before the fracture, the time after. There's no going back. I chose to find my father, and if I could go back and cross out one thing in my life, erase one decision, one moment, one second of my existence, that's the one. Because that's the moment when life went from being shit but manageable, to being completely out of control.

'Go on,' said Martin.

I decided on the potted version. 'I found him.'

'And?'

'He'd remarried, had another daughter – she is, was, only a couple of years younger than me. Fiona.' The name hurt my mouth. I hadn't said it for a long time.

'And?'

'And, well …' What to say. I didn't have the words. 'All hell broke loose. He hadn't told Fiona about me. He wasn't … he wasn't pleased to have me turn up.'

'Not your fault. Can't deny your existence in order to keep his skeletons in the closet.'

I gave Martin the glimmer of a weak smile. I knew he was trying to make me feel better and that alone was something to be treasured. He nodded at me to continue. I pressed my lips together.

'You can do it,' he said.

'Everything changed. Fiona – she was such a daddy's girl – had such a hard time finding out he'd lied.'

'Might be good for her. They say it's empowering to discover your idols are human.'

'It was like she was waiting for me to show up, so she could stage some kind of overdue teenage rebellion.' The sentence rushed out of me before I could check it for accuracy. Was it true? I don't remember thinking that before. It struck me like a

320

new idea, but I filed it. Even if it was true, it didn't change the facts. If I hadn't shown up, she wouldn't have had a clear-cut excuse to go off the rails. 'Anyway, to cut a long story short, she jacked in her A levels, got a job in Paris, as an au pair.'

'Not the end of the world.'

I cut him off before he could paint an imaginary reality. 'She had an affair with the father of the family she was working for, got pregnant. He killed himself afterwards, after it had all, you know ... Anyway, David, her dad, our dad, went apeshit. He went to France to bring her back. I think he thought he could force her into an abortion and, well, according to the police investigation, they had a row.'

Martin was staring at me in a different way now. 'I read about it.'

'You did?' I was relieved. He already knew the story, saved me the hell of repeating it.

'He killed her.'

Three little words.

Easy to say when they don't apply to you, to your family, when the 'he' doesn't mean your dad and the 'her' isn't your younger, quirky, gorgeous, ten-week pregnant half-sister. When you're not the reason that the sentence exists, when you have no moral responsibility, no culpability. Three simple words.

He killed her.

'They argued,' Martin continued. He wrinkled his nose. 'He said he pushed her, she hit her head on something?'

'The coffee table.'

'Accidental death. But he hid her body. Was his sentence reduced because of the crime of passion thing in France?'

'Seven years.'

'And this was what, two years ago?'

'Three.'

'And now he's out.'

The waitress brought over another cup of tea. I don't remember anyone asking her to. I waited for her to leave before I said: 'He turned up outside my house, after we'd seen you. No warning. He knocked on the window. I was in the van. I opened my eyes and he was just there. Didn't even know he was out.'

'No wonder then.'

'No wonder what?'

'That you were off your game. Anyone would be. Stop blaming yourself.'

'He had a set of car keys.'

'You won't help anyone by beating yourself up.'

'He said he didn't drive.'

'Your dad?'

'No, Col. Col said he didn't drive. But last night I saw he had a car key on his keyring. I should have realized.'

'But you didn't. Doesn't matter. Move on.'

'Easy for you to say.'

'Easy for you to do. Move on.' He poured a stream of sugar into his own cup of tea. 'Where's your dad now?'

'I told him to get lost.'

'And then?'

'I got stoned.'

'Heroin?'

'No.' I met his eyes for the first time since we'd arrived in the café. 'I'd never touch that stuff.'

'What then?'

'Spliff.'

'Whisky in my day.'

'We got completely caned and then Col showed up. Told us Wilkins had killed Karen whatever-her-name-was. A total fucking made-up fantasy. I fell for the whole thing. Hook, line and fucking sinker.'

Martin Blink popped another Fisherman's Friend. He crunched it, chewed it up and when he swallowed he shook his head. Like he was a judge – he'd considered the whole thing and decided there was no case to answer.

322

'Don't sweat it, kid. I was convinced Wilkins had killed his missus. We're all guilty of letting our issues cloud our judgements. Happens to the best of us and, believe me, I was the best. Tell me what happened at Wilkins's house.'

I said the first thing that came into my head. 'Jo saved my life.'

I told Martin the sequence of events, from the moment we got there to when Col had shot Jo. I knew that picture would never leave me, no matter how long I lived. Then I told Martin that Col had been about to kill me, that Jo had shot Col.

'They don't like to believe their undercover coppers are capable of going bad. Reflects badly on the whole practice. We're going to need to prove it to them.'

'How?'

'Let's go through it one more time. We must be missing something. Start from the very beginning. The minute you got hired.'

So I retold the story from beginning to end. Martin didn't say a word until the bit where I got to Martha's flat, and the keys I found under her bed.

'Where are the keys now?'

'I put them in the safe, at the office.'

'Come on, let's take a look.'

We didn't finish our tea. Martin paid the bill and drove me back to the offices. I liked having something to do, some sense of a purpose, something that helped me stop thinking about Jo. I unlocked the safe and took out the small bunch of keys.

'One for her flat, one for her car, and this one.'

I held it up, and he frowned. 'Looks like a key for a padlock. A lock-up maybe? Or a locker?' he said. 'Maybe she had a locker at the station.'

Lockers.

And that got me thinking. The lockers at the university. I remembered on the Saturday, that last meeting with Megan, or Martha as she was then. And how I'd been coming back from

323

the shop, and I'd seen her hanging out by the lockers. Had I seen her touch one of them?

Martin drove us down and parked his car behind Blenheim Square. It was the middle of the morning, and I held onto Martin's arm as we dodged the traffic on Woodhouse Lane. He was slow, limped along as we threaded our way through the university buildings until we reached the Union. We made our way down the stairs to the basement, and I know it sounds mad, but it was like I could feel her presence, watching us, propelling us forward. The last time I'd seen her. Where had she been standing? I forced myself to visualize the scene from outside the shop. She'd been bent over when I'd first noticed her, had straightened up almost straightaway. Only four days before but it felt like a lifetime ago.

I tried five different padlocks, holding my breath as I fiddled with each one, half expecting someone to shout at me for trying to break into their locker. Martin stood next to me, shielding me from view, until the sixth one I tried sprang open.

We both stepped back, like it might be booby-trapped. I tugged open the door. Inside was a bag that looked like every student's bag, a green canvas bag. It had a badge pinned to the outside of it, with a picture I'd seen a dozen times before, of a woman raising a clenched fist. I pulled the bag out by the strap. It wasn't heavy. The only thing in it was a notebook. My hands shook so much I couldn't turn the pages, so I handed it to Martin.

He scanned the contents. Then he looked at me and his blue eyes sparkled like raindrops.

'Bingo,' he said.

Chapter Thirty-Eight

And that was that. We gave the notebook to Simon, and Jo was released the same afternoon. On bail, but it's only a matter of time. Martin was something else – threatening the Detective Inspector that if he didn't ensure charges were dropped he'd be reading about the whole fiasco over his morning cup of tea, along with the rest of the nation.

Jo was shaky. She'd had an operation on her shoulder, and her arm was bandaged. She was still woozy from the anaesthetic. I had to tell her over and over, if she hadn't shot Col, I would be dead. She took a life but she saved a life. My life. Col killed Megan because she was on to him. Her death means there's another child out there, condemned to grow up in trauma, the odds stacked against them. The ripples spread, patterns repeat and so, to my mind, Col deserved everything he got.

Megan had suspected Col, and the final thing she'd written in the notebook we found was dated the last Saturday of her life. The day we'd met her on the Parkinson Steps. She'd known her life was in danger. She'd left a note to be passed to her son in the event that anything happened to her.

* * *

325

Two days after Jo's release, on the Friday, we went to the office. My replacement phone had arrived, and Jo was setting it up for me – can't say I was jumping up and down for joy, but at least it gave Jo something to focus on. The bell went, and Carly stepped into the offices.

'Wow,' I said as I caught sight of the young man behind her, holding her hand. I recognized him immediately, even though we'd been given so many different pictures of him – heroin addict, public schoolboy, bereaved child, boyfriend, best friend, turncoat. It was odd to see them there, all squashed into one human body. 'Where did you come from?'

'Sorry,' said Carly, although her grin made me think she wasn't really.

'You knew where he was all along.' It wasn't a question. And in that moment, looking at Jack, the colour in his cheeks, the truth hit me, and I cursed myself for not seeing it from the start, from the moment we laid eyes on the smack in the Old Holborn tin. If there's one thing I should know, it's an addict doesn't give away his stash. 'Rehab,' I said.

'Where?' said Jo.

'Devon,' Carly said. 'He's done it.'

'Early days,' Jack said, but I could see the pride in the way he held himself. 'Three weeks.'

'You've done the worst bit,' Carly said. 'Anyway,' she turned to me, 'I wanted you to know he's OK.'

'Do you know where Brownie is?' Jack asked. 'There's no one at the squat.'

'Right,' I said.

'I spoke to Pants. He said Brownie's disappeared, that it all kicked off. I feel like a right shit, but I had to get clean. I was no use to anyone.'

'Right,' I said again. Christ, where to start? I glanced at Jo but the look on her face made it clear. This was my job. 'Do you want to come through to the back?'

326

Telling Jack his father was dead was one of the hardest things I've ever had to do. I recognized the look in his eyes, and it's not one I'd wish on anyone. I tried to think of anything that might help. 'He was really pleased to know you had a girlfriend.'

Carly had her arm around Jack's shoulders.

'I bet. Always convinced I was gay.'

'He told us some things, about your mother. She didn't die in a car crash, Jack.'

He didn't look up at me. He sat with his head between his hands. I carried on talking, found that once I'd started, the words took on a life of their own.

'From what he told us, I think your mum was bipolar. She was always up and down, he said. He showed me a note she'd written.' I faltered, unsure whether to press on. I'd started now though, and I couldn't stop. 'Jack, your mum committed suicide.'

Carly stared at me.

Jack didn't speak for ages. When he finally looked up, Carly had tears running down her face.

'I know,' he said.

'You told me she died in a car crash,' Carly said.

'You told Brownie your dad killed her,' I said.

'I blamed him,' Jack said to me. 'I didn't want to know. It's all a mess. I had this recurring dream as a kid, of a car crash.'

'There was a crash,' I said. 'A year or two before she died. You were in the car.'

I watched Jack drink in the facts of his childhood. Try to fit them with his own ideas. I've been in that situation. Kept in the dark, piecing together your history, the titbits people throw at you.

'So who's the woman who paid you to look for Jack?' asked Carly.

'Martha.'

'"Martha"?' Carly's curls shook. 'Why?'

'Probably cos she wants to kill me,' said Jack. 'She'll blame me for abandoning Brownie.'

'She thought you had the cash to pay off Bernie and Duck.'

'What?' asked Carly. 'That's bonkers.'

Jack shook his head. 'I bet Brownie's told her my dad's loaded. But, I couldn't go to him. He hates, hated me.'

'He didn't hate you. He knew he'd fucked up. He didn't blame you.'

'So Martha wanted you to find Jack, so Jack could go to his dad and try and get the money?'

'Not exactly.' I took a deep breath. 'Martha was actually an undercover policewoman called Megan Parsons.'

'What?'

'It's true.'

'It can't be. She's screwing Brownie!'

'She genuinely fell in love with him. She also blackmailed your father, asked him for the twenty-four thousand pounds you needed to pay off your dealers.'

'She didn't.'

'She did. She got the money, broke into the squat and put it all in what she thought was Brownie's sock drawers. But you two had swapped rooms.'

'My dad paid?'

'He knew he was dying. He thought you were behind the blackmail, and he thought what the hell, you're going to inherit it all anyway.'

'I'm going to inherit it all?'

I nodded. 'That's what your dad said.'

'So where's the money now?' asked Carly. 'The money Martha put in Jack's drawers, I mean?'

'Pants cleared the room once it was apparent you'd done a runner. He bundled up all your possessions and put them in the cellar. When Martha realized you'd swapped rooms with Brownie, she went back into the squat, discovered all your possessions had gone and thought you'd skipped with the money.'

'So Bernie and Duck still haven't been paid?'

'I wouldn't worry too much about them. They've been arrested. Don't think they'll be any trouble in the foreseeable.'

'Yeah, but—'

'What do you mean "was"?' asked Carly. 'You said Martha was an undercover policewoman.'

I hesitated. 'She was killed.'

'"*Killed*"?'

'Last Saturday. In the line of duty.'

'Who killed her?'

'Well, that's the thing.' I knew this was a lot for them to take in, and I tried to break it down into bite-sized chunks. 'Did you ever hear Bernie and Duck mention a guy called T?'

'T killed Martha?'

'T was a bent cop.' I tried not to think of that kiss, the heat of his body next to mine. 'Martha was on to him. He killed her.'

'Shit.'

'"*T was a bent cop*"?' Jack repeated my words.

They both stared at me. I took a deep breath. 'We left our business card at the squat. Bernie and Duck went there, looking for you or Brownie. I think T was putting them under pressure to get you to pay up. Pants told them he'd given us your stuff. Bernie and T broke into our offices, trashed the place. I don't know whether T recognized Martha's signature on our client form, or maybe he staked out our offices. Whatever, somehow, T realized Martha was paying us to look for you. He needed to find out what she knew and how much she'd told us.'

'Where's T now?'

I swallowed. 'He's dead.'

'Brownie,' said Jack, and I saw real fear in his eyes. 'Where's Brownie?'

I breathed out and felt my shoulders relax. At last, some good news. 'Don't worry, Brownie's safe. He's in rehab too. Kind of.'

* * *

Me and Jo went to Megan's funeral the following week. She got the full works – the West Yorkshire police saw to that. I was strangely moved by the sight of them all in uniform, carrying her coffin. I got the sense that at least she'd belonged somewhere, that she had a tribe.

I saw her son – at least I assumed it was her son – I didn't speak to him, but he fit the bill. A teenager, pale-faced and spotty. His dad kept his arm around him all day – never let go of him once – and so I allowed myself to believe that maybe he'd be OK. I comfort myself with the fact that Megan's cards were marked long before we showed up on the scene. Thank God she'd plucked up the courage to walk through our doors, otherwise maybe Col would have managed to find a way to get rid of her without anyone ever finding out the truth.

The last person to turn up was Aunt Edie. She arrived the day Jo and I were painting the offices. Brownie was with her, half a stone heavier and wearing clothes that fitted him. She'd brought him back to Leeds on the train, wanted to make sure he got home safely.

'Wow,' I said, when Brownie had left. 'What've you been feeding him?'

'Sausages, mainly.'

'Vegan sausages?'

She gave me a sly look. 'Now, you're going to have to keep your eye on him,' she said. 'I've done my best, but these things take time.'

'We'll do what we can, but we're not a babysitting service,' I said.

'Speaking of which, I've been trying to ring you for the last week,' Aunt Edie said, stooping to pull the edges of the old pair of curtains we were using to cover the floor so that the paint didn't splatter the carpet. 'I've left a dozen messages.'

'Sorry, Aunt Edie.' I was standing on the desk, using a roller brush. Jo's shoulder was strapped, so she was doing the edges with a brush. The room already looked bigger, lighter. 'We've been up to our ears in it all.' I had sent her the cuttings from the newspapers – we'd been blazoned across most of them, which had been fantastic for business – the phone hadn't stopped ringing. 'We haven't had chance to listen to them all yet.'

'That's where I come in.'

'What?'

'I'm offering my services.'

'"*Services*"?'

'Answering the phone. Cook, cleaner, general bottle washer.'

'Oh, I don't know about—'

'You two need looking after. I've been going out of my mind with boredom since my Arthur, God rest his soul, passed on. This business has reminded me what I need.'

'"What you need"?'

'Something to do other than the blinking crossword. I can help you get this place straight for starters.'

I rollered the white paint over the last letters in 'Be Scarred' and watched them fade before my eyes. I turned to Aunt Edie. 'Where would you live?'

'I'll apply for one of those housing association flats.'

I looked across at Jo.

She shrugged her one good shoulder and, for the first time since she'd come out of the police station, she grinned. 'Business is booming.'

True. We'd had four requests for our services so far since the press coverage. Martin had done a great article that all the local press bought. The *Yorkshire Evening Post* had sent photographers, and they'd done some mean and moody shots down the Dark Arches, Jo's bright blue eyes, heavily mascaraed, staring into the distance, her shoulder in its black sling.

The piece ran to two pages and told how we'd busted a drugs ring, solved a seventeenyearold case about the disappearance of a young mother, and disposed of a bent copper responsible for the murder of his colleague. Made us sound like superheroes.

Aunt Edie's here now, on the telephone, chatting to a potential client, and I can't fault her. Five minutes on the phone and she's got people telling her intimate details of their lives, even the ones that were just ringing to sell us water coolers.

And she's managed to work out how to use the oven in the kitchenette without burning the place down.

I haven't told her about me falling off the wagon, about how good that whisky tasted, that I still smell it whenever I close my eyes. Better than food, better than sex, better than anything I've ever tasted. A need to know basis, I decided. I've joined one of those fucking AA groups. I figure a bit of help to get through the next few weeks can't hurt.

I didn't tell Aunt Edie about David showing up either. Jo reckons he's got the message and that's the last I'll see of him. I'm not convinced but I'm trying not to think about it. No one can know what's round the next corner.

So, that's it. A full report. Writing it down means letting it go. Time to finish the chapter, close the book. There is only ever the here and the now, and the smell of freshly baked parkin is making me hungry.

Lee Winters
Director
No Stone Unturned Ltd

332

Acknowledgements

Thanks to everyone who has read early drafts of this novel, particularly Martyn Bedford and Oz Hardwick, Rachel Connor and Anna Chilvers. Thanks to Nathan Ramsden for helping me when my own knowledge ran out.

Thanks to Jamie Cowen, the best literary agent ever, for his insight and for his belief. And also for his penchant for profanities. (All swearwords are his responsibility.)

Thanks to Bekki Wray Rogers for running through it, running with it, and for running with me in general.

And thanks to Kathryn Cheshire, Janette Currie and everyone at HarperCollins and Killer Reads who has worked to make this better than it was.

And last but not least, thanks to Mark, for understanding.

KILLER READS

DISCOVER THE BEST
IN CRIME AND THRILLER

Follow us on social media to get to know the team behind the books, enter exclusive giveaways, learn about the latest competitions, hear from our authors, and lots more:

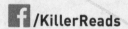 /KillerReads 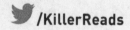 /KillerReads